Reflections

of Love and Loathing

*To Shirley
Keep on Truckin.
M Sntz M.D.*

M. R. GUTIERREZ, M.D

authorHOUSE®

AuthorHouse™ LLC
1663 Liberty Drive
Bloomington, IN 47403
www.authorhouse.com
Phone: 1-800-839-8640

Published by AuthorHouse   01/27/2014

ISBN: 978-1-4918-5342-9 (sc)
ISBN: 978-1-4918-5341-2 (e)

Contents

I dedicate this to Donna Lynch, a true friend,
ready to help whenever she can.

A major theme of "Reflections of Love and Loathing"
is finding love and finding the courage to be loved,
so I also dedicate it to friends from another time in my life,
Denise and Paul Brotherton, had a marriage, a true partnership.
Paul died looking for homeless people in a burning warehouse,
leaving seven young sons behind. Thank you for all the help
both of you gave to this displaced, confused friend.
Yours was a real marriage, an example for cowards like me.

Chapter 1

Heart Strings

Terry kicked the tire of his inert Chevy truck and groaned as the pain radiated from his toes up his leg. His expression of frustration was misspent on the uncaring truck. Intending to lean over the fender to glare at the engine again, he jumped when the hot metal burned his hands and nearly stumbled as his sore foot gave way. With a despairing look up, he counted a grand total of five small, fluffy, white clouds that mocked his frustration from the inverted bowl of cobalt blue sky.

Longingly, he sought the Sandia Mountains on the eastern horizon towering over Albuquerque. Those mountains should be behind him by now. Then he looked back at Mount Taylor, a mystical mountain to the local tribes, which marked one's arrival to Grants. At this particular moment he did not appreciate the view of the purple mountains or the color and clarity of the sky.

His well-cared-for, ungrateful, classic red Chevy truck had thrown a rod, leaving him stranded on the empty highway between Grants and Albuquerque. He glared at the passing vehicles that ignored his outstretched thumb and uplifted hood with glee and impudence. He felt invisible and miserable as he drank the last drops of water from his water bottle. His current circumstances boded ill for his plans to attend his father's funeral scheduled for the day after tomorrow in Amarillo. Empty and conflicted, he hadn't yet come to terms with the death of his father. Stubbornly, he held his thumb out again, unwilling to begin the long walk to Albuquerque, or Grants.

1

He glanced at the searing golden sun, perversely adding to the record high temperature of 105 degrees for early in June. He was so depleted from the heat that he expected to see vultures circling above him. After the next group of vehicles ignored his outstretched thumb, he gave up. He pulled his well-worn cowboy hat down to shield his eyes and leaned back on the hot fender of his treasonous truck and crossed his broken-down boots out in front of him and folded his arms across his chest and stared at his boots and as he considered the long, hot walk. Instead, he listed the personal failings that had led him to this untenable position.

First on his list was his misspent loyalty to old possessions that had served him well. Last year, he had had the money to buy a new vehicle, and had planned to do so, but it felt like a betrayal of the first truck he'd saved for so long to buy many years ago. That loyalty to possessions once treasured, then become burdensome was perhaps the only trait he had in common with his father. Then, of course, he had waited until the last minute to start the drive from Farmington, New Mexico to Amarillo, Texas. Right now he was ready to give up, walk away from his belongings and get drunk at the nearest bar. Pessimistically, he ruled out option after option for getting to Amarillo for the funeral. For one thing, he couldn't arrange anything from where he was with a dead cell phone.

Suddenly, he was distracted from that unhappy train of thought by the loud, rumble of a truck with a bad muffler as it gunned its way across the wide median between the east and west bound lanes. A thirty-year-old, dusty, battered turquoise and white truck squealed across the pavement; the contents of its bed banged around as the result of the wild U-turn. It narrowly missed a honking, black Mercedes sedan headed west. The driver of the truck ignored it, pulling up behind his truck, kicking up a cloud of dust as it skidded to a stop. A young woman with black and red spiked hair stuck her head out her window to yell over the roar of her truck, "Do you need a ride? Or are you planning to feed your bones to the vultures?"

With a smile of gratitude creasing the dust that covered his face, he pushed his hat back as he reached the window of the truck and offered his hand in greeting. The inside of the cab was occupied by a Native American young woman, a cooler on the floor, an open backpack, school books and snacks strewn across the bench seat, and the rearview mirror facing the roof. "I'd rather not feed the vultures today, but it's that, or sacrifice everything I own by leaving my stuff to human scavengers. My name is Terry Prentice, by the way, and I am very glad to meet you.""

"I'm Liliana Hunt," she said as she handed him a cold soda instead of shaking hands, "I guess I'm your knight in a rusty truck."

He laughed, opened and drank half of the orange soda before responding, "Well rusty or not, I am grateful that you stopped. I've been out here two hours and you're the only one who has noticed me. I felt invisible."

"I'm not surprised. There was a break out from the high security prison near Santa Fe. Nobody's picking up strangers until the bad guys are caught."

He narrowed his eyes against the bright sunlight to examine the pretty, copper-colored face of a young woman with large, dark brown eyes, high cheekbones and short, spiked black hair tipped an inch down in flame red. Her expression was friendly, despite a habitual guarded wariness and tension in her eyes. The ends of her full lips curved slightly upward and her manner was welcoming.

"Then, what are you doing stopping for a stranger?"

"And what are you doing standing out here like coyote bait?"

He laughed, "All right. You're safe; I am not an escaped prisoner."

With a sharp nod, she opened the door and he backed away to give her room to climb out. She pulled her cell phone from her pocket and looked at him questioningly. "Don't tell me you're the only white man left without a cell-phone?"

"I didn't notice that I'd let the battery die until I needed it. I've had other things on my mind."

"I bet. So what's wrong with the truck? Will a jump get 'er going?"

"Fraid not. She threw a rod and probably needs a new engine. I knew it was coming, but I kept putting off the overhaul."

"Other things on your mind, eh?"

"Yup." He liked her brash manner and no nonsense tone. He'd never met anyone quite like her. She moved with the same confident intensity that characterized her speech. Once out of the truck, he saw that she was around twenty years old and, just about five feet tall, thin with narrow hips and was dressed simply in a plain black tee shirt, cutoff shorts, and red, high-rise tennis shoes. He assumed that she was from a local Pueblo tribe, but it was hard to know for sure. Some Navajo lived in this region as well as several Pueblo tribes.

She walked over and looked under the hood, then inspected the contents of his loaded truck. "Nope, you don't want to leave all that stuff out here. My Uncle Mike is a mechanic and has a tow truck." She crossed her arms and gave him a sideways look that said that she was sure of what she offered, but worried about the consequences. He was intrigued.

"Tell you what," she said. "I'm headed home to Grants for summer break. Put the valuable stuff in my truck. If he can't come right away 'cause he's busy, you won't lose anything that matters. I have a stop to make before we get to Grants."

"I don't want to be any trouble. I can wait here."

"No, you can't. If you don't come with me, I'll call an ambulance. You look ready to croak." She tipped her head to one side while looking him in the eye. He was worn out, but he didn't think he looked that bad. He licked his dry, chapped lips with his dry tongue and decided he couldn't stand to wait any longer to get out of the heat. He shrugged and agreed; he couldn't resist spending time with this interesting young woman. He was hooked.

"Good. Believe me, heat stroke is no fun and you'll get a chance to wash off some of that road grit. Then you can repay the huge favor I'm doing you by going with me to see my Grants grandma. I'm a few days late getting back to Grants. If I'm alone, she'll rant for hours. She'll cool off faster if there's a good-looking man to flirt with."

The look she gave him dared him to refuse and worried that he might. There was a trace of guilt in her eyes, which made him wonder what he was in store for. He didn't want to get involved in her family problems, but two hours in the ferocious heat had worn him down. Besides, he was irresistibly drawn to her and found himself unable to even consider refusing. Even if he called a tow using her phone it could be another hour or more of waiting in the heat and would likely cost more than Liliana's uncle would ask of her friend, and his credit cards were maxed out. He knew his decision was influenced by his attraction to her; he hoped he wouldn't regret the decision.

"Well, it's hard to refuse such an interesting offer, but I hate to put you out." Just for a second, he saw relief in her expression.

"Too late. There's no backing out from a treaty with this Indian. Start moving your stuff, while I call my uncle." She flipped her phone open and asked, "You married?"

"No, no," he replied a little too quickly. She certainly got to the point. "And you?"

"Me? I'm just a kid. Can't you tell?"

Nonplused, he laughed to himself as he pulled back the tarp and started moving his electronics to her truck. The traffic on the highway made it difficult to eavesdrop on her phone call, but it sounded as if her uncle needed some arm-twisting to come for his truck. However, before long she was at his side.

"What goes next?"

He pointed out a couple of boxes and asked, "He didn't want to come out, did he?"

"You've got good ears," she laughed, but turned away from his interrogative gaze. He liked her laugh and wondered at her sudden shyness. "He says he's tired of my bleeding-heart ways, but he's good people… Actually, he likes helping people out, but you'll never get him to admit it."

After fifteen minutes of hot work, he was surprised to be dripping in sweat. He wouldn't have believed he had any more sweat left in him. He said, "I think that takes care of the most valuable stuff. The rest is mostly clothes and kitchen gear."

"He oughta be here soon. It'll be cooler on the road and I gotta get going."

"I doubt anyone would want what's left."

"It's too hot to hang around and worry about it." Once inside the truck, she handed him a bag of oatmeal cookies and started the noisy truck. "Have another soda, or a bottle of water. They're in the cooler."

She put the truck in gear and spun out backing up swiftly, then, without pausing, made a U-turn directly across the dirt median to reach the westbound lanes. He gripped the seat and happened to look her way as she grinned mischievously at his reaction. Her phone rang an instant later, startling him.

Watching him out of the corner of her eye, she said, "Hi Tío, yeah, I can see you coming over the hill. We're on our way to see Grandpa. Carla will hang me by my toes if I'm too late. Thanks again," she paused, and then said, "Oh, quit complaining, man. The truck is old, but when you see it you'll know that a loving owner has taken good care of it," she paused and crossed her eyes at Terry. She listened for a moment, "and when have I ever been wrong?" Pause. "Okay, once, but not again since, geez. See you in an hour or so, bye." She shrugged in response to Terry's questioning glance as she folded the phone into her pocket, and then accelerated into the fast lane. "It turns out that he just dropped off a car at Acoma Pueblo and was close by."

There was something about her that reached inside him, made his skin tingle and filled his heart. He hadn't felt that way about anyone, ever. It felt strange; strange enough to make him worry why he'd let her drag him into her life.

Once on the road, he attempted some polite conversation. "So, Liliana is a pretty name."

"I think Mom wanted a little girl in pink and lace."

He wasn't sure how to respond. She dressed and spoke with vitality, definitely not a dainty girl. From then on she seemed to have little to say; maybe she was shy despite her confident mannerisms. She turned off the highway onto smaller roads after twenty minutes, and then made several turns within a small, isolated community consisting of a mix of adobe and frame houses, with a helping of trailer homes spread out over dry low hills. She turned down what turned out to be a long, dirt driveway, which then turned to gravel as it neared a long, beige stucco adobe house, with a barn and corral in the back. She released the gas, coasting along the last part of the gravel road to the door of the well-maintained house.

She couldn't remember if she had told him she was visiting her grandfather when she knew he wouldn't be here. It didn't matter; she doubted this irresistible man would ever trust her. After getting out and slamming the contrary truck door shut, she explained to Terry, "This is my Laguna family's house. My dad grew up here. They didn't like my mother's family." Quickly she glanced over to catch the first reaction in his light hazel eyes; he returned her gaze with a nod.

"My parents died in a car accident when they were my age. The anniversary is at the end of the summer. Aunt Donna is great, but she's not very trusting and I like meeting new people. Once we had a bad situation that turned out okay in the end, so sometimes she can be a little testy. She makes the best lamb chili and fried bread and she'll be insulted if we refused to eat."

"It must have been tough to lose your parents. Do you remember them?" he asked.

"I was little. It was a long time ago."

Every time he spoke with his Texas drawl, she smiled inside. She liked his small build and sand-colored hair, cut short and professional looking. Probably in his late thirties, he would have been very fair, but it was clear he spent a lot of time baking in the New Mexico sunshine. Although this wasn't the first time she picked up some hapless soul on that empty stretch of I-40 going to or coming from Albuquerque, crossing the highway to help this particular white man was the result of the most powerful impulse she could ever remember having. It was like having a steel cable attached to her heart that would have ripped her heart out if she passed him by. She never questioned those feelings, even though, once he was in the truck, she couldn't think of anything to say. There were things she wanted to confess about what she was getting him into, but she couldn't spit out the words. It felt wonderful sitting next to him, and terrifying at the same time.

She was never in a good mood when she returned to Grants. Life with her Grants grandmother was mostly miserable, partly because she wanted Liliana to be there all the time. Her Laguna family didn't seem to want her around, even though she maintained her relationship with them. It would have pleased her father and it felt good to spend time in their calm, love-filled home. Stopping by on the way to Grandma Carla's was the easiest way to see them. Once she was with Carla it required complex deception to get free time to visit the Res. Despite all that, it hurt her heart to see how unhappy Grandma Carla was as she battled her own demons. No one understood why she went back now that she was old enough to be on her own. Liliana wasn't even sure.

In any case, as unpleasant as her time in Grants would be, she would at least have her own room. The aunt she stayed with in Albuquerque was kind and generous, but she had five kids, and the sofa Liliana slept on should have been declared a national disaster ages ago.

Looking up at the broiling sun and clear, sky, she added, "I have a few memories. My mother was fourteen when I was born and my dad was sixteen. I hear about how wonderful my father was when I visit here, so it's like I know him. He was already a football star when he married my mom and his family was very disappointed. Five years after I was born, they were driving home when they ran off the road. Carla said they were drunk; they had just had dinner with her. But everyone swears my dad never drank. So, there's the story. I guess we've stood out here long enough to be polite. Let's see what kind of mood she's in. We don't have to stay long."

Liliana banged on the screen door and called out, "Aunt Donna, it's your favorite niece. Are you home?"

Liliana shrugged and opened the door. Taking off his hat he followed her into the cool darkness of the adobe house. An annoyed woman's voice echoed from deep in the house.

"Why do you act that way, Liliana? You don't have to knock; this is your . . . ," she stopped speaking when she saw the handsome man looking politely down at the hat in his hands. "Oh, I'm sorry. I'm Donna Chavez." She wiped her hands on the kitchen towel she carried, and then waved them in. "Come in, come in. I'm sure she told you there would be a meal waiting, and, fortunately, there is. I stayed home with my sick kid, so I decided to get some baking done."

"My name is Terry Prentice. My truck broke down east of Grants. I'm sorry to inconvenience you, but I'd been there two hours when Liliana saved me from the vultures." The cool darkness of the hall was a relief from the heat. "I appreciate your hospitality."

He saw in Donna an attractive Native American woman who had Liliana's dark eyes and her appraising look that at this moment revealed a mix of friendly attraction, annoyance and old grief. Her face was oval shaped, with blushing high cheeks and nicely shaped lips. Her straight, long, black hair was tied back revealing a broad forehead and a graceful neck. He judged her to be in her early thirties. A little shorter than Liliana, she was also a little heavier with a more rounded figure.

She smiled up at him, "You're a ways from west Texas, Mr. Prentice. What brings you out this way?"

"Yeah," he said, exaggerating his drawl. Twisting his hat in his hands, he added, "I've been working in Farmington. My father just died and I'm on my way home to Amarillo. My truck threw a rod and I don't have the time or money to get it running right now. I may have to take a bus."

"I'm sorry to hear about your father. I lost my mother just a few years ago." Donna said as she led them to the patio in back of the house. "I thought they paid well up there on the oil fields."

He followed her through the hall that led directly to the back door, passing openings to the living room and kitchen, all very clean and neatly organized. Shelves carried assorted clay pots in a variety of tribal styles: Zuni, Acoma, and Navajo. They passed a nook with a statue of the Virgin Mary with several lit votive candles around her. On the walls hung many pictures, some very old, representing many different people of different ages. As much as he'd have liked to, he refrained from stopping to examine them. Out the back screen door was a large, shady, cool, honeysuckle-covered patio, ringed with rose bushes. Alongside was a garden of corn, chili, beans and squash. A child's bicycle leaned against the trellis that supported the honeysuckle.

"Come sit down. I'll get some iced tea." She smiled and took Liliana firmly by the arm, dragging her into the kitchen. Liliana rolled her eyes, dumping her backpack by the door as they went inside.

From inside Liliana called out, "There's a bathroom in the main hall to your left, if you want to wash off some of that road dust."

When the voices became hushed, he heard something about the danger of hitchhikers. Terry smiled shaking his head as he sought out the bathroom. Liliana was clearly the black sheep in this family. He understood the role well. As he entered the darkness of the hall, he was caught by the smell of lavender. His paused as his eyes were drawn to an open bedroom door on his right where a table with several beautifully painted pots sat. He jumped at the touch on his shoulder and turned to find Liliana and Donna standing behind him.

The two sets of brown eyes met each other; Liliana's were defensive, even though Donna's were only mildly suspicious. "My mom painted these pots. She was a well-known potter so they sell for a lot," Donna explained.

Liliana just shrugged, "He's okay, Auntie." She explained, "One time a new friend stole a couple of pots, but I got them all back." Terry could see by her stance that she was prepared for conflict.

Donna was embarrassed for revealing her suspicions. "You know you should be more careful about picking up hitchhikers," was all Donna said.

"I got the stuff back, didn't I? And it hasn't happened since."

"Yes. So now every guest you bring, you surprise with a search of their belongings." Donna glanced across Liliana to see Terry's discomfort with the conflict, so she desisted. "Here's the bathroom," she said, opening the door across the hall for him. "We just have to set the table. Come out to the patio when you're ready." She shut the pottery room door after he moved to the bathroom.

After he washed his face and hands, he combed his hair and changed into the clean shirt he'd pulled out of his suitcase on their way in. He looked at the shower longingly. Nope, that would be asking too much. He'd just have to wait until he got his room in Grants. He hoped they'd have a room ready right away.

The patio had a large, tiled table on which the two women were setting bowls of lamb in red chili stew, sliced squash cooked with onions and corn, and a pile of large, flat discs of fried bread in the middle. He was familiar with the spicy lamb stew from his Navajo friends in Farmington. He dug in, hungry after a long hard day and complimented Donna's cooking.

"So, Terry, you're from Amarillo. What took you so far from your family?"

Liliana coughed up her tea, then apologized as she dabbed up the spray from the table.

"Well," he said drawing out his words, "let's just say there was an incompatibility in our lifestyle choices."

Liliana started laughing and Donna smiled, slightly embarrassed. Terry sensed her interest in him and saw how she scanned his face, pleased by what she saw.

"What type of work do you do in Farmington?" she started again.

"I'm a civil engineer, which means I usually travel a lot from my base of operations in Farmington. After my dad got sick, I changed my job so I could stay in Farmington, the closest position they would offer me. The traveling gets old after a while, so I was planning a career change . . . teaching, maybe. But you know how expensive cancer treatments are. Dad had the ranch, but no cash flow. Now I'm just about tapped out. To top it off, the company used my frequent absences as an excuse to lay me off; I expected that fifteen years would have bought me some consideration.

"I'm all he's got except for my brother's widow and his grandchildren. Since I'm the only one left to run his large ranch, I locked up my house and loaded up the truck to move out there. Maybe I'll take over his ranch just like he always wanted." He seemed unhappy at the prospect. Changing the subject, he said, "There's still a lot of stuff in my truck, even though Liliana helped me transfer the important stuff to her truck. I hope Mike doesn't have any trouble getting it to Grants. I should've waited for him."

"Mike's reliable. He probably already has your truck at his shop. You've had a long day. Relax. I'm sure you could use the rest."

A young voice called out from inside the house. Donna stood up. "That's my eight-year-old son, Angelo. He woke up with a fever and a rash, so I had to take the day off. I guess it was lucky in a way. It would have been the first time Liliana arrived to an empty house. I'll fix up a plate for him. He's probably hungry since he slept through lunch."

After she left, Liliana looked up apologetically and said, "Sorry, my aunt is not usually so nosy."

"Don't worry about it."

"There's pie in the kitchen. Do you want some coffee to go with it, or is it too hot for coffee?" She smiled, already knowing the answer.

"It's never too hot for a cowboy to drink coffee," he smiled and finished off his second bowl of stew so she could take his dish.

She laughed, "I thought so. I'll be back in a flash." She scooped up the rest of the dishes in one hand, stacked the plate of bread on top, and took the serving bowl of stew in her other hand. Clearly impressed by her skill, he raised his eyebrows. "Intermittent waitress at work," she said as she elbowed her way through the screen door.

Promptly she was back with plates, cups and a lemon meringue pie, and then fetched the coffee and sugar. She served each of them a healthy-sized slice of pie, and then said with a full mouth, "We can eat it all if we want to. No one else likes lemon meringue." After drinking some of her black, heavily-sweetened coffee, she said, "So, you like my aunt?"

He smiled and nodded.

"She's been divorced for a while, which means," She paused as she concentrated on cutting herself another fork full of pie, "that she would probably go out with you." Looking over the pie, she gauged his reaction, and then lowered her eyes as she ate.

"You think so?" he teased, hearing a trace of jealousy in her voice. She shook her head pointed her chin to the house, and changed the subject as Donna's footsteps echoed in the hall.

"Mike will let you make payments on the tow, but I don't know how much work he'll invest in the truck if you can't pay most of it right away." She stopped speaking as Donna arrived.

"I see Liliana found the pie. Have all you want. No one else likes it, but Mom used to make it for her since she was little. Those two would sit down and eat a whole pie in two days. She used the excuse of Liliana visiting to blow her diabetic diet. I guess I got in the habit of making it when my niece got a break from school."

"You miss your mother," Terry said.

"We were close, especially when I moved back home after the divorce. She'd complain about my noisy boy, but she spoiled him rotten anyway. That diabetes just eats you up. I took a leave of absence to stay with her, because she didn't like having strangers come into the house and, after a while, they couldn't find a visiting nurse that would come to see her."

"Yeah," Liliana interjected, "the Laguna women said that Grandma would give them the evil eye."

Donna pointedly looked at Terry, refusing to respond to Liliana's attempt to annoy her. "She died two years ago. She'd been miserable once she got too blind to paint her pots. Even though she was ready to go, I still miss her." She shook her head. "Too much sadness. Are you dating anyone?"

"Not right now," he shrugged, "I travel a lot with my job and there have been a lot of trips to Amarillo this year. How about you?"

"No, it's too hard when you have a kid and a sick mother. It's been awhile since I even considered dating."

Liliana got up. She was annoyed that Terry liked Donna, even though she knew he'd never like her. She couldn't take anymore of the courting conversation. "I'm going to visit old Paint. We should leave in half-an-hour."

Donna looked up and said quietly, "Old Paint's been dead for three years, Liliana."

Liliana walked away as if she hadn't heard. Walking through the barn touching the dusty saddles and absorbing the smells and memories of her time with the pony her grandfather had given her, she wondered why everyone had to remind her of death. Of course Paint was gone, like so many others she loved, but it felt good to sit in his stall and imagine that she could still smell him. She took a deep breath of the stable smells, to distract herself from thinking about the lone cowboy she couldn't resist. Despite the distractions, she imagined how her skin would burn if he touched her, what his lips tasted like, and what it would be like to wake up to his eyes in the morning. The impossibility of that happening battled with the pleasant fantasy.

After half-an-hour, Liliana started back. She came in the front door so she didn't have to hear how easily her aunt talked to him. She went to wash up, wishing it was that easy for her.

When she entered the bathroom, she lowered her head and concentrated on the water. She needed to get to Carla's soon. Peripherally aware of the mirror hanging much too close, she heard Carla's gravelly voice, "¡Como parece a su tata!" Carla's taunt was a lie; Carla knew that man wasn't her father, whether or not Liliana looked like him. *Lord help me*, she thought, *let me be strong and not kill Carla this summer.*

13

She knew she couldn't keep Terry around for more than a day, but if she could just make it through the first few days she might make it through the summer. Every year got harder, yet she couldn't abandon the woman who brought so much misery into her life. Mostly it was because her mother, Susana, was a generous soul who had cared about Carla. Susana knew it hurt Carla when she left home so young.

She pushed some loose hairs back as she turned on the hot water. She forced the memory of that hateful statement away and avoided the face in the mirror that brought it to mind. Knowing that the person she was supposed to resemble was not her father didn't erase the feeling of disgust at the sight of the face that so many people compared it to, Joe Yazzie. The man she hated more than anyone in the world. She filled her hands with scorching water and splashed it over her face, burning away the filth of that memory.

No one noticed how she dodged mirrors if she could, or knew about the pain her reflection had given her for as long as she could remember. Her self-loathing was a secret pain she'd never shared with anyone. The hot water drove the pain away, but not before a desperate tear slipped by. No, the cowboy would never like her. Not only was she tainted with shame, but it was imprinted on her face for everyone to see.

She closed her eyes and mind, pulled her tough shell around her and tried to care more about Carla's health and less about her meanness. Her liver failure caused the swelling belly that was larger every time Liliana saw her. There wasn't much time left for her grandmother. *I will not hate Carla*, she promised herself. *That is not who I am.*

She focused on her hands. Aunt Donna said they looked like Liliana's father's hands. Everyone had loved her father. No one loved Carla; she was too full of rage.

And Joe, omygod, I cannot deal with Joe right now. I hope someone runs him over before I shoot him.

She leaned on the door, the offensive mirror out of her sight, until she was ready. Well prepared with her I'm-cool-with-anything Liliana look she returned to the patio.

Through the back door, she saw Terry laughing at something Donna said; she pushed her resentment away and maintained her look as she opened the door. As she leaned down to get her pack, she said, "We should get going. Maybe you guys can meet up in town while Mike checks out the truck." She fought the jab of jealousy; she didn't want that feeling. It was too much like Carla. "Thanks for a great lunch, Aunt Donna. Tell Grandpa I said 'hi.' And yes, thank you, I'll take the rest of the pie and some stew and bread."

Donna nodded with a slight frown. Liliana knew she should have waited for Donna to offer, but there was a bit of jealous satisfaction in knowing she had annoyed her aunt. Liliana helped package the food and Donna walked them to Liliana's truck.

"I'm amazed this old beast doesn't give you more trouble," Donna said.

"It's my dad's truck and he loves me. It will never leave me stranded." Liliana replied as she jumped in the truck and slammed the door shut.

Chapter 2

Meeting Carla

S he gunned the truck over the gravel spraying rocks around until
they reached the uneven dirt road to the road that led to the paved
road to Grants. "So, you and Donna got along pretty good, huh?"

Terry nodded watching the way her hands gripped the steering wheel.
"Yeah, we seem to have a lot in common."

"Maybe you could call her and take her out to dinner tonight."

He glanced over at the thinly disguised sarcasm in her tone. She kept
her eyes on the road, her lips pressed together.

"No, for several reasons. I like her, but I'm not staying. I have just
enough money for the tow, expenses and a bus ticket to Amarillo...
Speaking of money, are you sure your uncle won't be mad when he finds
out I don't have enough to pay for any work on the truck?"

"Oh, he'll be pissed, but he's a good guy." She blew out a big breath,
and then glanced at him. "I might have to remind him is all. Do you
want to be there, or should I make my mojo with you politely out of
hearing?"

"I guess I should be present to find out which of my body parts you're
offering him." She laughed. He liked her laugh and was glad to see her
face relax.

"Well, if he were interested in body parts, it would only be your scalp.
Even though he's Spanish, he's always bragging about how many scalps
his Apache great-great-grandfather collected in his day." She glanced over,
"It doesn't seem to bother you to be teased about being white."

16

He nodded, "Nah, I got used to it in Farmington with my Navajo friends. It was strange at first, being the only white man at a party, but I enjoy their dry humor and it's best when they're ragging on a white man."

"Yeah, right. You just wanted to hang onto your scalp."

He turned to face her with his back to the door. Her shoulders hunched automatically as if preparing herself for an attack; a stance he remembered from his own childhood. "So things are rough with your Laguna family?"

She relaxed, but only a little. With a tight smile, she said, "Yeah, well, decades pass but bitterness doesn't let go."

He decided to go with the truth as it appeared at the moment. "Donna seems to care about you."

She glanced over. "Grandma Carla has given them a lot of grief fighting over me. They'd rather have my dad alive than have me in any shape." She fell silent and Terry was reluctant to dig into her painful memories. Silently, he turned to look forward, watching the deprived streets of this part of Grants pass by.

"Oh, I guess I should warn you. My Mexican, or Spanish as she prefers to be called, grandma, Carla Gonzalez, had a fight with her boyfriend as the bar was closing last night. The cops had to break it up. Mike told me," she responded to his unasked question. "Anyway, she'll be primed and ready to explode. Just be your polite, good-looking self and maybe she'll flirt instead of yell. There won't be dinner, but we have enough left-overs. I have my own set of keys, so she can't deny you a room, but she might try. Unfortunately, she may make you wonder if you're crazy after you've been around her for a while," she paused. "Let's hope your truck doesn't need much work. We'll stop at Mike's shop first, while I'm in a negotiating mood."

Terry wondered what kind of mess he'd let himself in for. As he examined Liliana's profile, he was surprised to realize that he didn't mind. He wasn't ready to say goodbye yet. They passed a series of empty malls, service stations and decrepit motels. He saw the faded sign for Mike's Auto Service on a building with three working bays, a small office and a multitude of broken down cars parked in the attached lot. The offending red Chevy was parked to one side of the bays, with the hood open and someone's half-covered rear end hanging out. Liliana pulled up by his truck and Terry got out, prepared for the worst. The rear end dropped to its feet and the rest of a short, dark-complected, rotund person turned around. Mike's round, mustachioed face was not smiling as he wiped his hands on a blue rag. He pulled up his pants and tucked in his grease-spotted, blue work-shirt as he walked over to greet them.

Terry winced at the look on Mike's face. Again he was reminded that should have gotten a more reliable vehicle years ago, but he was attached to the old Chevy and the challenge of keeping it running. That challenge was going to present a serious problem in his current situation.

Before Liliana said a word, Mike started complaining. "Goddamn it, Liliana, when do you ever ask for my help with a customer who has more than ten cents in his pocket?" He turned to Terry, indignation colored with humor. "This engine is gone, man. Even a rebuilt engine is going to cost you a thousand and I'm not going to put that kind of money into it without most of it up front. I don't care if he's the next Jesus Christ, Liliana, without money, I am not relying on your judgment."

He turned to Terry, and put out his hand. "Sorry, fella, it's graveyard time. My name is Mike, as you might have guessed. I can tell you've really taken care of this antique, but you should've known it wasn't up to a cross-country trip."

Before he could respond, Liliana said, "You're just mad 'cause Martinsen sent you all the money he owed you. Now you owe me the hundred you bet against him. Terry, do you want a coke?"

"Yes, make it an orange drink and thanks for the straight story, Mike. I'm Terry Prentice and I can tell you I'm good for it, eventually. I'm not ready to dump her, yet. Do you mind if I leave her here to work on tonight? I've got my tools in Liliana's truck."

"I don't mind. It'll make it look like I got some business. The tow charge is a hundred bucks, hombre." He held out his hand palm up. Terry reached into his wallet and laid a hundred dollar bill on his palm. Mike's eyebrows shot up in surprise. Liliana returned with the soft drinks, handing her uncle a cold beer. Mike slapped Terry's shoulder and said, "Man, you have made a friend for life."

Mike dodged, but was not quick enough. Liliana snatched the money from his hand. "It's about time you paid up on one of your bets." She looked at him with defiance; he laughed and hugged her.

"So, how's school going, Chica?" he said.

"So, so. I learned a new one. How do you eat an elephant?"

"One bite at a time," the two men chorused.

"It's like that."

"Why don't you and your friend come over to my house for dinner tonight?" he asked. He saw her expression and said, "Okay, I know, Carla will have a fit if she finds out. Sorry, Terry, if you don't go, Carla will tell everyone in town that you're Liliana's new pimp. And a few just might believe her." His face was sympathetic. "I guess you might as well get it over with. Come on over whenever you want to work on your truck, or if you just want a beer and some gossip. You should get your stuff into locked storage, though. It won't be safe outside overnight. You've got time; I'm open until nine, so I can keep an eye on it." Terry shook his hand and thanked him. They got back into Liliana's truck and he waved goodbye as they left.

"Vaya con Dios, 'hita," Mike said as they drove off.

They drove down the main road until they reached a small, dilapidated motel. The unlit neon sign said simply Grants M_t_l with a faded vacancy sign swinging below it. They pulled up beside a beat-up, lavender 1980 Cadillac that was set up on cinder blocks instead of tires.

"Purple is my grandma's favorite color. Most of the time it matches the color of her face." Liliana's knuckles were white as she gripped the steering wheel.

Terry didn't respond. Liliana took a deep breath as they climbed out of the truck. Terry saw the dirty, empty pool behind the row of single-story rooms badly in need of stucco repair and paint. Next to the office door was a large, faded sign stating that the management had the right to refuse service to anyone. They entered the small dirty office with a cluttered customer counter. It was cooled by a squeaking air-conditioner, which competed with the noise of the country-western music blaring from an old radio on the shelf behind the front desk.

Liliana turned off the radio and unlocked the door marked "private" with one of a number of keys she pulled from her backpack, calling out, "Grandma, I'm here and I have company. Where are you?"

They stood in a living room rank with the smell of cigarettes, beer and stale, cheap perfume. The furniture was covered with dirty, fake fur throws and full ash trays. A kitchenette, revealing signs of a hasty, incomplete clean-up, occupied one corner of the room. Liliana walked over and kicked a pair of black, spike-heeled shoes inside the bedroom and shut the door concealing a pile of dirty clothes.

"Where do you think I am?" a coarse, female voice yelled from the bathroom. "Mike called to tell me you had a friend. Of course, you wouldn't be caught dead being courteous to your own grandmother and call me to tell me you were bringing company. Get your friend a beer. I'll be out in a minute."

Liliana whispered as she passed by him, "Mike prob'ly called to tell her I had a cute guy with me to cool her off some." Then she shrugged, not making any predictions as to what he ought to expect. "Do you want a beer?" Terry shook his head and held up his pop. Liliana whispered, "She only buys the cheap crap anyway."

She led him outside through the sliding doors to the tree shaded patio, and then returned to get three steel chairs with torn plastic seats and backs from the kitchen. As she sat down, she pulled an asthma inhaler from her jeans' pocket and deeply inhaled two puffs. They waited in silence for the appearance of her grandmother.

"Well, look what we have here," crooned a gravelly, female voice as the creaky screen door slid open. Terry looked up to see a small, dyed-red-haired woman wearing heavy make-up over a thin, hollowed out face, tight jeans over skinny legs, narrow hips and a swollen belly. A very low-cut, skin-tight top revealed a large bosom, obviously pushed up from beneath.

Politely smiling, he stood up to introduce himself, "Terry Prentice, Ma'am."

"This is my grandmother, Carla Gonzales," Liliana said, through clenched teeth as the woman ignored her, smiling flirtatiously as she held on to Terry's hand. Embarrassed, Terry wasn't quite sure of the safest reaction. He noticed that Carla had a swollen, bruised eye that her heavy make-up failed to conceal.

"Nice to meet you," he said, maintaining what he hoped was a safe smile.

"Well, it's very nice to meet you, too. What's the matter with you, Liliana?" she scolded. "Didn't I tell you to get this good-looking man a beer? I have to do everything myself. Kids have no respect anymore." She turned to re-enter the house, transferring her beer to the same hand that held her cigarette, but Terry touched her arm stopping her, to which she turned seductively as if he'd fondled her; so hungry for love she was. He pulled his hand away as if scorched.

"Thanks anyway, Ma'am. I already have something to drink, thank-you. Here, take my chair." He held the chair as if he were holding a basket for a viper. Once she had swung her hips into the chair, wiggling everything possible as she sat, he took the third chair on the other side of Liliana. It wasn't far enough he discovered as Carla leaned over to tap the ash from her cigarette on the cement, giving him a full view of her bosom. Glancing over at Liliana, he saw her watching the interaction with narrowed, glowering eyes.

"You sound like you're from Texas. Let me guess, Amarillo?" He nodded, and she continued. "I went to Amarillo, years ago. It gets really hot there from what I remember. What brings you to Grants? Did you pick up Liliana on the street?" She laughed at her joke. He strained to produce a small, polite smile.

"I was coming from Farmington, headed through Albuquerque. My truck broke down and Liliana gave me a ride when she saw me stranded on the road. Mike has my truck, but he doesn't give me much hope that we'll be able to get it running soon."

"Cars are such a pain in the ass, aren't they? Just when you think you've got yourself a reliable one, it breaks down. Kind of like men I guess." She inhaled her cigarette, oblivious to the insult. Terry felt Liliana's tension rise, preparing herself for what was coming next.

"And I know what I'm talking about," Carla continued, and then took a long pull at her beer. As she leaned over to set it down, she didn't seem aware that she was falling out of her blouse. Now on the her favorite topic, the unavoidable baseness of men, she continued, waving her cigarette in the air, ignoring Liliana's coughs. "I've been married three times and none of them was worth a piss," her voice was slurred, but she had found her rhythm. Liliana rolled her eyes.

"Those were the ones who had me fooled the longest. The others never got that far; I saw through them right away." She stopped to light another cigarette. "Honey, get me another beer will you, and one for our guest," she said, his refusal already forgotten. Liliana shrugged and got up to go inside.

Carla leaned over, "The worst one was that stupid reservation Indian that got her mom pregnant at fourteen. If he'd been one year older, I'd have had him in jail for state rape." The screen slammed open. Carla leaned back and said, "Now this child is the light of my life. My only grandchild; I was never able to have more than my one daughter. She messed up my womb and I could never have another kid."

Without acknowledging Liliana, she accepted the opened beer and took a long drink. "I could have had me a nice husband, but no one wanted a sterile wife with a kid. No sir. They all wanted their own kids. When my granddad died, we were on our own. Then, after everything I did for her, she got herself pregnant and then she got herself killed and left me to raise her Indian kid. Oh, I'm sorry, they like to be called Native Americans these days."

When she appeared ready to give a lengthy opinion on that issue, Liliana's crossed her arms and turned to look out at the street as if longing to escape. Terry attempted to change the subject. "How did you land out in the motel business? It must be hard in this town."

Startled out of her routine rant, her eyes blurred while she slowly processed the question. "It was my dad's place," she finally responded. "The only thing he left me. A stone around my neck. Barely makes enough to keep food on the table. Speaking of food, I bet she took you to see her Indian grandma's house before she brought you here? Dead two years, and the kid I raised still goes there first. Where were they when she was sick with her tonsils, or when she cried all night with her colds? God, every time I turned around she was sick again. Who paid for all that medicine? Well, she works it off now, but she still doesn't give me any respect. Just sits there like a wooden Indian, just like Joe. Looks just like him, too. Never has a word to say." Terry glanced at Liliana, and saw her desperately hanging on to her temper.

"Before I forget, Liliana, units four, five and six need to be cleaned and they all need to be painted. I hope you've got some of that Indian scholarship money left, because I don't have any money for paint. Hand it over. I know they give you lots of money, and I know you don't spend it living with me. Come on now. Show this man what a good kid you can be." About to fall off her chair, she grabbed Liliana's knee to support herself. "What's the matter with you? Do you think you get free room and board here or what?"

Liliana finally spoke, "I'm broke, grandma. I just had enough to get gas to get here. I have a lot of expenses at school." She ignored Terry, who tried to hide his surprise at the necessary lie. He could see that Carla would have immediately spent the money on alcohol. He could never lie that smoothly.

Carla stood up weaving, "Don't lie to me, you little squaw whore. I know they give you money. Hand it over." When Liliana didn't move, Carla slapped her, catching Liliana by surprise. "You little slut, just do what I say. I know how to punish little sluts. You may be taller than me, but I can still take you."

Terry had enough. He stood up, reminding Carla that he was there. "Oh, don't mind me," she croaked, brushing her hair out of her eyes. "Just a little bad mood. We get along just fine, don't we, 'hita?" Clumsily, she patted Liliana's shoulder.

Terry took her arm and said, "I think you've had a hard day. Don't you think you'd feel better after a little nap? Come on, now. I'll help you to your room." Liliana stood up, warning in her eyes, but he shook his head. She followed them inside. He pushed Carla's roaming hands away just before she fell onto the bed. He shut the door; the snores started almost immediately. Liliana picked up the lit cigarette Carla had dropped and threw a kitchen towel over the spilled beer. After she locked the patio door, she led him through the office, which she locked and put up the closed sign.

"You have to be careful with her," she said once they were outside. "A guy went to prison, because she convinced the court that he raped her. I was there. He was the one who got raped. I was only eight, so no one was going to ask a kid what happened. Come on, let's see which rooms are clean enough to stay in. She quits cleaning when it's time for me to come home."

They opened door after door and found that all twelve units were trashed. It looked as if they had been used for drunken parties for weeks. None of them were immediately habitable. Intensely embarrassed, Liliana stared at the floor.

"I'm so sorry. I didn't expect it to be this bad. I'll get one of these cleaned up. Why don't you take the left-overs to Mike? He loves Donna's cooking and it won't keep in this heat. You can work on your truck and get your stuff stored while I clean a room for you." He heard her desperation.

He asked, "Is it always like this?" He worried about leaving Liliana there.

She turned away from him before answering. "This is the worst it's been; I mean the rooms. I never brought anyone over before. Usually she yells and tries to hit me because I leave her for school. I let her get it out then I leave until she passes out. The next day, when she sees the rooms are clean, she's better. She's been going downhill for the last couple of years. She barely eats anything and she won't go to see a doctor and she won't tell me anything about what's really going on. It's one lie after another. I find out more from Mike than from her." She wiped her nose on her sleeve. "The place looks like a collection of junkie shooting parlors. While you're at Mike's, ask him if he has a couple of spare . . . you know those pole things you put under the doorknob to keep the door shut. You don't need any junkies visiting in the middle of the night."

She handed him the truck keys, let herself into the maintenance room for supplies and yelled out the door. "There's only enough stuff here to clean one room." She stepped out and looked up at him, embarrassed, pleading. "I don't want to sleep in my room in the apartment tonight. She's angry and her friends visit at all hours. I promise I'm safe, and the room's free. Maybe we could share a two bed room."

She didn't look up when he touched her shoulder. All he could think about was her alone with some drunk messing with her during the night, or even worse, having to endure Carla's poison all night. "I'm safe, too. And I don't mind sharing a room. Thanks." She turned to lean her forehead on the wall and nodded. "I'll be back before it gets too late," he said. He didn't ask her why she'd brought him into the middle of this disaster, nor did he offer to help any more than she had asked for, sensing her humiliation.

∞

As Terry drove off, she started sobbing. Having finally found someone who gave her so much joy made the mess so much worse. She knew Carla would drive him away. Falling against the wall inside the small maintenance supply room, she kicked the door shut and slid to the ground. Her head ached with unspent tears and rage. Finally, she was able to pull herself together and got started on the twin-bed-room farthest from the office. Moving fast so she couldn't think, she carted her supplies to the room and locked the door before she started to clean. Cars pulled up, and someone banged on the office door, but she ignored them. She tried not to jump at every sound from outside. When most of the smell was cleaned up, she loaded up the linens and carted them across the street to wash. The washer and dryer had gone missing from the maintenance room years ago, and the washer and dryer in Carla's apartment hadn't worked for years.

Too angry to read her textbook as she'd planned while the linens washed, she went through her calming ritual of remembering every single thing she could about her parents. She wished she had enough change to do her own laundry. Fortunately, she had clean clothes for tomorrow. Then she'd get her uncle to break the hundred she'd snatched from his hand. If she used it anywhere else in town, the news of her having a hundred-dollar bill was sure to get back to Carla.

The sun was setting as Terry drove up. She waved him over to the room she had ready and he parked in front of it. Dirty and discouraged, he had to face the fact that his truck was indeed not carrying him to Amarillo any time soon. He'd enjoyed his visit with Mike, however, who told him tall tales of his exploits as a hunter and enough information about Carla to prepare him for future encounters. After his encounter with the woman, he realized that he needed to know the risks since he was stuck here for the night at least. Then he'd have to decide if he was going to take a bus or call to borrow money from his sister-in-law for a flight. According to Mike, Carla was a force to be dealt with, even though she seemed to be on her last legs. She was mean and vindictive, Mike had said, and she never got busted for anything she did.

Terry learned how Carla had gotten pregnant in junior high school and had Liliana's mother, Susana. She'd married later, but it didn't last, so she returned to school. Then she managed to get pregnant by a popular, well-off football player believing that he would marry her. She bragged about how she had gotten money placed in an annuity from his family. Even though the baby was stillborn, the annuity continued to pay. That was the only thing that kept her afloat.

Mike was the brother of Carla's first husband and helped Liliana when he could. The rest of his family had left Grants looking for work. As a result of his marrying the daughter of the woman with the worst reputation in town, Liliana's father, Benjamin Hunt, and his parents were estranged. They were still estranged when Ben died in the car accident. Mike had known Liliana's parents well, and he knew they had loved each other and were responsible kids who took their marriage and child seriously. Terry asked him why Carla called Liliana a Navajo.

Mike shook his head, reluctant to answer. Finally he explained, "There's this drunk by the name of Joe Yazzie, a Navajo, who hung around Carla's mother, then around Carla since she was a teen. Everybody here knows Joe. Well, there are rumors that Joe slept with Anna and everyone knows he sleeps with Carla and some believe he got to Liliana's mom, too. I don't believe that he got to Susana. So Liliana has his blood, maybe twice over. Liliana does look something like Joe, like any Native American sort of resembles another, but you know how people love a scandal.

"I knew Liliana's mom and dad were dating, but they were good kids. Joe was around a lot when Ben and Susana ran away to Texas and got married. Then Ben's family abandoned them, but when Ben and Susana died they took Liliana in. Jim Hunt is still bitter about loosing his son and acts like he doesn't believe she's Ben's kid, especially when people started saying how much she looked like Joe. They had Liliana for two years until Carla got hold of her. Many times Social Services took Liliana from Carla, and Ben's family would take her in. Then Carla would find a way to get her back again. It became a huge war, and Liliana was the battleground. After a while, Ben's folks quit fighting. Nobody knew how Carla managed to get her back every time. I guess that was the worst of it.

"She's a good kid even if she's always been a little strange. I can tell you something though. If Liliana tells you something's going to happen, you can bet your life on it."

"Then why did you bet against her?" Terry asked, amused and curious.

Mike laughed. "Yeah, well, the kid's got it rough. I help when I can, but she's proud, too. I have to complain a lot, so I make losing bets against her." Mike patted Terry's shoulder. "You seem like a good guy, but, man, if you hurt her, Texas is not that far away." He eyed Terry with his forehead lowered like a bull.

Terry laughed and reassured him. "I'm going to stay the night at the motel. We'll probably share a room, mainly because it looks like a junkie flop house and I don't want her to stay alone with Carla or Carla's friends."

"Yeah, it's pretty bad. I don't think Carla gets any legitimate customers any more. It's too bad she can't even sell the place. Nobody's making any investments in this part of town." He sighed, "I appreciate what you have put up with. I think you're good for her. She was joking about Carla. She hasn't done that in a long time. Maybe she'll be able to leave Carla once and for all . . . soon."

When he arrived at the motel, Terry brought arms full of take-out Mexican food and pop into the room. Liliana sniffed deeply as he passed. "You've been to Concha's. Mike let you in on the best restaurant in town. Y'oughta feel special."

The room was small with bare walls, and only room for the twin beds, two small night stands and the table where a television had once sat. On the table two small electric deodorizers puffed their hardest, but barely made a dent in the smell. The tiny closet was in the wall at the back opposite the bathroom. There was a small dingy window in the bathroom. Liliana had managed to get most of the superficial crud cleaned up, but suspicious stains were scattered on the walls and ancient, reeking shag carpet. He'd given Mike a third of his cash for the tow. Now he was tempted to spend the last of his cash on a decent hotel for them both, but he was sure Carla would find them. Watching her set out the food, coughing with her asthmatic wheeze, he realized it was impossible for him to leave her there.

They sat on the bed with the door shut, despite the heat and the broken air-conditioner. "Maybe we should buy a fan," he suggested.

She shook her head chewing a mouthful of enchilada. "Carla left with her boyfriend. She'll be plastered when she comes back. Now that you're here to help me, we can get the air-conditioner from the office. She won't notice it tonight. We can take it back in the morning." He nodded and watched as she dug into the food, head and eyes lowered.

The room still smelled of old cigarettes and beer, but it was as clean as it could be without a paint job, new carpet and new furnishings. After they had the purloined the air-conditioner running, the room cooled until it was comfortable. After he took a shower, he found her lying on the bed with an anatomy book in her hands.

"Getting ahead on some school work?" he asked.

"Yeah, wishful thinking. There's a summer class in anatomy, but I have to stay here. When I'm in Albuquerque I stay with my aunt."

"So, is this an aunt on your mother's or father's side?" he asked around a mouthful of sopapilla and honey.

"Ooh, you're learning fast. Pretty soon you'll be downright nosy." He glanced up to apologize, but saw that her smile reached her eyes. "It's Uncle Mike's sister, Adela, and Mike is Carla's first husband, George's brother. George lives in California with his second wife, five kids and about a dozen grandkids. I've only seen Grandpa George twice since he left town. The last time he was in town, Carla shot him in the ass. Good thing she was drunk or he'd be dead. She's a good shot. Mike's a saint, but don't you tell him I said that."

She closed her book and laid it down. "I'm too tired to read. You can leave the lights on; they don't bother me. Good night." She turned off her bedside lamp and then said, "If it gets too cold, turn the air conditioner down to medium. I wouldn't open the window." She added, "I saw the truck was empty. I guess Mike warned you to lock up all your stuff. That's good."

"Yeah. That's why I got back so late. We found a storage place that would take a postdated check."

"That must be Gerry's place. He's good people." She pulled the blanket over her head and seemed to fall asleep.

Terry wasn't ready to sleep. He was angry at Carla and confused about his feelings for Liliana. He liked her, but he did not need more troubles with his own pile so high. Eventually he realized that her problems had managed to distract him from his own. And he liked her company, a lot. He lay down with a novel he'd been trying to finish, while thinking about how desperate she looked sometimes. Maybe she had latched on to the first stranger willing to help. No, he thought, it was more than that.

He woke to a crash of broken glass and the thump of someone falling, cursing and scrambling. The book was on his chest and his bedside lamp was on. Liliana was standing out of sight of the bathroom window. She motioned for him to lie still. There was drunken giggling and shushing going on outside the window.

A large hunched over man, with long, stringy grey hair, dressed in a faded red tee shirt and baggy jeans was trying to sneak, but he was too drunk to do better than stumble, over to where Terry's pants lay across the chair. Fortunately, his wallet was under his pillow.

Suddenly, Liliana stepped out, put a gun to the man's head and said, "Come on, you old bastard. Give me another reason to blow your brains out." The man immediately passed out, falling heavily to the floor. Terry rushed to the bathroom window to see Carla stumbling off toward her apartment, wobbling through the weeds in her spiked heels.

"Come on, help me get rid of this stinking corpse," Liliana said grimly. Terry checked the man's pulse and sighed in relief. They each grabbed a leg and dragged him and his stink outside. Liliana stepped out to the main street and waved down a passing police car. Terry noted the Laguna Reservation logo on the police car, but didn't realize that it was out of place.

"Hi, Liliana, who's your friend?" the policeman said as he got out of the car.

"This is Terry Prentice. Joe just broke into the room to steal Terry's wallet, with my grandma's help, so I guess we're not pressing charges. But you can take him in for drunk and disorderly, can't you?" Liliana's voice was shaking with anger.

"Sure thing, kid." He reached out to shake Terry's hand as he checked him out then looked over his shoulder at the single lit room. "I'm

Sergeant Jake Sanchez. And I'll even agree to ignore the fact that you're in possession of a firearm if you turn it over."

Liliana grimaced as she handed the gun to him. Once he found the gun wasn't loaded, he stuck it in his belt. He grunted as he leaned over the drunk to checking his pulse. "You scared the crap out of him, Liliana," he said holding his nose. "Do you have something to protect my car seats?" She nodded and went to unlock the next room.

Jake was dressed in a neatly pressed uniform; his black hair was cut military style. His eyes were widely spaced over a straight nose and narrow lips. His face and frame were narrow. Yet his muscular arms strained at his shirt sleeves. He turned his cool eyes to Terry and asked, "So, where did you meet Liliana? Aren't you a little old for her?"

With a tight smile Terry responded, "I guess you could call me one of her strays. My truck broke down and she gave me a ride, and a platonic offer of a room, since things are tight for me right now."

"Yeah, Mike told me. I'm sorry about your dad." Jake raised his eyebrows in response to Terry's reaction. "Don't look so surprised. You must know what it's like in a small town. And yes, I was checking up on you when I passed by." He looked down at the immobile figure on the ground.

"Carla and this one go way back. This old fool is always around to pick up the pieces when she fights with whoever she's seeing." He accepted the shower curtain from Liliana and Terry helped him lift Joe into the backseat of the Laguna police SUV.

After thanking Jake, Liliana stood with her arms crossed until the car drove off. She then turned and went inside without a word. Silently Terry watched the police car disappear around a corner, and then went inside. Liliana was sitting slouched over on the side of the bed.

"She's jealous and won't give it up." She got up and sat down again, restless with anger and frustration. "Why don't we leave now? We'll take my truck to Amarillo and get away from all of this crap. I won't be able to sleep here now; I'm that close to breaking her neck."

Terry heard the hard edge of the bitterness and despair that she had managed to conceal behind her dark humor until now. The sky had begun to lighten through the thin curtains as he considered her desperate plea. He should send her to her grandparent's house and get a hotel, but he'd learned too much about Carla to believe that would help. Then there was the way she made him feel. As stressed, angry and bitter as she was, he wanted to be near her. He wanted to hold her and comfort her. So, he agreed.

"You bet," he responded. "You know. Maybe it wouldn't have been so bad if you'd come home alone. She was performing for me, you know."

She kept her eyes glued to the floor. "Yeah, I'm sorry." She sighed. "I'm really sorry. It would have been different, but worse. She hates that I'm spending so much time in Albuquerque going to school. She'd make me pay somehow... Maybe we can get you a flight home tonight. I have some money hidden. This is totally screwed."

She leaned forward, arms tight across her stomach, until her chin rested on her knees. Despair oozed from her pores.

"Hey, kid, I'm sorry. I'm just tired. It's been a long year. I don't want . . . I mean I can see how desperate it must get here. Let's get an early breakfast at Concha's, and then we'll have to wait for the storage to open at nine. I have to get a few things from there." He touched her shoulder. When her eyes squeezed shut, he pulled his hand away.

"Great," Liliana stood and bent to get her pack without looking his way. "The sooner I get away from here the better. Thank you."

She went to the bathroom, brushed her teeth and changed from sweats to jeans and T-shirt. A spasm of coughing started while she was in the bathroom. When she stumbled out and grabbed her inhaler, Terry noted her pale hue and worried. After a few minutes the coughing stopped, but he could still hear her wheezing. He followed her into the bathroom and saw her leaning on the sink as she coughed. He watched to see her image in the mirror, but she managed to avoid it. She turned to him and he saw a strange look on her face when her eyes met his. She moved past him, coughing harder.

"Does Concha's have outdoor seating? I didn't notice last night and there were a lot of smoking customers. That's going to make your asthma worse." She shrugged without answering.

Soon they had their things together and started off. She was quiet at breakfast. When Terry opened his storage unit, Liliana exclaimed, "Oh, shit! I forgot to get my camping gear. I'll need it on the way back. You should bring yours, too. We might get too tired to drive and we could save a few bucks by camping out. I'll be back in twenty minutes, and then we can hit the road."

He watched her walk off, coughing and using her inhaler, not liking the sound of her breathing, or her color. As she backed the truck up, she returned his wave, and then drove off. It didn't take him long to pull out the stuff he wanted to take: his camping gear, summer clothes and his computer. When half-an-hour passed, he moved his stuff closer to the office and bummed a cup of coffee off the good-natured manager. Gerry, a fifty-ish, balding, pale complected man, gossiped with him about the recent scandals, including Carla's drunken brawls two nights in a row at a local bar. Like Mike, Gerry told Terry that Liliana was a good kid, and warned him to mind his manners.

Finally, after an hour, Liliana drove up with her gear in the back of the truck. Her eyes were filled with such dark clouds that neither of them asked her why she was late. Still coughing after they said goodbye to Gerry, she let Terry drive. When he got in he realized all the mirrors were twisted in strange directions. He straightened them and saw Liliana flinch when he brought down the rearview mirror. After ten minutes he turned the truck around.

"What are you doing?" she asked.

"You're going to the doctor," he said.

"No, I'll get better after I get away from the cigarettes for a while," she insisted.

"No, you won't. My nephew has asthma, and when he sounds like you he lands out in the hospital. I saw a sign for a hospital in town. Where is it?" He looked over to let her see she would not be talking her way around him.

"Dammit! I shoulda' drove. Take me back to the Pueblo. The reservation hospital won't bill Carla. That's where I see my doctor. By the time we get there, I'll be fine. You'll see," she said with conviction.

When they arrived at the Laguna-Acoma Hospital, she wasn't any better. He gave her a knowing look as he helped her out of the truck. "I thought you were never wrong," he said. "It doesn't seem to work so well when it's your own health."

She grimaced as she leaned on him, coughing. When the staff saw her enter the clinic, they immediately set her up with a nebulizer treatment and started an IV. A tall, black gentleman with graying, short hair, glasses and a white coat arrived soon afterward.

"I'm Doctor Frank Karnes," he said as he reached out to shake Terry's hand. "Thanks for taking care of her. I need to talk to her alone if you don't mind. Just for a few minutes."

Liliana pulled off the mask and called out to Terry, "Help me get outta here. Carla'll show up before you know it."

Terry just shook his head and went to the waiting room. True to his word, the doctor arrived ten minutes later. "She always gets worse when she's been at Carla's. I'd like to keep her here, but she's right. Once Carla discovers she's here, she'll be trying to pull her out to get her to work at her broken-down motel. I believe Liliana has reached the end of her tolerance for Carla. It would be good for her to get far away right now. Although I usually wouldn't advise her to leave with a stranger, desperate times need desperate solutions. Bless you for helping her get away and thank you. I've arranged a portable nebulizer and she'll need a treatment every four hours. She also has some tablets of prednisone she's supposed to take twice a day. Her sugar's a little high, so try to keep her away from the sweets, and make her drink plenty of water."

"You mean she has diabetes, too."

"Well, she's more of a pre-diabetic, but no one knows. She swears she'll scalp me if I let it get out. I never thought it would do much good to tell any of her family, anyway. She's pretty much on her own," the doctor eyed Terry warily. "She trusts you, so I trust you, too. Don't disappoint me."

"I've been warned by Mike and Gerry already," he grimaced. "She's safe in my hands. How far is the next hospital?"

"Here's a list of clinics, but they're pretty spread out. She said you have a nephew with asthma and you seem to know what to look for." Terry nodded. "Here's a handout and a spirometer to check her breathing. She's supposed to use it before and after every treatment and record it in this book. I'll be giving all this to her, but, since you'll be traveling together; you should know what to expect. Sorry to lay all of this responsibility on you, but you seem to be willing to help her. Thank-you again for that.

"She'll be able to leave as soon as she finishes getting her intravenous medications. Do you have a card or a cell-phone number so I can contact you if she turns hers off?"

Terry gave him his card, thanked him for his help, and went in to keep Liliana company while she finished getting her treatment. Her color and breathing were already much better. She glared at him over the blue breathing tube when he entered. As soon as the IV med bag was empty, she started buzzing the nurses to set her loose. Soon they were on the road to Amarillo. As they drove through Grants, she slid down in the seat. Her cell-phone rang as they passed the motel. After checking the number, she turned the phone off.

"The only thing she ever bought me. She likes to be able to harass me wherever I am. The miracles of the modern age."

They drove on in silence for an hour, and then Terry pulled over and retrieved his CD player from the back of the truck. He put on some sad country music. Silently they listened to stories of lost love. When Liliana fell asleep, he stopped to cushion her head with his jacket, not waking her from her exhausted sleep. She was wheezing less and her lips were a healthy pink. Lightly pushing her bangs from her eyes, he examined the features that had given her so much grief. He'd only seen Joe passed out drunk. As far as he was concerned, he didn't think she looked like him at all; he saw her Aunt Donna in her.

With anger and pity filling his mind, he started the rumbling truck and eased back onto the highway. He put on some more cheerful music and played it quietly. It wouldn't help her to deal with his anger as well as her own. After setting his cell-phone to vibrate, he settled in for the long drive. It was already two in the afternoon. She would need another treatment at five. He remembered a truck stop they would reach at about the right time. They passed through Albuquerque, unaware of the events that would drag them back there before long.

Mike had shoved a couple of hundreds in his pocket with a glance that warned him not to tell Liliana. It was sad that with so many people who wanted to help her, Liliana was stuck with a wreck like Carla. He decided that the reason Liliana returned to Carla, now that she was twenty, was typical for a child of an alcoholic, wasting their lives trying to take care of weak, ill parents, seeking the love those people were incapable of giving.

Compared to his own troubled childhood, Liliana's must have been a horror. Yet, he had seen her generosity, her own brand of honesty, and an incredible ability to adapt. She had anger and spoke of revenge, but he knew it was just talk, her only outlet for the frustrations heaped on her in her home life. Lost in memories of his childhood, he was startled by the vibration of his phone.

"Hi, it's me, Jake Sanchez, from earlier."

"Hello there. I didn't expect to be hearing from you. What's going on?" Terry responded.

"Well, not much good," Jake answered. "Is Liliana there? I can't get through. I bet she has her phone turned off."

"I had to take her to the hospital for her asthma. They gave her something to relax and she's asleep right now. Can I take a message?"

"Crap! She didn't look so good last night, either. Let her rest. It's just that we've got a bad situation down here. They found Joe dead at the Grants police station before dawn, and then Carla was in there screaming that Liliana killed him. They're sending him to Albuquerque for an autopsy. You'd think they'd lock Carla up for suspicious behavior. How the hell did she know he was dead? If you spend much time with Liliana, you'll learn that Carla is Teflon coated in Grants. The station is in a panic, so no one is thinking clearly. Anyway, I've held them off of Liliana up to now, but they've decided they want to talk to her. I should make you bring her back, but, God damn it, she needs to get away from this shit. I won't drag you back right now, but give me the address where I can find you tomorrow. Just in case."

Jake sounded worried. Terry wondered what it was he wasn't telling him. He gave Jake the address and their distance from Grants. He then asked, "Is there something else going on?"

"Well, it's just that there's a bruise on his butt where something was injected, and Carla says Liliana injected him with something and brought in a syringe as evidence."

He glanced over at the sleeping girl and hoped that she wasn't pretending to sleep; she wouldn't rest once she found out what was happening in Grants. "Maybe you should call Donna Chavez. Liliana might need a lawyer before this is done."

"I already did. Her Uncle Tony is a defense attorney. It's a shame. Sometimes I wonder if some bruja stole Carla's soul long ago. Well, I gotta get back to work. I'll let you know if anything important comes up."

"When will that autopsy be finished?" Terry asked before hanging up.

"Probably not before tomorrow afternoon, if then. It's not a real priority, given his age and poor health. Old Man Death has been looking over his shoulder for a long time. Be careful, and watch your speed. My ass is prob'ly cooked already, but Liliana doesn't deserve to be under this pile of garbage. Bye."

He hung up and Terry attached his phone to the charging unit, so they wouldn't miss any calls. It meant that the CD player had to run on batteries, but he could pick up some batteries later. What a mess.

Chapter 3

On the Road

Grateful as he was that they had made it through Albuquerque, he was even more surprised to pass through Tijeras Canyon to the other side of the Sandia and Manzano Mountains after his conversation with Jake. As the mountains began to fade into the distance, he felt his tension ease up. Liliana woke as they reached the flat, eastern high plains, so they stopped to stretch their legs and snack on the food Mike had sent with them. He didn't mention Jake's call. By seven they reached a small town east of Tucumacari, which he passed through nervously, even though it was a small town.

At the edge of the town, he pulled up to a restaurant parking lot and reached over to wake Liliana who had fallen asleep again. Her breathing was sounding rough again. As she rubbed her eyes, he got out and brought the nebulizer to her from the back. Grimacing, she silently set it up with the meds she needed and sat inhaling the medicated mist from the plastic tube. He could hear the improvement as her breaths came quieter. When she was finished, he checked what kind of battery it used so he could purchase a back up supply. She could be in serious trouble if she missed her treatments.

"Do you know of a decent restaurant in this place?" she asked as she glanced between the Mexican restaurant, a steak nightclub restaurant and a hamburger fast food restaurant that seemed to be the only choices available. There was also small grocery store in a strip mall on the other side of the street.

"I always drive right through here, so I'm not much help."

"I actually feel like eating a hamburger. That would be the cheapest," Liliana replied.

"Sounds okay to me," he responded. "Maybe we should check the hours at the store. I'd hate to have it close before we get our supplies."

Once they determined that the store was open until ten o'clock, they parked at the busy fast-food restaurant. An empty school bus with a high school banner on its side was parked in the lot. Inside a gaggle of teenagers yelling and carousing after a big win at basketball made Terry smile as he remembered those days from his own youth. As they walked through the restaurant silence fell and quiet stares followed their steps. He felt a strange, but familiar sensation. He couldn't figure out what was going on until he noticed that there was not one brown face in the place. This was something he knew. And he knew no good would come from aroused, intoxicated, homogenous teenagers when they were faced with anything different.

When he saw that Liliana was pointedly ignoring everyone, he put his arm protectively around her shoulder and felt her tense up as if to shake it off, but she didn't. Hearing the word "squaw" as they passed a table full of hefty boys in sweats with the high school logo, he resisted the impulse to turn around. There were too many of them and he couldn't afford to draw the attention of the local law enforcement.

After their order was slowly filled, they drove up the next hill in order to catch the cool evening breeze while they ate. He didn't know what to say and knew that nothing he could say would make a difference. He had run into the same thing when he was married, from his own father. He knew there was nothing to be done with well-preserved attitudes here and in his home state of Texas. Amarillo might be a little better since there were more Hispanics there, but there weren't many Native Americans, a factor he would have to consider when he took her out. She didn't need any more stress.

"You don't have to protect me, you know. I can handle myself," she said as if in answer to his thoughts.

"I'm sure you can, but I don't think your body can handle much more stress right now."

She nodded. Then she said, "Why was Jake talking about getting an autopsy on Joe?"

Damn, he thought, "Joe died at the police station and they found an injection site on his butt. Carla claims that you killed him with insulin and brought a syringe to prove it," he paused to watch her chew her sandwich in apparent calm. "Jake said to keep going and he'll let us know what happens. I figure on driving straight through the night. I don't think I could sleep anyway. We'll be in Amarillo by the time they know anything."

She nodded, apparently unsurprised by anything he said. His first inclination was suspicion, and then he realized that living with Carla had to have hardened her to shock. The police would be suspicious of her lack of reaction, at least those who didn't know her.

"That sounds like as good a plan as any. I suppose you don't trust me to drive," she said.

"You're right. You're too sick and that Valium knocks you out. I might fall asleep if I'm not driving, so I'd feel a lot better if I drove, if you don't mind." He leaned forward trying to see any reaction in her eyes.

She glanced over and said, "I'm all right. This isn't the first time Carla has pulled crap like this. I missed a whole semester in high school, when she told the principle I was talking about killing teachers and kids. She even forged entries in a diary, which was a big surprise to me, since I never kept a diary. She wanted me home so that I could paint the motel. As a result, I have a juvenile record of homicidal inclinations. I suppose Jake has called Donna and my lawyer uncle?"

"Yeah. He thought it would be a good idea to give them the heads up, just in case. I'm sure everything will be fine."

Her anger escaped in a snort. "You don't know my grandmother. Her brain may be pickled, but she's a sly old lush."

Finally, he heard the bitterness he expected and so was less worried about her. "You have a lot of friends and good family, too. They won't let her hurt you."

"They've never been able to stop her in the past," she responded, lapsing into silence as she ate. After they finished, they sat staring at the lights of the small town surrounded by the black of the surrounding, unlit open range and farms. Finally she said, "I'm tired. Do you mind shopping for supplies by yourself? Here's the hundred. Just take out my share."

He pushed her hand back. "We're using your truck. I'll take care of the food and gas."

He saw determination, gratitude then a strange wonder in her eyes as she looked into his. Those dark eyes, so full of life and pain, and love?, reached in and squeezed his heart.

"Your eyes are the color of sea foam," she said softly, as she reached out to touch his cheek. Embarrassed, she pulled her hand away. "Thanks for your help with Joe and Carla," she said coolly as if to distance herself from those emotions, then adjusted his jacket under her head and curled up to sleep.

Confused by his own surge of emotion, he watched her as he finished his soft drink, then he started the truck to return to the unpleasant little town.

When he reached the grocery store, he locked both doors and checked around for familiar faces before leaving her alone. The high school crowd was still celebrating across the street, apparently unaware of their return. With a gnawing sense of danger approaching, he grabbed a cart and rushed through the store gathering the few supplies necessary, in case they had to stop on the way. When he got to the register, which was run by a very slow, very old man, he was alarmed to see through the large front window that trucks with their lights on were parked on either side of the battered turquoise truck.

Young men in team warm-ups looking into the truck and banging on the doors. When they saw him watching, they stepped back and lounged insolently on their daddies' trucks, watching Terry fume as the checker broke open and recounted the change in several coin rolls before counting out his change. Terry forced himself to wait for the change, as he tried to see how Liliana was doing through the reflection on the windshield.

He held the last of the twenties above Terry's hand until Terry turned to meet the rheumy eyes of the ancient checker. "We don't hold with no injun-lovers," dropped the bill in Terry's hand, then turned away to walk to the back of the store. The old man had given Terry twenty dollars too much change, but he angrily pocketed the extra money. With all the bags in one hand, he wrapped his right hand around Liliana's bulky collection of keys, and then stepped out to see what kind of trouble she was in.

The belligerent, intoxicated eyes of eight large, young men holding beer bottles watched his approach. He knew the strength of rancher's kids, but they were still just kids, and he'd learned how to handle himself, a small man working with rough, hard men on oil derricks. Hopefully that would make up for their numbers and brute strength.

Pushing his way past two nearly identical, blond boys, he opened the truck door and shoved the groceries inside, ignoring their rude comments. One of the boys grabbed his shoulder trying to spin him around, but got an elbow in the gut instead. The big blond doubled over with a grunt allowing Terry to grab his neck under one arm, but, before Terry did anything, he heard an ominous click. He and the boy looked up to see a 38 revolver aimed directly at the boy's forehead.

Liliana's eyes looked ready to slaughter Custer and her spiked, red-tipped hair in the store's bright outside lights looked like a warrior's headdress. She said, "Are you the martyr type, Huedo? Do you feel like dying so your friends can have a little fun?"

When the boy sputtered and trembled, fear freezing his tongue, she jabbed the barrel between his eyes. Once the others saw what was happening the jeering stopped. Finally, the boy shook his head as the smell of urine wafted upward.

Loudly she said, "Well then I think all these boys should head back to join the rest of your friends across the street, and then I'll decide if your worthless hide is worth going to jail for."

With coldly furious eyes she looked up into the eyes of the twin of the damp-legged boy at the end of her gun. He motioned to the others who then climbed into their trucks and drove off.

"Quick. Dump him and let's get out of here before they remember that they all have their daddies' rifles in their trucks." Terry did just that, grateful that he'd managed to control his own bladder. The boy lay limp and crying on the ground as they sped out of the parking lot. "Don't be afraid to gun it. Uncle Mike gave me a great big engine for graduation. We can take any of them." She leaned out the window aiming the gun at the trucks that were lined up ready to chase them until she shot out one of their rear-view mirrors.

41

"Do you think pulling a gun on them was the best option, considering the situation in Grants?" Terry drawled. "When they run your license, the state police will find out about Joe." Despite his wry tone, his glance was worried as he checked the rear-view mirror.

"Don't worry. I keep my license plate covered with mud. I never know what surprises Carla will cook up when they hire a new cop who doesn't recognize her bullshit."

As the lights of the town disappeared in the distance, she sat down, put the safety on the gun and stuck it under the seat. Terry waited for his stomach to drop from his throat, before he considered a reprimand. Liliana leaned back in the seat and took a deep breath from her inhaler.

"Those two blond scalps would've looked good in my hogan, don't you think? Too bad they cut that pretty, white hair so short," she said dryly.

Terry choked, and then started laughing, more from relief than anything. He could only shake his head as he watched her set up another nebulizer treatment and take her tablets. As she breathed from the hose clenched in her teeth, she checked her blood sugar. When he glanced over he saw fear and uncertainty in her eyes that disappeared as soon as she caught him watching her.

"So, are you going to give a good report to the doc for me?" She started coughing until she could clear her chest, and then wearily lay back with her eyes closed. This wasn't good, but he was sure she already knew that.

Keeping his disapproval and worry to himself, he drove for a while, thinking that she was asleep. He was surprised to hear her ask, "So, tell me about your brother. Were you close?" Her eyes were still closed, her head leaning back, her bare feet resting on the dashboard.

"My brother's name was Michael Robert, named after my grandpa. He took after that side of the family, big and strong as an elephant. He was a genius at math, but Dad had decided that he would be the one to inherit the ranch and I was supposed to stay and work for him. Michael accepted his fate, even though he liked physics. My dad thought college was a waste of time for a hard-working man. Eventually my brother adapted the same attitude. I think he was happy with his choice. I left the ranch for school, but we were both in the Marine reserves when the Gulf

War hit. He died and I made it back without a scratch. My dad never forgave me for being the one that survived.

"When we were young, my brother and I got along fine. Our friends lived miles away, so we mostly just had each other. Mom died of complications after I was born and my dad never remarried. He did a lot of things to keep us from getting too close. I guess he thought there wouldn't be any love left for him if my brother and I got along too well." He ran his hands through his hair. "Now, I guess I'll be a rancher since I have no job. The old man will get his wish in the end. Sometimes I wonder if he would've been a happier man if my brother had lived, or if I'd given in and stayed with him. Probably not." He glanced over to see her nodding in agreement.

"Carla's always tries to keep anyone from liking me so she can have me to herself. I would have liked to have a sister, though. So do you think your dad loved you?"

"Yeah," he replied thoughtfully, "but sometimes I'd see him looking at me strangely, like he saw Mom in my face. You can stay as long as you like. Maybe a few weeks in the country air would be good for you." Glancing over, he noted her grim look.

"No," she replied, "Thank-you for the invite, but Carla won't let go for that long. I wonder what she'll do after I go to prison." She coughed hoarsely. "I bet she hires a guard to harass me for her. I think they only allow one call a day, so at least I'll have some peace there."

Terry drove in silence, wondering how Liliana could stand returning to that place every summer. As the miles of black asphalt passed beneath them, everything he thought of saying sounded like a platitude. It was hard to believe that Liliana could go to prison on her grandmother's word, but strange things happened, and fate wasn't fair. Keeping his anger to himself, he soon heard her soft snore. He pulled the truck over to get her a blanket and check on her. Her breathing was regular, but her skin felt cold and clammy. Something else was going on that was making her sick. He would have his sister-in-law Jeannette's second husband check her out before she returned to Grants. He stood quietly for several minutes listening closely to her breathing over the loud rumble of the truck, but she seemed to be doing okay for the moment.

As he drove down the well-lit highway, surrounded by the black, empty flat-lands, he thought of her brown eyes, dark and sensitive to the feelings of everyone around her. Her forehead was wide, her cheekbones high and prominent above a strong jaw, all covered with flawless, burnished copper-brown skin. Brows like bird's wings flew above eyes framed with nests of long, black lashes. He caught himself smiling as he thought of her dark beauty and precocious spirit and had to remind himself that she was nearly young enough to be his daughter.

As he tried to listen to his conscience and clear his mind of those fancies, he remembered the look in her eyes when she commented on his eyes. As impossible as their situation was, he knew she liked him, maybe more than liked him. Afraid of what he felt for her, he tried to laugh at his weakness for rescuing damsels in distress, but he couldn't convince himself that that was the source of his feelings. Fantasies of holding her close and kissing her full lips while he looked into her eyes persisted despite his best efforts to drive them away.

Liliana was funny, strong-willed, and intelligent. Her loyalty seemed indestructible, proven by the fact that she loved her family despite the pain they caused her. Liliana needed a break from that place, badly. He had become intensely protective of a young woman he'd known for less than two days.

Suddenly he felt doubt as remembered that Liliana had referred to Joe's unconscious form as a corpse, although he knew she had had no opportunity to inject him. Carla's lie was insidiously infecting his trust of the young woman he could guarantee was innocent. He wondered how Carla managed to get her way since she was obviously an irresponsible drunk and a devious liar. If he believed in witches and spells he could easily believe Carla was a true bruja. No, there had to be something else, a secret, someone with influence that she could blackmail. Exhausted by one day of Carla's games, he couldn't imagine how Liliana managed to live with them day in and day out.

After half-an-hour passed with no sign of anyone following them, he began to relax. As they passed into Texas, he realized that he was now taking a murder suspect across state lines. If the fates ruled against them, he could land out in Federal prison. Well, he thought glumly, at least in prison he wouldn't have to worry about where the next meal was coming from. Despite the darkness that hid the familiar west Texas landscape, memories of drives to and from home, mostly in anger, came to mind.

As he slowed down to turn off the interstate onto the road that led to the ranch, Liliana sat up, rubbed her eyes, and started coughing and wheezing again. She hadn't made it to the scheduled treatment without her asthma kicking in again. Using her rescue inhaler, she coughed until she cleared her chest. Finally, she laid her head back on the seat and turned his way.

"So, are we there yet?"

Terry nodded. "We just entered the outer edge of the ranch. It's slower driving on the dirt road, but we should be at the house in about twenty minutes."

She whistled. "That sounds like a big ranch. Will there be servants and everything?"

He laughed, "There would be. One anyway. But Rosa had been waiting to retire for years, so we'll have the place to ourselves. We won't have to wake anybody up in the middle of the night."

Liliana glanced at her watch and nodded. She looked into the darkness not reached by the headlights and said, "So what did your dad run? Texas Longhorns?"

"He kept a few of those for old time's sake, but mostly mixed breeds, some Angus. He was in the beef market, but he also farmed and grew most of his own winter feed. With the drought, he had to buy a lot of his feed the last few years. With the city growing, he'd gotten offers from land developers, but he refused to allow good ranch land to be buried under cement. I'll get an update from his lawyer this morning."

They were both quiet then, lost in their own thoughts of what the morning would bring. Finally, he turned onto a well-kept gravel road. After driving for another ten minutes, they came to a large ranch-style house with the yard brightly lit with halogen lights. He parked the truck in front of the plain front door. The house had been kept up, but revealed the stark personality of the owner in its lack of landscaping or any other sign of decoration.

The lights of a smaller house set fifty feet to the right and behind the main house came on. The front door opened as Terry opened the door to the main house. Terry reached in and flipped on the lights and pointed

Liliana to the kitchen. He waited outside for Luke, the tall, rangy cowboy who had helped his father run the large ranch for as long as Terry could remember.

Luke reached out to hug Terry. Without a word, Terry led him into the kitchen where Liliana was starting a pot of coffee. She looked up and smiled as Terry introduced her and explained the situation with his truck.

Luke grimaced, his dark, tanned skin crinkling around his thin lips and deep-set brown eyes. "I told you that old heap would fail you when you needed it most."

"Yup, you were right there. But I would have missed meeting a whole crowd of interesting people if it hadn't quit when it did," Terry responded, ignoring Liliana's choked cough. "How's the family?"

"Well, it's quiet now that it's just me and Maggie. The boys are doing well at college in Dallas. They want to own their own place like your dad. He was there for them when they went through the stage where they hated us. I guess it's easier to parent someone else's kids."

He looked around the house, clearly missing the man he had been close to for so long. Terry reached out and hugged him again. They held on longer this time.

Liliana stepped out of the kitchen with her cup of coffee and went to explore the house while Terry reconnected with his old friend. Wandering through the dark rooms, she discovered a well laid-out home that was still furnished in the style of the late 70's. Everything was in perfect shape as if no one had lived there since then. She passed through the living room into a family room, and then came to the back patio, which led to an empty pool and a tennis court sans net. Turning back inside, she explored the left wing of the house. Just on the other side of the kitchen was the office and past that the bedroom that had obviously belonged to Terry's dad.

Pausing at the door, she imagined Terry's dad sitting on the edge of the bed. It wasn't hard for her to believe that because Terry looked so much like his mother, that his dad was unable to show him consistent love. She found the boys' rooms, filled with old high school trophies.

Then she found the room that had been his mother's studio. Her paints and brushes were still set up as if she would return any moment to finish the painting that still stood on the easel.

Liliana flipped on the lights and walked up to a canvas painted with a large tree and a horse corral in the background. Next to the canvas there was a yellow, curled up picture of a boy on a pony and a smiling man standing beside him. Sketched over the painting was the shape of the boy on a pony. It was a picture of Terry's older brother. It looked like a moment of perfect bliss. Maybe it captured the last happy moment in the old man's life before the beloved artist died. It had sat on this easel for more than thirty-five years. This unfinished picture held so much love and pain that she had to leave the room, turning off the light as she left.

When she arrived back at the kitchen, Luke was leaving. He shook her hand politely and invited them for breakfast in the morning. They accepted.

After Terry shut the door, Liliana said, "You didn't tell him about my trouble, did you?"

"Nah. I figured that if everything goes well, he won't have to hear anything and if the shit hits the fan, he'll have had less time to worry. There are some messages on the answering machine, let's see if any of them are from Grants."

He returned to the kitchen and rewound the tape on the old answering machine. She handed him a cup of coffee while they listened. There were several messages from people his father must have done business with, who apparently hadn't heard about his death. There was one call for Terry from a lawyer who wanted to see him as soon as he arrived. Then there was a call from the Grant's police to confirm that the phone number Terry had given them was a real one. They wanted a call back as soon as he arrived. When he glanced her way, Liliana covered her anxiety with her unreadable mask.

He dialed the number and the receptionist put him through immediately. It was the Grants police chief, Molina, who for some reason was still at work. Terry handed the phone to Liliana. Reluctantly, she took the phone. She gave a summary of what had happened the night before and denied injecting Joe. Her voice remained cool and calm, although Terry could see the tremor in her hands. She said she had no knowledge of any injury to her grandmother, other than the black eye she'd had when she first saw her when she arrived in Grants. She hadn't seen her undressed, she said, so she couldn't say if there were any other injuries, then reported that her grandmother was drunk and unsteady and could have fallen. After agreeing to return to Grants first thing in the morning and assuring him that they didn't need to send a car for her, she hung up. Terry looked up over his cup of coffee and saw that she was pale.

"What happened?" he asked.

"Nothing," she responded, her expression closed. "Just more of Carla's crap. Let's get your stuff unloaded. I'm not ready to sleep yet."

She turned to walk out the door and he followed without a word. After they finished unloading the truck, she set up another breathing treatment. When he left to freshen up a room for her, she struggled not to cry. Her head and chest ached with anger and grief. The phone dialogue looped through her mind over and over and over. She turned to the window when Terry returned to tell her he had a room ready for her. Before he took her pack, she pulled out a package.

"I'm going to make some medicinal, relaxing tea for us. It actually tastes good, unlike most of the herbal medicines they make."

Terry smiled, "Then I guess I'll join you in a cup. Let me take this to your room." He picked up the bag and left. Liliana saw the sadness the house brought down on him and she hated deceiving him, but there were some things you had to do for yourself. She carried the nebulizer to the kitchen and brewed the tea, holding on to the blue tube with her teeth. By the time her treatment was finished, he returned and they drank their mugs of tea in silence.

When he showed her the guest room with the large windows open to catch the breeze, she said that she was going to bed. She was glad he didn't try to get her to talk about what was happening in Grants. She didn't know if she could carry out her plan if she started talking to him. When he gave her the money Mike had shoved in his pocket, all she could do was laugh, so she wouldn't cry.

"Thanks for all your help. I hope I haven't gotten you into trouble," she said quietly, looking suddenly vulnerable as she looked down at the money in her hand. He walked over and hugged her, she felt stiff and uncomfortable, her deception a wall between them.

"Listen," he said, holding on to her anyway. "I'm not worried about me, but I am worried about you. It's safe here. And I know a good lawyer who also works in New Mexico. We won't let your grandmother hurt you anymore. It's okay to accept help. You're not taking anything you don't deserve, or I am not giving to you wholeheartedly. You're a good person and we all help you because we want to. You don't owe me anything in return."

He heard her sniffle and released her to hand her his handkerchief. She managed a tense smile through her tears and said good night, holding on tightly to the sobs that threatened to break through.

After he patted her shoulder awkwardly, he turned off the house lights and decided to try to get some sleep in this house so full of memories. As he passed his father's office, he went to see what his dad had been working on. He picked up a stack of papers and aimlessly leafed through them. Surprised, he found a sealed envelope addressed to him. He set it back down. He wasn't ready to hear his father's last words.

Unlike his father, he'd traveled all over the world, but in New Mexico he had finally found a place that held his heart. The dry highlands of the Four Corners area and the gentle quiet way of the Navajo that called that place home brought him back every time he left. He was fascinated by the rugged, arid beauty of the land and found the Navajo culture intriguing and comfortable.

He thought about the eulogy he would have to give at the funeral. He tried to remember positive things about his father and he found many, if he considered every relationship outside of their own. Yes, he had plenty of good things to say. He would just have to forget the cold eye and rejection that was all his father had to give his younger son after he lost his wife, a son who had the same pale hazel eyes and light sandy hair that she had, as well as the small frame that was distinctive in her family. Terry closed off the part of his mind that wanted to tell his father just how much pain he had suffered as a result of his reflection of his mother's face while he tried to compose a eulogy.

He went to his mother's studio, a place of refuge when he was little. He lay down on the chaise lounge she used to rest on when she'd been on her feet too long during the pregnancy. He fell asleep before he knew it.

∞

Liliana appeared at the door, glad that the potion she put in the tea had finally worked. When she'd gone to the medicine man last summer to ask for a tasteless, sleeping potion, he'd been reluctant to give her one. "What do you need this for?" he had asked. "It doesn't set right with the spirits to put people to sleep without asking them and I don't believe you should be using this with the white man's medicines you take."

After an uncomfortable pause, she responded, "It's for Carla. It's getting harder to get away to Albuquerque . . ."

He nodded with a grunt and handed the packet over with brief instructions on how to use it. The first time she'd spiked Carla's beer, she'd been terrified Carla would figure it out. But things had gone smoothly, and she'd been able to pack and leave in peace as Carla snored away on the sofa.

With a stab of guilt, she set the alarm next to Terry so that he wouldn't be late for the funeral. She stood looking at his peacefully sleeping face, wanting so much to kiss him, but she couldn't take the chance that he would wake. She lifted her pack to her shoulder and slipped out of the house quietly. With some old rags from the bed of the truck she wrapped the hole in the muffler. By the time they got hot enough to burn, she would be out of ear-shot of the ranch house and could remove them. Once she was inside the truck she shoved the mirrors away. With a prayer that it would be as quiet as possible, she started the truck up and drove slowly with her headlights out until she reached the road.

When she reached the highway, she turned toward Mexico. It would take a day to reach the border; hopefully Terry would cover for her. If not, she would be caught.

Texas was not a good place for a Native American to run. She'd be better off if she were among her own people. She spoke Spanish so she could live in Mexico, but she didn't know anyone there. No, she would be safer at home. She was sure that there would be a cousin or two who would help her out as she hid from the white man's police.

So she turned back toward New Mexico. If she could get to the reservation, especially up near the Four Corners area, a desolate area where four states met at one spot, they could look for her forever. Dating a Navajo a year ago had advantages other than pissing Carla off, and his good company, of course. He'd loved to hike and knew most of the reservation like the back of his hand. He had shown her many excellent hiding places during the spring break, while he told her stories about the Navajo who hid there from the forced Death Marches decreed by the government's resettlement policy. She could make it through Albuquerque and Grants by dawn if she didn't stop at all. Then she'd turn onto the reservation roads and get very lost.

The news from the chief of police had not been good. Carla had presented them with a syringe she said she found in the room Liliana was using. It had Liliana's prints and Joe's type of blood on it. The missing tip of the needle turned up in Joe's buttocks during a cursory exam of Joe's body after Carla insisted that it was there and before he was sent to Albuquerque.

Her grandmother had set her up well this time. With the record of her high school death threats, she doubted that anyone would believe she was innocent. They also knew she had motive. When she was eight she had reported that Joe had tried to rape her. He'd claimed that he was in the wrong room by accident and Carla had forced her to drop the charges. She was in deep shit, especially since he had died so soon after breaking into her room. Carla had, of course, denied being anywhere nearby.

The final straw fell when the chief of police informed her that Carla was in the hospital with a concussion and bleeding on the brain. They found Carla unconscious that afternoon on the floor of her apartment with a lamp with blood on it nearby. When she'd reached consciousness in the hospital, according to the Chief, Carla managed to report her fight with Liliana the morning Liliana left, and asserted that Liliana had hit her on the head with a lamp that would likely have her prints on it. Carla had then slipped into a coma. Now her status was critical, mostly because of the liver failure that hindered her body's ability to stop the bleeding.

Carla's health was too unstable to do more than drain the blood from her head. Because of her liver failure, they predicted that the bleeding would start again and that her grandmother would probably die of her injuries despite massive infusions of blood and platelets.

Liliana had plenty of reasons to kill Carla, too. She doubted she would escape both charges and imagined what it would be like in prison. For as long as she could remember, she'd fought for survival and sanity; she couldn't do it anymore. There was no desire in her heart to see her grandmother before she died. She was done with all of them, with everything. Her only option was losing herself in the wilds of the Res. As she drove, she tried to remember as much as she could about the years she had with her parents. Sifting through her memories, savoring each one, she sped along the nearly empty, dark highway, the wind blowing the river of tears and guilt away.

Suddenly there was a steer in the middle of the road. She swerved too late to miss it, skidded and hit the steer on the driver's side, flipping the truck. She lost consciousness the first time her head hit the roof as it turned over and over through the short, steel railing into a creek. The truck finally settled deep in the heavy underbrush along the arroyo that disappeared into a culvert beneath the highway. No one was on the road to see the accident.

Chapter 4

Lost

Terry awoke to the alarm and found himself in his mother's studio with a blanket laid over him. He grabbed the clock to figure out how to turn off the loud alarm and saw that it was eight o'clock. The funeral was at ten. There was just enough time to get ready. Having been raised on a ranch, he automatically awoke at 5:00 every morning; it was not like him to sleep so late. Raising his hand to his thick, heavy head, he became suspicious.

He went to the window, and saw that Liliana's truck was gone. Checking her room he confirmed that the bed hadn't been slept in and her things were gone. He went to the front door in the hope that she had simply moved the truck to a spot out of sight of the bedroom. No such luck. She had skipped.

He couldn't blame her. Anyone would have been overwhelmed by the avalanche of bad news from Grants, and he couldn't even imagine how it felt to have her own grandmother make such terrible accusations. He thought of her brown eyes that always seemed to be laughing at some private joke, and the high cheek bones that would become more prominent when she gave one of her rare, all-out smiles. Then he remembered how sick she was and his worry intensified. After finding no note, he wasn't sure what to do. He was worried, but didn't want the police to know that she'd run. Maybe she had simply decided to leave for Grants early.

He tried her cell-phone and got no answer. After hesitating a moment he called Mike.

"Mike, I've got some bad news. Liliana took off."

"Damn," Mike said, "I'm not surprised; she knows the shit Carla can lay on her." Then, sounding like he was reassuring himself as much as Terry, he said, "Liliana has a good head on her. When she realizes how hopeless it is to run, she'll come in. She knows she has family to help her. We won't let Carla send Liliana to prison as her last act before she dies."

Terry was caught off-guard. "What do you mean last act? Is something wrong with Carla?"

"Didn't Liliana tell you? Jake said the police chief talked to her last night," Mike responded.

"She didn't tell me anything about Carla."

"When the police went to look for Liliana at the motel they found Carla unconscious on the floor. They took her to the hospital with a concussion. Molina says that when she woke up for a few minutes, Carla said that Liliana had returned in the morning bragging about killing Joe. When Carla tried to make Liliana go to the police, Liliana hit her on the head with a lamp. The lamp has Carla's blood. Her alcohol rotted liver is keeping her blood from clotting. They don't expect her to survive for more than a day or two, if she's lucky. She's been in a coma since yesterday afternoon. As a matter of fact they sent the FBI for Liliana, since she crossed state lines. She was supposed to wait for them to come and get her." Worry filled Mike's voice. "I guess it was finally too much for her to handle so she ran. Carla's last poisonous act in a life filled with venom."" Mike asked, ""How sick was Lili?".

"Her breathing was still pretty bad. She took her nebulizer, but she'll need refills for her medicines soon. God, I can't believe she just took off without leaving a note. Where could she have gone?" Terry leaned his forehead against the wall. He couldn't leave to find her, even though he now had his dad's truck to use. He had to go to his father's funeral and he had no idea where to start looking. "I tell you what. Just as soon as the funeral and reception are over, I'll head for Grants. I know she was never alone with Joe long enough to stick a needle in him."

"That would work anyplace else, man. There has been something weird between the law and Carla and Joe for as long as I remember. I just hope our girl pulls her head together and turns herself in. The prednisone they give her when her asthma is bad sometimes makes her wild and impulsive. Her doctor can testify to that. It may help her to keep from being jailed for running. Don't you think?" Mike had to wait a few seconds for a response.

Terry's mind was filled with the memory of Liliana calling Joe a corpse as they dragged him out of the room. He was sure that was only her dark, bitter humor. But then there was extra time it took her to get her stuff from the motel while he waited at the storage rental office. She was angry when she left for the motel and even angrier when she returned.

Yet she had always seemed in control of her anger, even when she was pointing a gun at the head of an obnoxious teenager who pissed his pants in fear. He was sure that incident would get reported and, with her luck, someone would connect it with her being in that area at the time. Damn, he wished he was a better liar. He would lie until he was green to keep Liliana out of trouble, but he'd never been good at it. Well, he was good at keeping his mouth shut. If they didn't ask, he wouldn't tell.

"Mike, was anyone else around the motel when they found her? A witness maybe?"

"Another of Carla's drunk friends was sleeping in the maintenance room. He's also a Navajo, Eddie Chee. But after what he said happened to Joe, they won't believe a word he says. Carla's current boyfriend was with his wife, so I don't know. Carla has lots of enemies, but lately she's been too out of it to target anyone. It's not looking good for my girl. Send some prayers for her at that service, would you?"

"Sure thing, Mike. It seems everyone knew that Carla was a liar, which should count for something."

"God willing," Mike responded. "I'll call you if she turns up. Let me know the same, okay?"

"Yeah, of course, Mike. See you later today." Terry hung up the phone, his heart full of misgivings. His chest ached in sympathy with Liliana's pain. Why hadn't she trusted him enough to let him help her?

As he got ready to shower, he called Jeannette to tell her that he'd arrived. They agreed to meet early at the mortuary to have some time to talk alone. After he hung up, he found himself looking in the mirror, seeing his mother's face as he knew it from his dad's photos. The image he saw had ruined his chance for a relationship with his father, because his father couldn't manage his grief. It must have been terrible to see the face of your tormentor every time you passed a mirror, especially a man as despised as Joe Yazzie was.

Dressed in his new black suit, he stepped out the front door to see Luke walking toward his house, looking like a different person in his good blue suit.

"I overslept. Sorry I missed breakfast."

"Don't worry about it. I'm sure you needed the rest. Where's your friend?" Luke asked.

"She decided to get an early start. Her grandmother's sick," Terry responded, uncomfortable with the lie.

Luke responded, "I'm sorry to hear that. Bad luck seems to come in runs doesn't it?"

Terry sensed words hanging in the air between them so he replied, "It sure does," and waited. After standing still, scratching his long chin in thought, Luke made up his mind.

"My mom was Indian. Her dad was a Kiowa medicine man. I knew your dad didn't like Indians, so I never mentioned it to him. Liliana seems to be a nice girl. I think she likes you a lot," he said. Then embarrassed he turned to walk away.

"Maybe the three of us can sit down to talk about it one of these days," Terry responded.

Luke turned back to say, "Yeah, maybe we can." He smiled having finally acknowledged the heritage that had troubled him for so long.

Luke then turned toward his house. At that moment Terry heard a car approaching and turned to see a black sedan headed for the big house. He wished that he had run as well as he stepped forward to greet them. Out of the corner of his eye he saw that Luke was waiting, curious to see who was driving up at this inconvenient hour.

The sedan pulled up in front of Terry and two men in dark grey suits climbed out of the car, straightening their jackets as they surveyed the area, nodding in Luke's direction. They both seemed to be in their mid-forties, but that and the color of their suits were the only things they had in common. One was over six-feet tall, thin with reddish hair, brown eyes and lips that wanted to smile. The other was medium-height, with a stocky build, dark hair, pale eyes and a face that seemed like it would crack before a smile could break through. Terry assumed he was the one in charge, but it was the tall man who walked up and reached out with his hand.

"Hello, you must be Terry Prentice. I'm Ian Ferguson. Agent Ferguson with the FBI." He pulled out his badge with his other hand as he firmly grasped Terry's hand. His eyes were friendly, but calculating. "This is my partner, Agent Martin Spence. I assume you know we're here to pick up a young lady who seems to have found herself in quite a lot of trouble back in New Mexico. You must have known that it was illegal to take her across state lines with such serious allegations against her in Grants." Deliberately looking around the grounds, he added, "I don't see her truck. Is she still here?"

Terry wasn't sure what to say. He had failed in his promise to keep an eye on her by letting her slip free, probably in a state of panic. Finally, he settled for the truth.

"Yeah, well, I think she panicked in the night and left. She's on a medication called prednisone that can trigger impulsive behavior. I'm sure once she's had time to think she'll return home." This didn't even come close to explaining all the factors that likely led to her panic, but the less said the better, he reminded himself.

Agent Ferguson frowned. "Yeah, my kid has asthma and he turns into a hellion when he's on that prednisone. How long ago did she leave?" He made notes in the notebook he'd pulled from the inside pocket of his suit.

"I fell asleep around eleven and woke up at eight o'clock." Terry replied.

Luke, now at Terry's side, added, "The truck was gone when I came out to do chores at six. I assumed she headed back to see her sick grandmother." Terry was grateful that Luke, despite having no clue what was going on, was ready to help Terry no matter what kind of trouble he was in.

"She helped me out by driving me home for my father's funeral, which is in a little over an hour. I don't know if I would've made it if I had had to take a bus."

"Well, you have aided a murder suspect to flee across state lines and now that suspect is missing. You know that you are in trouble, Mr. Prentice," Agent Spence added.

"Yes, I do," he replied, "and I'm willing to cooperate." He paused for a minute, torn between obligation and worry, then he said, "I'll be glad to return with you, but I really need to be at my dad's funeral and there's some urgent business I have to take care of today. If I could go to the funeral and speak to my sister-in-law and my dad's lawyer before we leave, I would sure appreciate it."

The agents glanced at each other then nodded.

"Also, if you wouldn't mind, could we take my dad's truck and could you guys keep out of sight? I don't want to embarrass my family, since this has nothing to do with them. I will not try to escape."

With skepticism born of experience, the agents hesitated, but finally agreed with a nod and a warning. When he was ready, they loaded up in his father's four passenger truck. Luke and his petite, blonde wife followed as they headed into town to the funeral parlor. The detectives waited across the street during the service and Terry had some time before everyone arrived to talk with his sister-in-law. He told her about Liliana and reassured her that everything would be fine.

"You always were too trusting, Terry. I just hope it doesn't get you thrown in jail this time," she responded. Then Luke and his wife turned up close behind him. Terry could see that Luke was going to make sure he was close by in case Terry needed him; Sheri, Luke's wife looked worried and sympathetic. "Anyway," Jeannette continued, "There's good news. Your dad finally got an excellent offer for the ranch from a ranching corporation. Les Chancery will be here with all the papers for you to sign. Your dad left Luke and me and Rosa well-taken care of, and the rest is yours. You're a rich man, Terry Prentice. The ranch sold for four million. You'll have one and a half million in your account as soon as you sign the papers. I'll call Les and have him bring the papers with him. He can recommend a lawyer from Albuquerque for whatever help you need for this business with the FBI."

Terry was surprised to recognize most of the flood of people who walked up to give her their condolences. The next two hours passed in a blur of people he hadn't seen in years, a eulogy he fumbled his way through, and finally carrying the casket to its place next to his mother and brother. When he saw his father's still face, he could believe that his father had found peace. Yes, he could forgive his father.

Yet all the while, he was wondering where Liliana was, expecting one of the FBI to walk up any minute to report that she'd turned herself in. During the services, he kept checking his cell phone to see if she had called while he had it turned off. At least he knew she had some money and hoped that her commonsense would kick in soon. She would have been in Grants already if she'd driven through the night.

Then he was reminded of his grief and loss as he signed the papers that in a flash increased his net worth from the hundred in his pocket to more than a million dollars. Luke would manage the place until the new owners showed up in a week. They had left Terry time to deal with his father's personal belongings, except that now his time was going to be spent looking for a frightened, desperate, young friend.

Terry and Luke were finally leaving Jeannette's house with the FBI with more than a few curious looks at the two silent strangers in dark suits; Terry finally loosened his tie and took a deep breath. He wondered if he weren't so worried about Liliana would he have been able to feel like he was grieving as much as he should. He doubted it. Being at home reminded him of his arguments with his father. Standing at the door, ready to say goodbye to Jeannette and the kids, he remembered the only time he confronted his father about his silence regarding his mother's death. Words had passed that were not meant by either one, and now would never be forgiven.

His stomach soured with the memory of that last argument, and then he was startled by a tap on his shoulder. Turning, he saw Agent Ferguson standing behind him with a sympathetic, but determined expression.

"Your friend hasn't shown up in Grants and the state Patrol has seen no sign of her on I-40. It's time we got going."

"Just a minute," he said as he turned to Jeannette. "Would you mind getting my mother's things from the house and whatever you think my father would have like saved? I may not get back in time." There was nothing he could say to relieve the worry in her eyes as he returned her hug.

Les, a large, pale blond man, was wearing an expensive suit tailored to fit his large frame perfectly. He shook Terry's hand as he said, "If they press charges, we can get enough bail to get you home to see your dad's house again before they take it down. Don't worry; I'll take care of anything that comes up." He then hugged Terry, and said, "Your dad missed you. He would never have admitted it to a soul, but he was sorry for a lot of things he said and did."

He gave Terry a reassuring slap on the back and watched as they returned to the truck and headed for the ranch. Once they arrived, Luke offered to drive with Agent Ferguson in their car so that Terry could take his father's truck with Agent Spence. Luke had decided to remain at Terry's side for as long as his support was needed.

As they finally left Texas, Terry watched the flat, dry grasslands pass in the daylight. Racing down the interstate, it seemed as though nothing had changed since he left the first time. Spence was driving in silence as Terry thought about his father. Flat highway and small towns passed unnoticed until he saw a large, dead steer on the side of the highway about twenty miles east of Tucumcari. It was clearly road kill, but it triggered an image of Liliana lying broken on the side of the road. A large flock of crows had already started the cleanup. He turned to look at the steer after they passed and saw a damaged railing where large drainage pipes allowed an arroyo to pass under the interstate.

Spence noticed Terry's first motion since they left Amarillo and asked, "What did you see?"

"Nothin.' Just a road-killed steer." He looked back once more as his worry intensified.

The agent nodded and started a story about taking his kids to see the amazing, ancient cliff dwellings in the Four Corners region of New Mexico and Colorado. He called Tucumcari police to see if there was any news from the local police and hospitals as they passed. There was nothing new.

Terry was glad, and disappointed, but mostly worried, and it was wearing him down. He wished, again, that Liliana had talked to him. She didn't know him well enough to know that he would have let her make the decision that was right for her. It hurt, whether she was protecting him or just didn't trust him. He was anxious to get to Grants and get this mess straightened out.

Jake called to inform him that Joe's autopsy was finished and some of the blood tests would be back in a few hours. When Jake learned that Terry was with the FBI on the way back, he postponed giving him any more information until he arrived in Grants. Spence was clearly not happy that Sergeant Sanchez had called Terry instead of him or Ferguson, but Terry decided to ignore the change in his mood. He had to be careful not to slip and give away something that could be used against Liliana.

He took a turn driving half-listening to the agent's stories, while a storm of rage and worry filled his mind. Damn Liliana's stubborn pride. Again he wished she had trusted him enough to discuss her plan with him before taking off. Her fear of what Carla could do was what drove Liliana to run. If Carla was alive when he got there, he imagined everything he would tell her about the horrible life she'd given her grandchild and how she deserved to die. And then he knew he could never say those things.

It was dark when they reached Albuquerque, but the coroner was waiting, so they postponed dinner. Ferguson wanted Terry to take a look at Joe Yazzie and identify how much of his trauma occurred after he saw him last. Terry figured they wanted to see his reaction to the corpse. Apparently, Joe Yazzie had arrived at the coroner's office looking as though someone had beaten him to death. Terry had already told them that except for a minor scrape on his forehead Joe was intact.

He hadn't seen a traumatized dead body since the Gulf War, and he wasn't looking forward to the experience as they parked near the University Hospital that held the coroner's office. They entered the air-conditioned building, left Luke in the waiting room, and walked down a hall that smelled more strongly of formaldehyde the farther they followed it. Finally, they arrived in the room set aside for the viewing. Swallowing his nausea, he wished that he hadn't had chili for lunch.

They entered the cool, plain white-walled viewing room where the coroner joined them from a side door. He was a fifty-ish, slender and fit man, nearly bald, but with bristly eyebrows that almost made up for his lack of head hair. The steel gurney with the body was rolled in by a tech that left immediately. The coroner lifted the sheet back to Joe's chest, allowing Terry to see why they wanted him to see the body.

"Most of the trauma happened just before he died," the coroner began. "In addition to the facial bruising he had a fractured left orbit, and nasal fractures, as well as significant contra-coup swelling on the brain and some bleeding. As you can see the bruises on his face and head are linear and vertical as if he was struck directly from the front by a rod shaped object. Two of the front teeth were found on the floor. The only bruising on his torso was from the injection site on his buttocks and some bruising on his forearms." He turned the body and showed them where the tip of the needle had been removed in Grants.

"He had severe congestive heart failure, but the final cause of death was a massive heart attack while or soon after he suffered the head trauma. That is supported by the finding of very little intracranial bleeding; his heart stopped almost immediately after the head trauma. His labs came back consistent with a diabetic alcoholic. His liver and kidneys were barely functioning. And his clotting factors were extremely low. I'd say this old man was living on borrowed time. I'm surprised he lived so long. He had insulin in his blood stream, but his glucose level was still over four hundred and his alcohol lever was over .20 %, high enough to prevent delirium tremens. That's all I have for now. A more complete tox screen will take a day or two, but I'd be surprised if anything unusual turned up."

Silently, the agents waited to hear what information Terry had to offer. He assessed the bruised and broken face with a puzzled frown. "He looks a lot different from when I last saw him. I guess bruises could show up later, but his face was intact. There was only a small cut on his forehead when I helped Sergeant Sanchez load him into the car. His pulse seemed normal."

Ferguson waited and when Terry remained silent, he asked, "Why did Liliana open the front door before calling the police or an ambulance?"

"His breathing and pulse were regular and the smell was pretty bad. Joe had shit his pants when he passed out. Liliana got a shower curtain to keep him from fouling up Sergeant Sanchez's car. I helped Jake wrap Joe in the shower curtain and load him in the car. We were as gentle as we could be, but he was a heavy guy and it was awkward. No one ever struck him."

"Why didn't you call an ambulance to come and get him? A sick, old man just fell through a window and was unconscious, weren't you worried he could be sick?"

"Liliana and Sergeant Sanchez knew this guy real well and thought he'd just passed out, which would be pretty normal for him. I figured the Sergeant would know if Joe needed to go to the hospital." Terry tried to keep his face calm as the agents watched him. He wasn't going to say that they just wanted to be rid of Joe as quickly as possible and he hadn't even thought of calling an ambulance. He added, "I just remembered something else. As I woke up to the sound of him falling into the bathroom, I heard a man say, 'What the hell did you do that for?' and a woman laughed. Maybe that was Carla sticking him with the syringe."

Agent Ferguson asked, "Did you see him wake up at any time after he first lost consciousness?"

"No. I never saw him awake after he passed out. He was snoring when I shut the car door."

"Thank-you, Mr. Prentice. Is there anything else you would like to add?"

Terry thought for a moment then shook his head, holding onto the urge to tell every detail. They wouldn't hear about the gun from him, if he could help it. A worried man stared back at him from his distorted reflection on the shiny, stainless steel gurney. He had his own questions as Agent Ferguson suggested they head for Grants.

After thanking the medical examiner, Spence and Ferguson stepped out of his hearing for a short discussion. Luke followed close behind when they left the building. Agent Ferguson rode with Terry, reviewing everything Terry had reported. Terry felt he did a good job keeping the story consistent, but these were pros and he wasn't sure what they read from his expression.

When he jumped down from the truck at the Grants hospital, he almost fell because of a sharp pain in his left shin. He stopped and lifted his pant leg once they were inside the Grants hospital to see what hurt so much.

Ferguson commented, "You've got quite bruise started there. What did you do, run into something?"

"I'll be damned if I know." Terry took a breath. He couldn't lose his temper. This was just the beginning of the scrutiny he was going to have to tolerate.

Carla was in the small ICU unit at the Grants hospital. Her status was too unstable, and her prognosis too bleak, to move her to a bigger trauma hospital. No one would operate while her liver and kidneys were failing. They had a drain in her skull, so they knew that the bleeding inside her head persisted despite infusions of the blood clotting agents to give her what her scarred liver was unable to provide. When Terry arrived at her bedside, he saw the bandages and new bruising on her forehead.

Pity and outrage fought to win his voice as he explained, "She had the black eye when I saw her the night before last, but the bruising on her forehead and face is new. She was drunk when I met her, barely able to walk. According to what Mike told me later, that was her usual state. Apparently she'd had a fist fight with her boyfriend at the bar the night before."

Ferguson responded, "We questioned him. He has a solid alibi for yesterday morning. Let's go see what Liliana's doctor has to say."

When they arrived at the Laguna-Acoma Hospital, Terry saw Dr. Karnes watching him through his office window at the front of the building. Their eyes met when Terry stepped into the parking lot light, then the doctor turned to answer a nurse who was talking to him. Once inside, Agent Ferguson told the receptionist that Dr. Karnes was expecting them and they were escorted to his small, crowded office. The doctor had his dinner spread out on his desk, along with a pile of charts. He turned off his tape recorder and stood to greet Terry warmly, then allowed the FBI to introduce themselves, followed by Luke, who had made himself a part of the team. Although he was grateful for the presence of his old friend, Luke made Terry feel like a kid whose father was accompanying him to the principle's office.

As Agent Spence prepared to take notes, Agent Ferguson settled into questioning mode. "We'd like to speak to Liliana Hunt. Do you have any idea where she is?" After Dr. Karnes shook his head, Ferguson continued, "We've been told that there's the possibility that the medications she's on could be affecting her judgment and that she has diabetes and could have syringes in her possession. Can you confirm that?"

"Well, this is confidential information, but I suppose that you already know about her asthma and the prednisone. She's pre-diabetic and only has to watch her diet. I've known Liliana since she was two. She's always had a lot of commonsense. Even though she's survived several kinds of hell, she's definitely not a murderer."

The doctor was clearly upset, ready to defend Liliana with every word. Especially since words were his only weapons. "I've never known her to maliciously hurt anyone in her life. Once she's had some time to figure things out, she'll come home. I bet she's already on her way home."

"Would Liliana know that an insulin overdose could kill someone?"

"Yes, Carla needed insulin for her diabetes and Liliana helped her manage it. Every insulin using diabetic needs to know the risks," he paused, twisting the shaft of his pen, "So, they've confirmed that Joe died from hypoglycemia?"

"The insulin didn't kill him, but I want to know her intentions. He was worked over and was pretty badly bruised. Did the local police call with any reports of trauma at the station?"

"Well, since he was in the Grants' station and not on the Reservation, they would have called the Grants hospital. As far as I know, Joe never came to this clinic. He could have been seen by someone else here at some point, but you'll need a warrant to see his records. The Pueblo Council is strict about protecting patient rights."

"I thought he was picked up by a Laguna policeman, Jake Sanchez. Why was he taken to the Grants station?"

"You'll have to ask Jake. I would assume it was because he picked him up in Grants."

Ferguson frowned. The smell of the doctor's sandwich made Terry's mouth water. The doctor handed him half of his sandwich, with a wink.

"It's not that important," Ferguson said. "I really came here hoping that Liliana had contacted you. From what Mr. Prentice says, she's pretty sick and trusts you."

"I would have hospitalized her, but every time I do, Carla shows up to check her out against my advice. Now that Liliana's twenty, Carla would have shown up just to create chaos. Liliana feels responsible for taking care of her grandmother and chooses to go with her."

"So, Liliana had reason to be angry with her grandmother?"

"More exasperated and fed up, I'd say. She'd always go home and help her grandmother with that broken-down motel. She would never harm her grandmother."

"What about Joe Yazzie? Did she have any reason to hate him?"

"She wished him out of Carla's life, because he encouraged her drinking and stole from her, but I don't think it was ever more than a wish." Dr. Karnes examined the pen in his hand as he considered the pattern of Liliana's life with Carla and Joe. Many of her secrets were not written in records, he kept them in his memory to preserve the privacy of the young woman. In such a small community, even medical records were not completely secure. If they kept digging, they might even find the link they were looking for.

"Before you go. I saw Terry limping. Is there something you'd like to show me?" His gaze was direct as it captured Terry's attention. He lifted his pant leg. The doctor leaned over and examined the now swollen, purple bruise. He glanced up with suspicion in his eyes.

"I don't know how I got it. I just noticed it as we walked in. Maybe I bumped into something and forgot. It's been a long, hard day." He finished his half-sandwich and raised his eyebrows at Agent's Spence's hungry stare.

"Let's get something to eat, Ian," Spence said. Ferguson agreed.

Liliana awoke with bright light glaring in her eyes. The hot sun scorched her face and a jackhammer pounded inside her skull. Her lashes were stuck together by something sticky, and her vision was obscured by something red. Once she pulled her right hand free, she tried to wipe her eyes. The cut on her hand made it difficult to know if the blood was from her face or her hand. Her throat was parched and when she tried to push herself upright with her left hand, she cried out in pain. She saw that her left arm was at a strange angle from the mid-forearm down as it lay against the bashed in door. Her left leg was a miasma of pain that became excruciating when she tried to move it. She could wiggle the right leg and almost get it loose from beneath the steering wheel, but the left seemed to be pinned between the door and the dashboard which was crushed inward. She turned the ignition off.

When she tried to raise her head to see where she was, the motion magnified the pounding in her head tenfold. She lay still for a moment with her right hand over her eyes. The tinted windshield was shattered so there was nothing to protect her from the blistering sun. Avoiding any sudden movement, she looked down slowly to see where the sound of water tinkling over rocks came from. She discovered that the truck lay on its left side in a deep creek bed; a hole in the floor allowed the shallow water flowing by to enter the truck. The water had reached her left leg, where she saw the deep gash with a bone protruding from her shin. She hoped the water was running fast enough to be clean. With excruciating effort, she edged her head around until she could see the upper bed of the creek and the overpass and hear the sound of cars whizzing by.

With a groan she realized she was out of sight of the highway and if someone had seen her go over the side, help would have already arrived. She was in big trouble. Closing her eyes to rest them from the pulsing sunlight, she reached out with her right hand to drag her jacket over her head. It helped with the glare, but the heat was still unbearable. The sight of her nebulizer machine on the floor just out of her reach reminded her to take inventory of her body functions.

She had lost both bowel and bladder contents, probably during the accident. It had happened awhile ago, since her sense of smell had adapted to the odor. Her chest was tight, so she fumbled in the pocket of her jeans to find her inhaler. After two inhalations, she felt her chest loosen up a little and her headache eased just a little as well. Her face was cold and clammy to the touch, in spite of the heat, telling her that her sugar was either very low, or she had a severe infection, probably both. Looking up at the back of the rearview mirror, her heart thumping with fear, she forced herself to turn it so she could see behind her. Thick brush and sky was all it showed her. She shoved it back up to the roof, closed her eyes and spoke to her mother.

"Okay, Momma, I know it was stupid to take off. I wouldn't be in this mess if I had just waited. You would tell me that I can't blame Carla for this one. This is all on me. You knew I could do better."

Her voice was hoarse; speaking triggered a fit of coughing, each cough triggering an unbearable spasm of pain in her head and ribs. *Please*, she begged silently, *don't make me cough anymore*. Despite the pleas, the coughing continued. She finally passed out from the pain in her head. Somewhere in the dark dream of pain and blood, she heard musical chiming. Confused, she wondered if it was the signal for her spirit to leave, but the sound went away.

Terry closed his phone in frustration. He wished she would answer. She had to know it was him calling. He couldn't shake the feeling that something terrible had happened as he listened to the unanswered ring tone. Something was wrong. Even though he hadn't known Liliana for very long, he knew that she had more commonsense than to think she could hide from the law indefinitely.

After an hour of questioning by Chief Molina of the Grants Police, he was left in the interrogation room, a plain, grey-tiled, green-walled room with a table, four chairs and a camera on the wall. Through the open door, he watched the weather report on the television in the corner of the office. There was an intense weather front in the Midwest that was sending tendrils of thunderstorms into the Texas panhandle and eastern New Mexico. There was a lot of moisture in the storm, so there were flash-flood warnings for the rest of the day. Terry's chest tightened at the news. When Agent Ferguson came for him, he almost turned on the agent with a surge of anger at the delays they were forcing on him, but if they had asked what felt so urgent, he wouldn't have been able to answer.

From Molina Terry learned that in the early dawn hours of the day before he and Liliana breakfasted at Concha's, Carla had gotten Joe's wife, Lorraine, and her son Eugene to go with her to the Grants police station. There Carla reported that she had discovered that her granddaughter had murdered Joe for an old grudge. Lorraine added to the drama, echoing Carla's dramatic cries, insisting that they arrest

Liliana immediately. Eugene was there because he wouldn't let either of the intoxicated women drive, but he tried to stay out of the whole thing, sitting in the farthest corner until the police threw them all out.

Confusion and panic had already ruled the police station since Joe was found beaten to death alone in his cell before daybreak, but no one was going to tell either woman anything about the beating until they had a reasonable explanation. According to the on duty officer who had helped to wash the intoxicated prisoner when he was brought in, Joe had only a few minor bruises. The video cam for that cell block had broken two days before, so there was no record of anything that happened in his cell in the few hours between the times he was processed and when he was found dead before shift change. They had figured it was delirium tremens, the DT's, which sometimes caused terrifying hallucinations and were a common problem when a chronic alcoholic stopped drinking suddenly. Before they could make any sense of it, Carla had arrived, slowing the investigation with her own version of chaos.

Later in the day, when questioned about what could have happened to Carla that morning, Eugene reported that Carla was fine when he dropped her off at eight in the morning, along with Eddie Chee, an old crony of Carla's, who had asked for a ride from the police station where he was in for public intoxication. After the story he told about what had happened in Joe's cell that night, he was labeled an unreliable witness. They didn't bother to ask him what happened at the motel. From Gerry, and confirmed by Terry, they learned that Liliana had left for the motel at nine to pick up her stuff from the motel and returned more than an hour later.

As the Grants police and the FBI reviewed their information, they brought Sergeant Sanchez in to consult with regard to the reservation side of the story. He knew just about everyone in the Pueblos and in Grants.

When Jake arrived at the Grants police station, he saw that the FBI had a firm grip on Terry. Anger radiated off of Chief Molina who was powerfully built, though a little less than average height. He was still handsome at sixty, though some of his muscle had gone to fat. He and the agents kept asking the same questions over and over again, trying to make sense of a case that made no sense. The fact that Terry had taken their suspect across state lines kept him in their custody.

After watching silently, Jake finally spoke up. "You know, I hate to interfere with your case, but I think there's a roadblock here. These are answers that only Liliana can give us and she's not here. Carla's in a coma, and Joe's dead, so we're not going to learn much more from them," he paused. "Why don't you let me try to take our reasoning in a different direction for a while?" he suggested, Terry watched him edge his story through the room full of powerful egos.

Agent Ferguson looked up and said, "What direction were you thinking of, Sergeant?"

"Well," Jake said thoughtfully, speaking slow and reasonably, careful not to antagonize these two, or any chance at cooperation would be lost. "Carla has filed false charges on half the population of Grants and the Pueblos. Also the nurses at the hospital told me that she was confused and answered every question with 'Liliana did it' until she went into a coma. What if we set aside her claims from this morning and start from scratch?" He sent a conciliatory smile at Molina, whose report he was contradicting.

"Now what have we got? The only trouble Liliana she had in school was based on Carla's accusations. So we have a good kid with no record, who works like a dog to help her grandmother keep her business running, in addition to attending the University of New Mexico and working to help support herself.

"Now, we have Liliana's new friend, Terry here. His truck breaks down on the highway and he needs a ride to his father's funeral. He accepts Liliana's offer of a room at the motel and a ride so he can get to Amarillo in time.

"According to Mr. Prentice, Carla hit Liliana in front of him, but Liliana did nothing. Then we have Joe's break in, his transport and exam when he was arrested and his much changed state when he was found dead. Carla and Lorraine showed up at dawn, drunk and raising hell while everybody was trying to figure out what happened to Joe. That afternoon Carla is found unconscious in her apartment. Both victims had lots of enemies and were dying from liver disease. Carla was mean and liked to hurt people and sleep with other women's husbands. Joe's been shot several times, because he, allegedly, liked to mess with little girls. No one ever acted on any of the charges against either of them and there are too many incidents for all of the claims to be false. All Joe and Carla's victims have motive. Someone has been protecting them from the legal consequences of their actions. Maybe that someone got tired of protecting those two troublemakers. That would be someone else with motive, and maybe the power to arrange their deaths." He paused to let that information sink in, and then added, "Just a thought."

The FBI agents looked at each other. Terry could see that neither one was happy. Chief Molina hadn't mentioned any of this background. He saw the Chief's face go pale and Terry figured the accusation of murder by police could ruin him.

"Now, I have some new information that you might find interesting, but it doesn't do much to solve the case. Let me tell you what Eddie Chee, a crony of Carla's, told me. He was in the cell next to Joe's and was released just after they found Joe dead. By your face, Agent, I guess you met Eddie." He ignored Molina's glare. "They let Eddie loose and he got a ride with Eugene and got out when Carla got out at the motel. That afternoon, when Eddie got to his sister's house, he started talking about seeing ghosts. She took him to see Dr. Karnes. Dr. Karnes called me in and Eddie told me that there were ghosts in the cell with Joe Yazzie, and they were giving him hell. Joe was shaking and crying out that he was haunted. He seemed to fall all over like someone was throwing him around. He looked too scared to yell for help, Eddie says. Then he started begging the ghosts to leave him alone. The Navajo do not like ghosts at all. Joe began to throw himself against the bars of the cell trying to escape. He tried pushing his head through the bars, until he was bleeding from his eyes and mouth. Finally, he just fell over and stopped moving. Mr. Chee never saw anyone enter the cell until after Joe was dead."

Jake smiled at the disgruntled, disbelieving looks the other law enforcement officers gave him, he hadn't had this much fun with a tale since he'd started on the force ten years before. He knew they didn't believe a word he said, but that made it even more fun.

"Okay, so we've got a ghost or the DT's that made Joe beat himself up. If we believe that, who killed Carla?" Agent Spence asked interested in the story despite himself.

"Both Carla and Joe had serious cirrhosis. It was amazing that they were still alive in the first place. Carla's death was probably an accident."

Agent Ferguson spoke up curtly, "Internal Affairs will supervise Joe's case. Now do you have a mystical answer for the blow to Carla's head and Liliana's missing hour?"

"I started checking with the regulars that hang out around Carla's place, but Eddie Chee was the only one hanging out at the motel that morning. After Eugene dropped him off, he hung around and fell asleep by the maintenance room. He heard Liliana's truck, and then he heard Liliana and her grandmother arguing. Carla accused Liliana of killing Joe. The yelling stopped, and then Liliana came into the maintenance room and collected her camping gear.

"He fell asleep again, but later he heard another truck drive up. He heard Carla yelling, and a man's voice and then silence. The truck left. He didn't see it and swears he didn't recognize the voice, but he begged me to lock him up for his own protection. For now that's all I've got. One less murder, but still one assault to solve, and one sick, scared kid to find." There was no change in the skeptical faces in the room. Terry sighed.

"We'd like to speak with this Eddie Chee. Maybe you can introduce us," Agent Ferguson said.

Sergeant Sanchez studied the FBI Agent and leaned forward. "I can have a deputy introduce you to him. He's in lock up right now. I'd like to ask a favor though. I'd like to start a search along the highway between here and Amarillo. I don't think she made it this far. No one on the Res has seen Liliana and her truck is so loud someone would have noticed if she passed by. She was sick and then there are those punks who were harassing her. I'd like to take Mr. Prentice and someone from the State police to check those kids out. Liliana's sick and afraid. I have a bad feeling about this."

"Sorry, Sergeant, but Liliana is headed underground on the reservation, until we have evidence otherwise." Agent Ferguson's mind was set. He'd done his duty and listened to what the local cop had to say, but he didn't agree with any of it. The sergeant had no authority since none of the events had happened on the reservation.

"Has there been any sign of her truck on satellite?" Jake asked.

"The satellite systems are occupied elsewhere. There's been no sighting of her truck. The tire tracks she left on the main road showed her leaving some rubber behind as she made a sharp U-turn from east to west just outside the turnoff to the Prentice ranch. If you insist on looking for her I suggest you start looking there," Agent Ferguson said coldly. He stood and motioned for the others to follow. Terry and Luke stood up. They would all be traveling to the Laguna police station in the dusty sedan, leaving Terry's truck at the station as they followed Sergeant Sanchez to see Eddie.

As they walked to their vehicles, Officer Sanchez added, "We're letting everyone know she needs medical attention, so maybe the more reluctant residents will cooperate. If she runs to the Res, we'll find her. I'm just worried she didn't make it that far, especially after what happened near Tucumcari. What if those kids ran into her again as she passed through? She could be in hurt or dead."

"We've contacted the Tucumcari police. They have found no evidence of her having been in that area this morning. I think you should let everyone do their jobs and you can do your job. Maybe one of your shamans can ask the spirits where Liliana is hiding out." Agent Ferguson turned and walked to his rented sedan taking his sarcasm with him.

Insulted, but refusing to give the white man the gift of his reaction, Jake gave Terry a shrug. He had tried, but the FBI had their own way of doing things. Jake decided to stick with them anyway. A more opportune moment could arise.

At least the Sergeant had had his say, Terry thought. He had expected the FBI to shut him down the minute he contradicted Chief Molina. They had nothing for a case and they might land out with an innocent, but dead suspect.

Chapter 5

Desperation

Again Liliana woke to the blazing sun and a parched throat. Thick and dry, her tongue tried to choke her. The jacket had slid off her face letting the pulsing sun add to the pounding in her head. Her face burned and her whole body ached, but her left foot was suspiciously numb. When she saw the sun setting in the west, she hoped that it was still the first day. Without moving her head, she scanned for any sign that anyone had been near. Then she looked for something she could hold up and wave. The effort to look and think was exhausting, and then she realized what had awakened her.

She could barely draw a breath of air through her constricted airways. It was past time for her prednisone, but she couldn't remember where it was. When she found the bottle of pills in her jeans pocket, she couldn't decide what to do. The prednisone would keep her body from fighting off an infection as it reduced the inflammation that narrowed her airways. She got some relief from her inhaler, and decided to hold off on the prednisone.

With her right hand she explored everything within reach. She found an empty paper coffee cup and tried to reach the water, but it was too far away. Her pocket knife was in her pocket, and her backpack was behind her head. As she looked around she saw how crumpled the roof was and she was glad she didn't remember the accident. She stopped to rest and remember if there was anything in her backpack that could be useful.

Dust kicked up by a burst of wind stung her eyes. A shadow passed across the sun, bringing the fear of the very vultures she had used to get Terry to accept her offer of a ride into town. She lost herself for a moment in the color of his eyes and the smell of him in his jacket as she slept on their way to Amarillo.

Forcing her attention back to her inventory, she remembered that she had a portable clothes line. She could attach a T-shirt to the string and see if the wind would lift it. That is, if she could do it with one hand and get it out of the passenger-side window that seemed so far away. The driver's side window was lying against the creek bank.

When she moved her left arm, the pain made her cry out. She closed her eyes as she slowly laid the throbbing arm across her chest. If she could splint the arm, it would be easier to move around. The thick backpack straps and the clothes-line together might stabilize the arm, but then she wouldn't have enough line to fly her T-shirt. Another fit of coughing started and she desperately held her abdominal muscles tight so that she wouldn't move and trigger more pain. This time she managed to remain conscious. Maybe her concussion was getting better.

The sound of water running just out of reach was torture; her parched throat ached for relief. Hopelessly, she lay back and began listing her sins. She had to make up for not having Carla around to list them for her.

She was stupid. She shouldn't have run. She was being punished for being stupid. She was mean. She'd said horrible things to her grandma yesterday morning and wished she could forget them; Carla could die. She was selfish. All she wanted was to go to school, she tried to explain to her inner accuser, but it wasn't accepting excuses. Carla's home was turning into a junkie hovel and she was in danger living there alone, still Liliana dreaded every minute she spent with her grandmother and made sure Carla knew it. She was weak and afraid. She could have worked in Albuquerque and found a place to live. Still she kept torturing herself trying to please a woman who could not be pleased. If she had tried harder she could have gotten away. Maybe she should have gone to California. Carla wouldn't travel that far. Again, she was stupid to have ever hoped that Carla would change.

She was completely alone, no parents, brothers or sisters. The few family members she had left were distanced by Carla's venom. If she was so smart, she should have figured out how to get around Carla by now.

Despair filled her heart. Feeling sorry for herself was a weakness, but she was good at it. Wallowing in self pity, she listed the things Carla had done to her. If Carla lived, Liliana would always be alone. Carla would destroy any relationship Liliana might try to nurture, just as she had tried to destroy her chance at school, the only place Liliana had ever found pleasure. She loved science and she remembered how her teachers had been pleased to have an eager student. They offered her opportunities to go to science camps with scholarships, but Carla would never give her permission. Finally, her biology teacher had contacted Social Services and gotten an okay for Liliana to go to a science fair in Albuquerque. A day trip. She would have been home before dinner.

That was why Carla had again ruined Liliana's pleasure in school by faking Liliana's journal with pages of forged entries that threatened the lives of teachers and popular students. Carla had used her skill as a forger in the past to alter checks from customers and had been arrested a couple of times, but nothing ever came of it. Liliana didn't even try to tell the teachers that it was all lies. The result was that, not only was Liliana not allowed to go to the science fair, she was suspended from school. They sent her to a psychologist, but Carla's threats kept her from talking. So she spent the sessions in silence. A few of her teachers tried to defend her, but her silence didn't help.

Fortunately, she had passed over two years of school, without Carla's knowledge, so she still graduated at sixteen. She learned from her grandmother and forged Carla's signature on the forms that made it possible. Liliana let Carla believe that Liliana had dropped out and told everyone about her useless, dropout granddaughter. Liliana skipped the graduation ceremony and even took the GED so that Carla wouldn't find out that she had managed to complete school early, with an A average. She told Carla she was going to TVI, the vocational school in Albuquerque, and entered the University of New Mexico on scholarships and grants. Again, her forging skills had come in handy when the financial forms needed to be filled out. They were truthful, just filed without Carla's knowledge. She had sworn to secrecy everyone who knew her family on the topic of her going to the University. She then had to fight an unrelenting battle with Carla to be able to go to Albuquerque. Finally she just left, turned off her phone and hid from the disinterested cops who came looking for her on Carla's behalf.

Carla had no true friends, but the woman had a network of spies and eventually found out that Liliana was enrolled there. Liliana convinced her she was in a remedial program to help TVI students get better jobs. She was fortunate that her Aunt Adela, Mike's sister, lived in Albuquerque and was willing to take her in without asking for money for food and bills. Without her Aunt Adela, she wouldn't have been able to carry the eighteen hours a semester schedule that she managed to complete with a B+ average. Still she felt alone. Even with the love of Aunt Adela and Uncle Mike, the fact that she had to hide everything from her vicious grandmother drained the satisfaction from her achievements.

The memory of her mother and father lifting her into the air with pride when they discovered that their three-year-old daughter hadn't just memorized her books, but could read a book she'd never seen before, brought sparse stinging tears to her burning eyes. They had rejoiced, calling her their genius child. That was one of the few memories that was still clear in her mind. It was what made school so important. Every night before she fell asleep, she would tell her parents about her day at school. She had been loved, once.

Liliana remembered climbing into their bed on Sunday mornings and staying very still so that they could sleep in and not send her back to her own bed. Broken, feverish and afraid, she concentrated on making those memories real: sunlight filtered through the lace curtains curving over her mother's arm and her father's leg; their warm skin against hers; the scent of their bodies; her father's snore; their feet sticking out of the sheets, her mother's pale, short feet, and her father's long, dark-brown toes. Sobs welled up from her chest.

It was a long time since she'd let herself cry for her parents. When Carla caught her crying, she would torment her about how tears weren't going to bring her parents back, so she might as well get over it. The sobs triggered a coughing spell that wracked her head with pain. Her eyes were clenched as she stifled her cries of grief and pain. As she lost consciousness, she felt a cool hand stroking her forehead.

∞

Frank Karnes finished his charts as quickly as he could. As usual, when he needed to get out early, he had a full day of complicated patients and had no reasonable sounding excuse to cancel them, only the urgent feeling that something terrible was happening and he had to do something. As he passed through the waiting room, he saw the evening weather report: thunderstorms predicted for eastern New Mexico. Maybe they'd get a little of that rain here. His garden was suffering in the early heat. Finally, he got into his jeep and drove over to Jim Hunt's house.

He arrived as the scorching sun drifted toward the horizon. He walked up to the blue door and knocked firmly, not expecting a friendly reception. This was going to be tough. Acting as Liliana's advocate had gotten him crossways with this family in the past.

He heard heavy footsteps on the wooden floors approaching the door and took a deep breath. The door opened and a square-jawed, clean-shaven Pueblo man with short, graying black hair appeared in the doorway. The unhappy face turned to a scowl when he saw who was at the door. He kept his voice polite, however. "Hello, Dr. Karnes. What brings you this far out of your way?"

"I came to ask for your help to find Liliana."

"She's not here. The police have been here and they call every time I turn around. If she's running, she would know not to come here. I wouldn't put up with such nonsense." There was no invitation to come in. Jim Hunt knew what the doctor was looking for.

"I understand how you feel about Liliana, but I know her. She might have had an impulse to run, but she's a smart girl. By now she should have come in. I think something has happened to her. She was having a bad attack of asthma when I saw her yesterday. There's a chance that the asthma has gotten worse and she can't get herself here."

"Well, if she was so sick, why did you let her go? You should have known better. If anything happens to her because of your carelessness, you're responsible." Anger and fear blended in the stubborn man's voice.

"Yes, I know that it seems like a bad decision, but you know what's happened every time I've tried to hospitalize her in the past."

Mr. Hunt interrupted him, very unusual for a Pueblo person. He was that upset. "Yes, I know. Everyone knows about Carla. She pulls the kid out, or else screams and curses our family so that everyone in the tribe knows that crazy drunk is related to us. So now the crazy woman is dying, and her boyfriend is dead. Liliana wouldn't have run if she was innocent. You're wasting your time. Maybe she's chosen to die, instead of dragging our name through the dirt. She made her bed. Goodbye, Doctor."

Frank reached out to hold the door open, praying to be able to forgive the hurtful words spoken in frustration. He heard Donna call out. "Daddy, I know it's the doctor at the door." He heard light, quick footsteps hurrying to the door. Flushed and worried, she pleaded, "Dad, don't be so stubborn. Liliana is ours. Maybe the doctor can help; I know something bad has happened to her. Please, we have to try." She arrived to stand beside her father.

Jim Karnes took the chance to plead his case again. "You may think Liliana is foolish, and willful, especially after everything Carla has said about her, but you're wrong. Do you know that Liliana has nearly finished a four-year degree in science at the University in only three years? Do you know that she has been accepted to medical school? The youngest woman ever admitted. The youngest Native American ever admitted! You have a special grandchild, Mr. Hunt, and you don't deserve her. I would leave, but Liliana needs our help. With your influence in the Council, maybe we can get a search going. I'm not asking for a lot. You don't have to go with us. Just make a call."

The two figures lit by the sunlight from behind the doctor had faces filled with shock and surprise. Finally, Donna said with regret, "Medical school. I never really believed her."

Both sets of eyes dropped in shame as they stepped back, inviting him inside. They never gave Liliana a chance to be anything but the bad kid, the troublemaker. The reason their dear son and brother was dead. The idea of medical school had seemed so improbable that they had assumed she was lying to gain their favor. She had sworn her doctor to secrecy until she actually started. She was such excellent applicant that she was accepted early with a small proportion of those who would clearly have been admitted for next year. The doctor, who had encouraged her and conspired with her to outwit Carla, had known of her hard work and the amazing things she had accomplished.

Frank Karnes was sure that the Hunt's had known in their hearts that Liliana was not at all like Carla. He watched the faces slowly begin to comprehend what he'd just told them. It didn't matter now whether they believed everything he said, as long as they agreed to help.

He'd spent a lot of time with the emotionally abandoned child during her visits to his ER as she worked to get past her asthma so she could get home before Carla showed up to embarrass her yet again. He or his life partner, Peter, had dropped her off close to her home many times so that she could walk the rest of the way and tell Carla that she'd been in detention at school for getting in a fight, rather than report that she'd been so sick the teachers had someone take her to the clinic. Somehow, Carla was never around to answer the phone when they called about her sick grandchild.

He glanced into the room where Dolores Hunt had painted her beautiful pottery. Through the window the colors of the sunset entered to lay themselves in graceful curves over the table, the last pots Dolores had been working on, and the sweater that lay over the back of her chair. He stood silent in the hall. He felt worry and panic. Speechless, his mind asked for more. Then he knew. The cowboy could find their girl. Donna took his arm and led him to the living room.

"Okay, so we set up a search for Liliana," Jim Hunt sat in his lounge chair and waved for the doctor to take a seat. "Where do we start? This is a big state; she could have left it by now."

"I don't think so. She's too smart to wreck her life over Carla's bullshit." He saw Mr. Hunt's grimace and reminded himself to watch his language. "She was sick. She was driving in unfamiliar country. Maybe she took a wrong turn or ran off the road too far for anyone to see her from the highway. I think we should search the highway between Amarillo and here, maybe with a small plane. Laguna Pueblo has a search plane."

"They do, but it's not for any fool to use."

"Daddy. You're being rude. I know you are worried. It wouldn't hurt to ask. Everyone knows her truck and no one's seen or heard it. Dad, we have to help look for her."

Jim stared at her, thinking. Finally, he got up. "I'm going to the kitchen to make some calls," he said as he walked out.

Frank Karnes leaned back into the sofa. Then sat up again. "Oh dear, I forgot to call Peter when I left."

Donna sat quietly, worrying silently, while the doctor updated Peter. She didn't offer a greeting to be passed on to Jim's life partner.

Not long after he hung up, Liliana's grandfather appeared in the doorway. "The FBI at the Pueblo station making a ruckus. The pilot will get the plane ready, but first we're going to talk to that Texan."

On the way to the door, he pulled his cowboy hat off the rack and his keys from the telephone table. Donna grabbed her purse and they went to his truck. He stopped and turned to the doctor. "Where are those FBI men now?"

"The last I heard, they were headed for the Reservation police station to talk to Eddie Chee. He was at the motel and heard someone arguing with Carla after Liliana left."

"That Eddie Chee. Another wino. He spent a lot of time around Liliana and Carla, didn't he? Do they still have that Texan with them?"

"Yes, they're keeping him with them. They don't want to arrest him so he can bail himself out. That's how Sergeant Sanchez reads it, anyway."

"Let's go find this Texan. Come ride with us."

Relief filled his heart, but the doctor kept his face neutral. Donna sat in the middle and Mr. Hunt started the truck and roared off, spraying gravel behind them as he sped out of the yard.

The Pueblo police station was simple square building with a windowed entrance facing west, opening into a small waiting room with a television high in one corner. It was different from the station in Grants because of a mural of Native American history on one wall, and several dark, wood shelves holding a variety of Pueblo painted pots.

Terry, filled with a growing panic, watched the sun heading for the horizon through the window above the entrance in the waiting room. He looked back to see Sergeant Sanchez watching him, then looked over at Luke who rolled his eyes and yawned widely in response to Terry's glance.

They were wasting precious time. The FBI had spent two hours with Eddie at a desk on the other side of the room and every time they asked the same question, the devious old man gave them a slightly different answer.

Eddie Chee was clearly playing games with the white men, with a perfectly serious and cooperative expression. Terry guessed that he was insulted that the white men were treating the Reservation police in a disrespectful manner. He didn't care how they treated him and was enjoying the payback, since he didn't expect them to help find Liliana no matter how hard her friends tried to convince them. No one else, except for Sergeant Sanchez and Luke detected the humor in his rheumy eyes as Eddie ""remembered"" more details, conflicting details of the wild story of what had happened to Joe Yazzie in his cell. Agent Spence finally looked up to catch Terry covering a smile.

"Okay, what's so funny, smart guy?" Agent Spence walked over to ask, his voice tight with frustration.

"Well, this is only my opinion, mind you, but I think this guy is getting even," he replied.

"What do you mean, getting even?" Detective Ferguson snapped.

"Well," Terry drawled, "I'd say Mr. Chee gave his story to his own people, and you are showing a lack of respect when you come and repeat the same questions. When you ask the same question over and over again, you're insulting him. If you didn't like the first answer, he'll give you a different one. I've been keeping track, and I don't think he's repeated himself once. Pretty good for a booze-pickled brain."

The object of their discussion gave Terry a wink that the Feds didn't see. Terry kept his face neutral and leaned forward on the desk. "I'd like to ask again. Can we please go see her grandfather? I think he can help us."

Luke watched him and then turned his gaze to the agents. He was worried that Terry would lose his temper and they'd arrest him.

"The last I heard she wasn't there. I don't see any benefit to a trip out there." This time Ferguson's temper was apparent.

Terry had suspected early in the day that Ferguson's friendliness was a veneer that would crack with enough stress. When he realized the agent was red-faced and pacing, Terry saw that the panic was not just dominating his own mind. Now that he thought to look around, he saw the stress on everyone's face. Tension, worry, and panic lay over the room like suffocating smog. He couldn't breathe the thick air. His chest hurt and he could get no air. Panicked, he stood up and leaned on the table heaving, trying to pull air into his lungs. The room began to swim in front of his eyes and then it went dark. As their only credible witness fell unconscious, Jake and Martin grabbed his arms to stop his fall and eased him into a chair.

Just then Mr. Hunt, his daughter and Dr. Karnes pushed their way past the front counter. The doctor rushed to Terry's side and heard the wheezing. He pulled out his own inhaler and sprayed it into Terry's mouth, which he held open as he held his nose closed as he noted Terry's blue lips. Jake laid Terry on the ground and the doctor told Jim to call for an ambulance. He cursed to himself as he remembered that his medical bag was in his car that was sitting at the Hunt home.

Terry's breathing seemed to ease. Karnes touched his left wrist to check his pulse and Terry cried out in pain. He was mumbling under his breath and the doctor leaned forward to hear what he was saying: talk of water and a ditch sounded like Terry was delirious. Outside the ambulance siren started up and was soon followed by the appearance of three paramedics with a gurney.

As they loaded Terry carefully onto the gurney, he cried out again when his left leg was moved. His left arm and left leg lay at awkward angles. Luke remained by his side, concern clear in his eyes. Mr. Hunt and Donna followed in the truck, the FBI in their sedan and Jake Sanchez took a rookie, Felipe Chee with him in his jeep.

Jake waited with everyone in the emergency waiting room while the doctor worked on Terry in the small, well-equipped ER. After about twenty minutes the nurse came out and asked for Liliana's grandfather and aunt. The FBI seemed upset, but the nurse was firm and several staffers seemed ready to back her up. Jake sat back and waited, watching the waiting room television and the news flashes running along the bottom of the screen warning of flash-flooding northeast of Tucumcari, thinking about how the people who needed to be together were finally in the same room.

His cell phone rang as the others disappeared into the emergency room. It was the station calling to report that Carla had died fifteen minutes ago without regaining consciousness. Jake felt his heart lift, then felt guilty for being glad that someone had died. He informed the FBI and then said a prayer for her soul, knowing he would need to confess the fact that he could feel no sorrow at her passing. He only hoped that she hadn't destroyed her granddaughter's life as her last wicked act in a life filled with cruelty.

∞

Terry was sitting up in bed, breathing medicated mist through a tube. Luke was standing in a corner, trying to keep out of the way. Terry smiled when he saw Donna. His color had improved. The doctor was making notes in a chart and looked up.

"Well, it appears that Mr. Prentice has experienced his first asthma attack and it nearly succeeded in killing him. It's a good thing the police and ambulance headquarters are so close to each other. Mr. Prentice, this is Mr. Hunt, Liliana's grandfather. We had a short visit and he wants to speak with you urgently. Fortunately, you are now on my turf so we don't have to filter everything through the FBI."

Terry nodded, transferred the tube to his splinted left arm, and reached his right hand out to shake the older gentleman's hand. Mr. Hunt eyed him closely and Terry noted his discomfort with the entire situation. A young granddaughter hanging out with an older Texan and then getting herself accused of murder would not improve his standing with the Pueblo Council. He nodded and waited for the question that was in the man's eyes.

"The doctor tells me some white boys were picking on Liliana out east." Terry nodded. "Do you think they followed you to Amarillo?"

Terry shrugged, removed the tube from his mouth and said, "It was dark; I would have seen their headlights. But she did have to pass by there on the way back. If some of them were still out drinking they would have recognized the truck."

"Frank told me that I needed to talk to the Texan. That you had some idea where she is."

"I . . . ," coughing interrupted him. The nurse put the tube back in his mouth. There was silence, broken by the sound of the nebulizer and the doctor's scribbling. When his breathing eased, he said, "While I was sitting at the station listening to Eddie Chee, I remembered that I saw a pretty banged up, fresh steer carcass on the side of the road east of Tucumcari." Terry looked down at his arm and leg, wondering about the pain that was gone as quickly as it had come on. "I don't know anything for sure. All I know is that I have a very bad feeling that Liliana's in danger. Her asthma was still bad the last time I saw her, and I don't think she's foolish enough to keep running. She panicked and made a bad choice, but she'd be here by now, if she could. I feel her fear.

"Last night, we ran into some hooligans that were drunk after a basketball game and were harassing Liliana while she was alone in the truck," he explained to Jim Hunt, needing to convince him to start a search. "They surrounded her truck with their trucks and banged on the windows. I was inside the store and couldn't hear what they were saying. When I got to the car, they threatened me until she pulled out a gun and got them to back off. I'm afraid they got hold of her on the way back and did something to her to get even. I think we need to go to that town near Tucumcari and look for her."

Mr. Hunt nodded, "Sounds right to me," and left the room. When he returned, he had Jake by the arm. When Ferguson and Spence sensed that they were being kept out of the loop, they appeared in the doorway. Before they could say anything, an angry Mr. Hunt rounded on them, his guilt and worry finding a target.

"This man told you that my granddaughter might have been attacked in that town and you ignored him. You did nothing to find out if someone hurt her. You think that it's okay for white men to call Indian girls names. It's only a joke for your kind. You never listened to him tell you that she was a victim. She's a victim of fate, a victim of that drunken grandmother and now a victim of white boys who see an Indian girl as a piece of dirt to be stepped on. If anything has happened to her, I'll be sure that our council gets an investigation and your badges."

He shook his finger in their red faces, daring them to retort. He seemed much taller than his 5'6" as he reared up in fury. Finally, he stopped and turned to the doctor. "Can he travel? We're going to Tucumcari, now. The council will let us use the search plane. Jake will use his sirens to get us to the airport. There's room in the plane for one gurney and medical gear, so," he told Terry, "you have to be better when we find her, or get left behind." He turned around to look at all the faces in the room. After so many years of denial and inaction, he was on the move. Donna had a proud look; this was her father at his best. "Maybe the doctor could come, too. Maybe he'll bring one of those breathing machines. Liliana can't breathe. I feel her terror in my heart. We need to find her."

He turned to see that Terry had dropped the breathing tube and slid off the bed. Luke stood at his side ready to catch him if he should fall. Terry, voice now clear, introduced Luke Harris to Jim Hunt, while the doctor and a medic put together the equipment they would need for her asthma, diabetes and possible trauma. The medic carried the large metal box with supplies and the doctor had a portable nebulizer in his arms and his stethoscope around his neck.

Ferguson and Spence stood in their way, not consulted and not giving way. It looked as if they were trying to find something to say, but finally they changed their minds and allowed them to pass. Before anyone could get in their cars the agents stopped the crowd.

Agent Spence said, "I'm sure this is a wild goose chase, but we'll arrange for a search plane to start at sunrise, on our dime. I don't want it said we didn't do everything in our power to help this girl."

Mr. Hunt grunted and pushed past them to his truck. Without another word the agents took Terry and Frank to their car Jake, Luke, the medic and the rookie were in the lead car, followed by Mr. Hunt in his truck with Donna, followed by the FBI sedan with the agents, Terry and Dr. Karnes. Jake had given the Tucumcari police a description of the boys who had harassed Liliana early in the day. Terry watched all the action, amazed at how at Jim Hunt's word, everyone found their task and moved quickly and efficiently.

The FBI agents called Tucumcari once they were on the way and told them that those boys and anyone who knew anything about their activities of the night before were to be picked up and held for questioning. They then called the Albuquerque office and arranged a search plane to be ready for the morning search. When Terry called to tell Mr. Hunt that a plane would be ready to search his only response was to grunt, "Finally."

Despite the weather system that had moved southwest over the northeast quadrant of the state their flight path was clear. They reached the airport, sirens wailing, in a record fifteen minutes. When they arrived at the plane it was clear that no one wanted to be left behind. Even Jake was too worried to stay behind and his skill as a tracker would be useful. He had to be there for the girl he"d watched grow up, and had done his best to protect her from a situation he was helpless to change. The doctor sent the medic back with the emergency medical equipment once he learned that they would have the Tucumcari emergency services ready when they arrived. Worried about Terry, he kept the portable nebulizer at his side. All were loaded and settled in fifteen minutes. They were finally in the air, leaving the rookie, Felipe Chee, to drive the Laguna police car back to the station, and Donna, who would wait at home for Liliana"s call.

Liliana woke again. She couldn't get any air. She used the inhaler every thirty seconds until she could get a breath, praying that it wouldn't run out while she still needed it. Her backup was in her box of belongings that had been in the bed of the truck. It was pitch black outside the halo the halogen lights threw on the highway; a thick layer of clouds hid the moon and stars. The small chance of a passing plane seeing her was gone until the morning. Shaking with fever and chills, awkwardly she drew her jacket over her. When she reached for her inhaler again, her hand was shaking so badly that she knocked the inhaler off her lap. Panicked, she felt for it in the dark until she found it lying next to her hip.

She was desperate for a drink of water. With her right foot she could reach the water flowing beneath and into the cab through the hole in the floor. Gritting her teeth against the pain it caused in her other leg; she tried lifting her foot so she could grab the cup with her toes. Her jeans were too tight to allow her knee to bend far enough. She pulled out her pocket knife and started to cut at the leg of her pants. Her hand was shaking so badly she feared to cut herself and braced her hand on the steering wheel to steady it.

She fought to hold back bitter, hysterical laughter. *I'm probably already dying from a blood infection; one more cut won't make a difference.* With the fist that held the knife, she thumped the steering wheel trying to calm down. When her hand had steadied somewhat, she carefully continued to slice at the jeans. Thankfully she kept the knife sharp.

It seemed to take forever, but finally she had a slit cut down the inside leg of her jeans. As she rested with her eyes closed, she remembered some breath mints she had grabbed from the kitchen while trying to escape her grandmother's screaming. Shifting her hips she dug the small box from her pocket, managed to get the little plastic container open with one hand and tipped a couple of the tiny mints into her mouth. They tasted wonderful, but triggered no saliva. She was that dehydrated. This was not good.

Slowly she brought her right foot up, and then had to put it back to press the clutch to move the gearshift out of the way of her knee, breathing a sigh of relief when it slipped aside easily. In order to maneuver around the gearshift, she would have to move her left leg. Terrified of the pain, she was even more afraid of the unconsciousness it brought with it, fear of never waking up again. Again she brought her right leg up and rested her foot on the seat. She wished for her father's long toes as, with her first two toes, she grasped the cup and carefully lowered it to the water below. As she lifted the cup up, she felt some of the water spill out. Holding her foot still, she carefully reached down with her right hand to grab it. Pain stabbed through her left arm and leg as her body shifted position.

Suddenly, the truck slid deeper into the creek bed, jarring her with the motion, nearly knocking the cup from her grasp. The shock of the truck's sudden movement left her breathless for several minutes.

She forced herself to breathe deeply and slowly, knowing that, if she panicked, her asthma would get worse and she didn't know how much was left in the inhaler. Eventually the worst of the pain passed and her head cleared a little. The water tasted of motor oil and mud, but it was sweeter than honey to her parched tongue. She wondered how much motor oil a body could tolerate, but she decided she didn't care. She replaced the cup between her toes and was eventually able to get five small drinks of water. Her fingers and toes began to fumble with fatigue, so she stopped to rest. She couldn't afford to lose the cup.

At least it was cooler now. Her face stung from the sunburn. Then she began to shake again and she wished for a blanket. As soon as she rested for a bit, she would see what other clothes were in her backpack.

Thinking about her father's long toes as she sat holding the cup, she savored another mint, but the memory of her argument with her grandmother shoved all positive thinking away. She had planned on slipping in and out as her grandmother slept off her usual hangover. Liliana entered through the office to get her sleeping bag from her bedroom closet only to find Carla waiting for her, all cannons primed and ready to fire. All cleaned up and made-up, Carla sat behind the desk, as if she was there at nine every morning.

Carla started at a high pitched scream and escalated from there. "You think you can just leave me whenever you want. You don't appreciate a damn thing I do for you. Well, Joe's dead and you killed him." she yelled. "You and your white fucker killed Joe. The best friend I ever had."

Liliana tried to ignore her insanity, made it through the side door to the living room and had her sleeping bag in her arms by the time Carla blocked the side door. Liliana turned to the patio slider, but Carla grabbed her arm hard and leaned into Liliana's face, spitting as she screamed, "Didn't you hear me? Joe's dead. You don't care. Well you're going to fry for killing him. It serves you right. You never had any respect for your grandfather. You and your friend killed him. I told the police. They're looking for you now. They're going to hang you for murder, you stupid squaw.

"You think that your Indian family will help you leave me. Well, let me tell you, you little bitch, they don't care about you. They never did. When their kid knocked up your mother, they tried to make her get an abortion. They wanted to kill you before you were born. They knew you were evil from the day you were conceived. Your mother, too, she wanted to get rid of you, but we didn't have the money. Then her stupid Indian boyfriend stole her from me. He kidnapped her and no one would help me get her back. The whole bunch of them kept me from her. That whore grandmother of . . ."

Liliana slapped her hard and faced her grandmother, shaking with anger. For a moment, they stared at each other in shock, but Carla was recovering rapidly, so for the first time, Liliana yelled back. As she thought about it, shivering, bleeding, in pain, but worst of all, alone in the blackest night, she remembered every cesspool word that had come from her own mouth.

"Don't you say anything about my grandma, you stupid drunk. You wouldn't know love if it shoved itself down your throat. Oh, I'm sorry, I forgot," her voice sneered with disgust, "you like having things shoved down your throat. You let Joe shove his thing down your throat every chance he got. That's all he wanted you for, an open mouth and your monthly check. Don't give me any bullshit about him being your friend. When you weren't around, he called you a drunken slut and he told all of his friends what kind of things you did for him. You want to know how I know. His friends told their friends and it was all over the school. Everyone in town knew exactly how well you sucked his cock. What? Are you shocked, Grandmother? He was such a *good* friend."

She was out of control, but now her voice was low and deep with rage. "You taught me how to use those words. Every word that falls out of that polluted trap of yours is foul. I learned real well how to curse, but I never wanted to be like you. I tried taking care of you, because it made my mama sad that you wouldn't speak to her, but I don't care anymore. You can lie in this hell pit you call home and rot with all the venereal diseases you've got from doing all the drunks in town. You call my grandmother a whore. Well, you're the whore everyone talks about. Even the little kids at school know what you are. A drunken slut. And you can take your words, and your shit, and your junkie motel and ram it all up your ass."

Carla had passed from pale to purple with fury. She picked up the heavy lamp from beside the sofa and tried to swing it at Liliana, but Liliana swung the sleeping bag, deflecting the lamp aside and Carla fell back, the heavy, square-based lamp pulling her to the floor. Liliana looked down and saw that Carla was glaring at her from the floor, her face bleeding from where it hit the corner of the lamp, but Liliana turned and left anyway.

When she saw Eddie in the maintenance room, she told him to steal everything he could. She got her tent and the rest of her gear from where she'd hidden it deep in a storage box and loaded it in her truck. Then she drove to the empty school yard and parked so she could calm down. She didn't want to face Terry in this state. No she wouldn't cry. She'd shed enough solitary tears. She let the flames of anger burn away the last of her feelings for Carla until she realized she was in danger of burning herself up in that inferno.

Then the image of what Terry would think if he had heard her screaming like a bar-hag made her burn with shame. She pulled out her brush and started brushing her hair as if it were still long. For a long time she brushed her imaginary hair, trying to remember how good it used to feel when her mother brushed and braided her hair before bedtime, trying to calm herself so she could face those kind, sea-foam-colored eyes.

Finally, she began to hear her mother telling her stories. Native American stories she'd learned from her husband and others she'd looked up in books. Susana wanted her daughter to be proud of what she was. Liliana knew, because her mother told her when she was too young to understand, that her mommy and daddy had not made her until after they were married. Susana reminded Liliana of the true story of their love and her conception, so that she would always remember.

Susana told her that she and her daddy had told a lie, but it was a secret lie. Only Liliana would know the truth. They had told everyone that she had already been made when they got married. They were afraid that, because they were so young, no one would let them stay together if they didn't have a baby coming. So they had prayed very hard and on their wedding night they made their daughter. Other people might tell her bad things, but she could always remember that her making was blessed, because they had wanted her so much. Even then, Liliana knew her mama was trying to protect her from Carla.

As she sat desperately trapped in the truck, she tried to feel sorry for the things she'd said to her Grandma Carla, instead of allowing the raging anger to burn her heart black. She had betrayed her mother, but she just couldn't listen to Carla's poison anymore; she couldn't stand to hear those filthy lies from that foul mouth one more time. She was finished with Carla. The thought was followed with the conflicted love and pity she held for her.

There had been a few times when Carla had the illusion of love with a new man and felt happy enough to shed a little of it on her granddaughter. There were occasional events that included jokes and laughter, and acting silly while making cookies together, but it wasn't enough. Liliana was finished, but she doubted Carla would ever truly be out of her life.

Then she knew. She felt Carla Gonzalez leave the world and join others like her. She believed that Carla would be given a chance, because she had suffered as a child, but it would have to out-balance the suffering she had caused. However, she had given much more suffering than she had ever received. With a sudden wave of nausea, Liliana then remembered the spark that had freed the flame of uncontrollable fury. It was a piece of information that her grandmother, in all of her drunken tirades, had never before let slip.

Joe the drunken child-molester had more than once fondled her in her sleep, waking her to his stench and filth. Carla had called Joe her grandfather and Liliana believed it. The story of Joe and Anna, then Carla and supposedly Susana was popular gossip. They all assumed that he was her father, because he had messed with Susana before she fled into the arms of her true love.

One time when they thought she was asleep Liliana heard her mother and father talking. Liliana was too smart and understood more than she should have from those painful conversations. Because of the way her mother was crying, Liliana knew that they were talking about something terrible. When she was older, she realized what it all meant. Now she knew how horrible it really was. Joe had almost succeeded in raping her mother, his own child.

As bitter, foul tasting bile rose in her throat, Liliana fought to keep it down. Finally, her body ejected the filth of the man who had haunted her life; she cried out with agony from the stabbing pain in her head and chest as she vomited. She went away again, but this time she dreamed of her mother and found some peace.

Chapter 6

Following His Heart

Terry anxiously watched the ground approach as the small plane landed at the small, private air strip that serviced the area around Tucumcari, searching the area for any sign of Liliana's truck, even though, logically, he knew she would not be there. The local police had a car waiting for Terry, who had to go where the FBI took him and Frank stayed close, because of Terry's alarming asthma attack. Terry's goal was to face the young men and decide if they had hurt Liliana, but as he transferred to the police car, Terry could only think about heading east to find Liliana as he felt the wind from the north-east and smelled the rain soaked ground.

He started to shiver and clenched his jaw with pain as he entered the local police station with the FBI agents and the doctor. There he saw several sets of worried, angry parents in the waiting room. Terry was impatient and suspicious that the local police were intentionally marching him in front of the distressed, glaring eyes. Terry glared back from behind the officers and some of them looked away.

He knew that the boys were guilty of harassment on the base of ethnicity, a hate crime, which carried a higher penalty than a bit of juvenile rough-housing. They had committed a federal crime, even if they had nothing to do with her disappearance. Maybe there was a benefit to having the Feds with them after all. With his testimony, at least they might learn consequences that would inhibit further unacceptable behavior. That is if the agents believed anything he said.

They were offered coffee and an officer led them to the interrogation room. The County Sheriff had been called from his home when the FBI called earlier that night and was waiting at one end of the table. He stood, holding his hand out in greeting, and Terry found himself accepting it automatically and was informed by the forceful grip that the chief didn't like someone causing trouble for his people.

The crisply uniformed officer introduced himself as he completed the handshaking ritual. "I'm Sheriff Nick Plates from Tucumcari. I have jurisdiction over this area. When I got word that the FBI was coming out to look for a lost murder suspect I figured I should get out here and offer my help." He indicated that Terry and the two agents should take seats around the table.

Impatiently, Terry spoke out. "I appreciate your interest and help, but I really think I should be out there looking for Liliana."

Plates waved a dismissive hand, saying, "Don't worry Mr. Prentice. We've got some of the best search and rescue people in this state looking for her. They'll find her if she's out there. You've made some serious allegations against some of our boys. Why don't you tell me what happened last night that makes you think that our boys have something to do with the disappearance of your friend?"

Terry swallowed his frustration, not wanting to antagonize local authorities, and spit the whole story out as efficiently as possible. Then, to his dismay, the officer excused himself without responding. When he returned, he said, "We have some local boys here. Do you think you could identify the boys that caused you all this grief?"

"Yes, of course," he responded, as he despaired of getting out of the station before sunrise, feeling like he was running out of time as he slowly suffocated. Plates ambled out of the room, and after another long delay returned to lead Terry out past the waiting room to the line up room.

When he arrived, Terry wasn't surprised to see the line up of kids who looked so similar they could have been clones. All were husky kids with short blond hair, dressed in jeans and T-shirts. He easily identified the three that had been around the truck. He had gotten a good look and had a good memory. Obviously disconcerted that Terry did not hesitate to identify the boys, the Sheriff led Terry out to set up the next line up. Just as easily he picked the two dark-haired boys from the line of dark-haired clones. Five was all he could be sure to identify, although there had been from eight to ten kids involved. He made that clear to the chief, who nodded curtly and accompanied him back to the room.

The kid who had pissed his pants was named Todd Reeves. His brother Joe was the other one closest to the door when Liliana pulled out the gun. The FBI agents, who accompanied Terry during the line-up identification, questioned the suspects. The doctor was allowed to join Terry in an office as the suspects were questioned.

Frank voiced his concern about Terry's flushed face and cough. "I think we should get a chest x-ray. You look sick. We didn't have time in Laguna. Pneumonia could trigger asthma-like symptoms and your fever."

"Not now, Doc. Quit worrying about me. When we find Liliana, I'll feel just fine." He clenched his right hand around his left forearm and leaned forward, resting his elbows on his knees, staring impatiently down the hallway. Frank stretched out his long legs and leaned back, keeping an eye on Terry's color, praying for some news from the search.

As Frank and Terry waited for the interrogating officers to return, Luke, Jim and Jake were arguing with the head of the search teams on the side of I-40 five miles west of where Terry had reported seeing the steer. Apparently, no one had reported the road kill, so Terry's report was dismissed by the head of the team. Luke figured someone had taken home enough meat for a month. Jim grunted in agreement.

The lean, athletic, white-blond, forty-ish man had seemed angry from the minute he walked over to their car to greet them. "I'm Jim Reeves, Emergency Search Coordinator for this area."

Jim Hunt stepped forward from the small group saying, "I'm Jim Hunt, Liliana's grandfather. We have good information that she might be at least five mile markers from here. Is there an arroyo overpass near there?"

"Yes," the search leader said clearly dismissing their suggestion out of hand. "But this here's where most all of the accidents happen along this stretch of road. The hill and the curve give intoxicated and sleep-deprived drivers a surprise and they tend to run off the highway here-about."

"Can one of your cars drop us off farther east while you search here?" Jake interjected before Mr. Hunt blew his cool. He shared the boiling temper and urgency of his respected elder and was insulted at the way he was treated, but knew that they needed to keep these people on their side.

"Well, if you want to find this young woman, I suggest you let my people do their job. If you're so worried about her, you won't want one less person to be looking in the right place. She could be a ways off the road if she was speeding; we'll need to search pretty far out in the dark." His voice and posture informed them that he was in charge of the search and he would decide who went where.

Jake set his hand on Jim's shoulder to remind him to remain calm, and said, "We have good reason to believe that she's farther down the road."

Looking down his nose at the two short Pueblo men, he said, "And how would you know that? Did some medicine man ask the spirits where to find this girl?"

After that open provocation, Jake knew they would get nowhere by arguing with this man. It was unfortunate that they had allowed themselves to be dependent on the will of with this angry man, who appeared determined to contradict any of their suggestions. Luke watched with his arms crossed, his expression deceptively placid.

Once the search leader walked off, Jake turned to Jim and Luke. "We have our phones and flashlights, but only our feet for transportation. We can walk to the spot Terry described and examine the sides of the road as we walk." The other two nodded. Jim sent a special glare at the white-headed man. Luke crossed the highway to search for tire tracks on that side. The old man was cursing under his breath as he and Jake walked rapidly along, scanning the road and the land nearby for any sign that her truck had stopped or left the highway, but not expecting to find anything this far from the arroyo.

The moon was only a sliver and heavy clouds were moving in quickly from the north occasionally blocking its dim light. This section of highway was well-lit with glaring halogen lights, which made searching the pavement easier, but blinded them to anything more than a dozen feet off the road.

Jim sniffed the rain on the wind and looked north to the heavy storm clouds he'd watched from the plane as the sun reached the horizon. His heart clenched at the sight of those storm clouds. He fought the urge to run blindly along the road calling out to her and forced himself to systematically run his light into the dark past the lights looking for any sign of Liliana's truck.

The traffic was light, which was fortunate since the part of the highway they were searching wasn't blocked off by the police who were determined to search where they chose. Occasionally a car would whiz by a little too close and Jim would jump farther onto the shoulder. He decided to stay on the shoulder of the west-bound lane, running his flashlight across the dry grass and mesquite bushes. Jake and Luke joined him as they looked for the spot Terry described.

As they searched, the Sheriff and the two agents rejoined Terry after a suspiciously short interview of the young suspects.

Ferguson started, "Well, Mr. Prentice, it turns out that while you and your friend were being harassed, these five young men were home in their beds. Their parents confirm their alibis. They didn't leave their houses all night. So now I ask you again, do you know where Liliana Hunt is? It seems that if something has happened to the girl, you're the prime suspect. What did you do with her? Did she refuse your advances and so you killed her and dumped her here to throw suspicion on to these boys?"

Terry's face was pale with anger even though he knew Ferguson was purposely goading him. "I know you don't believe that story. When Liliana's truck is found, you should have fingerprints, unless they've wiped it down already. Are you going to arrest me?"

"Well, now you know how these good people feel when you accuse their law-abiding children of harming an unknown woman. It doesn't feel so good does it?"

"The only difference is those good people are lying through their teeth, because I know what those kids did in front of that grocery store. I can't accuse them of anything else, because I don't know, but you don't seem too interested in finding the truth. If you release me and have someone drive me to the search site, I can find her."

"No," Ferguson responded, "whatever happened to Liliana, you are still guilty of aiding in the escape of a murder suspect. You will stay right where you are. Meanwhile, we'll be contacting the police in Amarillo and have the premises of your father's ranch searched. Dr. Karnes, do you know if she had any friends in Texas that might be helping her escape from the law?" The doctor shook his head, too angry to speak. "We suspect that, other than the reservation, her most likely goal would be Mexico. We already have a bulletin out for her truck, and then there is the fact that she is known to be armed. I find it interesting that you didn't mention that she threatened these kids with a gun." He grimaced and turned away as he realized what he'd just said.

Terry would have laughed if he hadn't been so angry. "You have to pick a story, sir. Either these kids were innocently spending the evening home in bed, or they were being threatened with a gun in the parking lot of a grocery store. You can't have it both ways."

Ferguson flushed, but remained silent until he regained his calm. "One of the boys says that a Native American woman threatened him with a large gun as he passed innocently by the window of a blue and white truck at the fast food restaurant near the grocery store."

"Which boy is it? One of the three blond-headed kids or one of the dark-haired ones? I'd like to have him tell me that lie to my face." He swore to himself that he would report everything that happened in this room to his own lawyer and sue this self-righteous town into some respect for the truth. "Look, I can understand that these parents want to protect their kids, but don't you think they ought to consider it more important to teach these youngsters respect for the law. A prank now may lead to criminal behavior with worse consequences later on in life."

He spoke with a loud voice taking advantage of the fact that the agents had left the door to the interview room open. He could see the anxious parents through the open waiting room door across the hall, eavesdropping on the man who accused their kids of crimes they would not admit to. The agents stood up and left, closing the door behind them.

Terry leaned back in the chair and closed his eyes in frustration. He knew better than to argue with the police. He'd been in a few scrapes when he was a kid in Amarillo and he knew how they hated to admit making a mistake. Suddenly his phone vibrated. He got up and stepped into a corner away from the door. It was Luke.

"Say, Boss, how's it going?" Luke drawled.

"Well, they're about to arrest me for aiding and abetting her escape, or murdering her myself. How's it going there?"

"Well, it turns out that the man in charge of the search operations has the same white hair as those kids you told me about. Do you believe in coincidences?" Terry's heart sank. "It seems that nobody's reported the road kill, so they're ignoring our suggestions and are spending their time searching a bad turn in the road where drunk drivers get into trouble. It's about five miles from the mile marker you gave us. He wouldn't even give us a ride to the arroyo. We're on foot, checking the roadside as we go. It'll take us awhile to get there, but I feel good about the direction we're taking. Do you remember anything about the roadside?"

"When I looked back, I saw that the railing that prevents drivers from accidentally swerving into arroyos was damaged. It was quite a ways back from where I saw the steer and I wasn't really paying attention. I have to hang up. Call me if anything turns up."

He quickly closed the phone and shoved it in his pocket as the door opened. He didn't want them to confiscate his cell phone. He looked over at the doctor, who looked to be in a slow boil himself and was glad for the company and another witness to the local police's treatment of the situation. Without the presence of the doctor, he might have felt frustrated enough to take a swing at Sheriff Nick Plates' smug face.

"We've spoken to the parents again," Agent Spence said, "and they have remembered that maybe the kids got home later than they said initially, and that they had been drinking. They are all adamant, however, that the kids were home by midnight and woke late this morning with hangovers. It's unlikely that any of them slipped out during the night. They'd had a good time celebrating after the game and went to sleep after sharing their experiences with their parents. Of course they denied drinking, which the parents knew was untrue, and none of them mentioned the incident involving you and Liliana."

He stopped and waited for Terry's reply. Terry took a deep breath and asked again, "Please take me to the highway. I want to help with the search. If we find nothing, then you can try to convict me of any crime you choose."

He looked up at the clock. It was close to four in the morning. The sun would be rising in an hour. It was at least a twenty-five minute drive to the place he wanted to search. Finally, he stood up, "Since Joe wasn't murdered by anyone, as far as they can tell, and the verdict is out on Carla until we get more information, you have nothing to hold me for since Liliana is likely innocent of any crime. The doctor has arranged a rental car that's waiting for us. If you don't mind, we're leaving now."

He resolutely headed for the door, imitating Liliana's bravado, eyes straight ahead, secretly hoping he didn't have to punch anyone to get out the door. Although Ferguson and the Sheriff looked as though they wanted to stop him, they held back. Once he and the doctor left the building, they looked at each other with relief. The rental agent the doctor had called was waiting outside, sleepily rubbing his eyes.

When he heard that they were going to search for a sick, missing woman, he offered his help. Several of the parents followed them outside to offer their help. Terry shook their hands and thanked them. He and the doctor left and the others followed in their cars and trucks. Several of the vehicles carried some of the chagrined young kids who had been called in for the line up. *You never know what people will do*, Terry thought, shaking his puzzled brain. They started out with a caravan following them.

Liliana woke up in the dark. Again, she couldn't breathe. She used the inhaler a couple of times and realized it was empty. The truck had settled into the creek, or else the water was rising. With a distant rumble of thunder, a different, more urgent fear filled her. As much as she longed for a drink of water, she knew the danger of flash flooding in any waterway in New Mexico. Most of the land was too hard to absorb much water and rain often came in sudden torrents that rapidly flooded arroyos, creeks and rivers.

She filled the cup and drank the water she could now reach with her hand. Other than mud, the water tasted cleaner, so she drank as much as she could. An apple floating in the water bumped her hand. Surprised, she grabbed it, but when she bit into it pain lanced into the left side of her head. The sweet fruit was worth it.

She could still wiggle her right foot, but her left was pinned and she couldn't tell if it moved. After eating the apple, she felt a little better, but she was completely exhausted. It was as if her life force was being sucked away into the dark maw of the huge drainage pipe that led under the highway. Her truck faced the opening, like a carriage headed into the black depths of Hell.

Forcing herself to ignore the ominous blackness, she wondered if they would be able to save the leg if she was found before she died. She wasn't sure if she wanted to live with only one leg. She closed her eyes, losing the last vestiges of hope as the hours passed and her misery overwhelmed her.

The memory of her last words with Carla refused to give her any peace. A well of self-loathing surfaced as she remembered the things she'd said. She had dropped to Carla's level and would always remember that she was capable of the same cruelty that she so despised in her grandmother.

That was the hardest to take. She'd tried so hard to be like her mother, to get along with good kids and do well in her studies. Her teachers liked her, at least the few who hadn't met her grandmother. It seemed that after Carla turned up at school with some pretense or another, the teachers' attitudes toward her would change. Her first realization that the damage Carla did to her school relationships was rooted in jealousy occurred when she was in the fourth grade and was the apple of her teacher's eye. Without telling Liliana, the teacher decided to call her grandmother, to congratulate her on having a wonderful grandchild, and to tell her that they planned to pass her to sixth grade, since she had already mastered fifth grade work.

When Liliana saw her grandmother in the hall, prancing in her stiletto heels, skin tight leopard pants, and a blouse open down to her navel, Liliana felt something precious slip away. Although Liliana was passed to the sixth grade, since her achievements could not be denied, the teacher became cool and distant. Her new teacher never offered Liliana interesting work that was above her grade-level.

Within a few weeks, in a drunken tirade, Carla was calling Liliana all the usual names and told her then that she had asked for the teacher's help with Liliana after telling her that she'd caught her nine-year-old grandchild having sex with a thirteen-year-old boy. Carla laughed at the shocked look and the tears on Liliana's face. "You think you're so good. Well, guess what? You're not better than me," Carla mocked. It would not be the last time Carla broke off pieces of her heart.

Liliana had suspected her grandmother's meddling when she was sent to the counselor's office, but since she wasn't doing anything wrong, she hadn't understood the questions they wouldn't ask directly. In any case, she knew better than to report Joe to anyone. When he was around Liliana slept in the locked maintenance room, even in the freezing winter. By morning she would return to her bed and Joe couldn't ask her where she'd been. An experienced predator, he knew to keep his night visits from Carla since he couldn't always predict how she would react. Liliana suspected that some of the things the counselors asked about were a part of her life, but she was terrified of foster care, so she never told.

Besides Carla's horror stories of foster parents using kids as prostitutes or punching bags, it seemed to Liliana that Carla was the only real family she had. She visited her Laguna family, but she didn't believe that they would take her in. They didn't believe Liliana was of their blood and had let her go to Carla when she wanted so desperately to stay with them, despite the cold way her grandfather treated her. She was sure she would land out on the street if her grandmother threw her out, as she frequently threatened to do.

Foul memories continued to torture her fevered mind. Liliana felt long suppressed bitterness as she remembered how, once summer break arrived, Carla would fire the help and make Liliana clean all the rooms and change the linens. By that time the washer was gone, and all the laundry had to be done at the Laundromat across the street. She would roll the awkward cart with the wonky wheel across the street and sit and read until the laundry was done. It was her only chance to be alone and read.

When she was eleven, one of Carla's intoxicated friends found her there and tried to talk her into sharing a room with him. There were several women and men doing their laundry, and they saw how she shook her lowered head mutely, while the drunk kept trying to paw her. Finally, when he tried grabbing her arm, one of the men told him to get out or he would call the police. The nice man gave her his name and told her which nights he did laundry. One of the ladies also told her other nights when she would be there. After that she would see who was at the Laundromat before going to do the laundry. She had found new friends and would visit with them while they all waited for the machines to finish. Sometimes she would help an overwhelmed mom with her kids or the elderly man to fold his clothes. The Laundromat, strangely enough, became a safe place for her.

Winos bothered her a few times after that, but her new friends chased them off. Once they had to call the police when it was Joe who was after her, accusing her of thinking that she was too good for him. She was twelve that time. Jake got the call from a friend in the Grants dispatch office, who knew the Grants cops would ignore the call. So he came to lock Joe up for the night, and caught hell for arresting a man out of his jurisdiction. Carla had just gotten her check, so she was the one Joe called to make his bail. Her grandmother used a heavy leather belt to beat her that time, for the bruises that appeared on Joe's face that day. Carla knew that Liliana would never tell.

Liliana's eyes were getting heavy, but she didn't want to sleep, afraid that if she fell asleep with her asthma so bad she wouldn't wake up again. She tried reviewing how the kidneys worked from her physiology class. It helped, but eventually her thoughts returned to her remaining family. Struggling to find positive thoughts, she remembered how her Laguna relatives had been reasonably kind to her and they had continued to fight for regular weekend visits. She could taste lemon meringue pie and hear Grandma Dolores' laugh if she concentrated.

Among the flotsam being lifted from the truck floor by the rising water, she saw a package of peanut butter and crackers. It was just out of her reach. After shifting her hips in that direction, she was forced to wait for the pain to ease so she could breathe again. She grabbed the crackers and the cup that had drifted away without her noticing it and gobbled the crackers down until she was down to the last two. She then forced herself to slow down and savor them.

When she went to fill the cup, she was alarmed to see that the water was up to her knees. The banks of the creek were as tall as the top of the cab, she knew that if this was the beginning of a flash flood, the truck would soon be covered with water. She trembled as the fear of drowning threatened to overwhelm her.

Waiting inside the truck was no longer an option. It was time to bite the bullet and pull her left leg free. She set her right foot on the front of the dash board and her right hand on the gearshift for leverage. With as deep a breath as she could manage, she pushed her self upward toward the passenger window, the highest point in the truck. The pain was excruciating; she wept and pushed.

Too soon she had to stop, unable to bear the pain, but she was a few inches higher than before. After resting for a moment, she tried again. Her leg came free and she had several minutes of excruciating pain and the threat of darkness at the edges of her vision, followed by hope. There was a chance she could get free.

Suddenly the water pushed the truck away from the side of the creek on which it had been resting; the water was up to her chest. Now was the time to think hard, but panic nearly replaced reason. She froze in place afraid of destabilizing the truck further. It didn't help to be still; the truck shook as the swiftly moving water gained force. She pushed on the roof with her right hand fighting to hold her position, terrified that she would be dragged out by the water that had begun to pour into the windows and out the smashed windshield. By the time the truck stopped traveling, all four wheels were on the creek-bed, bringing the water up to her chin. It continued to shake and shudder as the powerful currents pushed and pulled at it.

She needed to figure out how to get on top of the truck. If she couldn't get above the level of the banks of the arroyo, she would drown. She started crying, completely worn out and drained of her last drop of hope. Frantically she pushed at the drivers' side door now that it was separated from creek bank, but it was too badly damaged to budge and the window frame was crushed to where it was too small for her to squeeze through. In order to get out, she had to get to the passenger door. The windshield was shattered, but the top was too far for her to reach and there wasn't anything to hang onto once she was out. It would be her last resort.

Reaching over as far as she could, she reached for the door handle, lifted it and tried to shove the door open. The force of the water was too powerful. She was trapped. The window was only half-open, so she couldn't fit through it; then the handle broke off in her hand when she tried to open it. She remembered the gun under the seat and was glad she had been the passenger the last time she had it out. The water was rising rapidly; she didn't have time to rest or think. She grabbed the seat bottom, took a deep breath and went under water reaching frantically under the seat for the gun, fighting the pain. She came out of the water choking and sobbing with an empty hand.

Her breathing was worse. After struggling to take in a few gasping breaths of air, again she reached down farther beneath the seat. This time she felt the familiar metal shape, and pulled it loose. When she came up, the water level was nearly over her face. Painfully she pushed herself higher up, bracing her hip against the back of the bench seat.

She shook the gun to try to clear as much water as she could from the inside. In order to get her face above the water, she dragged her mangled left leg over the gearshift and sat on her backpack, which gave her a few more inches. But the water was rising rapidly. She aimed the gun at the passenger window and was gratified when it fired. The echoing blast ripped her poor head apart. Ignoring the pain, with her hand wrapped in her jacket, she pushed out the remnant shards of glass.

She could fit through the window, but she didn't know if she had the strength to manage it. Her leaden limbs responded only with her greatest effort. She fought off the desire to simply let her head sink into the water and let go of all her grief and pain in a few minutes of breathing dark water. All she could hear was running water, her racing heart and her own wheezing as she took a moment to rest. She tried her inhaler again, but it was completely empty. Empty as her heart. Empty as her soul.

It felt like her lifelong struggle was finally over. The time had come to accept the horror of her life and give up the fight. The accident was a sign that there was no hope of escaping the fate her grandmother had picked out for her, either dead in a ditch, or in jail for life. Well, she'd finally fallen into the ditch Carla had reserved especially for her. Remembering

Carla's bleeding face on the floor, Liliana wondered if the lamp hit her as she fell. It didn't matter; she'd left Carla there to die. If she didn't drown in her ditch, she would die in prison. There was no hope.

Then, as the rising sun glinted on the water rushing by the window, she remembered eyes the color of sea foam. Those eyes held her. She desperately wanted to see them again. She wanted to kiss those eyes. She wanted to kiss those lips. It was the only thing she really wanted in the whole world. Her need to see him gave her the strength to try again.

The creek was nearly full to its banks with a torrent of muddy water. She knew there was no hope of spending any time with the kind soul behind those eyes, but she had to see them one more time. Just one more time. Reaching out of the window with her good hand, she grasped the slippery outside door trim, and pulled herself upward with all the strength she had left. If she didn't make it on the first try, the water would be too deep to make much difference. She hoped to make it to the roof where she could hold on and pray that the water didn't rise much higher.

Slowly she strained to pull herself into the rushing water that tried to drag her out of the truck and into the black maw of the drainage pipe. She banged her injured arm and leg, but had no time for pain. She forced her way out and upward. Finally, she was bending her elbow to pull herself to where her hips reached the edge of the window. She reached across her body to grab the rear of the roof trim and hold on.

The current was even stronger than she'd expected. She didn't think she could fight it for long. When she tried to push herself up with her good leg, it slipped out from under her and her weight fell on the left arm she held close to her body. Tears of pain mixed with the rushing, muddy water.

Water filled the cab of the truck. Lurching and shaking, the front of the truck slid into the opening of the cement pipe that ran under the highway, blocking the flow of water. Watching the water rise behind the blockage to create a lake that would soon drown her, she sobbed with pain and hopelessness. She had no more strength to attempt to fight the rushing water and swim to dry land that was moving farther and farther away on both sides. She laid her head on her arm and cried.

∞

Terry started up the rental sedan as the doctor signed for it. He was impatient of even the few minutes the willing attendant took to rush the paperwork. Once he was on the road, he saw the FBI and the Sheriff following him. Anxiously watching the mile-markers, he realized he didn't need them. He knew he was getting close to Liliana and she was in trouble. He passed his friends without seeing them. Frank called to tell them they were on their way in a rental. Finally he reached the railing he remembered on the trip to Grants.

He whipped the car around, driving recklessly across the highway divide. He parked the car on the north side of the highway and jumped out, followed by the doctor. He leaned over the railing. The truck was stuck in the drainage pipe; the arroyo was full to its banks with a torrent of muddy water. With the help of a sliver of sunlight sneaking over the horizon beneath the layers of clouds he saw Liliana hanging half out of the passenger side window of the battered turquoise truck. She had her head on her arm and her right hand was holding desperately onto the back rim of the roof against the current that threatened to drag her into the six foot wide drain pipe.

He turned to the police car that was parking just ahead of him. "Do you have a rope?" he shouted over the rushing water. The sheriff took a quick look over the railing, then hurried to open his trunk and grab the rope and harness he kept there. Terry climbed into the harness while the chief radioed for help. Men and women were jumping out of cars all around them.

Several men lowered Terry over the side to stand on the cement drain. He pushed off the drain to land on the hood of the truck and had to grab inside the edge of the broken windshield, cutting his hand, to pull himself against the current to Liliana's side. The truck jerked suddenly as the force of the water pushed it forward. Holding onto the rope with one hand, he reached down to touch Liliana's face, but had to grab the rim of the roof as the truck shifted again. She looked up at him with a pale, feverish face and eyes that believed they were dreaming.

When he tried to grab under her arms, she cried out with pain. He stroked her head and said, "It's going to be okay, kiddo. The cavalry has arrived."

Her eyes cleared as she realized he was really there. She replied weakly, "Then we'd better hurry and get out of here before they kill this Indian."

Grimly smiling he wrapped his arm under her right arm and around her back as he felt the force of the water trying to pull her under. It felt like he fought the current for hours in the twenty minutes it took for the rescue team to get there. Finally he looked up to see two men in harnesses being lowered to his level. When they arrived, initially the angry rescue coordinator insisted that they first pull Terry out to allow his experienced team to take over the rescue. Liliana's grandfather and Jake arrived at the same time and placed themselves firmly between the coordinator and the men holding the rope, insisting that there wasn't time for political nonsense. It was clear that Terry was tiring quickly and Liliana was exhausted.

When they got the call for a water rescue, the two men trained for that situation changed into wet suits as the SUV drove to the site. One of the harnessed men in wet suits stood on the edge of the cement drain pipe while the other struggled to gain a footing on the hood of the truck. Even then the roar of the water rushing around them complicated any communication with Terry, but they were pro's and moved in concert, using military sign language to signal each other and then shouted to let Terry know what they were going to try.

The man on the hood climbed down the side of the truck with an underwater flashlight to see what was happening to Liliana's lower half, holding onto the door with all of his strength against the powerful current. When he came up, he returned to his partner's side to explain the situation.

"I'll pull her hips to get her legs out of the truck. When she's free, I'll signal for you to pull her up." His partner nodded just as another harness arrived beside them. The diver again moved onto the roof of the truck and told Liliana, "Try to push your hips up and I'll pull you out of the window and take you up with me. It looks like your legs are free is that true?"

She nodded, and then croaked, "My left arm and leg are broken."

The diver braced his legs against the door and grasped her hips, his partner, who had come over to stand on the truck, held his line to stabilize him. He counted down to three and Liliana pushed with her right leg, but her foot slipped and the diver lost his footing and fell back into the swirling, dark water. Flailing as he was pulled into the drain pipe, only the strength of his partner kept him from passing under the highway.

A gasp, inaudible to those in the water, passed through the gathering crowd on the highway. A cheer accompanied the reappearance of the diver's head above water as his team pulled him up, so he could climb to the top edge of the cement drain. Once stable, he signaled his team to allow enough line for him to again swing out to the truck. Terry held his precarious position with one foot on the dashboard and one on the doors window frame, holding Liliana's head above the rising water. Her skin was cold and her eyes were closed, but he knew she was conscious, moaning with pain as the current battered her injured left side, as if the fates that had let a woman like Carla raise her were trying to drag her spirit into darkness and death.

Responding to the team's signal, Terry moved to Liliana's other side to stand in the bed of the truck. From there he leaned outward to protect Liliana from as much of the forceful current as he could. The second rescuer kicked in the rest of the windshield and looped a line through the windshield and the door window to hold his place on the truck. He held Liliana's waist, calling out words of encouragement as the diver got in position to pull her loose. This time he wrapped himself around her torso, his feet braced on the door, his partner holding his lines taut, and grasped her thighs just below her hips. With a nod to his partner, the diver pulled her up, but was again knocked out of position by a surge of water. Terry heard his curses as he flailed in the dark rushing water.

Terry bent his head close to Liliana's ear, "It's okay. There's been a glitch or two, but we're going to get you out. Don't give up. I'm not leaving without you." She seemed to lean into him, so he kept repeating his reassurances.

The rescuers paused as two men who had stationed themselves on either creek bank threw them rope to stabilize their position from the sides. Once the diver was tied to both stabilizing ropes, he returned to his position behind her.

When Terry glanced up at the road, he saw Jim Hunt in front of the crowd of people that had followed to help in the search on his knees, leaning on the railing, rosary gripped in one hand and lips moving as he watched his granddaughter with a face filled with fear and struggling hope. Terry signaled the doctor for an inhaler and luckily caught it. While the rescuers managed to get her halfway into, and tied to a sitting harness he gave Liliana a couple of puffs. It wasn't much, but it did seem to help her breathing. She seemed more alert as a result. He turned to the diver and shouted, "You have to do it this time. I don't know how much more she can take."

The rescuers glanced at each other, sharing their frustration at their failed attempts. Finally they got her free in a last desperate heave. The exposed left tibia caught momentarily on the side of the window frame and she screamed hoarsely. The diver signaled the crew at the rail who then raised her and the diver who kept her from banging on the wall of the highway with his outstretched legs. A cheer broke out from the onlookers, even from the boys who had harassed her, then a gasp as they saw her mangled leg, but all Liliana heard was Carla's voice carried in the roar of the water cursing her to Hell for getting free of her once again.

Next Terry and the second rescuer were lifted to the highway. When Terry's feet touched the ground, he heard a screeching noise and looked down to see force of the water push the truck farther into the pipe. The level of water rose so rapidly that the rescuers beside the creek rushed to get to the relative safety of the highway. He turned to find Liliana's broken body being carefully arranged on a gurney and covered with thermal blankets, an oxygen mask in place, and a paramedic starting an IV.

Their eyes met and she called out his name. Her grandfather was standing with his hand on her forehead. When Terry arrived at the head of the gurney, she looked up into his eyes and said his name. She tried to reach up to touch him, but they were trying to start an IV. Once the line was in, they moved the gurney toward the ambulance. Her eyes begged him to come with her, but there was only room for her doctor, who had entered without asking permission.

∞

"I'll be there soon," he promised, and lifted his hand in good-bye as they closed the doors.

The doctor was giving the orders for her breathing treatment, fluid, antibiotics and morphine for the pain while monitoring her low blood pressure. As soon as the morphine eased her pain, she drifted into uneasy sleep. Terry, Jake and Jim followed the ambulance to the Tucumcari hospital.

Once she arrived they continued the antibiotics and intensified the treatment of her asthma. The x-rays revealed pneumonia, compound fractures in her tibia and fibula of her left leg, the radius and ulna of her left arm, as well as two broken ribs. Her skull was fractured, but she had seemed neurologically intact when she was conscious. Since her breathing seemed relatively adequate on oxygen after a shot of epinephrine and albuterol inhalation they did not immediately intubate her, but she needed intensive trauma care so they readied her to fly to Albuquerque. They used the Pueblo council airplane for the trip back to Albuquerque since it was ready. Fortunately, the plane, which was used for transport of rescue teams on the Reservation, was large enough for all the equipment, as well as all of those who did not want to lose sight of her, each for his individual reasons.

Her grandfather sat holding her hand. When the pain of being jostled in the move woke her, they looked into each other's eyes, guilt in his eyes and forgiveness in hers. She then turned to look for Terry. When she found him, sitting with his head bent, out of the way of the medical personal, she watched him until he felt her gaze and looked up to her.

"You found me," she whispered.

He smiled, understanding the movement of her lips, and nodded. Not surprising to his new awareness, the ache in his limbs had resolved once Liliana got morphine for the pain. They landed at the Albuquerque International Airport and a helicopter took her to the University Hospital. They immediately took her to the intensive care unit, because she was severely dehydrated, septic and anemic from the blood loss. Her blood pressure was low from shock and infection in her leg and blood. Even though her breathing was better, she needed to be stabilized before she could handle the anesthesia for the surgery necessary for the open fractures in her left leg.

They waited anxiously in the waiting room while the ICU team worked on her. Once her blood pressure was stabilized with fluids and medications, they moved her to surgery. Before starting her surgery, they took her grandfather aside. Terry watched as the old man's face paled and he gave a worried nod, and then turned away to hide his tears. Terry came over and touched his shoulder, glancing over at Frank Karnes' grim face.

"What is it?"

"There's a chance that they'll have to take her leg. The two lower leg bones are fractured into so many pieces she'll need multiple surgeries. But right now they don't know how damaged the circulation is and the wounds are probably infected. Bone infections are hard to clear," Frank explained. "They'll know more once they get a look inside. If the blood vessels can be repaired there's a chance she'll heal. She's young and strong; she can do it."

Terry nodded, and watched as they wheeled her sleeping form down the hall while her grandfather signed the paperwork. He, Jim and Frank waited in the hospital. The agents went to the FBI offices to work on their paperwork and Jake had to return to Laguna and report to his boss who had not approved his jaunt to eastern New Mexico. Luke went to arrange a hotel, by a change of clothes for Terry and him and take nap. Donna arrived with a basket of food and a change of clothes for her father.

After five hours of surgery, Liliana was returned to the ICU. Her grandfather waited at her side until she finally woke up. Donna, Terry and Frank were eventually joined by Luke, Jake and the two FBI Agents to wait nervously in the waiting room. When it was clear that she would likely be unconscious for another day, the agents got up to leave.

"So, are you going to cart her off to jail once she can move?" Terry's voice was frigid.

"We would like to talk to her,'" Fergusen responded, ""but her doctor says she won't be coherent before tomorrow or later. I just wanted to let you know I'm sorry she had to wait so long for help. Spence and I will return to Denver and leave the rest of the investigation to the local authorities. Good luck. Let us know how she does, okay?"

Terry nodded numbly and turned away. The agents shook Frank's hand, nodded to the rest and left. After several hours of waiting, Jim finally came out to report what her doctors were saying. The vascular surgeon gave her an eighty percent chance that the repaired circulation would be adequate to save the leg. The orthopedist reported that fragments of bone had to be removed and the wounds in her leg were infected. An infectious disease specialist would help plan her therapy. Once the infection cleared, and if the circulation was good, they would be able to place steel plates and bone grafts so that the leg would heal to the same size and strength as before the accident.

Donna went to sit with her. Terry was surprised to hear from a nurse that Liliana wanted to see her fiancé. She was awake enough to write that message down. He sighed with relief that she was well enough to make him part of the family and took his chance to see her.

He entered the ICU with apprehension. Liliana was pale, her dark eyes sunken into deep hollows. She had a breathing tube down her throat taped to her face; her left arm and left leg were in traction and she had several IV's with multiple bags, one of which contained blood, hanging from the pole. Heavily sedated, she had fallen asleep again soon after asking for him, so Dr. Berger, the family practice doctor who would coordinate her care, called him outside.

After she introduced herself to the group, she explained. "The surgeons are optimistic, but she has a long road of recovery ahead of her. Unfortunately the staph infection from her leg is also in her blood. Staph is one of the worst bugs for causing sudden death, but we got to her in time. Fortunately, this is a weaker form of staph than the one giving hospitals so much trouble. My plan is to get her stable and out of here so we don't risk the MRSA type contaminating her wound. Her asthma is responding to treatment so we may be able to remove the breathing tube in twelve to twenty-four hours. I'm optimistic that will happen, but things can change quickly with staph infections. She's been through a lot, but she was healthy and I believe we can pull her through this. For now, Liliana needs all of the emotional support you can give her, so, I'm going to loosen the ICU restrictions on visitors. If she's stable, someone from her list can be with her all the time. My advice is that you get some sleep. You all look ready to collapse from exhaustion. She'll sleep for hours. She's in good hands."

Jim gave Terry a strange look, "So, my granddaughter has a fiancé."

Terry held his hands up palms outward after the attending physician left. "We are just good friends. Honestly, Mr. Hunt, I have not taken advantage of your granddaughter."

Her grandfather nodded curtly, "Just be sure she understands that. She needs someone now. If you don't want to be that person, tell her soon. I want to be with my granddaughter." He returned to her bedside. Terry was finally able to accept the sandwich and soda that Mary offered him. He called Luke to relay the doctor's report. Then he sat staring at his hands, remembering the sight of Liliana being pulled into the flood waters. Frank called Peter and Mike and was about to leave when Jim returned.

He asked, "Why are you out here? Is something wrong?"

Jim accepted a sandwich and started sipping the coffee from Mary's thermos. "Her blood pressure dropped. They say she's in a coma caused by the blood infection and it will take time for the antibiotics to start working. There's a whole posse of them circling the bed. I was in the way." He paused, tears leaking from his eyes. Terry couldn't think of anything that he could say that would make a difference.

"I only wish." Jim's voice was tight, "that I wasn't such a damned fool. She just needed someone to be on her side. Her family should have been with her. I abandoned her. I blamed her for the death of my son. I don't know if I can give her the love and hope she needs to survive. She could die, because of my failure to be a true father to my son's spirit. He loved his child. That should have been enough for me. It was because of Joe that my son married Susana so young. He loved her so he had to save her. I never spoke to him after he married Susana.

"After they died we had Liliana for two years and then all we could get was visitation rights. People talked about how she looked like Joe and like a fool I believed it. She felt the hate I had for him. I failed his child by not trying hard enough to keep her in my home, letting her to return to that unclean place."

Dr. Karnes placed his hand on Jim's shoulder. "I don't know what you've heard, but Joe is not Liliana's father. He'd been harassing Susana since she was little, but she had managed to stay clear of him. I did the premarital blood tests on them. She wasn't pregnant when she married Ben. They wanted you to believe that she was already pregnant so you wouldn't try to annul the marriage. Ben and Susana were good kids. When they told me that they waited until their wedding night to have sex, I believed them. Joe was Carla's father, but he didn't tell Carla until about eight years ago. And," he sighed, "he's also Susana's father according to Carla"

"I should have killed him when Ben asked for my help to protect Susana. There wasn't anything else that would have stopped him. Everybody knew the cops never arrested him for anything. He stole, destroyed property and they say he messed with a lot of kids. He should have died then and I'd still have my son."

"But you'd be in prison, Jim. Ben wouldn't have wanted that. Your home was a refuge for Liliana. It reminded her that her parents were good and that they loved her. That was a huge benefit for Ben's little girl. She also had Ben's friends to check on her. They did the best they could, too." The room fell silent until hours later a nurse came to tell them that Liliana was stable and someone could come in to sit with her. Terry stood up and looked down at Jim who only nodded, so he went into sit with Liliana.

"So, who killed my son?" Jim's face was streaked with tears.

"No one knows for sure," Frank replied. "You know about the cut brake lines and the gossip that Carla did it to get even because Susana left her, but she must have had help. I don't think she wanted them dead, but she wanted to take Liliana from Susana. Jake tells me that they've been looking under all the rocks for some way to prove it. I guess it doesn't matter now that Carla is dead."

When Terry came to the door, Frank looked to Jim and her grandfather nodded his consent for Frank to spend some time with her before heading back to his obligations at the clinic.

Terry sat down next to Mr. Hunt and, without thinking, he put his arm around the proud man's shoulders. "It looks bad now, but she's tough. Pretty soon she'll be sitting in your kitchen eating lemon meringue pie."

"I never could figure out why Dolores liked that pie so much. It's too sweet for me," he sighed.

Terry pulled his arm back. Donna arrived with an elderly Native American man wearing a ceremonial robe. Mr. Hunt stood up and greeted the man respectfully in his native language, Keresan. He introduced Terry and Dr. Karnes and told them that this was William Crane, one of the medicine men for the Albuquerque hospitals.

Jim spoke at length with the medicine man and soon Donna was crying. Frank came out and Donna went in.

Mr. Hunt then introduced the medicine man to the staff in the ICU and they agreed that they could work around three people in the room if Liliana remained stable. It was just a matter of waiting for the steroids to help her asthma and the antibiotics to work on her blood infection and adjusting the medications that helped to keep her blood pressure stable.

Mr. Crane was accustomed to working in hospitals and the University Hospital was accustomed to accommodating Native American religious ceremonies. He carried a large flat wooden board upon which he would create the spirit designs that would call the good spirits to help Liliana heal. Donna and Jim joined him, waving branches of sage that they were not allowed to burn. He began the chant and was joined by Donna and Jim, as he created his sand painting.

Terry was alone in the waiting room, listening to the muffled voices singing the repetitive chant. The waiting room was rectangular and plain, except for a dusty fake ficus in one corner and a few Gorman prints. At least the chairs were cushioned. The chanting went on while the machines beeped to their own rhythms.

After seeing how pale Liliana was, Terry was having a hard time holding onto hope. She hadn't moved a lash when he kissed her forehead. He thought about how little time they had spent together. He had feelings he didn't understand. She'd been careful to keep her distance, joking and teasing from afar. There had only been two moments that her barriers had come down, and those moments lingered in his thoughts.

He could feel the touch of her hand on his face and see the lost look in her dark eyes when she paused for that moment and commented on the color of his eyes. The intensity of her feelings was clear in that moment, but she had quickly raised her defenses again. The second moment he felt special to her was when she had beckoned him to her in the ambulance. She had seemed amazed to see him and intensely glad. Otherwise he could only rely on what he knew of his own feelings. She had left the ranch alone not trusting him to take care of her, leaving him devastated. When the FBI arrived, he was glad that she'd gotten away even though it was a mistake to run.

She was such a strange mix of self-confidence and vulnerability, gentleness and violence. His surprise when he saw the gun she held to the kid's face had nearly caused him to lose control of his own bladder and he'd faced guns in his time in the Middle East. Her strange sense of humor and her ability to deal with an angry, alcoholic grandmother who used her as a verbal punching bag, earned his admiration. When he thought about how suddenly she had turned her truck around to come to his aid on the highway, and how natural that felt, he realized that they were linked somehow. When he remembered how his breathing failed him in Laguna, the hair on the back of his neck lifted. There were a lot of things they had to work out to maintain their friendship. At that moment he decided that he would keep his imagination in control. There would be time when she was well and free of Carla. She was so young, with such a bright future.

When someone sat down next to him and laid a pale hand on his, he looked up into Dr. Berger's face and saw concern. "You look almost as bad as Liliana," she said. "Are you going to be all right? Do you need to lie down?" He shook his head, unable to say a word. She squeezed his hand. "She'll be fine; you got to her in time. An hour later and she could have gone into shock before she got help. By tomorrow we should start to see improvement. She's going to be in the hospital for a while. She'll need you and her family when she wakes up. We'll keep her on tranquilizers for a while until she's strong enough to deal with everything that's happened. Dr. Palley is the attending for the Family Practice resident's team this month, so she'll be working with me. The nurses will always be able to get one of us, if she needs us."

"Thank-you for all your help," Terry said earnestly, holding her hand.

"You're very welcome," she said, then added. "Have you set a date yet?"

He laughed, and then said sadly, "Don't tell anyone, but we've only known each other for a couple of days. She only said that so that I could visit her. We've become good friends."

The doctor smiled and said, "Well, maybe you're not engaged, but she called for you for as long as she could speak. We had to keep reassuring her that you were close by. By the look in your eyes, I would say that she's more than a friend to you as well." He looked down in confusion. Smiling she said, "I'm being a busybody, but believe me when I say that she'll get past this crisis. She's a fighter."

After squeezing his hand once again, she left to enter the ICU. He closed his eyes and leaned back against the wall, thinking about the difference in their ages and backgrounds. After all, he really couldn't know her that well after just a few days. Yet, somehow none of that mattered; he was glad that he never got a good look at Joe. He would never have that face in his mind when he saw Liliana.

He tried to remember prayers from church, adding them to the quiet chanting, giving his strength to the call to Liliana's spirit to remain in this world with those who loved her.

Spence and Ferguson had succeeded in their primary assignment, the recovery of a suspected murderer who had crossed state lines. They gave their report on the search and recovery of the young woman at the Albuquerque office. Then they asked for an update on the results of the lab tests; they were unsurprised by what they learned. The final autopsy on Joe Yazzie stated that he died of heart failure complicated by perimortem trauma.

Carla Gonzalez' death also seemed to be the last page of a long book of self-abuse. Although the condition of Carla Gonzalez' body when she was discovered suggested foul play, the only identifiable prints on the lamp were Carla's. The position of her body also suggested that she had tried to lift the heavy lamp and had fallen back, the lamp striking her head as she fell. The coroner was sure that her death was mainly due to her multiple ailments complicated by a mild skull fracture with intra cranial bleeding. After reviewing the report Spence concluded that Carla's death was likely an accident.

The next case would be more difficult. According to Terry Prentice, Liliana had suffered from a racially motivated hate crime in eastern New

Mexico that had affected her state of mind, resulting in her running from the authorities and her subsequent accident. Spence was in agreement with that assessment. In any case, the federal prosecutors would decide if the case was worth their time. His next assignment was waiting for him in Denver, as well as a reprimand for the amount of money they'd spent on the plane they never used to search for Liliana. Well, he didn't mind that reprimand. It made him feel better about harassing her friend, and he was glad they found her in time. However, the little devil inside him did enjoy jerking people around once in a while, all in the name of justice. He tried not to make a habit of it. He decided to stop by the hospital before he left for his next assignment.

He arrived at the hospital in the middle of the shaman's ceremonies. When he asked the head nurse why this patient was allowed special treatment, she said that the hospital considered the spiritual treatment of its patients as important as the medical. It was also known that Liliana was a medical student due to start school in August. The influential Dr. Ben Kauffman, one of the chief faculty at the School of Medicine had gotten together with Dr. Sharon Berger and obtained approval for the ceremony.

Spence was surprised that Liliana was academically successful, considering her living situation. Raised by a cruel, manipulative alcoholic, he would have thought that she would have had a hard time breaking that cycle. He left some flowers and a card he'd picked up at the gift shop. Martin Spence had to return to Denver to get his next assignment. He nodded to Jim Hunt when he looked through the ICU door's window. The old man nodded in return.

As he left, he shook Terry's hand. "Why didn't you tell me she was starting medical school this year?"

Terry simply stared with his mouth open. Spence laughed and chucked him under the chin to close his mouth. "So, you didn't know either," he said. "Well, I guess that makes us about even. So, do you have anything else to say?"

He figured he'd give the man a chance to recover and have his say. He and his partner had treated him pretty rough. He knew that his partner, for all his superficial congeniality, could be a real jerk. Ferguson was probably chewing on his antacid pills, trying to get past the anger he felt every time he'd been steered in the wrong direction, whether by his own bull-headedness, or someone else's. Terry shook his head and offered his hand, his attention on the ceremony. Spence shook his hand and walked off. Maybe they would meet again under different circumstances.

Chapter 7

Questions

Terry was sitting with Liliana; Donna and her father were in the waiting room when a group of medical students and residents led by two attending physicians approached. The group stepped into her cubicle and introduced themselves to Terry. Dr. Kauffman, a senior faculty member, was of average height and build with graying brown hair, kind, brown eyes and a mustache and a short beard. He held her hand for a moment, giving her a blessing of his own, and then they left.

Terry sat, still dumbfounded that Liliana had managed to conceal her achievements from most of her family. Terry had come to sit by her side after the ceremony was finished and William Crane left to visit his patients in the Albuquerque Public Health Service Hospital for Native Americans next door. If there was a turn for the worse he would return.

Terry worried about her left leg. The toes were dark and he had heard the word gangrene mentioned. He gently massaged the foot and toes until they were warm. A nurse came by and handed him some lotion, which he used to continue to massage the toes and half of the foot to where the cast began. Patiently, slowly and gently he rubbed the square, brown toes.

He felt the calluses from running barefoot on hard dirt, and the scar from when she'd stepped on a broken liquor bottle in Carla's house when she was little. He didn't know how he knew that; he didn't remember her telling him that story. Maybe he wasn't paying attention when she told him. Just like a man, his ex-wife would say. He massaged the foot as he watched Liliana's face, lost in worry and confusion.

Jim arrived at his side to trade places. As he left the ICU, he thought of how Liliana needed his help to survive the struggle of the next few years. He'd known a few medical students and knew it was a rough haul. Hopefully, Liliana, a child of the Laguna Pueblo, would have all the help she needed.

The Pueblo would be proud of her, and, after many years, maybe it would forget her beginnings, or at least those beginnings would be pale shadows compared to the brightness of her spirit.

Jim took the lotion and massaged her other foot, then her hands and arms and again started on the toes of the injured leg. When he was ready to let Donna sit with her, he held Liliana's hand and felt it squeeze back. He looked to her face and saw no sign of consciousness, but he knew that she was aware of his presence. Tears filled his eyes as he returned to the waiting room.

Donna would spend that night after insisting that her father should also go to rest. Luke arrived with the keys for the four person hotel suite. Terry finally agreed to leave and sleep. Luke offered to take him and Jim since he needed to arrange for someone to bring Terry's truck to town. Terry silently showered then fell into bed, asleep at once.

Jim couldn't rest. He had one of the rooms of the suite to himself and he was exhausted, but the things he wanted to tell his granddaughter kept him from sleeping. He wanted to tell her so much that he sat on the side of the bed and spoke to her spirit for hours in Keresan. He told her the story of his life and the joy of his marriage. He told her of his anger when he had believed that his son had thrown his future away at the irresponsible age of sixteen, and of the overwhelming grief when his son died before he made peace with him. He remembered one specific incident clearly.

Jim believed that Carla had killed his boy. She had ranted and raved for five years to anyone who would listen about the evil Indian that stole her pride and joy. He wasn't sure if she'd planned on killing her daughter as well, but he wouldn't put it past her. Susana had found her independence and Carla needed a victim. She wanted the child for herself, along with the financial assistance she would get from the tribe.

After the death of her daughter, Carla started a vicious lawsuit to get custody. He had no idea where she got the money, but she had the help of an expensive lawyer. One night, after the courts had taken Liliana and given her back to her alcoholic grandmother, again, he'd been unable to sleep, hating the feeling of helplessness that Carla's repeated victories gave him; he resented that there was nothing he could do, but worried about what could happen to Liliana with all those drunks hanging around. Restless, he had gone to weed the bean patch by the light of the full moon. Alone in the quiet cool night, he felt the weariness of the painful, never-ending battle with Carla. Her constant verbal assault and the financial strain of paying lawyers wore him down and drained away his desire to the fight. Discouraged, he decided that he had no responsibility to the child rather than accept his reluctance to continue fighting and spending money in the seemingly hopeless struggle. After two years, he gave up the fight. Now, as he spoke to the young woman in a coma two miles away, it was as if he was back in the bean field.

He knew Carla's history. Despite fraud, check forgery, assaults and public lewdness, she was never officially charged for any crime. Fortunately for Dolores, Liliana's caseworker also knew Carla so they were able to get a few days here and there to spend with Liliana. He knew there was someone with influence helping Carla, probably unwillingly. It was the only way she could have gotten away with all of those crimes.

Ben had tried to tell him why he had chosen the child of a drunk to love, but Jim would not listen to his son. He blamed Susana; then he blamed Liliana. Carla got a lot of blame, too, but he'd missed the person most at fault, himself. Ben could have taught his father to love Sana, as he and his friends called her. Jim could have learned to love her, but he let five years pass, then his chance was gone. They were taken from the world too soon.

As he sat there he realized that he *had* to find out how Carla evaded the police, and where she got the smart lawyer and the annuity she constantly bragged about. He owed it to his son. He owed it to Liliana.

He would find the ace Carla had up her sleeve. He knew there would be risk to his family and Liliana if he started down that road. Whoever had enough money and influence to protect Joe and Carla all those years would be able to come after them if they were afraid their secret would be discovered. He was still determined to find out who provided Carla with the power to take his son's life and never be punished.

Liliana was safe here in the hospital, he hoped. He would use the time she spent there to poke the devil and see where the fire started. When Liliana was stable, he would go to Grants to look for the secrets lost in the world of ghosts, the secret of who Carla and Joe knew. He should have paid more attention to that secret thirteen years ago. Then he let himself remember, and finally accepted that he had been intimidated by a veiled warning to let go of his fight against Carla. What made it so painful and shaming was that it came from a man he respected, and it had worked. No clear threat was made, but the message got through and he let go of the fight.

He couldn't be the only one who had been influenced to give up a struggle. Joe was infamous for his crimes against children. He'd been shot by three angry fathers and survived. It made sense now why those fathers had given up on the law and risked life in prison; the system failed them. There were too many unexplained, unpunished acts of evil done by both Joe and Carla. Until now he had chalked up the evil deeds he and his child suffered from Carla and her friends to the unknowable will of God and accepted them. Jim had known what Joe and Carla were, but the anger that had festered in his heart left no room for reason. Now his mind was clear. It was time to drive the vermin into the light.

With a decision made, he finally went to bed and slept, keeping company with his son as they weeded the garden, in the silence of two men who needed no words to communicate.

Sitting up with a tight chest and fear clouding his mind, Terry awoke wondering where he was. Rubbing his hands over his eyes, the events of the last two days came to him and he knew he had to get to the hospital. He pulled clean clothes from the closet in a rush when Jim Hunt stepped out of the bathroom with a determined look on his face. The sight of Jim helped him realize that his anxiety was probably due to a bad dream. However he couldn't ignore the tightness in his chest.

"I know you have something to say, but would you mind if I called to check on Liliana first?"

"I called already. She's had a set-back, but she's better."

Running his hand through his hair Terry sat down on the edge of his bed to wait for the breathlessness to resolve. After a moment, he asked, "So what has you up so early?"

"Are you okay?" Jim asked, worried that Terry was going to collapse on him. "Relax. She's in good care."

"I know. There's nothing I can do there anyway." Terry sighed, and then looked up. "You look like you're ready to walk into a grizzly bear's den. What's up?"

"I have something I want to run by everyone at once. Do you think you can hold off seeing her for a couple of hours?"

"Sure, if you think it's important."

"It is. I already called Jake and Dr. Karnes. They'll join us when they get into town."

"You've been busy; it's only seven in the morning."

"Yup. They weren't too happy when I woke them up. They'll be here in half-an-hour." When Jake and Frank called to say they'd reached Albuquerque, Luke and Terry were ready. Jim drove his truck and Luke and Terry followed him to the other side of I-40 to the North Valley and the Pueblo Cultural Center. Jim ate there whenever he was in Albuquerque.

He liked where the Center lived in an area of Albuquerque close to the Rio Grande River, an area of older homes rapidly becoming gentrified sending children who had grown up in the North Valley to buy homes much farther south, or north, or west on the high and dry side of the Rio Grande along a ridge of dormant ancient volcanoes where housing was more affordable.

Jim was a fan of the excellent restaurant associated with the Pueblo Cultural Center, which was a delightful mixture of a museum and Native American run trading post selling only Native American made goods and using the profits to fund the Center and to support Pueblo culture. Jim, Terry and Luke didn't have long to wait before Frank and Jake arrived.

The host had reserved a private dining area at the request of Jim, a tribal elder.

"I just checked with the hospital," Jim explained, "They're still trying to wean her off the breathing machine. Eventually, she needs to know everything we discuss here this morning."

When the waiter arrived, Jim said, "I think this will be easier on a full stomach." They ordered and patiently waited for him to ready himself.

It was difficult to begin the story he'd put together. Meanwhile, the others spent the time getting acquainted and sharing their stories about Liliana. Jim was gratified that the policeman, a good friend to his son, had taken it upon himself to be available to rescue Liliana when she needed him. He expressed his gratitude to Jake.

Jake thanked him and responded, "My boss almost had a heart attack when he found out that I and my partner Clint Hernandez had a child in the car when we responded to Arnold Baca killing his wife. When we told him that it was Liliana, he cooled down and asked why we had her. He was pissed off at Carla for leaving the kid alone with all the doors open so her drunken friends could walk in. He knew it wasn't the first time and that social services were worthless when it came to protecting Liliana. Finally he said he didn't want to know when we had her with us and suggested that we find someplace safer to put her when her home was dangerous. So we asked Mike if we could drop her off at his place. His wife is good people and didn't mind, thank God," Jake explained.

Jim responded, "So many people took care of her."

"It was not a problem. She was a good kid," Jake responded, "most of the time."

"But you risked your jobs to help her." He turned to Frank Karnes and said, "I apologize for being rude to you. I am glad you were there to help my granddaughter reach her potential despite Carla."

"She did all the work herself." Frank adjusted his glasses, inconspicuously brushing a tear aside, "All I did was to be there to listen when she was sick. After all, especially in Liliana's case, it takes a village to raise a child."

"Yes, it does," Jim responded, "but I know you gave her hope and a role model. Why else would she choose medicine? You are important in her life." The others nodded in agreement.

The embarrassed doctor then told his own secret. "I felt a special bond with her. My mother fell in love with a Kiowa man when she was a college volunteer on the reservation in Oklahoma. Her family took her back to Georgia when she told them she was pregnant. That's where I grew up. I guess that's why I decided to work for the Indian Health Service. My mother made me promise never to contact him, since she'd never told him she was pregnant. She knew it would break his heart. He lived a good life and died awhile back."

Jim reached out and shook his hand, "Welcome to the tribe, Medicine Man." Even through his dark complexion, one could see the deep flush on the doctor's cheeks.

Jim then turned to Terry, "First of all you have to call me Jim, Terry. We are now friends, and every time you speak to Mr. Hunt, I keep looking for my father." Everyone laughed, but Jim was serious.

"You saved my granddaughter. There is nothing I can say or do that would repay what you did for me. I have only my humble thanks to give to you." Terry tried to wave it away, but Jim was determined. "Without your help, I would never have been able to make up for the injustice I have done to her." He paused. "I would see her bright shining light and I would be amazed, but I held my praise inside. I would hear her speaking to my wife after she passed, and I would get angry and jealous," he looked down in shame.

"I know Donna gave her money in my name and I never tried to stop her, but I never added my support. I let Liliana suffer Joe's evil in her life. If I had used my resources in the Tribal Council I could have helped more. I don't think my ancestors will welcome me when my time comes." He waved their protests aside, "I felt like a righteous man. I never feared that I had done any wrong that would keep me from joining my wife. Now I'm afraid that if I don't right an old wrong, I will never see her again. My son asked me on the last day we spoke to care for his child if anything happened to him. I was too stubborn to listen.

"Now I ask: Why did my son have to die? How did this long chain of devilry start? Why does it continue? I would like to find out what Ben knew. They got to me too, even though I never thought about it. We fought Carla for two years; I was sick of it. Then the head of the counsel, he's dead now so I won't say his name, came to me and warned me that maybe it was better to stop fighting Carla. I never asked him for his opinion, or why he chose to poke his nose in my business. I was only glad that I had support for the decision I wanted to make. I am ashamed that I made that choice. Now that all the buried truths are trying to sprout, I think there is one more truth that needs to be uncovered and this is my best chance. Now that everything is stirred up, maybe I'll find the meat in this stewpot."

He paused, as the waitress removed their plates and laid a basket of fried bread and several bottles of honey on the table. They all reached for the delicious treat.

Jim gave Frank a warning look and said with finality, "Today we do not worry about cholesterol."

Frank nodded and bit into his hollow puff of fried bread filled with sweet honey. Soon they were all sticky. The waitress brought wet towels and more coffee.

Jake finally asked, "What have you learned, Mister, uh, Jim? What do you know that can expose those responsible?"

Jim twisted his coffee cup in his hands. "Donna saw Senator Fowler in Grants years ago and wondered what an influential, well-dressed man was doing walking with someone like Carla hanging on his arm, barely dressed and too drunk to walk a straight line. It was right before that that Eddie Chee called Jake when he found Liliana locked in a closet where Carla left her for two days while she took off with a new boyfriend. Carla's custody of Liliana was reinstated without any investigation. Since then I believed the Senator was involved, but I never did anything. I had given up.

"The Pueblos have no influence with the Grants police. The FBI does, so I requested that Agent Spence be reassigned here to help us today. We need the Feds to get the records on Carla and Joe. I'm not too crazy about Ferguson, but Spence is a straight shooter."

Jim continued. "I admit that I have selfish reasons for looking for skeletons in this closet, which would never be allowed in respectable Pueblo families." He got a chuckle from the group, and finally allowed himself a small smile. "I think the crimes and tragedies of these last few days are broken branches of an old tree with deep roots. Joe and Carla can't hurt her anymore, but I worry their protector will want to silence

Liliana, who probably knows enough about this mess to cause trouble. If we focus enough attention on the old crimes, we can track down who has been misusing their power. Maybe it started with the one who raped Joe's mother." He paused, "I need to know if he had anything to do with my son's death.

"That's our task. When she's feeling better, we'll ask Liliana. Meanwhile, Agent Spence can get cooperation from the police in Grants before all the records we need get 'misplaced.'"

"Do you have any idea which cases to look for?" Frank asked Jake.

"I tried looking in Grants for molestation charges against Joe Yazzie I heard about when I joined the Laguna Police Department, but I got chased out once they got wind of what I was looking for. Then there is Emelina Yazzie; there is no record of her report. She lives with her older sister way out on the Navajo reservation. Maybe they can start us in the right direction. If we want to protect Liliana we have to find Joe's protector. I've been digging for this bone a long time.

"Joe knew who his father was, and the grapevine says it's a Fowler. If Joe told Carla, he probably told others. I actually think that most of the word on the street is from what Carla and Joe leaked as their alcoholism rotted their commonsense. The word is that the only reason Carla was kept off the streets, was that old man John Fowler, the father of the state senator, set up an annuity for her. Carla told everyone the money came from the family of the father of her stillborn baby. I know his family; they don't have that kind of money. They were used as a cover for someone else.'"

"Why did you start your search?" Terry asked.

"For the same reason as Jim. I wanted to know who killed Ben. I knew Joe and Carla had a secret. I saw her smug look every time she got Liliana back. I couldn't believe that an irresponsible alcoholic would get custody when there were decent relatives willing to take the child in. There had to be some action going on under the table. Carla spent a lot of time with Joe; she knew his secrets. I started with the secret I knew. I have a friend in Gallup, who told me that Joe's mother was raped when she was just thirteen by someone rich and she got pregnant. In those days it didn't matter; a Navajo girl reporting a rape wasn't likely to get any help. We could start a search on other rapes in the area that could be linked to the same rapist." Jake looked down at his folded hands. "The FBI would come in handy, but we need a place to start."

"Why don't we rent a plane and fly out to talk to the Yazzie sisters?" Terry suggested.

Frank looked up, "I thought you were broke."

"It turns out that my dad finally sold the ranch effective at the time of his death. I have plenty to spare and I owe Liliana big time," Terry responded. "If she hadn't given me a ride, I wouldn't have made it to my father's funeral."

Jake said, "They've kept this secret for a long time. If Carla was blackmailing someone, that would give them motive for killing her. Then there is Eddie Chee's account of the argument with the unidentified man in the truck that hasn't been resolved."

Terry said, "I'd forgotten about that."

"It'll be hard story to sell. Our only witness is a drunk and he's been telling everyone that ghosts killed Joe," Jake said.

Terry leaned forward, "We should let Liliana make the final decision. If we start down this path, she might be exposed to state or even national press. We can't make that decision without asking her."

"Have you ever seen Liliana back down from a fight?" Jake retorted. "She lived her life in a fish bowl full of shit. Everyone knew her business. I don't think she would let that stop her from finding justice for her parents."

"Is it her that wants to punish someone, or is it you?"

Jake stood up and looked down at the fair Texan. "I've known Liliana her whole life. You think you know her after a day. It sounds like you want to let the dead bodies lie in the well, poisoning the water of her life and everyone in the Pueblos. You have no idea how many people Joe hurt. Some have come to me asking for help. They need to know why the law wouldn't punish this son of the devil. It's not just for me or for Liliana. She'll choose the good of the Pueblo."

"You're right," Terry said. "Like she chose to return to take care of Carla every summer. She's twenty, a working student; she could have found her own life. She'll sacrifice herself for the Pueblo the same way. Think about what you're asking her to do."

Jake stood with his arms crossed, hands in white-knuckled fists. "I know what I'm asking her to do."

"We should wait until she's gotten home and adapted to her losses. This situation is more than forty years old. What makes it so urgent now?" Terry asked.

"Despite the coroner's report, Carla and Joe might have been murdered by professionals that we'll never find. Did the same thing happen to Ben and Sana? You don't know how much pain Joe and Carla caused and nobody's ever made them pay. It would be real easy to kill Liliana even in the hospital since she is barely holding on as it is."

Jake turned and strode out of the meeting room slamming the door. When Terry's attention returned to the table he saw understanding in Jim Hunt's eyes.

"I see two young men trying to take care of their friend. The white man wants to wait, but we have waited centuries for justice for what was done to us. Maybe Liliana will agree with you; maybe she'll agree with Jake. I am tired of waiting. And I have to piss. When I'm done we'll go see my girl."

He pushed himself up from the table. Terry could see the stiffness as he straightened his knees. Terry's mind was filled with the fear in Liliana's eyes, even when she was joking. He had to admit he didn't know what she would decide. He sat and remembered his time with Liliana, then he saw Jim wave at him as he left the bathroom and headed for the exit. He turned to Luke who had been keeping his opinions to himself.

As he stood up, he realized they hadn't paid yet. He opened his wallet looking even more confused and lost. Luke started shaking and covered his mouth to smother his laughter, as Terry tried to decide to use the last of his cash or take a chance that the credit card company would let him past his limit. Luke slapped his back as he pulled out his wallet.

"Hang on there, Mr. Millionaire; I'll take care of it." Terry smiled, afraid that if he started laughing, he would cry. Luke laid out the cash with a generous tip. Then he hugged the man who felt like a son to him. "This has been a terrible week: your dad dying, the funeral, meeting this strange girl and Carla. There's a woman who would make you doubt your sanity. You've been accused of aiding a murderer suspect and dragged all over the state. Then you nearly die trying to rescue her yourself. It's okay to let go."

Terry hugged him back then shook his head. "No I can't. Not yet. I need to . . . God, I don't know what I need to do. I just need to hang on for a while longer. Then I'll rest. What would your Kiowa blood tell you to do, Luke?" Terry turned to the doctor and only got a shrug. Frank was keeping his opinions to himself.

Luke ran his fingers through his hair returning it to its usual tousled state. "Sorry, kid. I got no idea. I am ashamed to admit that I kept my mother secret as if there was something wrong with her, so I never went back to Oklahoma. I think they would tell me to fight, but to remember the balance of the world. Waiting would be okay. This fight has been going on for centuries, like Jim said. Would a week make a difference?"

Terry stood studying his face, and then turned to leave. "Maybe it's better to catch them unawares. They could leave the country or hurt Liliana if we wait too long. Let's go see what that family has gotten away with all this time."

Chapter 8

Digging for Truth

They found Jake standing by his car as he called the Navajo police force looking for someone who knew where Joe's mother lived. He left a message then joined the others.

"Lorraine Yazzie has been at the Grants' police department since 2 A.M. drunk and hysterical. She's demanding that Liliana be imprisoned immediately for the murder of her husband. They couldn't reason with her and she wouldn't leave so they arrested her for drunk and disorderly and put her in a cell to sleep it off. Well, she's awake and the circus is on again. I'm glad I'm not the one who has to tell her what happened to her husband."

Frank joined him, while Terry, Luke and Jim took Jim's truck. Frank and Jake had to get back to work after they saw Liliana.

"Will the police come after Liliana?" Frank asked Jake.

"I don't think so, but they're looking at an ugly lawsuit when all this comes to light. I'm going to call my chief to bring him up to date on what we've discussed. I think we should take care of this while we have all this help. If Liliana gets mad, she'll just have to get over it."

Frank nodded, "Should I call Donna to tell her to watch out for suspicious looking strangers?"

"I don't know. We could just be paranoid and make them worry for nothing. There'll be someone with her all the time anyway, won't there?"

"Maybe not. If I get tied up in Laguna and Jim and Terry decide to go to Gallup, it'll be too much for Donna to stay all the time." Frank was worried. He'd grown up black in the Deep South, so he knew what powerful white people could get away with. "I think Terry should stay with Liliana. Miss Yazzie will be more talkative with her own people. The rape counselor in Gallup is Joan Birdsong. Maybe she can go with them. I wonder if it's too late to prosecute her rapist."

"If she was thirteen or younger, or he caused her great mental anguish or bodily harm, it would be first degree rape. There's no statute of limitations for that in New Mexico. If it happened on the Reservation then their law would apply. Even if she's willing, it'll be hard to get any traction on a prosecution. Hell, right now we don't even know who we're after. We could be chasing our tails." Jake shifted his weight to lean on the arm rest as he looked out the window in frustration.

"I hope that we'll have some answers soon. I would like to tell Liliana that the past can't haunt her anymore." Frank's expression revealed a mix of doubt and hope. "You know if it's one of the Fowlers, it's going to be nasty. We could be making her life worse. At least this way, with her two biggest troublemakers dead and her grandfather determined to make up to her, she may find some peace,"

Jake glanced over and they shared a look of uncertainty. "The only thing we can do is follow our instincts. Right now, I want to find out who killed Carla, so we can get Liliana's name cleared. If we don't get rid of the rattlesnakes hiding in the rocks, she'll never be safe.

"If it is the old crime that's causing this chaos, it's going to be tough on her. Her history will be known by everyone. God, Doc, we think that her great-grandfather and her grandfather were the same man. The tribe will see her as a product of sin, an abomination. Are we doing her a favor by confirming that?" Jake pushed his hat back and scratched his head. "I wish we could ask her what she wants, but we need to move fast, before they realize we're on their trail. And you know Liliana. She'd say to leave it be."

"First we find the truth. Then we tell her."

"Yeah," Jake said, "that's the best we can do."

Donna scolded her father after Jake told her about their plan. "I know that stubborn look. You're talking about tearing her life open and spreading it across the news. Do you know what that will do to her? You know she wouldn't let you do this if she could speak. You men always think you know what's right for women. I think you should wait until she wakes up before you do anything."

Jim sat staring at his hands. It was clear that he would do what he believed was right whatever Donna said and hope that Liliana would understand in the end.

Meanwhile at the Albuquerque International Airport, Agent Spence called the Denver headquarters as he was finally about to leave Albuquerque and was surprised to hear that his services had been requested by Jim Hunt, a tribal elder of the Laguna Pueblo. Somehow no one had thought to call him earlier. He was to contact Mr. Hunt to see what use he would be to the Pueblo council leader. He had wondered if the unusual delay in flights portended that he was on the wrong path in returning to Denver, but never would he have admitted such superstition to anyone.

This had been a strange case from the beginning, especially the eerie psychic connection between the man they had in their custody and the young woman they sought. If he hadn't seen Terry Prentice collapse, he wouldn't have believed it. And not a wheeze from him once Liliana was safe in the ambulance.

Yes, it had been strange and he was clearly not finished with this case yet. Ferguson was not invited, so he returned to Denver to deal with an ongoing case there. Spence could see his partner was fed up with all the psychic bull and was fine with leaving town.

When the nurse came in to see if Jim Hunt was there to pick up a call from Agent Spence of the FBI, Jim looked at Donna waiting for her approval.

"You already requested his help. There's no sense sending him away now." She shrugged and turned away.

He picked up the hospital extension and told the agent that Liliana was not out of the woods yet and gave him a short summary of their discussions. Politely Jim told him that they could use his help to step across police jurisdiction to get to the old records Jake had seen in Grants. After hanging up he said, "He almost sounded glad. I bet he keeps unsolved crimes in his file forever."

"I can believe that," Terry responded.

Within the hour, the taciturn agent arrived in the same wrinkled shirt looking like he would rather have a nap first. Yesterday had been a long day. Jake called in and got permission to continue on the case.

"I guess Mr. Hunt has a lot of political pull around here." Terry saw the faint glimmer of humor in the tired eyes. "Well," Agent Spence sighed and pulled out his notebook. "Where are we and what do you need from me?"

Jake summarized the details of the case Spence didn't yet know and the plan they had decided on. The agent was not surprised by anything they told him, but kept his opinion to himself until he had actual evidence and testimony.

"So, Joe's widow thinks she's hit the jackpot," he remarked as he wrote in his last notes.

Terry added, pessimistically, "If she lives long enough to sue. Someone in the department has to be involved with this circus. Maybe the only reason Lorraine is still alive is that three unexplained deaths could not be written off so easily."

Spence nodded without raising his eyes. "I agree there could be risk, or this whole thing is just coincidence juiced up by Carla's scheming. In any case, even if there are crimes and conspiracies, there might not be enough to prosecute anyone. The news of this much incest in Liliana's family may make the Grants paper's front page. If it were my family, I would be devastated."

Agent Martin Spence leaned back in his chair, allowing his concern to show. "I know you care about her and I know you want justice for the legacy of pain that act left her, but you have to decide how far you want to take this. Once the dominoes start to fall . . ." he made toppling motions with his right hand, "you may wish you never started."

Donna was stonily silent, as her father responded, "I think we need to move now." The other men nodded; mixed feelings on all their faces.

"Okay. Jake and I will head for Grants with the allegation that they conspired to suppress reports of a sexual predator so we can access their records. If we shake that tree, some useful evidence may fall, but I have to say it's been the norm to ignore these kinds of cases until recently. There may be no records. Even with reports, they're damn hard to prove. And, we don't know how the suspected powerful family will react to us putting our collective nose up their ass. It's likely they will try to bury Liliana in dirt. For now, she's not likely to be charged with a crime. That could change. If the old crime is left alone, if you let the past fade away, she could go on to live a good life." He leaned forward to give them another chance to back out. "How will all of this help her in the end? It's up to you to decide how far we go. I'm assigned to the case at your request, Mr. Hunt. I'll follow through, but, if you want my advice, I'd say to let it go."

Thoughtful silence filled the room. Finally, Terry spoke up. "Liliana's a tough kid. In the short time I've known her, she's never shrunk from facing the truth. She takes the hard stuff straight on. From what I've heard the town already knows the worst about her family. She wouldn't back off from a fight just because her life would be at risk. If she thought there was a chance to discover which bastard started the train that wrecked her family, I think she'd say, go for it." He laughed to himself as he recalled the image of warrior Liliana scaring the piss out of the white-haired punk.

"What's so funny?" Spence asked.

"Aw, nothin'." Unwilling to share that image with the FBI, he said, "When I met her, her hair was spiked in all directions. Those red-tipped spikes looked like a warrior's headdress. So where do we start, Agent Spence?"

"Call me Martin. Jake and I will visit the Grants police, and then talk to the guy who heard the second argument at the motel. Is he out of jail?"

Jake shook his head, "Eddie Chee asked for protective custody, so he's in the Laguna Jail, dining well, I'm sure."

Eyebrow arched, Martin asked, "Do you think that's why he came up with this story?"

"You never know with these winos. He's been sober for a day; we should talk to him first and see how his story hangs together."

Martin Spence nodded, "I think talking to Joe's mother is a good idea. Someone from the Navajo police should go with Jim and that counselor. Emelina Yazzie is his mother's name, right? This is sure to be a traumatic subject for her. Did she have any other kids?"

"No," Jake responded, "She never married."

"I'm just curious, Jake," Martin said, "what happened to Joe? From what you say, his mom was just a kid. Didn't her family help her?"

Jake shook his head. "Her dad was a religious, bitter widower, on disability for Army related injuries. There wasn't much money or love in his house. The community tried to help when Joe was little, but he started running wild when he was still a kid. Somebody was giving him money, I heard. He started taking his buddies drinking by the time he turned fifteen. I've heard people say that his father's family ruined him with money."

"So all the neighbors knew who his father was, and it seems like Carla got her hands on some of their money, as well?"

"That's what the gossip says."

"Then we have a plan. By the way, who's paying for the flight to the Reservation? I'm already on the hook for the wasted flight to Tucumcari. The FBI's wallet is closed."

"I'd like to take care of that," Terry said, and then added, reluctantly. "I would also like to go to visit Ms. Yazzie. I feel like I'm not doing my share sitting here in Albuquerque."

"No," Donna interjected, "she'll be asking for you the minute she wakes up. If you're not here when she wakes up she'll think you don't care."

Terry stared at her for a moment, relieved and confused. He was sure Liliana would be glad to see him, but he'd been burned badly by women who needed him. Deep inside he still wondered if she only held on to him to help her with her grandmother. Carla was one of the first topics she had brought up when they met. Right now, confusion ruled his heart and mind; he hoped it would clear when he could talk to her again.

"All right. Then how do we go about this?" he asked. Then he said, "My sister-in-law told me that the money is in my account already. Should we rent the plane here or in Grants?"

Jake said, "I have a friend in Laguna with a plane. It'll be easier to figure out how to pay afterward. I'll call him and by the time we drive there he'll have the plane ready." He slapped his knees, "That sounds like a plan. Mr. Hunt can save time by flying. I'll call Ms. Birdsong to let her know who's coming and ask her if she can introduce them to Emelina Yazzie."

Agent Spence, Sergeant Sanchez, Doctor Karnes and Laguna Pueblo Council member James Hunt got up and said their goodbyes. Spence and Sanchez would drive to the Laguna jail, Karnes was returning to the clinic and Jim would take the plane to Gallup.

"I sure hope Liliana doesn't suffer for whatever you stir up today." Donna stated in a last attempt to reason with them. "I honestly don't believe that the Fowlers, if they have done what you say, would be brazen enough to try to hurt Liliana. They know they can protect themselves from one young woman."

Jake pulled her into his arms and hugged her. "Try to get some rest, Donna. We will take small and careful steps. Today, our only goal is to talk to Joe's mother and make sure certain records don't disappear forever. If Liliana wakes up, give her a kiss for me, okay?"

After another squeeze he stood back and their eyes met. Donna, with tears in her eyes, nodded, then dabbed her eyes and sighed. Jake kissed her forehead. Jim hugged her, shook Terry's hand, determination in his grip.

After they'd gone, Terry said, "I guess we're left to keep watch."

Donna smiled, "Go on. I know you can't wait to see her."

Nervously, Terry entered the ICU. His episode that morning had frightened him. When he closed his eyes, he could still see her pallid, sweating face covered with small cuts and blood. The sound of her scream and the sight of the mangled leg were as bad as anything he'd seen in Iraq. His stomach clenched in reaction to the image. He put on the blue gown and gloves at the door. Once they had confirmed that she had a staph infection they put her in the ICU isolation room.

His head started to spin as he saw her small form with tubes in her nose, mouth and a bag from the tube in her bladder. Her left arm was in a cast bent at the elbow that lay on her chest. Her leg was in a split cast because of the swelling; further surgery on her leg would have to wait until her infection cleared. They'd reconnected the blood vessels and straightened the bones as best they could, but her tibia and fibula bones needed metal supports that couldn't be put in until the infection cleared. Two intravenous sites were connected to multiple bags. The blood bags were gone, which seemed like a good thing. White leads from the sensors on her chest led to a complex machine that reported many wavy lines and numbers. A plastic device with a pink light clipped onto her index finger kept track of her oxygen on the same machine. A thin tube went into her nose to drain her stomach.

The hardest to take was the unnatural way her chest would rise and fall with the hissing rhythm of the ventilator connected by a large, blue tube that connected to the clear tube that entered her mouth, disfiguring the shape of her face with the tape that held it in place. He sat down next to her until the spinning sensation in his head and stomach settled. It wouldn't help to pass out here.

Her face looked puffy and pale. Bruising, cuts and bandages covered most of it. Her lashes were gooey with lubricant. Holding her right hand gently, he wanted to talk to her, but he wasn't sure what to say. He stroked the short, brown fingers, and then brushed her bangs from her eyes, as his mind went back to the nightmare at the flooded arroyo where he had almost lost her. If he'd been paying attention, he would have made the connection when he first saw the dead steer on the side of the road. No, if he'd been thinking, he would have acted on his sense of her panic and talked her into returning to Grants with him right away, instead of falling asleep. One day he would ask her if she drugged him and then he'd have to decide if he would believe her whatever she said.

It had been so close. Half an hour later and she would have drowned.

He thought of the way she'd handled the drunken boys and her tightly contained rage in response to the abuse Carla spouted. "Liliana, I wish I had been there for you like you needed. Maybe then you wouldn't have taken off. I hardly know you, yet I feel like I've known you forever." He leaned over and pressed the back of his hand to her forehead. He couldn't talk, because he would cry and he wouldn't let himself cry. He didn't know how much time had passed when the nurse told him it was time for them to finish bathing her. He glanced down and saw she still had blood under her nails. It was a good thing that she was stable enough for them to finish cleaning her up, he told himself.

Terry left the ICU to join Donna in the waiting room. She had a sandwich and a soda ready for his lunch. "Thanks," he said, "I hadn't even thought of eating."

"This place can do that to you," she responded with a smile.

"They're giving her a sponge bath."

"Thank-you for telling me. I'm going to go help with the bath."

Her face was hot. The sun was blazing through her eyelids. She felt lost, unable to think a clear thought. Something was moving her around and it made her leg hurt. Was the truck getting pushed around in the flood water? No, it couldn't be that. He had come for her. When she saw his frightened, pale eyes beside her she was relieved and terrified that he would die with her. She could feel him holding tightly to her hand as they were tossed around by a torrent of water. The sound of water faded slowly as she struggled to open her eyes. She felt as though she was stuck in a strange place with real pain and a dream of love.

Drugged. Yes, she knew this feeling. They had drugged her twice when her asthma got really bad. So much felt familiar, but why was she in so much pain? She heard whimpering and knew it was her. Then she heard a woman's voice say, "I think she's in pain. Push the button for another dose of morphine so we can finish."

Liliana felt the pain easing and tried to fight the loss of consciousness that came with it. Finally she let go. She couldn't fight it. *Somebody's going to pay for this*, she thought vaguely, *they know I hate being drugged.* The light and the pain faded away.

∞

After the bath, Donna left to get some sleep at the hotel. The day passed slowly for Terry. When they got a call from Grants, she was back with Terry in the waiting room while the respiratory therapists tended to Liliana. Jake and Martin were in the police station reviewing the recovered file filled with complaints and reports against Joe Yazzie.

Jake reported that Spence had obtained the files, but Jake was suspicious. The faces of the staff and officers hinted at secrets withheld. Without cooperation, their progress was slow. Frank had to return to the clinic and would return to Albuquerque when he could. Peter was planning on coming that evening even if he wasn't on the list to actually sit with her.

Jim had found Mrs. Birdsong, the rape counselor, and they were on their way to Emelina Yazzie's remote home with a Navajo reservation policeman. Jim learned that Mrs. Birdsong knew about Joe. He was banned from the Navajo Reservation by tribal elders because of the number of complaints against him. Jake promised to report anything new.

Just before they were ready to order take out for dinner, Dr. Berger came by to update them on Liliana's progress. Donna, who had been sitting with Liliana, entered with her. Mike's sister, Adela Ramirez, had arrived while Donna was with Liliana. When they arrived Adela was complaining to Terry about her overprotective brother. Mike had waited until after he learned from Donna that Liliana was taken from critical to serious condition to tell Adela that Liliana was in the hospital.

"I'm going to hang him by his toes. He always does this. Typical machismo. He can know she almost died, but oh no, don't worry Adela. I mean, what if she'd died and I never got to say goodbye, you know. I had five kids and made it to the hospital for four of them. I know about hospitals. Darn him, any way."

She turned her tear streaked face when Donna touched her shoulder. She jumped up and hugged Donna, rocking her from side to side. "Oh my God, Donna, what's happened to our girl? She didn't have to go anywhere. I have friends. If she'd called me I could have had her on the Reservation or in Mexico in a flash. How is she? He said she might lose her leg. I bet she looks awful, but everyone looks awful in hospitals. It's the lights they have here. Don't worry; she'll be back to her old self before you know it . . ."

Donna took Adela's distraught face in her hands and leaned her forehead against Adela's. "I'm sorry I didn't call you. I thought Mike had. She's going to get better, Adela."

Adela started sobbing; soon Donna joined her, embracing her once again. Terry struggled to control himself, but tears escaped down his cheeks.

Dr. Berger laid her hands on each woman's backs, rubbing gently to calm them. Finally, Donna said, "This is the doctor in charge, Dr. Berger. She just checked Liliana out."

"I'm sorry I'm such a crybaby. It's just that she's become one of my own the last three years. How is she? Is she going to lose her leg, Doctor? I'm glad she has a woman doctor. Those men don't know how to treat a woman right."

"Thank you, Adela. She has a team of men and women taking care of her." She pushed her loose white blond hair behind her ears, leaving a fraction of an opening for Adela.

"Wow, you have the blondest hair I've ever seen and it looks like it's natural with your white eyebrows and all. Oops, sorry, foot-in-mouth disease. I'm sorry. I talk too much."

"No, it's just fine, Adela. I know you're scared. Liliana is a fighter. She's very sick, but we've been able to keep her stable for a few hours now. The plan for tonight is to see if we can slowly wean her off the respirator. It will all depend on how she responds. In general, she's young and healthy. I'm sure she can get past this."

"But she has pneumonia," Donna protested.

"Yes, the x-ray does show a small area of possible pneumonia, but sometimes it's hard to tell for sure. We'll know how bad it is by how she does with less oxygen and we'll do follow up x-rays. We'll keep her on tranquilizers even after the tube is out since she's been through so much stress and it triggers her asthma attacks. I have to go, but I'll check in again in the morning."

"Yeah, I had to take her to the emergency room a couple of times for her asthma. What about her leg, Doctor?"

"I'm sorry, but we won't know for a while. They repaired the arteries and veins as best they could. Now we wait to see if it was enough to get good blood flow to the lower leg. Dr. Palley is covering tonight. I'll see you tomorrow, okay?"

"Thank you so much, Doctor."

"Yes, thank you," Terry and Donna chimed in as the tall, graceful blond left the room.

Donna covered her face and sat down, then looked sharply at Terry. "You were checking her out. I saw you."

Startled, he frowned, trying to understand what she was talking about. "I don't remember. Was I? Maybe I was staring, but all I saw was Liliana hanging half out of that truck."

The teasing look in her eyes was replaced by guilt. Terry patted her hand. "I'm glad I didn't see that part. This is nightmare enough for me," she said.

"I can't see her through the window in the door," Adela complained. "I'll just have to pray she gets better fast so I can see her. Tell me what happened to her out there. Mike didn't know any details."

A nurse came out to say that Dr. Berger had added Adela to the list of visitors. Adela jumped up and left with the nurse.

"Saved by the nurse," Terry quipped with relief.

"You should talk about it. Talking can get it out of your head."

"I'm not ready yet." He sat down next to her.

"Adela's been a good aunt, even if they're not blood relations," Donna commented. Terry looked at her curiously. She explained, "Carla already had Susana when she married Adela's brother, George. She was doing okay at the time, trying to be a responsible mom. Eventually she started drinking again. George had been a heavy drinker before they married. They both got worse while they were married. Their fights got violent until Susana got a broken arm.

"After that he moved to California and got rehab. He's been sober since then, but he only came twice to visit. The last time Carla shot him."

"Yeah, I heard about that."

"Mike keeps him up on how Liliana's doing. George loved Susana and sent child support. It was hard for him to leave. Susana was a sweet little girl. After she died, George, Mike and Adela kept on helping Liliana as much as they could. I don't think she would have made it if not for them. Mike would stop by to see if there were groceries in the house and when Liliana was old enough to drive, he asked Dad for Ben's truck and got it running for her so that she could escape once in a while. That was when she started visiting us more regularly. Carla got mad, but Mike threatened to wring her neck if anyone messed with Liliana's truck. I guess she believed him. Then, when Liliana started school in Albuquerque, Adela let her stay at her place, even if all she could offer was a sofa to sleep on. Carla threw fits, but Liliana had learned to manage her better, or maybe Carla was too sick from her cirrhosis to fight like she used to. I'm glad Adela came. I should have called her right away."

Terry's cell phone rang, and he answered to a signal with a lot of static. He listened, and then asked loudly, "Do they have any idea where she's gone?" He paused, then, "Sure, we'll let you know if she shows up here. What if she goes to Jim's house thinking that Liliana's there when she doesn't find her at the motel?" He paused, "Okay, well good luck. I'm glad you got some answers anyway. Call me if anything changes. Are you going to try to come back tonight?"

After he hung up, Terry reported, "Emelina left home in her sister's truck this morning. Her sister Francis says that Emelina's been acting strange for a week. She told her that the owl that sits in the tree by their house has been telling her to go see Liliana. She's been having nightmares and talking in her sleep. Francis was worried about her and walked to the shaman's house this morning. By the time they returned, her sister had left in the truck.

"When Joan set up her group a couple of years ago, Francis enrolled Emelina for therapy for sixteen weeks. Old memories were giving her nightmares. She seemed to do better after talking with other women who had been raped. After that, she began talking about her obligation to her son's victims. She believed that if she'd been a better mother, Joe wouldn't have hurt so many children."

"That poor woman, she's blaming herself for events she had no control over. She was just a kid herself, how could she have done any better? I hope she doesn't hurt herself. That would be too sad. I hope we have some good news for Liliana by the time she wakes up," Donna worried.

Donna went to pick up the Mexican food they had ordered while Adela was with Liliana. When she returned Luke was there checking on Liliana and Terry. He'd decided it was time to head home. Terry had plenty of support with all of Liliana's family and Luke had business to take care of at the ranch. He'd slept most of the day so he was ready to fly home that evening.

Again Terry sat next to Liliana wondering what to talk about. Finally, he decided to tell her his life story, starting at the beginning with his birth and his mother's death. As he relived his childhood, he discovered good times that had gotten lost among the bitter memories. He told her about his father teaching him to ride and rope, and about his favorite horse, Spook, named for the way his white coat glowed in the dark. Lost in memories of his father and brother, he realized that the only close relatives he had now were his sister-in-law and her children. He then switched to puzzling out what he was going to do with his life, and where he would live.

Without realizing it, he stopped talking. The ranch was gone, and the bank had confirmed the deposit of one million five hundred thousand dollars to his account to which he had no checks yet. Out of work, but with his living expenses now taken care of, he could live wherever he chose and do whatever work appealed to him. It left him feeling lost. He'd worked hard all his life and now he felt like a man taking a bungee jump off of a high bridge. The hours passed as he watched the nurses and therapists come and go, checking monitors and making adjustments on the ventilator. The sky began to lighten in the distant window, reminding him of early mornings on the ranch. He glanced up from stroking Liliana's hand to see her watching him. When she had his attention, she pulled his hand to her cheek.

He smiled and stroked her hair with his other hand. She started coughing and the nurses appeared. They had been able to wean the ventilator to where there was no assistance. She'd been breathing on her own for an hour. The resident for the night appeared and removed the breathing tube. Terry stood back against the wall, trying to stay out of their way. The respiratory therapist arrived to help Liliana turn to one side, so she could cough. He watched her struggle to clear her airway as the therapist thumped her back to help. It seemed to take forever, but was actually only a few minutes until she stopped coughing up green goo and they let her sip some water to clear her mouth. The nurse gently wiped her face with a damp cloth, removing the remnants of adhesive from the tape that had held the tube in place. Once they had her comfortable up on her pillows, they did a breathing test. She was able to manage with just oxygen. The nurses, doctor and therapists all moved out, the last nurse waving Terry to return to her side.

Liliana turned to look at him, with a damp cloth in one hand, and clear plastic tubing in her nostrils carrying extra oxygen to her, coughing occasionally. Finally she said, "You stopped talking."

"You were awake?"

"Kind of in and out." She coughed. "So who won, the cowboys or the Indians?"

He smiled and squeezed her hand. "I think the Indians won this one."

"You're just trying to humor me. The Indians never win."

She wasn't smiling and his face became serious. He leaned forward and kissed her cheek lightly. "I think this Indian beat them all," he said before sitting back. "Do you want me to call your aunt?"

She shook her head. ""Tell me what's been happening. That calendar," she pointed to the calendar on the wall in front of her, "says I've missed at least three days."

"You were missing one day, before I finally figured out where you were and then I had to convince the FBI that I wasn't crazy. You're at the end of your second night here." He stroked her cheek.

"How's Carla?" He remained quiet, touching her gently. "It's okay. I can handle it. Tell me."

"She died. They think it might have been an accident." He saw the fleeting guilt and fear in her eyes before she closed them and turned away. "It looks like Carla fell back with the lamp in her hand. If her liver hadn't been so bad she would have survived. They just couldn't stop the bleeding on her brain. A man named Eddie Chee said he heard her arguing with a man who arrived in a truck after you left, so there's another suspect if they change their mind and decide she was murdered. Did you see anyone around?"

Her voice was hoarse, "Just Eddie. He was sleeping in the maintenance room." She wouldn't tell anyone that she'd given Eddie a set of keys years ago. Fortunately no one thought to ask how Eddie had access to the locked maintenance room.

"Yeah. He's not a real reliable witness, but he's consistent in telling that story anyway. Jake, a man from the FBI, and your grandfather are trying to solve the mystery of who was protecting Joe and Carla from the law. Jim and Jake really want to find out if there's a link to your parent's death"

"Does Molina still think I killed Joe and Carla?"

"I don't think so. The place is chaos after Carla's accusation and Lorraine showing up with her craziness after Joe mysteriously died in their custody. He looked like someone beat him to death. The insulin Carla gave him wasn't enough to kill him. Your grandfather's worried that someone put a contract on Joe. Someone professional who could have drugged him or a crooked cop could've finished him off."

"If it was a pro, Carla would have arranged it. The only way she could control me was to have me arrested for murder, besides half the town wanted to kill Joe. They don't need to go hunting for some professional." Her voice was hoarse, echoes of old anger lingered.

"Maybe you should rest."

"No. I want to know."

"Somebody hit him with a rod, or something, that left deep bruising and some fractures on his face. Eddie Chee was in the next cell and he swears ghosts drove Joe to bang his head on the bars trying to get out until he died. It's a wild story, but the trauma pattern could fit that story."

"Joe's drinking finally did in his brain. His liver was as bad as Carla's."

"Yup. He would have lived if his liver and heart weren't so bad."

"So what's Grandpa stirring up?"

"Well, Jake and your grandfather have put some information together about Joe's father, his life and his connection to Carla." He watched her eyes and took a breath. "They think that if a rich, powerful man raped Joe's mom, then paid Joe and Carla off and then later maybe he had them both killed to keep it all quiet, you could be next. Jim's determined to find out so he can make you safe."

She lay staring at him. Confusion, anger and grief flitted across her face.

"That old fool's going to get himself killed and for what? It's all over. They're both gone."

"He wants to help you, Liliana."

"He wants to help his guilty conscience."

Terry sighed. He, the stranger to the family, was the one left to explain all this. His gut twisted with old grief and anger, even though none of it was his.

Liliana saw his reaction. "I'm so sorry I got you mixed up in all my shit." Their eyes met communicating tension and confusion.

"No. Don't be sorry, but to tell the truth, I am . . . annoyed." After the failure of his marriage he'd sworn to be truthful about his emotions, but when he saw the tears well in her eyes, he kicked himself. "Oh Lili, this is all a mess, but I'm not angry with you. You helped me, and then I saw how much help you needed from me. I could have made different arrangements when we got to Grants, but I wanted to help you."

"Yeah. Liliana always needs help with something." Her voice was bitter.

Terry didn't know what to say. He watched as her damaged face close down, her swollen eyes filled with bitterness and she looked away. She let loose of his hand, letting hers fall onto the bed.

"Liliana. Look at me."

With a grimace, her eyes turned to him. He said, "It's okay to need help, but that's not why I'm here now. I'm here because I can't leave. The idea of leaving you makes me hurt inside. I felt like I would die if you died. I've never felt this way about anyone before, even my wife. We hardly know each other, but I only want to be with you."

He could see the struggle in her eyes. Doubt warring with hope. Finally she said, "It's just because you rescued me."

"All I know is that right now I am very confused. I felt this way before you left the ranch, but you are so young and we're strangers, really. If this is because of the rescue, it'll wear off. But I don't think so, Liliana Hunt. If you're willing; I think you're stuck with me for as long as you'll put up with me."

She squeezed her eyes shut, but unruly tears poured from beneath the long, black lashes.

"Please, don't cry," his voice choked. "It might make you sick. Just put it aside for now. Please, you need to breath, Liliana."

A sob broke through sounding raw and strained. He pressed his cheek to hers and whispered into her ear. "I'm here. Don't be afraid. I'm not going to hurt you."

She pressed her cheek to his, unable to speak. Alarming noises arose from several machines at once. He tried to back away, but she had hold of his shirt. He held her fist as nurses arrived to check the alarms.

It was simple to fix the oxygen monitor that had fallen off her finger. It took some waiting and careful watching until her heart rate and breathing recovered. They tried to send Terry out, but Liliana wouldn't let go. Every time they tried to separate them, the heart rate monitor went off. Eventually, she calmed down; the machines quieted and then the nurses calmed down.

Terry, however, was terrified. He'd pushed too far. When the only nurse left was the one recording the incident, he saw a trace of mischief in Liliana's eyes.

"Gotcha," she said and coughed.

He remembered that this place and these machines were familiar to her and was able to give her the smile she needed.

"Girl, don't do that to me again. This old man just about had a heart attack."

"That's okay. There's room in here for two." She was studying his face, absolutely serious. He took a deep breath. "Good boy," she said, "just keep on breathing and you'll be okay. That's what everybody tells me anyway."

Denise, the nurse responsible for Liliana, a tall, pale Irish woman with a long red braid, said, "No more fooling around. The machines don't like it." She winked at Liliana, put the chart on the rack, and then shook her finger at them as she left.

She coughed again. "So, are they going to throw me in jail?"

"No, but they will want your statement. Fortunately, Martin Spence, one of the FBI agents they sent for you, is in Grants with Jake, buried in old police records. Your grandfather went to the Navajo reservation, looking for Emelina Yazzie to see if she'll report the rape so they can . . ." He shrugged.

"Yeah, that's the question. Do what? What are they going to do if she does? Nothing will happen. They'll just upset her for nothing." She fell silent looking down at his hand as she twisted it to examine it from different angles.

He nodded. "Yeah, well, the boulders are already rolling down the hill. We'll have to wait and see who gets out of the way and who gets smashed."

"Carla knew John Fowler and his son Steven, the senator." She looked up at him. "She said they were family and if I played my cards right, I'd be set for life."

"Do you know how they were supposed to be related to you?"

"You're asking me if I know about Joe."

He nodded. This kind of horrible didn't seem to bother her the way the idea that he cared for her did.

"Yeah, I heard enough drunken arguments to get a pretty good idea. Grandma Emmy came to see me when I was ten. She's Joe's mom. She was raped when she was thirteen and had Joe. She never went with another man again. Carla saw her talking to me and had a screaming fit, but she'd already told me all about Joe and his father. Grandma Emmy knew all the awful things he'd done. She told me she used to pray for him to drink himself to death or walk in front of a semi when he was drunk, but God wouldn't listen to her prayers. Finally she confessed her sin to the priest and stopped praying for the death of her son.

"She warned me to be careful and I told her I already knew I had to be careful. She's a nice lady; Joe must take after his father." She sighed, coughed and continued, "Carla told me that she loved Joe when she was a kid. She said he was good-looking and hung around the school. She was only thirteen when she got pregnant with Mama. I was eight, I think, when she freaked out and stabbed Joe during a huge fight. She was ranting about how he was her father and he knew it and never told her. He was denying everything. The cops didn't do anything to either of them. Later, she'd get drunk; he'd come around and it would be the same as before. She was addicted to him."

Exhausted, she leaned her head back into the pillow. Terry stood up, and then leaned over to kiss her forehead. "I'm going to tell your aunts that you're awake. If your grandfather calls, do you want me to tell him to stop what he's doing."

She shook her head. "Nah. He's too stubborn. Anyway, it'll make him feel better to do something. Then he'll get frustrated; when he gets no results, I'll hold his hand."

They were silent, holding hands tightly. Suddenly, he said, "I forgot your Aunt Adela is waiting. I'll go get her." She frowned, but he kissed the back of her hand and went to call Adela to come in.

∞

In the minutes before Adela arrived, Liliana closed her eyes to look for the lit candle she used for meditation. She'd awoken in the midst of a dream of Carla crying, asking for forgiveness while she was being dragged away into the darkness. Liliana was crying, but she could not get free to help Carla. As she slowly awoke she saw Terry holding her hand, and remembered why she wanted to stay in this world. She would miss her grandmother, despite her anger, but life and love held her back.

Chapter 9

Old Rage

Soon Terry found himself comforting Donna. She was sobbing, after he reported most of his conversation with Liliana. "I always believed, or tried to believe that Liliana didn't know what everyone knew. I wanted to believe it wasn't as bad as it seemed. I was so lucky to have parents who loved me. We were so angry when Ben got involved with Susana. He loved her, so he sacrificed his future and his relationship with Papa. I can't imagine what Liliana's life must have been like after Carla took her from us. I wish we had helped more."

"The cards were stacked against you. The only one to escape was George and he had to move to California to do it." Once she calmed down, he said, "You should call your dad and tell him she's awake."

Terry called Jake and Frank. He heard the catch in their voices when they thanked him. Donna was crying on the phone to her father. It seemed like all the old grief was overwhelming everyone now that it was loose. When Adela, red-eyed and tearful, returned he went to tell Liliana that he had to get some sleep.

"I see your warrior headdress is back."

"Yeah, Adela does it every time she can get me to sit still. I usually just let it hang."

"I like it."

"Come back soon."

"Soon. I need a good six hours. Then I'll be back." She nodded and watched him leave. She looked too sad to just be missing him. There was

153

a lot to make her sad, but he couldn't help her to identify which part was the worst. Maybe after some sleep he'd be more help.

∞

Jim Hunt was glad for the plane. The drive to Gallup wasn't that far, but he needed all the energy he had left for what he had to do when he arrived. The task of bringing up painful memories for Emelina Yazzie distressed him, but he was determined to get some answers. The plane landed at a small private airport on the edge of Gallup, where Joan Birdsong, the counselor, and a Reservation policeman, Officer Bill Two Horse met Jim. Bill had a youthful, round face, a fine, sparse mustache and a slightly receding hairline. His skin was the color of the shadow side of a desert rock; his eyes and his hair were light brown; he was built solidly with short legs and a round belly. Bill drove Jim and Joan to the Yazzie mobile home while the sun was on its last legs, lending long shadows to every tree, bush, large boulder, valley and butte. Joan, a short, moderately overweight, fair skinned, soft-spoken woman told Jim what she knew about the two sisters.

"Emelina and Francis have lived together most of their lives. Francis never married. Some said that was because she hated all men after what they did to her sister, raped by a white man, then betrayed by her father. They were always close. Their brothers help when they need it and they have a slew of doting nephews and nieces. No one gets between those two and no one pisses Francis off. She can be a hard woman, but she took good care of her sister once she could support her. When they were kids, Francis fought any kids if she even heard about them talking about her sister's shame. Once she grew up, she made it clear she would get back at anyone who talked about her sister. She made sure she knew everybody's secrets. Francis is an interesting woman, strong, smart and giving, but still mean as a bear protecting her cubs when it comes to Emmy."

Bill added, "The last time Joe came to their home drunk, demanding money and threatening his mother, Francis shot him in the leg. Boy was everyone riled up about that one, but not how you think," he laughed. "Many people bet that she'd kill him if he ever pissed her off enough to pull out her shotgun. A lot of people lost money on that one, except for me. I cleaned up. Nobody bothered to report it to the police. He didn't even go to the hospital, just hid out for a month or two."

"Has the council ever ruled on any of his crimes?" Jim asked.

"Yeah. There were a couple of half-hearted resolutions. Then they'd forget anything happened," Bill said.

"Mrs. Birdsong, do you think Emmy will be willing to put in an official complaint after all this time, if it would help her granddaughter?"

"I don't think so. She seemed satisfied to let it all go. It was like she'd been waiting for a chance to share her pain with others who understood. It's been a long time. Francis, though, Francis will do something, but it won't be official . . . unless she's sure there will be results . . . maybe."

Bill looked up to see Jim in the rearview mirror. "So how's the rain down your way? It's been bone dry here."

Jim let Bill steer the conversation away from Francis' anger. He was an insightful young man. Jim had felt his blood boiling as he contemplated the crime against the Navajo child. He would need all his calm if he was going to succeed in enlisting the help of the sisters.

It was an hour drive on two lane paved road, then another twenty over pitted dirt roads. The sky was clouded, giving the landscape a shadowy, ominous look. They were on a high, elevated plateau with dry grass, large boulder formations, and sage and pinion trees. The horizon was uneven with the distant collections of mountains. They drove by several deep canyons and down into and up out of several deep, dry arroyos. Occasional hogans and trailer homes resided along the dirt road. The Yazzie's white trailer sat at a point where the road ended at a deep canyon. Several pine and pinion trees clustered around the trailer and a huge boulder occupied the space between the trailer and the edge of the canyon. The view of the layers of orange, brown and sand colored walls in the canyons was captivating. It had been awhile since Jim had been out this far.

They waited politely in the car outside watching the owl in the tree until one of the women who lived there came out to greet them.

Francis Yazzie, a retired teacher, was nearing seventy, but still walked erect as she came down the steps of the mobile home dressed in loose cotton pants and a shirt in a pale floral pattern. She was lithe and graceful and her strong featured face held eyes dark with secrets and hard decisions. Her graying brown hair was long and loose as if she had just been brushing it.

It was nearly six when Francis invited them in for coffee. When she was introduced to Jim Hunt, she turned her back to him, apparently placing him in the category of evil men who failed the women of the family. He looked appropriately ashamed.

First Joan asked after Francis' nieces and nephews and received curt responses. Then she told her about the school concert her daughter sang in. Finally, Joan said quietly, "Francis, we are here to ask you if Emelina would help if there is a way to punish the one who raped her. There's been bad trouble in Grants. Liliana's family worries about that man coming after her. We'd like to talk to Emmy. Is she around?" Finally, Francis nodded and turned to allow Jim a look of limited tolerance.

"No," she responded coolly, "she was gone when I woke up this morning. Why do you need to talk to her now?"

"Well, we have some bad news. Her son Joe is dead and so is Carla who is Joe's daughter," Officer Two Crow responded.

She barely blinked. "That's not bad news. Her prayers for Joe's death are finally answered. I don't care about Carla."

"We understand that," Jim responded. "I heard Joe was hard on his mother."

"He was evil, just like his father." She said with finality and lifted her cup to take a drink of the bitter, black coffee.

Joan Birdsong softly filled face and round shape was a contrast to Francis's lean, sharp features. Joan's eyes were wide, soft brown and set wide apart over high cheekbones. Her kind face expressed her unwillingness to cause more pain for the sisters. "That's why we're here, Miss Yazzie. You see, Carla Gonzalez and Joe died suspiciously. Liliana's people believe Emmy knows something that will help explain their deaths. We know that Joe did many evil things and they believe that someone was protecting him from the law. We also know Carla was getting money from the Fowler family and that she has been seen with Steve Fowler." She waited for Francis to absorb the news, but it appeared this was old news to Francis.

When he saw no response from the angry woman, Jim added. "My granddaughter might be in danger because she might know things that would give the Fowler's trouble." Francis Yazzie's face remained closed. "We are also worried your sister will come to harm. If the one who raped her arranged the deaths of Joe and Carla because they were talking too much, he may come after Emmy or Liliana next. We want to help her."

"Why didn't they kill those two thirty years ago and then decide to kill them now? It doesn't make any sense. Anyway, what will anything you do to help Emmy?" Scorn colored Francis's words. "My sister has suffered for fifty years and no one helped her. Only me. Many girls and boys were victims of that family of living evil and nobody has done anything to stop any of them. Why should I believe you? Why should I help you?"

Jim responded, his eyes on the cup of coffee he held in both hands. "I'm guilty of causing pain for Susana and Liliana, because of my scorn for Carla. It's too late for Susana and my son, but I want to help my granddaughter. This evil caused the death of my son through Joe and Carla. I want to stop it before it takes his child, too."

"You men. You talk, talk, talk. You never listen to women. My father was the same. He kicked my sister out of the house for the shame of having a baby with no father. He knew what had happened, but he wouldn't help her. He was too proud, like you. But he was afraid, too, because he found out who did it. That family has tormented my people for generations. Women take care of things now. Your chance has passed."

Officer Two Crow leaned forward, regret and concern clear on his face, "I'm sorry, Miss Yazzie. So many people have failed you for so long. A friend of mine, Jake Sanchez in Laguna grew up with Ben and Susana. He has searched for the truth since they died. We want the guilty ones to pay. Please, Miss Yazzie, tell us where Emmy went. She could be in danger." He saw only cold refusal in her eyes and made one last pitch. "Tell us who it is that poured the tainted water from the jar of evil. We'll find a way to punish him and protect her."

Francis snorted rudely, "You can start with Columbus."

Jim sat back and looked down at his boots, glad he hadn't brought the FBI agent with him. He looked up and asked, "Do you know where she's gone?"

"No." She said sharply. "If I knew, I would have gone with her." She looked out the window, avoiding their eyes. "Three nights ago, the owl came to her and told her that the child needed her help. My sister was afraid. She thinks she's been cursed, because she didn't do enough to help the children." Her eyes turned to meet his. "I don't know where she is."

Without another word she got up and left the trailer. They followed her to the door and watched her walk to the outhouse. If Francis knew who violated her sister, she had no intention of telling them. Worry filled Jim's mind as they drove over the bumpy dirt roads to the highway in silence.

At the entrance to the highway, Bill pulled over to the side and turned to his companions. "If you don't have any other ideas, I would like to talk to two people who lived near Emelina's family. One is my grandmother, the other is my great-uncle. I've never tried to talk to them about this, since it was such a private thing that had happened long before I was born. They might have an idea if one of the Fowler's was hanging around the school. I'm not sure they'll tell me, but I think my grandmother had a lot of sympathy for Emelina. No one ever talked about it openly. I only know Joe's story because I'm a policeman and Jake Sanchez is my friend. I handled a couple of complaints that made it here from Navajo people living near Grants. I was told it was a Grants problem and to keep my nose out of it. He was already banned from the Reservation when I started."

Jim said, "I'll talk to them."

Bill nodded to the elder and turned the SUV onto the highway.

Francis came out of the outhouse as soon as she heard them drive away. She returned to the mobile home and picked up the cell phone her brother had given her for Christmas and called her cousin, who lived three miles down the road. He agreed to let her borrow his truck and would meet her on the road to his house. She changed to jeans, boots and sweatshirt and put on her good LL Bean camping jacket. It would be chilly when the sun set and the coat had handy pockets, which she filled with her pain medicine, her phone, and her glasses and a bottle of water and some beef jerky.

She drove her brother home and told him that he'd have his truck back by tomorrow evening. All it took was a look from his older sister for him to know Francis Yazzie would not answer any questions he might ask. He had no intentions of going anywhere, but she saw he was curious why she wanted to use his truck when she had her own. He would find out eventually. She drove toward the highway as the western horizon exploded in yellow, orange and blood red.

Francis first went home to get her shotgun and hunting knives. Then she drove onto the highway blacktop. She knew where Emmy went, but she had her own destination. Their lives, so close for so long, had been very different. With a mother too young to take care of him, Joe became a wild, unruly teen. Emmy had collapsed under the weight of the assault and shame while he was still a little boy and she turned to drink. The added weight of her fear of her grown son destroyed the last of her true self. Once Francis had a home, she, with the help of the community, finally got her sister off the booze and nursed her back to health. She tried to help Joe, not very hard, since she'd already decided he had too much of his father's bad blood.

After watching her sister suffer years of torment, Francis maintained her path of secrecy. Some of the people who helped Emmy wanted to help her, but at a young age she had learned to make a face as cold as stone, keeping everyone at a distance. Helpless to protect her sister when she needed her most, Francis' guilt and rage had turned inward. She never sought peace by giving up her wish for revenge as her sister had finally done. Her sister had been tormented; Francis believed Emmy had to change in order to survive, but hate still burned Francis's heart.

No one knew how to help her when she was young. Alone, she had tried to heal the burning wounds that tore at her mind, destroying all joy. Finally, she accepted that she would live a cold life. She gave her sister all the love she was capable of. Yet, as the years passed, she found herself loving the new nieces and nephews Emmy invited to the house to walk with her when Francis was delivering jewelry to various vendors. Francis would come home to find Emmy teaching a couple of the nieces how to make jewelry, or telling them Navajo stories. It gave her some peace to see how happy Emmy was when they were there. The children hungered for the sense of identity their Navajo legends gave them. Life had been peaceful for a long time. Now that peace was threatened.

The arrival of the owl meant that it was time to finally act on her wish for justice. Now these people had come to her house offering her the law. The law they represented was worse than useless, it was complicit in many crimes against her people. And she knew these people would never act outside the law. That made them helpless to fulfill any of their noble goals. Their efforts were worse than useless; they could trigger reprisals against Emelina. Francis knew she was the only one who could, and would, destroy the root of the problem and cut down the rotten tree, instead of chopping off twigs, pretending it would make a difference. It was time to end it. Her sister had chosen to act on the owl's message in her way. Francis was ready to commit to the plan that had shaped itself in her heart for decades. Her destiny was different from her sister's.

She thought of her trips to see the white doctor after the medicine man couldn't help her pain. He told her she had cancer in her bones and that she needed to stay in the hospital to have treatments that would make her sick and possibly kill her. All of that for a small chance at a few more months of life.

She didn't want to live her last days in the hospital; every moment in the land she loved was precious. When her time came, she had planned to walk into the wild country to die, so that her sister could live in their house without fear of being haunted by her ghost. It was beautiful on top of the butte that overlooked the valley that began with the canyon near her home. That was the last sight she wanted to see, the view from that butte, to die with the wind in her hair and the cry of the eagle in her heart. The only medicines she wanted from the white doctors were the pain pills that allowed her to hide her illness from her sister.

Now she knew that it was not her fate to have the death she had imagined. She would have to remember the wind and the call of the eagle. She would never climb the butte again. After driving for a long time, she reached the gate that kept strangers off the private property of the rich man. The pain pills made her so sleepy that she'd found herself almost veering off the dark, empty road several times.

Now she was there and very much awake. She cut the chain with her new chain cutter and opened the gate to a pasture; she drove closer to the house over barely marked tracks and parked the truck behind a clump of short pinion trees and sage bushes, out of sight of the road. Francis called and left a message on her niece's answering machine telling her where the truck was. Her niece would return the next day after visiting her children in Denver. She would tell their cousin where the truck was then. That would give Francis plenty of time to complete her task.

She picked up the shotgun from the floor and loaded it, shoving extra ammunition in her pocket. After leaving the keys under the floor mat, she started the long walk to the big house. She only hoped that the police didn't find her too soon. They would be suspicious as soon as they found out that she had left her home alone.

It was a long walk. She pulled out her bottle and chewed several of the bitter pain pills, and then drank a little water to wash them down. Not too much water, she didn't have time to stop to pee.

Martin Spence was surprised at the instant results his request for Joe Yazzie's police record got. It was as if they were ready for him. While he sat with Jake going through the stack of files, he'd taken stock of the officers who came and went from the office. Some were curious, some angry; several were nervous and two were terrified, failing to maintain the blank faces that could protect them. The police chief and his captain passed them frequently, clearly on edge. Finally, they left the station with a box of records.

Martin shook his head in frustration, "How is it that so many people have accused Joe Yazzie of the same crimes over and over again and nothing has ever been done? Sure some of them have retracted their stories, but how can these reports just sit in the files and be ignored? Do you have any idea who in the department is responsible?"

Despite his vindicated expression, Jake seemed hesitant to voice his suspicions. Finally he said, "Well, the chief and the captain are the most likely. They've both been in the department for years. Maybe their predecessors were involved as well, but now they're retired and I doubt that we can touch them."

"What kind of leverage do you think was used on them? I know you don't work under them, but you seem to know a lot of the officers in the Grants department."

"There are rumors, but I don't think that I can say for sure. I'm sorry, but all I have is hearsay and it could destroy a lot of lives if it isn't true."

Martin leaned back in his chair and eyed the younger officer. It would have to be something nasty for Jake to be unwilling to bring it up to help in the investigation that meant so much to him. "Okay," he said finally, "what say we check out a few of the recent allegations and see if there's enough to start an investigation? Whoever has been protecting Joe will be flushed out. Maybe we'll get some answers then."

They picked two of the most recent and reliable reports and went to speak to the victims and their families, hoping to learn whether bribes, fear or hopelessness was the reason for their acceptance of the police's inaction.

By the end of the afternoon, they had enough credible testimony to investigate why Joe Yazzie had never been tried for two forcible rapes on young teens in the last five years. No evidence had been gathered at the time of the crime, but there were two young children who did look a lot like Joe. Spence was surprised that such an old man was still capable of these crimes, but then he'd had decades to hone his skills.

The people they talked to said they had always been willing to testify if the police had ever asked. They had assumed that the police had worked on the case and hadn't gotten enough to prosecute Joe for his crimes.

"Okay. I think these families will stand firm and testify." Martin turned to the Sergeant. "What do you think? Will they come through?"

"I know these women. They have enough commonsense not to beat a dead horse, but if someone is willing to help, they'll follow through. So what's our next step? Since Joe's dead we can't prosecute him."

"Yeah. I know. If we let on we're after cops and cover-ups, everyone will shut down."

"Maybe if we focused on finding out if there's evidence of contact between Fowler family members and Joe Yazzie and Carla Gonzalez, someone will feel safe enough to talk. Once we've ID'd the more cooperative officers, we can ask them if any officers in the department knew the Fowlers."

"That's the plan then."

They called in Officer Evan Jones, who'd been hanging around since the morning. A tall, pale, lanky, man with thin brown hair and watery blue eyes, he folded himself into the chair across the table. Jake shut the door and joined them at the table.

"So how can I help you fella's?" The officer gave them a self-satisfied smile.

"I don't know if you've heard," Agent Spence began, "but we're looking for an answer for Joe Yazzie's apparent immunity from prosecution for some terrible crimes. But first I want to know why you've been hanging around all day, when you worked night shift last night."

"Well, I'm real curious, so I took a shift today to cover for a sick officer. After they found Joe Yazzie dead, I figured IA would show. Besides," he smiled, "I've accepted a better paying job with a security firm. After twenty-five years with no promotion, I figure I'm wasting my time here. Since I don't have anything to lose, I can talk for the others who need to keep their jobs. You know what I mean."

"Maybe you get a little payback in the bargain?"

"Only doing my duty to the community, sir," he smiled. "Why don't we meet at Lenny's restaurant after this shift and we can relax and talk?"

They went to interview Carla's neighbors and the homeless alcoholics that hung around her motel while they waited until their dinner appointment. After a frustrating afternoon of denials and evasions, they went to the restaurant to wait for Sergeant Evan Jones. After waiting an hour, Jake called the desk sergeant. Martin's face turned red with fury as Jake told him that Sergeant Jones had been killed by a hit and run as he stood on the side of the road ticketing a drunk driver. Jake called his boss with the news, while Agent Spence immediately put in a call to the Albuquerque FBI office and requested agents to come and keep track of records before evidence started disappearing. Then he contacted the State Police Internal Affairs office and they agreed to send a team out right away.

As they returned to the station, Agent Spence was glad they'd taken the box of files with them when they left the office, despite his misgivings at the regulations he broke. When they arrived, he ordered all phone records for the station, starting with those belonging to the chief and captain's office and their cell phones for the last five days. At first unwilling to cooperate when asked for the location of the chief or captain, the desk sergeant eventually broke under Agent Spence's glare and told him that the chief and the captain occasionally had dinner together at a local bar. He and Jake were on the way to the bar when Jake saw the captain's car parked in front of Carla's motel.

After parking next to the car they heard loud, angry male voices and, with a nod to each other, they drew their guns as they ran to the apartment where Carla had died. They stooped under the one remaining strip of yellow tape, walking as quietly as they could across the gravel to the lighted apartment. The angry voices escalated and a shot was fired. As they rushed through the door, they saw the Chief of Police standing over the body of the Captain with a gun at his own head. They yelled for him to stop, but he blew his brains out without giving them a glance.

Jake dropped to his knees, his lowered gun held in both hands. He'd known these men for many years and felt responsible for their deaths, because of the investigation he had promoted. Martin leaned on the doorframe and covered his eyes. Jake holstered his gun, and stood up slowly. He checked the pulse of the Captain to confirm what he knew.

Answering Martin's questioning look, he said, "There have been rumors around that these two were lovers at one time," Jake said. "They're both married now, but I think that's the information that was used to control them. The chief was going to retire this year after working in the department for forty-five years. He has four kids and six grandkids. If that got out, I don't know. It would be awful, but how else can we explain this?"

"We have to tell what we know. Their past is hearsay and doesn't have to be mentioned. All we know is that something they were afraid of triggered this . . . tragedy. We can follow up on that line of inquiry, and conclude, as far as you and I are concerned, that the secret died with them. What we need to know is who manipulated them. Their phone records will let us know if someone has been blackmailing them to protect Joe. At least I hope so. Someone has to pay for this." Martin ran his hand over his buzz cut hair and began to examine the room, grimly systematic.

"Should we call the others?" Jake asked, after calling for police support and an ambulance.

"I'd like to know how the kid is doing, but let's wait until we have more information. It'll take time to get the phone records; we should wait until tomorrow. She might sense something's happened and she doesn't need anymore grief right now."

Jake agreed. It was going to be a long night. They found two notes in the left hand of the police chief while they waited for the FBI and Internal Affairs police to arrive. The first page sent his love to his family; the second had a name, address and phone number written on it. When they saw the name, they called Jim Hunt.

Jim and his companions were experiencing a frustrating evening with Bill's senior relatives. None of their pleas for the truth had any effect. The elders believed that the tragedy was long past and secrets belonged to the sisters. They remained impassive despite all persuasion. It was late, and Jim, Joan and Bill were exhausted. Bill wasn't surprised at the elders' silence, despite his hope that they would change their minds once they understood what had happened in Grants. Jim struggled to contain his impatience. Using his role as a fellow elder of his tribe, he'd gone in circles with the old folks, telling him how important this was to his grandchild.

Finally, Bill's grandmother said, "This knowledge can't help your granddaughter to heal. She must find peace in her heart and in the hearts of those that love her. You seek revenge, because you abandoned her. This thing you want to know can only bring more pain. You won't be able to punish this man with our suspicions. If Emmy's word was not enough; what difference will our suspicions make?"

"You mean she gave a name to the police," Bill stated. "We thought she'd never reported it. I looked for some record when Jake first called and I couldn't find anything."

"Francis made the report. You remember that fire at the station, a long time before you started working there?" his grandmother asked. Bill nodded. "Those records and the night dispatcher were burned that night. Do you wonder why the sisters live so far and so alone?"

Jim had seen the way years of fear and anger borne in silence had marked Francis Yazzie. He now recognized the look he'd seen on Francis' face when she refused to discuss the crime against her sister. It had seemed strange that she had the look of one who knew that her time had come. He had thought it was because someone was finally investigating the crime. He stood up.

"We need to get to Francis' house," he said.

"She has the cell phone her brother gave her. Here's the number," Bill's great-uncle picked up a small tablet and leafed through it to find the number. Bill dialed the number and was surprised when Francis answered right away.

"I'm sorry to bother you, Miss Yazzie. I just wanted to be sure you were okay," he said.

"I'm just fine," she said.

"Have you heard from your sister?"

"As a matter of fact I have. She's in Albuquerque at the hospital. She called to tell me her granddaughter is doing well and has good friends and family with her. She's going to stay with Liliana's aunt and come home when Liliana doesn't need her anymore. I told her it was okay. I won't need the truck."

Bill was still suspicious. "Where are you now, Miss Yazzie?"

"Where else would I be? I'm at home you young idiot." She hung up.

Jim looked to Bill. "Is there anyone who lives near their home?"

Joan responded, rubbing her eyes wearily. It would be another two hour drive back to the Yazzie house and she was beat. "She has a cousin that lives three miles away. I think I have his number. I kept tabs on Emmy while she went through the worst depression." She leafed through her notebook, and showed him the number. "His name is Eugene Crow."

Bill dialed the number, and asked Eugene if he'd seen Francis Yazzie. They watched Bill run his fingers through his hair and ask, "Did she say where she was going?" Then he said, "Thank-you. Don't worry. We just wanted to ask her some questions. Okay, thanks a lot."

"No idea where she went?" Jim asked. Bill shook his head.

"So what do we do now?" Joan asked.

"We go to bed," Jim replied. "We have no grounds for questioning the Fowler's. Let's have dinner, I'll check into a Gallup motel, and start again in the morning."

They thanked the elders and said goodnight. They received patient smiles. The old folks seemed to find it interesting that they had been included in the exciting turn of events.

Once they were on the road watching the setting sun paint glorious colors on the clouds above, Bill got the call from Jake. He listened silently, asking no questions about the tragedy that was being unfolded to him. He pulled out his notebook and took down the name, number and address Jake gave him. The ranch named on the note was twenty minutes south of Gallup.

He hung up and turned to Jim and Joan. "We need to get to the Fowler ranch. I've got a bad feeling about this." He called dispatch and found a Reservation officer who was near the ranch dealing with a DUI. The officer agreed to get to the Fowler ranch right away. Bill called the state police and reported his suspicions about Francis Yazzie's intentions. Now that they had the proof of the connection of the Grants police and the Fowlers they had an excuse to get onto their property and question them.

"You know," Bill said, as they raced to try to prevent what they were sure would be another tragic event, "Steve Fowler was in the morning news. He arrived yesterday at the Albuquerque airport coming from Washington and announced that his father was seriously ill. He was going to see him at their ranch." He returned his full attention to the road and increased his speed. "Francis could know that all three Fowler men are at the ranch."

Francis hung up on the policeman as she paused behind some scrub bushes within sight of the sprawling ranch house. She had expected to have more time. She had seen servants leaving the main house for the smaller house just behind it. Cautiously she reached the house and she went to check the glass sliding door to the dining room. It was open an inch as if someone closed it without paying attention. From there she could see through the open doors to the library. Phillip the eldest and Steve the younger son were arguing with John, their father. They all looked so old, their good looks rotted away with evil. Francis wished that her shotgun had three barrels so she could be sure to get them all. Adjusting the sheathed knives she'd strapped to her waist, she pushed the patio door open while she watched the red, angry faces yell at each other among the luxurious comfort of the huge, richly furnished library. She saw the glass display case filled with a variety of rifles, guns and automatic weapons near the old man. The way the argument was going, she would have to move before they started pulling out weapons and killing each other.

After hearing some of the content of the argument, Francis thought of how strange it was that the old man was obsessed with impregnating his son's wives, since the two brothers were sterile from episodes of mumps in their childhood. He refused to accept their adopted children as his grandchildren. He was so determined that he threatened to disinherit them if they did not allow it. She wondered what the wives would say to being referred to as breeding stock with no consideration by their father-in-law.

So that's why I never got pregnant, she thought, remembering the shame of being violated and betrayed. She had been surprised by the violence of Phillip's attack. Initially, his seduction had been shy and sweet. Francis remembered Phillip's stuttered invitation to his house after he had finished with her. He must have seen the hardness in her eyes when he left and never spoke to her again. Her heart bled as she realized the true degradation her sister must have suffered. Emmy believed Steven Fowler had loved her and betrayed her by raping her.

However the old man had gotten his hands on her sister, he was obviously the only one who could have fathered Joe. Emmy still believed Steve was Joe's father. Francis's resolve solidified. Emmy would never learn the truth. This was the right path. It was time for this horror story to end. However, if the raging men continued as they were now, everyone would know whatever dirty secrets they did not already know. She sent a prayer to her sister. Francis could only imagine how degrading it must have been.

She slipped inside to hide behind the heavy drapery in the dining room. Fortunately the house alarms hadn't been activated for the night. *I'm getting old*, she thought as she realized that she hadn't even thought of alarms until it was too late. From behind the curtain she couldn't see the arguing men.

Francis heard how this was the first time in his life that Steve revealed his rage to his father. It had taken this last demand to free the anger his cowed sons had withheld all their lives. Old man Fowler believed that his blood line was sacrosanct. He didn't care or even understand why they protested. He had already stripped away every shred of self-esteem his sons possessed. Francis thought it was strange that this subject brought up so much ancient family history. She waited, listening and learning the sordid history this man had with his sons.

Finally, she learned that Emmy was not alone. Apparently, the old man had trained his sons to bring girls to the house and drug them for the old man. He didn't like any fuss when he used children. All the times Joe was shot or beaten and this demon acted as though he had never once been confronted. It was time for his evil to end. For a while Francis wondered if she would be disappointed if they killed each other before she had her chance.

The sound of a thud and someone falling brought her attention back to the raging men; she took a chance and edged silently in a crouch across the dining room to look around one of the library doors. Steven was on the ground with his eyes closed, his left temple crushed and bleeding. Smiling, she pushed the door aside with her left foot; the rifle steady in her hands. Philip and his father were screaming in each other's faces. Philip had a grip on the trophy his father had used to bash Steve's head in. They didn't notice her watching their struggle.

Having only two barrels on the shotgun was no longer a problem. Even if Steve survived, she doubted that he could prevent her from finishing him off. She couldn't take a chance that the snake spawn would recover. When she raised the shotgun to aim at the back of the old man's head, Phillip glanced over and saw her. His red face paled and he stood frozen in place. The father turned, "Who the fuck are you? And what the hell do you think your doing?" He started toward her. He always was a man of action.

When she blew a hole in his gut at three feet, she saw no fear, only fury in the old man's eyes as he fell slowly to the ground clutching his belly. She watched the old snake and his son carefully while she quickly reloaded the empty chamber with another shell, just in case. Phillip's shock had cost him a few seconds of opportunity. Shut the doors, Phil," she said, as she stepped back against the wall in order to keep them all in her sights as he obeyed.

"Why have you done this?" John croaked from the floor.

Ignoring the father, she asked Phillip, "Do you remember me? You were twenty and I was only twelve, your favorite age. I hear you still prowl after little girls, Philip Fowler; it seems to be a family trait. First you get me, and then your brother went after my sister. I didn't know you had raped my sister, too, Old Snake. She never told me about you. You must have many children, Snake, why do you need to argue about keeping your blood flowing? I knew you liked little girls and boys, but I didn't know that you liked your own sons, too. You passed your evil blood to my nephew then brought him here to teach him your evil ways. How many other criminals on our reservation owe their deviancy to you?"" Too incapacitated to respond the old man glared at her while he clutched at his guts.

"You white men think you can do anything you want to my people. This has been an enlightening evening. I would have enlisted your sons' help if I had known how much they hate you. I'm sure we could have agreed on which ant hole to bury you in. Your sons might have enjoyed carving you up a little while we waited for the ants to sting you to death. Too bad. My time is limited, so you will die too easily." Her voice was low and even, a stark contrast to the chaotic uproar of a few minutes ago. Yet, when compared to the raging men, her voice was infinitely more deadly, filled with a purpose nursed for decades.

"I know you like little white girls, too. My sister told me that there were other women in Joan Birdsong's therapy because you gave your sons your gift for evil. Joe liked little girls, too. Actually, maybe he preferred his daughter above all. By the way, what really happened to the little girl your wife bore you? The police tore apart every hogan on the reservation looking for the Navajo that you said stole her from you. Then they jailed the poor Mexican who had worked his whole life for you and they killed him in that prison. We all knew he was innocent, but no one could help him. Does he visit your dreams like he does mine?

John moved suddenly, reaching for her ankle. She shot him in the face at point blank range. As Philip vomited, she again reloaded her shotgun, calm and steady. When he heard the click of the barrel, Phillip looked up with the realization that he'd missed his last chance to live.

"I almost feel sorry for you, but not enough. You gave more than you got and you deserve worse than death as well."

Phillip looked up, his face white with shock and his chin covered with vomit. Somehow he had nothing to say. Glancing down at the open skull of his brother, she asked, "Did you kill him?"

He shook his head.

"Are you ready?" she asked.

He dropped into a chair and covered his face with his hands. When he heard sirens, he looked up. "If you let me live, I'll say I did everything. You won't go to jail. I will. I promise I'll take all the blame." His voice shook, but his eyes lied.

"You don't really want to live, do you?" The eyes that watched him were icy black in the shadow by the door. "You can't even lie well enough to try. You're a good one for promises. I remember all your promises. You promised to take care of me, but you threw me aside the minute you had what you wanted. You promised to take care of my niece; instead she died at the hands of that butcher you sent her to for an abortion. Yes, you make lots of promises. Well, I can promise you something right now. Your spirit will never find peace. I will follow you and your family for eternity, reminding you of the monsters you are."

Suddenly activated by the flashing lights of a police car in the window, he lunged at her. Her shot caught him in the middle of his chest. He fell against her, smearing blood down the front of her clothes. She had to hurry now.

No one came. The house seemed to be as empty of people as it was of love, filled with trophies and hate. If there were any servants in the house, they would be hiding, but the police were close. She pulled out her skinning knife, castrated the dead men, and shoved their testicles in their mouths as the doorbell rang and rang. The police had arrived too late to hear the shots, so she figured they would hesitate to break in, because of the wealth and power of the owner of this house. The front door bell rang over and over again. She worked fast. She was ready for her own death when she heard the patio door open. She should have locked it after she entered.

She dropped the first knife, and pulled out a clean one she had prayed over in preparation, after the owl spoke three days ago. She set the tip firmly above her heart, angled so it would pass easily between her ribs. She didn't want to survive this. She was ready. The door to the study was kicked in as she pushed the knife all the way in and pulled it out to let the blood flow free. When she saw the shock on the young policeman's face, she asked for forgiveness for the suffering she caused him. She had not intended for anyone to see this. He rushed to her as she fell and eased her gently to the ground. Her great-grandnephew held her hand as she died. Because of the fear in his eyes, she blessed him with her last words and saw his relief and his tears. She had no intention of haunting the living; her spirit would haunt the dead.

Just after dinner, they moved Liliana to a regular room. Her breathing had been stable for twelve hours. It was a two bed room, but she had it all to herself and all of her guests. Once she was settled, her family and friends came in to sit with her. She looked at the collection of people in the room and was glad they were all there. Terry had been around since late afternoon, looking rested. She had no lack of company with her aunts and her uncle Mike who closed the shop to spend time with her. Mike brought Edward Chee, looking a little ragged around the edges, but better than he'd ever looked since she'd known him.

He pointed his chin west and winked slowly. Eddie was taking care of her.

She remembered the time he'd come into the office while Carla was hitting her, when she was little. He pushed Carla away and ran away holding onto Liliana's hand. He took her to hide at the empty warehouse where he was sleeping at the time. She was only nine, but she knew she could trust him.

The police looked for her after Carla called them, but she didn't go home until morning. After showing the police the bruises Carla had given her, she told them that she had run away alone and Carla was lying about Eddie. Lt. Molina had little interest in the truth; his only wish was to shut Carla up. So, he promised to arrest Eddie, but he never did. When he was promoted, he assigned an officer to keep Carla out of his hair.

A shy, tiny Navajo woman, with grey hair bound up traditionally and the loose skirt and blouse with a large squash blossom necklace that were also traditional Navajo, was led in by Denise. Her appearance sent those dark memories flying away from Liliana's mind.

"This little lady says she's one of your grandmothers,'" Denise announced. ""She came to the ICU looking for you. Here she is, Miss Yazzie." Denise smiled, swung her red braid over her shoulder and left.

Liliana called out, "Come here, Grandma. It's been so long."

The shy woman nodded to the others and walked slowly to Liliana's bed.

"You remember me?"

"How could I forget my great-great-grandmother?" she hugged her and asked, "How is your sister?"

"Oh, she's okay. I didn't tell her I was coming. She worries too much."

Liliana remembered the strong-spirited woman who had kept watch as the two talked at the edge of the school yard. Emmy had told Liliana that her sister Francis was a teacher. Francis's face seemed hard, yet when she looked at her, Liliana saw compassion and knew this woman would die to protect her sister. She knew this woman would kill for her sister. Then she remembered how Carla had shown up. *She had to be part witch to have known Emmy was there*, Liliana thought. Carla yelled, but was too intimidated by the strong woman to abuse Emmy or slap Liliana in front of them.

Liliana reached out her arm and let Emmy Yazzie welcome her great-great-grandchild back to life. The frail, little woman wept in the respectful silence of the others as Liliana held her close, rubbing her back gently.

She looked up as Adela said to Terry, "Why are you paying for a hotel? You are welcome to stay at my place."

"Before anyone answers," Liliana interceded hoarsely, "I should warn you the sofa has springs that will turn your back into a sieve, and there are four teenagers who have a hundred friends who talk all the time and play their music at full blast."

Emmy stepped back to see Adela's surprised look. "Okay, maybe my place isn't the best choice. Come to think of it, maybe I could join you guys at the hotel. I would enjoy peace and quiet for the first time in forever," she laughed. "I actually have an empty bed while my youngest is at music camp. Your grandma could stay with me awhile."

Liliana could tell Adela wanted to take care of this gentle woman who had come from so far all alone. Liliana smiled at Adela's generosity. Then she looked out at the darkening sky and her dark eyes became sad.

Chapter 10

Tragic Resolution

The squad cars began arriving at Carla's motel minutes ahead of the ambulance. Agent Martin Spence and Sergeant Jake Sanchez told the police what they'd found without mentioning the other case they were investigating. Many on and off duty officers arrived at the scene. Almost none of them were surprised, but, still, they grieved for their old friends. The dead officers were liked and respected. Since Joe was found dead, they had been enveloped in thick walls of tense secrecy. Everyone had felt the strain rebounding off the walls of the station. Yet, their superior officers kept silent, if not calm, in the presence of officers from outside their jurisdiction. Their men took their lead, e.g., if not asked, don't tell.

Jake knew that they would stand together. Other than it's handling of Joe and Carla, the department was well-run and proud of their record. Overwhelming stress after the mysterious death of a man in their custody would explain the suicide/murder. Jake stood next to Agent Spence as he made his report to the FBI by phone, watching certain men move from group to group, setting the story straight. Jake wondered how many had heard the rumors that these two were a couple. It would be denied by all. Meanwhile, all of them kept clear of the two outsiders.

Agent Spence guessed that huge resources would be expended to find an acceptable answer to this tragedy. He made a mental note to check on the investigation periodically; he would return if it looked like the local powers were trying to prosecute a scapegoat. He stood next to his car in the cooling evening breeze. The katydids sang louder than the whispered human conversations, lights flashed, but sirens were silent. A crowd of curious onlookers was gathering outside the ring of police cars. He'd be glad to get home to Denver. The air was too dry for him, even though he liked the landscapes of New Mexico.

Once the medical examiner arrived, Jake and Martin left to join the State Police who were arriving at the Grants police station to secure the records until the FBI and Internal Affairs could get their people there. More were being sent to monitor the investigation of the murder/suicide. When they arrived at the station, the telephone records were immediately handed to Martin by a nervous middle-aged woman; the clerk had been instructed to give the records to Agent Martin Spence only. The stocky man with the deep, penetrating eyes, and grim look, gave the nervous woman a reassuring smile, and got a less nervous smile in return. The main room was peopled with employees and desk-bound police trying to look busy, as they strained to hear any clue as to what was really going on.

Martin and Jake commandeered the chief's office and sat down to look through the phone records and other pertinent records. Their suspicions were confirmed. The number on the paper from the Chief's hand appeared intermittently on the Chief of Police's records. Some of the dates coincided with arrests of Joe Yazzie. Martin was sure that, if they looked that far back, they would find that there would be phone calls from that number with dates that coincided with Carla's efforts to maintain custody of her grandchild as well.

"Well, there it is," Martin said, leaning back in the chair to observe the grief as each new arrival learned of the deaths of the men they'd known for years. There were tears, brushed away by the men, and wept openly by the women. Martin wondered how many knew of Joe Yazzie's connection to the deceased. After the deaths of Joe and Carla within days of each other, many in the office must have been waiting for the hatchet to fall. Joe committed some heinous crimes. It was unlikely that there was anyone oblivious to his free ride. No one had been willing to break the silence and now they could only prepare for the inevitable questions.

"I think we'll get some answers now," Jake commented.

Martin nodded, "Yeah, but we already discovered what we need to know. Internal Affairs can take over. Once they get here, we can return to

Albuquerque and see Liliana. I would like to finally meet that young lady. She was the center of a tornado." He looked over to the Laguna cop he'd grown to like. "Then we can get very drunk."

Jake smiled grimly, "That sounds like a great idea."

Spence reached out his hand and said, "And real New Mexican food."

"And real New Mexican food," Jake smiled and shook his hand.

They each pulled out forms from the desk and started writing their reports. By the time the internal affairs officers arrived, the two men were quite finished with the whole business. After quickly filling in the bare essentials, they left for Albuquerque. On the way, Jake got a report from Bill regarding the events at the Fowler ranch. Bill would be tied up all night, but Joan was headed home and Jim would return to Laguna to get some sleep.

Jake pushed the button on the hospital elevator with obvious reluctance. He would be the one to lay out the story for Liliana and knew it would be harder on him than her. She'd lived with this filth all her life. Although he and Mike had tried their best to protect her, they couldn't protect her from the past that had haunted her from her first tiny step-like motions in her mother's womb to this moment as she sat in her room quietly watching as her new, larger family was getting to know each other.

Jake stood at the door to her room, thinking that the whole town must be here. Martin stood at his side until Liliana looked up to meet his eyes. Jake ducked his head as the group turned to see who she was looking at. Mike and Terry stood and offered the two exhausted officers their seats. No one spoke, so Liliana started.

"Come here, Jake and give me a hug. You look wiped out," she reached out and Jake leaned over and gave her a hug, carefully holding her shoulders and kissing her forehead.

Wiping tears from his eyes, he said, "You don't know how good it is to see you up and talking so soon." He took a deep, breath and couldn't say anything for a minute as he sat down.

Martin took her offered hand and squeezed it between his two huge paws. He had a kid her age, and until this moment he hadn't realized how much Liliana's plight had affected him. He couldn't hide the glimmer of unshed tears from Liliana, whom he had silently worried over all day, despite never having met her. She pulled him down and kissed his cheek. "Thank you for helping my friends, Agent Spence."

He laughed, "Well, I don't know if we did much more than hinder them in the beginning. They are a persistent bunch, and call me Martin."

"Okay, Martin, sit down and rest. I think we have some takeout around here somewhere. You've had a busy day." She looked over to Adela, who pulled out a sack of wrapped burritos, and sodas from a cooler. "My auntie believes that being prepared for anything means there should always be food around in case someone is dying from hunger."

They each took a burrito and a can of pop, while Terry introduced the entire group. "We've been here waiting for the sky to fall," he said. "No one wants to go home."

"It's called circling the Pueblo," Liliana said. "You never know when the cavalry will show up." Some laughed, Martin just nodded. "So tell us what happened in Grants." By her expression, she did not want to know, but was willing to hear what they had found out.

Jake finished swallowing his last bite of burrito and turned his eyes from the sack to meet hers. Adela handed him a second and he took a drink before he started, delaying the inevitable.

"We finally got the records on Joe Yazzie. The single consistency we found was that either Mack Jones, Captain of the Grants police, or Fred Molina, Chief of Police, signed off on every report that resulted in no action. Molina has been on the force forty-five years, and the first records concerning complaints against Joe started forty years ago." He glanced over at Martin who had agreed that they would not spread the long-held secret. "They were over our shoulders all day. One officer was willing to talk because he was moving to a better paying security job. When he didn't show, I called the station and found out that he was killed in a hit and run this afternoon. We were on our way to the bar Molina and Jones frequented, since they weren't answering their phones, when I saw Chief Molina's car at Carla's motel."

"You know," Liliana remarked coolly, "the motel is way out of the way from that bar."

"I guess I'm just used to turning that way when I leave the station," Jake said. "When I realized where I was going, we were nearly at the motel. I figured, what the heck, maybe someone suspicious would be hanging out there. The lights were on; so we parked near the office. They were in Carla's living room. Molina was yelling about how it was all over and they were ruined. Jones was trying to calm him down telling him that they could handle Fowler and make him protect them. Then we heard a shot. When we got to the door, Molina was standing over Jones. He saw us and put the gun to his head and fired before we could get to him. They're both dead. The FBI and Internal Affairs will complete the investigation. If it hadn't been for Martin's help, they would have continued to stonewall any attempt to get at the truth. He knew how to get things done; that tipped the scales in our favor."

Mike cursed softly to himself. He'd known and liked those two all his life; he didn't care that they liked each other, but they had forfeited their very souls by allowing a child predator to accumulate what must be hundreds of victims, worst of all, his Liliana. He felt a little guilty for the gossip he'd participated in at their expense. He sent a silent prayer to their families and their spirits.

Terry asked, "What have you heard from Jim?"

Jake shook his head; weary of sad news, he couldn't look up to meet Emelina's eyes. Martin took over the story. "Jim went with Sergeant Bill Two Crow and the rape counselor, Joan Birdsong, to see if Miss Yazzie here could tell us who was responsible for obstructing justice in the cases against Joe Yazzie. I guess you were already on your way here." He looked up at Emelina. Liliana watched him, nodding slowly, her eyes wary, as if she was waiting for a snake to strike. "Francis refused to tell us anything. So Jim went to see Bill's grandmother and great-uncle, who knew you and your sister when you were girls. They hoped that they could get enough information to justify an investigation into the Fowlers."

Emmy nodded, holding on to Liliana's hand. He continued, "Well, the old folks would only say that Francis would do anything to protect you. Bill Two Crow got suspicious and called Francis Yazzie. She said she was home, but he called her cousin who said she'd borrowed his truck and left several hours before. Bill got hold of an officer in the area and sent him to the Fowler ranch. He called us while we were on the road here.

"The father, John, the senator, Steve, and his brother, Phillip, were there. When the reservation policeman arrived at the house it was quiet, but the lights were on. When no one responded to the doorbell, he went around the house and found the patio door open. He entered just in time to see your sister stab herself in the heart. Steve was dead from a massive head injury; John and Phil were shot dead. The shotgun was at Francis's feet. I'm really sorry, Miss Yazzie," he said to the little woman who sat weeping into her hands.

Emmy whispered through her tears, "She talked in her sleep. I pretended that I didn't know she was dying from cancer, because she didn't want to worry me. She was afraid that he would come after me when she wasn't there to protect me. She must have heard the old ghosts whispering... A long time ago, Joe's father found out I went to see Liliana and sent me a letter. Francis tore it up before I saw it. She figured that those people would come after me if they thought that I would talk. But then she told me about it later, because she thought I should be careful."

Adela pulled her chair over and sat with her arm around the tiny, weeping woman. The room was quiet for a long time. Donna broke the silence, "I think Liliana needs to rest. Since my dad's going home, I'll go, too, and we'll come back early." She stood up with a sigh. "Emmy, do you want to come to my house to sleep?"

"No, no," Adela insisted, "that's too far. Emmy's going to my house."

"Do you still have that hotel room, Terry?" Martin Spence asked.

"Yeah, here's the key. I slept today so I'll stay here tonight."

Jake leaned over and kissed Liliana's forehead. "Be good, okay. No evil thoughts tonight. Only good dreams."

She held his hand and nodded. Donna kissed her and Eddie shyly patted her arm.

Mike hugged her awkwardly around all the casts and IV's. "I'll call tomorrow, 'Hita. I want good news, yeah?"

"Sure, Uncle Mike. Rainbows and lollipops." He stroked her cheek. "Don't worry. I'm better, okay. As soon as I can get these casts off we'll go get my truck, right?"

"Oh yeah. When do you want to do that? Next Monday okay?"

"Sure, I'll bribe the guard and escape. Be ready."

He nodded and they bumped fists. Then he patted her spiked hair and left, following Donna, Eddie, Adela and Emmy out the door. Once they were all gone Terry looked down at Liliana who was watching him through half-closed eyes. She patted the bed beside her, so he came to sit next to her. She pulled him down, saying, "I'm tired of talking so loud. Come here where I can whisper."

He lay on his side, his head next to hers, and his arm over her waist. "So what kind of things did you want to whisper about?" he asked. He was comfortable lying so close to her for the first time.

She smiled as she looked into his eyes, "I guess I just wanted to ask you if you would like to share a hogan for a while. I always wanted to seduce a rich man."

"I wouldn't have figured you for a gold-digger."

"It's easy to fool belagana men."

"I guess I'll have to get a prenup written before you take me for everything I have."

"I guess you'd better," she said. She kissed him long. It wasn't their very first. They'd found a few moments alone between visitors and nurses, but to her every kiss felt like the first, an experience filled with tingles and blood rushing all through her.

She laid her head back and closed her eyes. "So Carla killed the Fowler's and Francis, too."

Startled, Terry paused then agreed. "Carla sent a letter about Emmy's visit to the Fowler's, so they threatened Emmy, and Francis decided that they had to die. How many more threads are linked to this web?"

Liliana didn't respond. He looked down to see that she was asleep. He shifted position to get comfortable and watched her sleep. He woke up at midnight when they came with her breathing treatment and arranged a cot for him to sleep. Liliana finished her treatment, said goodnight and they both slept as much as they could between the every four hour breathing treatments.

Lying on the cot watching one of the treatments, he thought about how she hadn't commented on any of the events of the day. It was as if none of the horror surprised her, or she was dealing with so much she couldn't react to any more. She seemed embarrassed and overwhelmed by the number of people who had come to support her and give her their love. Being Liliana, she played it cool and wouldn't have admitted any of those feelings to a soul, but he'd learned to see through her cover. He thought of all the loved ones she'd lost. Sadly he wondered if Francis's spirit would rest after killing the man who had threatened to hurt her sister and if she had wasted the last days she could have spent with her sister.

∞

After a few drinks with Jake, the exhausted FBI Agent settled at the hotel. Then he called home, leaving his daughter wondering why her dad had wanted to talk to her about every detail of her day. He was glad he was returning to Denver after finishing off his paperwork the next day.

∞

Jim Hunt dreamt of dancing with his wife, and woke in a good mood for once in a long time. He and Donna drove in to see Liliana, after picking up Edward Chee on the way. He was sober, clean and dressed on time.

∞

Terry was sharing Liliana's breakfast when she looked up at the footsteps approaching the door. Her eyes lit up when she saw a tall Indian monk, head shaved and dressed in red robes.

"Indy, I didn't know you were in town."

"How could I ignore the news that my little savior was so terribly injured?" He looked at all of her paraphernalia and shook his head sadly. "I am so sorry you have suffered so much." He turned to Terry. "I am Indra. I have yet to see the movie about this Indy person." He smiled and shook Terry's hand. "Liliana rescued me when I broke my ankle when I was knocked over by a skateboarder on campus. Then she carried my books until the semester ended a week later. We have had many long talks in the two years since. She has taught me much."

"I thought you'd already left for India."

"A member of the Sikh community asked me to participate in a two day seminar. Then who did I see, but my Liliana, being pulled out of a raging torrent. I'm sorry I couldn't get here until today."

She smiled. "This is Terry. He saved me."

"And much more, I see in your eyes."

For once Liliana had no reply, only blushes. He held her hand and prayed over her.

"I wish you could stay," she complained when he finished.

"It is my choice to return to the temple. I have learned what I can from Americans for now. One day I will return; until then it will be my honor to write to you to remind you of the path, as you have asked me to do many times." He leaned over and kissed her forehead. "I have someone waiting to take me to the airport so I must go. I will write and send my address. You will heal, Liliana." She held on to his hand, tears in her eyes. "Remember, child, I live in your heart. I am not far." He released her hand, and then shook Terry's hand again and left.

Terry turned to her. "So you're Buddhist?"

"I don't know."" She brushed a tear away. ""Who ever really knows? We had some good arguments. Was Carla evil in all her lives? Do I have to deal with a different version of her in my next life? That kind of stuff. Oh, and lots of love and acceptance." She nodded sagely, and then sighed. "Now I have to start missing him all over again."

She looked up to the door as her grandfather, Eddie and Donna arrived. Eddie and Donna waved, watching as her grandfather sat closest to her bed. He looked like he was having a hard time starting. Liliana took his hand and pulled him close to kiss his cheek. "It's okay, Grandpa. Don't worry."

He hugged her, and then stood up. "No," he said, "it's not okay. I was unfair to you. I have to say that I'm sorry and that I was wrong. Now it's done." He nodded sharply, and she smiled and squeezed his hand.

"I'm so glad to have my grandpa with me," was all she had to say. Donna, who had spent most of the day before apologizing for not doing enough to help her, came to hug her, but didn't repeat her apology. Liliana had threatened to have her thrown out if she didn't accept her forgiveness.

Liliana looked from face to face and shook her head. So much had happened while she was "away." There were so many changes in her old relationships that it felt like she had grown new limbs in strange, uncomfortable places. She wasn't sure what her role was now that she was free of Carla. Being sedated and sick had served her yesterday, but, as her head cleared, the changes in her life sometimes threatened to overwhelm her.

The surge of emotion she felt every time she looked at Terry was difficult to hide. She knew her grandfather didn't approve of their age difference, but she couldn't even be sure that there was something to disapprove of. Terry seemed to share her feelings, and she remembered the kiss they'd shared the night before. As chaste as it was for a first real kiss, she still found herself avoiding everyone's gaze as strange feelings filled her heart.

Despite the welcome distractions her family provided, the fact that Carla was gone from her life continued to occupy a portion of her mind. She was too ashamed to talk to them about the grief and guilt she felt for their last encounter. After two nights and a day anticipating death in the truck, she understood what it must have felt like for Carla to lie dying all alone. Despite what she had said and as angry as she would get, she had never been able to hate her grandmother. The last things she said made her heart ache.

She knew Carla was ashamed of her drinking and especially of her weakness for Joe. It was part of what made her so mean. The other part was her jealousy of Liliana who had so many people fighting to take care of her, while all Carla thought she had was Joe. Trying to distract herself from disturbing thoughts, Liliana stared out the window at the cobalt blue sky, watching the rare puff of white cloud pass by. Unfortunately, the mountains were not part of her view, but she could see them in her mind, the steep incline that led a mile up to the sharp ridge from which gliders would launch themselves to float down to the rugged feet of the mountain like eagles floating on the wind. At sunset, the mountain reflected the orange glow of the sun, which had given it its name. The Sandia Mountain, watermelon mountain, was named by Spanish explorers long ago.

That was the beginning of the complex relationships between the natives and the Spanish conquistadores. The killing and exploitation continued when the other Europeans arrived, and now into her own life. The crimes were uncountable; the death and pain immeasurable. It was better now, most of the time, anyway. There were laws to protect the exploited, but there were always those with the means to evade those laws and harm their own kind and every other kind of people.

Thoughts of Carla and death dragged her unwilling mind to Joe. She didn't want to cry. She struggled to erase the memory of his face that night when she was ten. The night he'd come to her room and she'd stabbed him. The nice, Navajo woman who had come warn her about Joe had given her the knife that she always kept with her under the old, battered pillow.

She tried to push those memories aside with good memories of her mother making cookies, but, instead of the smell of cookies, her mind was filled with the foul stench of Joe's breath as he leaned over her bed. His smell woke her before he had time to pin her down. She had her knife out and in his belly before he grabbed her right arm. Cursing, he pulled back and she kicked him. Carla never woke up.

After he ran out of the house, she got up, changed her clothes and sheets and washed them in the machine that still worked in those days. When the Grants police came by later that night after Joe showed up at the emergency room, the sheets were dry and folded away. She denied even knowing that Joe was in the house. He could have been, she told them, since he was her grandmother's friend. Neither cop mentioned the scent of fresh laundry.

That night it was policemen she didn't know. She had wondered why Jake didn't come. Later she learned that Jake and her dad's other cop friend, Clint, weren't supposed to be coming by her home. It wasn't in their jurisdiction so no one called to tell them that Joe had been stabbed there. That night she'd thought they had abandoned her to this white man who walked through the filthy apartment looking like he smelled something foul. He found Carla naked and passed out in her bedroom with all the doors unlocked and called Social Services.

Before they took Liliana to Social Services, they looked for the knife, suspicious of her story. He found blood spots by the bed that she had missed. Jones asked her where the knife was, but she put on a blank, confused face. She would learn to perfect that look through the years.

When Carla finally woke up, she was furious that Social Services had Liliana, but she never asked why Liliana had stabbed Joe. Carla never found the knife. It was gone now in the truck that was stuck in an arroyo miles away. Liliana thought of retrieving her truck and her knife and gun. Danger could catch her unprepared. The fear filled her chest and suddenly Terry's face was in front of her; his hands were on her cheeks.

"It's over," he said, trying to reassure her. "You're safe now. They can't hurt you anymore. I'm here. You're safe, Lili. Breathe. Let yourself breathe." He leaned his forehead against hers as Donna and Jim rushed to get the nurses. "I'm here, Liliana. They're gone. That part of your life is over. Come on now, breathe. Let the air in."

Coughing, she pushed him away. The smell. Joe's smell. The smell of his foul breath, his stinking body and blood filled her nose. She covered her nose and mouth with her hand, trying to keep him out of her. Joe's smell was trying to fill her mind. She fought to free her left arm, tearing at the casts. Someone put a mask over her face as someone else held her other arm. She tried to fight them, but she started getting sleepy. Terrified of being drugged, she lost the battle and finally drifted off.

Dr. Berger looked up to Terry's worried eyes. "I don't think we'll have to put the tube in again. The sedation is working and she's responding to the nebulizer. What happened?"

"She was quiet, and then she started looking scared. I think everything hit her at once." Terry was kicking himself. He should have reacted when he first saw the fear in her eyes. Fear he'd never seen, even when she was facing down a gang of belligerent white boys.

Dr. Berger put her hand on his shoulder and said, "It's not your fault. I'm going to place her on tranquilizers until she sees a counselor. Who has she seen before?"

Donna responded, "She's never seen a counselor that I know of. Carla wouldn't let her. Her medical doctor has been her support most of her life. Dr. Karnes is at Laguna Hospital."

"I'll give him a call," she responded. "She'll sleep for a few hours. Let the nurse know when she wakes up. Don't worry. She'll get through this, Mr. Prentice; she has all of you to help her."

Adela and Emmy arrived just after the doctor left. Donna told them what had happened and Emmy sat on the side of the bed, holding

Liliana's hands with tears running down her face. "I didn't know what to do. I didn't know what to do."

Jim said, "There was nothing you could've done. You were just a baby yourself when it started. Then Joe was big and you were small. You were brave to go to talk to Liliana when you did. She remembered you and she's glad you're here."

"No, it's not that," she paused, guilt stealing into her eyes. "I knew the old man took Joe to his house when he was little. I was afraid to take my son far away before they corrupted him. It's my fault he became evil."

Adela took her hand and said, "That white man with all his money would've stomped on you like an ant. There was nothing you could do. Now you can help Liliana."

"I don't know," she said with a voice full of doubt. "We don't know each other. How can I help her now that Francis is gone?" Her voice and hands trembled with emotion.

"For now, just take care of yourself. When you feel stronger, Liliana will be there so you can help her," Terry said gently. "I know she wants to talk to you. She told me last night that she was glad to have a grandma again. Do you like lemon meringue pie?" Puzzled, she looked up and Jim laughed.

It had been years since he remembered laughing. When he learned his wife had cancer, he'd forgotten how to laugh. Now he stood there, chuckling and shaking his head. He looked down at the little woman and explained, "My wife was a diabetic, but she loved lemon meringue pie. The only time she would eat it was when she'd make it for Liliana. She made it to cheer Liliana up; she was such a sad and angry little girl. They would sit down together and eat half of the pie. She always had a stomachache after Liliana visited. When Liliana got her truck, she'd stop by every time she was on her way home, or back to school in Albuquerque." He paused and looked out the window, "Lemon meringue pie," he said wistfully.

He stopped himself before he said that it probably contributed to his wife's death. That was a cruel thought and he was going to stop that. His wife always had trouble controlling her diet. The pies were only a small part of the problem. Liliana had made his wife laugh with her stories from school, or what the local winos were up to in Grants. He missed his wife's laugh.

When Emmy calmed down, she lay down next to Liliana, her head next to her grandchild's head. In a soft, whispery voice, she sang to her in Navajo. Jim saw Terry yawn, and sent him to the hotel to sleep.

Once in his room, Terry set the alarm to wake him for dinner and slept soundly, exhaustion winning over worry. He had planned to eat at Liliana's side, but when he returned to the hospital other plans had been made. Dr. Karnes was there with his life-partner, Peter, and Jake. They wanted him to join with them for dinner. Liliana had said she wanted time with her grandma, who was too shy to talk in front of so many strangers. She looked like she had had a rough time. Her eyes were glazed over from the tranquilizers and were surrounded with dark circles and grief.

Terry reluctantly agreed and took Liliana's hand to say goodbye; she pulled him down and kissed him. When he paused to look into her large, brown eyes, he knew she was as attached to him as he was feeling toward her, despite whatever else was going on in her head. He would have to wait for her to tell him about her grief. Again his heart overflowed with emotion as he remembered how close he'd come to losing her.

With a suspicious smile, Jake pulled him away, and they all headed out for the Nickels Bar that was close by, a popular source of excellent ribs and crab legs, served in a rustic environment.

Liliana helped her shy great-great grandmother to open up by asking her about where she lived and what her sister was like. Once she started, Emmy realized she had a lot to talk about. Her grief for her sister was balanced by the knowledge that now her sister was free of pain. She spoke with reverence of the home she already missed and of the sorrow of losing her sister. Their walks in the crystal clear air. The smell of sage and mesquite, and sheep. The swiftly passing shade of the clouds, eagles and hawks gliding over the rugged buttes and canyons. How the colors of those canyons changed with each passing hour of the day. She told her about the owls hooting in the night, and the hawk's cry in the day, of how the family of rabbits lived under her trailer, feeling perfectly safe from their fat, lazy cat. Finally they talked about what it was like to feel abandoned by everyone in your family, except for her devoted sister. She told Liliana how Francis was also raped, but refused to tell anyone; she didn't want anyone's sympathy.

Francis had learned through the grapevine and told Emmy about Carla, Susana and then Liliana. Emmy was too afraid to try to help Carla or Susana, but by the time Liliana was ten, she was ready to do something. She took the truck and her sister, to find the little girl who looked just like her, gave her the knife and told her how to hide it and use it. Liliana had understood why Emmy was telling her those things.

It turned out that Emmy was Eddie Chee's distant cousin on his mother's side. When she and her sister moved to the mobile home, the Chee family lived nearby. She knew Eddie when he was a kid. When his family moved to Grants and he dropped out of school and became an alcoholic, she grieved for him as she had for her own son.

They lay side by side on the narrow bed talking about the beauty of the Navajo badlands and that is how the others found them when they came back with bags full of ribs and crab legs. Emmy was willing to try the ribs, but she was unsettled by the sight of the crab legs. Finally, Jim sat next to her and cracked one open and fished out the sweet meat. Too polite to say no, she discovered that she liked the new taste. Terry sat and fed Liliana crab until she'd had enough. He then washed the buttery drips from her face while they laughed at the mess.

Reluctantly, Liliana looked up at Terry and said, "Isn't there some business you need to take care of in Texas? You were pulled away the minute the funeral was over."

"Are you trying to get rid of me?" he asked. She looked into the eyes that had captured her heart at first sight then blushed.

"No," she said, "but I don't want you to miss doing something that will cause trouble for you later."

"Everything was taken care of by my dad before he died. I am officially a free and rich man. Now you can be the gold-digger and marry this old man for his money." He turned at the gasp from Jim and Donna. He'd forgotten that no one had ever been around as he and Liliana joked about marriage.

Liliana saw Emmy smile. Jake stared in shock. He'd been busy and hadn't been aware of the glow of new love growing brighter the more time they spent together. Clearly some of her friends and family weren't sure if they were happy about the situation, as much as they seemed to like Terry. She brushed the worry aside and looked up at Terry.

He was looking down at her again, when she responded, "I think you'll have to wait until I'm no longer under the influence of drugs. I might agree to anything right now." With effort she managed a defiant look and he laughed and kissed her buttery lips.

"So you invite me to share your hogan, but you're not sure you want to marry me?"

"I think a trial run is in order." She paused to take a breath. "Uncle Mike always told me never to buy a truck until I've driven it through the hills."

"All right. You want to run me across the cactus and sand first?" He stood with his arms crossed, feigning annoyance, "Can I at least wear my boots?" It was good to spar with her again. This was the girl he'd loved from the first day.

"Well, every Indian knows white men are unreliable. I think watching you run across fields of cactus would help me make the decision."

Peter's blue eyes twinkled as he commented, "I think that you need to get out of those casts before he makes his run. That way you'll have a better chance of chasing him down when he tries to keep running."

Frank started laughing at what must have been a private joke, his dark eyes lit with good humor. Then everyone laughed as Liliana and Terry remained serious, watching each other with calculating eyes.

"Right," Donna said, and reached out to hug her father. Shaking his head, he shook a warning finger at Liliana, and then laughed.

"You are just like your grandmother when she was your age. I'm going to have to keep on my toes. I've gotten out of practice since she died." He eyed Terry, "I know you're old enough to make this decision, Liliana, but he's a little old for you. Just saying."

Donna squeezed his arm. "It's their decision, Daddy. Besides, I don't think she wants to be pushed down the aisle in a wheelchair, so they have time to think about it."

Liliana looked down her leg and doubted that he would want her if she was crippled for life. "I just worry," was all Jim said.

Chapter 11

Healing

Dr. Karnes arrived after finishing his day's work, late in the evening. Donna left for a walk around the hospital so they could talk alone. Dr. Berger had called him regarding Liliana's asthma being triggered by panic attacks. She suspected that Liliana wasn't sharing her emotional triggers. Once they were alone, he sat watching Liliana watch him.

"Well, Doc, here we are again," she said in her driest of dry tones.

"It is a familiar place," he smiled.

Looking away, she said quietly, "I'm sorry I caused so much trouble for everyone. I shouldn't have run."

"I would've run if Carla had been gunning for me."

She turned back, surprise in her eyes, and then began to blink, trying to clear the tears. He sat on the edge of the bed, cupping her face in his hands. When she started sobbing, she reached out for him and he leaned in to hug her.

Finally, when the tears began to slow, he released her to get a damp cloth to wipe her face. Carefully avoiding the stitches on her forehead, he washed away the tears, letting the cool, damp cloth sooth her emotions. She lay still, letting him take care of her. When he finished with her face, he started with her hands, wiping them clean, and then he pulled out his nail clippers to clean the old blood from beneath her nails, and trim the sharp corners of broken nails which he'd noticed were driving her crazy as she fiddled with them with her other fingers.

"Do you like him?" She immediately blushed, and he smiled. Now he knew her sensitive spot. He would use it when necessary, as he had been able to since she was six and had her first crush on a boy.

"Yes, . . . but we've hardly spent any time together. He doesn't know me very well."

"He knows you well enough to like you. And despite what you may believe, you don't have any deep, dark character flaws that will scare him away."

"It's too soon."

"Of course, but that doesn't make the feelings any less real." He released her right hand to start on her left, pulling the fingers free of the gauze hanging out of the cast. She looked down at the neatly trimmed nails, rubbing them with her thumb, avoiding his eyes. "That doesn't mean he's the love of your life, but you don't have to be afraid of enjoying what he has to give. He's a good man and he fought hard to find you. Give him, and yourself, some time."

"I don't know. It's just that . . ." Tears began to well up again.

He finished with her left hand. Noting the ominous darkness of the fingers, he hid his fears from her. "It's just that too much has happened to know what you think."

"Yeah. It's like that."

"And you can't handle the idea of getting hurt deep inside where it really hurts, again."

"Yeah." She said in a whisper.

"Well, I can tell you that, although he may not be sure that this is a lifelong thing, he will do anything to avoid hurting you. The only thing that will tell you how it will be is time."

"Yeah. Time."

He could count on one hand the times Liliana had been at a loss for words. Fortunately, he knew most of what went on in her head, whether she was chattering to cover it up, or brooding silently in his office. So he changed the subject to one on which he knew she would be vocal, but moved away from her fists to work on her toenails when he brought it up.

"Dr. Berger believes that you are suffering from severe post traumatic stress, along with the trauma to your leg and arm, which may get worse before it gets better. She thinks you should let yourself heal and consider delaying your entry into medical school for a year."

"No!" She almost sat up, but was stopped by the pain in her ribs. "I don't start until August. I'll be able to get around by the time school starts. She didn't talk to Dr. Kauffman, did she? Does he agree with this? They can't keep me from starting . . ." She stopped suddenly and eyed him suspiciously. She remembered the time he'd suggested giving her only teddy bear away, because she got so upset when Carla teased her about it. "You're trying to make me mad," she said accusingly, and fell back on her pillow, glaring at him.

He chuckled, scratched his head, and grabbed the wayward right foot firmly. "You'd better be still. If I slip you could lose another foot." He watched her from the corner of his eye. That statement would have shocked anyone who heard it, but they shared a dark sense of humor.

"Then I'll be set for life, because I'll sue a rich doctor and take everything he has."

"Sorry. If you're thinking of suing me, there's not much to get. Peter spends every meager penny I make."

"Peter, the coupon queen? Never! You must be spending it all on your secret lover."

"Now that would be interesting," he nodded. She was quiet, watching him work on her foot. He'd nearly finished when she spoke again.

"It's up to me, isn't it?"

"Of course, you can decide and you have plenty of time to think about it, and to heal. Your spot is safe. They don't have to know until the end of July to get an alternate. Dr. Kauffman will protect your spot. That gives you five weeks." He paused, to examine his work, then checked the left foot and decided to leave it alone. The dark purple color of those toes was disturbing, but they were definitely not gangrenous, which was good news. He wouldn't take a chance with a nail clipper.

She saw the look on his face and asked, "Do you think I'll lose it?"

He came up to her side, took her hand in his and said, "Liliana, you are strong, young and healthy. Right now you need to focus on healing your body, not trying to protect everyone from what's going on in that head of yours. Only time will tell if the leg heals, but *you* will heal whether you have it, or not."

She closed her eyes. He waited.

"What are they doing about Carla's funeral?" she asked.

"She can wait in cold storage until you're ready to decide." He stroked her forehead. "You don't have to think about it today, or next month. I'll put it all on hold in your name." He cocked his head. "So now you have another grandmother. She needs your love, now that her sister is dead. Even though she and Adela seem to have bonded, it will be good for her to have another friend."

"Adela is the best. You should hear Grandma Emmy's stories about Adela's place. I think she gets a kick out of being around a noisy group of teenagers. She never had a chance to be a rowdy teenager. She misses her nieces and nephews. She worries about her sister's spirit after the violence she committed."

"It was Francis' choice."

Her dark eyes turned to watch him from under her long lashes. "Too many bad choices by all of us."

"Not that many, really, just complicated by a lot of bad luck. After a life of good decisions, she decided to sacrifice it all to protect her sister and to satisfy her desire for revenge. It was her choice to make. She'll face St. Peter and he'll judge her good and bad intentions. We can't help her, but we can stop blaming ourselves."

He watched her struggle with the deep breathing exercises he'd taught her years ago. When she finally relaxed he said, "You know, I haven't had a chance to give you that graduation party I promised you. How many hours do you lack to get your bachelor's degree?"

"Ten. But I don't need a degree for med school. I've completed all the required courses."

"But that means Peter will have to wait four more years for the big bash."

"But it's only time, Doc."

"Touché, mon petit." He leaned back in mock offense.

"All right. I get the message. I'll think about it. Let's see how the leg does," she sighed. "You can have Carla cremated. Would you put an ad in the obits that the date of a memorial will be announced? That will give her drunken cronies time to sober up enough to shut up for an hour."

He picked up her right hand, slowly opened the tight fist, straightening one finger at a time, and then laid it over his heart. "Can you tell me what started it this time?"

She closed her eyes, "When I stabbed Joe."

"That was a terrible night, but now he's dead and gone. Now that you don't have to see him all the time, that memory will fade, I promise. Practice your meditation and call me when it gets scary. Okay?"

She nodded numbly. He kissed her forehead. "I guess I'll let someone else enjoy your gracious presence."

Hiding her grin under a mock frown, she pushed him away. He opened the door and Peter was the first in. "So did Frank talk you into letting us give your graduation party, sooner rather than later?"

"He tried," she said and smiled as Peter leaned down to kiss her. Peter was nearly the exact opposite to his partner in his looks. He was just as tall, but despite hours in the sun he failed to darken more than the almond colored stove in his kitchen. His eyes were dark blue, large and spaced widely apart. His shoulder length hair was so pale it was hard to see the grey that threatened to take over as his hairline receded. His face was oval, his mouth was small, but since he was always talking no one noticed. His frame was narrow with the touch of a paunch that only showed when he forgot to pull it in.

"Well, you have to let me know. It will take time to prepare the perfect menu. It's been ages since I've danced with Twinkle-toes. You should see him after he's knocked back a few. He's an absolute smoothie on the dance floor."

"I said I'll think about it."

"Okay, Sweet Thing. You think, and I'll plan. I'll check in tomorrow. This old thing of mine needs his beauty sleep."

Frank laughed and they swept out the door as Jim, Donna, Emmy and Adela crowded in. Conversation was limited since they were afraid to discuss their concerns lest she get sick again. They finally loosened up when they realized she seemed more herself after talking with the doctor. Terry returned from his nap; Jim and Donna returned home to get some sleep, now that Liliana seemed better. Adela and Emmy went to check on Adela's brood, conveniently giving Terry time alone with Liliana.

"I think you almost made Grandpa drop his pants when you asked me to marry you. He could've had a heart attack," she told him. "You shouldn't kid old people like that."

"I wasn't kidding," he said as he sat on the edge of the bed, "I'm in no hurry, but I had to ask you. You have plenty of time to think about it, but I'm sure about this."

"You don't know me very well. It's too soon."

"And you don't know me, either. So, we take our time."

"I'll be in school and you won't see me much," she said, watching his reaction.

"Okay, I admit that it feels like I'm joking by proposing marriage so soon. I just want you to believe that I care for you. I feel you holding my heart; I can't describe it. I just want to be with you."

"It feels the same for me," she admitted. "From the moment I saw you. But crushes start like that, too, and fade away when people get to know each other."

"Yes, my wise one. We will wait however long it takes to be sure. Lets' just say I want to get my bid in early. Don't doubt that I'm committed."

"And to which asylum are you committed to?"

"This one." He kissed her.

Chapter 12

Time Together

Almost two weeks in the hospital and Liliana was ready to lose her mind. Time in the hospital passed so slowly. Her days ran together in a miasma of nightmares, pain, guilt and performing for the people she cared about. Sometimes she wanted to throw everyone out and wallow in self-pity for days. She knew she needed every one of them, and it made her angry. Right now everything made her angry, but she would not let them see it. She couldn't risk losing their love.

She found herself waiting for her phone to ring. Carla used to call her at least three times a day. It never mattered what she did or said. Carla wanted her. Carla's reasons were selfish and malicious and they had terrible fights. But Carla never remembered those fights. She'd pass out and the next day would be the same. If she was mean, it was about stuff that had happened years ago and, of course, anything Liliana wanted to do that Carla hadn't told her to do, most recently it had been Liliana's time in Albuquerque.

Here there was always someone around, someone to hear every frustrated snarl. It was the main reason she hated hospitals in the first place. There was nowhere she could go to scream and kick the walls. It was why, she believed, her asthma wasn't as bad at home with Carla as it was at school, at Adela's and when she was stuck in the hospital. She always had an empty motel room for a good yelling, kicking and cursing session that never resulted in asthma, or personal consequences. She couldn't control the asthma here, because she had to keep that part of her

198

personality secret. No one knew about those sessions. She'd never even told Dr. Karnes. Sometimes she got sarcastic and "bratty" as Peter called it, but she always pretended she was making a joke.

Most of all, it disturbed her that she needed these people. Loving them was all good; she liked that. But needing them was sick. Carla bragged all the time about how she didn't need anyone, but she needed Liliana and fought tooth and nail to keep her. She'd never be like Carla.

God, I wish I could just cry when I want to without someone calling a nurse.

She remembered times when a half-sober, sad Carla would talk about her life with her grandfather. He just wouldn't leave her alone. Night or day, it didn't matter. She was never safe. There was nowhere else to go; she had no other family and she was ashamed to tell anyone.

Carla had told her what it was like when Joe started hanging around her junior high school, flirting with the little girls. She knew she was one of the prettiest and that's why he teased her. He was so handsome and he didn't give a shit what anyone said. He could take care of himself. He didn't need anybody. He was big and strong, and in her dreams, he convinced her that he could protect her. Her grandfather did something to convince Joe to leave Carla. She was sure it was his fault. So Joe married Lorraine. She hated Lorraine, but nothing she did could break them up.

One day Joe let it slip that he probably was her father. She was furious until she realized she couldn't turn him away even with that knowledge. When he showed up, wanting her attention, it was a small victory over her grandfather and Lorraine. Other than complaining about Lorraine, after that she kept her talk about Joe in the present, most of the time. Carla continued to fight with him and to fight for his attention, never trying to understand why she couldn't let go. Liliana decided that Carla drank to forget, and being drunk gave her an excuse for the behavior she was helpless to control.

Now Carla was gone and Liliana was an adult, the only one responsible for her own life. Indra had tried to help Liliana manage her rage when a call from Carla resulted in an asthma attack. She refused to go to the University Clinic so he helped her manage the attack with her inhaler. Later, he taught her about the self-destructive nature of anger, the healing of forgiveness. It all helped, some.

Dr. Karnes helped her face reality. There was no way to leave when she was little, so she had to learn to set aside her anger sometimes and learn to ask for help. He began teaching her to talk to him during the times when the school sent her to his clinic and before someone found Carla to tell her where Liliana was. For some reason, Carla never used her vicious revenge tactics on him.

Terry returned after the nurses finished changing the bed and her bandages and she shut the door to the past. She took a deep breath and smiled in welcome. It wasn't that hard to do. Whenever she saw him her heart sang.

"You look like you've been doing some heavy thinking."

"Maybe. I have a lot to think about."

He waited, but she didn't continue and wouldn't look up.

"Okay, let's talk about something else. Tell me about this guy you hiked the Res with."

She looked up sideways. "Jealous much?"

"Well, he was younger than me, probably cuter."

She snickered, "Cuter?"

"He wasn't cute?"

"Yes, he was handsome, but it was only a semester. Tell me about your wife, first."

"Ancient history. You don't want to hear about her."

"So you have a secret. Tell me, I want to know how it was with her. Consider it contributing to my education. I don't know very many married people. I need to learn about long term relationships."

"Long term relationships, eh? Is this for a sociology paper?"

"Maybe an archeology paper."

"Ha. Ha," he said flatly.

"Come on, tell me about her. Do you still love her?"

"I don't know, maybe. We had some good times." He settled into the chair after pulling it closer. "We met in college in engineering classes in St. Louis."

"What was she like?"

He leaned over and kissed her lightly. Oh, how she wanted so much more.

"Okay, if you insist. She was a knockout and since guys outnumbered girls in engineering, she got a lot of attention."

"What did she look like?"

"She was 5'2", a hundred pounds with all the curves in the right places. Some of the guys called her God's most successful engineering project. She could be teased like that. Then she'd turn around and walk away slow and sexy and they knew they'd never get out of the dugout, much less to first base."

"Big tits, uh?"

She got a sideways glance for that. Damn she always went too far. She had to learn to think like a normal person, or at least to keep her trap shut when the jealous Carla part of her spoke.

"Well, a little, I guess. It was the whole perfect package. I guess I fell for her body before I even met her."

"She was blond and oh so perfect?" Did it again, jealous bitch. Shit!

He squeezed her hand. "It was a long time ago. We divorced seven years ago." She looked down at his hand. "Anyway, she was half Irish and half African American. About your coloring, but with crazy, curly long hair. She kept it long and loose and it would float in the breeze. Her eyes were gold, the same color as her skin. I used to call her Catwoman, but she didn't like it. She was not at all athletic and was ashamed of not being perfect. She was a real nerd, just like me."

"Was she nice and proper?"

"Proper? Yeah, I guess so, until she got mad, then she would swear and hit. She slapped one of the nuns at the Catholic high school her parents sent her to. It was one of her favorite stories. I should have figured there'd never be much compromising with her. She could be nice, especially if she wanted something. I like that you're different that way. You lay out what you want. You don't play those pretty girl games."

"Oh, so I don't act like a pretty girl."

"Well, no, you're smart and sassy. She was spoiled and knew how to get stuff from people by laying on the sugar."

"No, I guess I never learned how to use sugar that way." She paused a minute, "Maybe it's the diabetes. Did the sugar work on you?"

He looked over to see the smirk. "Yeah, it did. I didn't realize it until things started to go sour. You're two different people that's all. Sometimes she'd use some of the more needy guys to do stuff she couldn't get done because she was always taking on more projects than any single human could manage. She wanted it all: a successful job, a lot of kids, and a big house with the perfect yard, charity work, a political career. Her list went on forever."

"Too bad she didn't wait. You could give her a mansion now."

His eyes became thoughtful. "You know, one day she'd give the shirt off her back to some poor kid, and other days she'd get mad if I borrowed her shaving cream."

"No shirt, huh. Was that bra or no bra?"

"That's what you got out of that?" He laughed. "You take things in so many directions. I can't predict you at all."

"Is that good or bad?"

"All good. What is life without surprises?"

"Yeah, sometimes I think you have me figured out better than I have."

"I wouldn't have a chance if I were your age. I've lived long enough to have met some unusual people."

"So she left you?" It was getting too close. Change topics.

"It was mutual. I couldn't give her the kids she wanted and my job took me out of town a lot."

"She cheated?"

He sighed. "Yeah, she needed more than I could give."

"Bullshit."

He shook his head with a half smile. "Well, I forgave her and she cheated again and again. Then I met someone else. She found out and wanted out, but I was ready by then."

"What happened to the someone else?"

"She's a friend, and that's enough of the third degree. Your turn. Tell me about the guy you hiked with."

She looked down at her leg and shifted her body, trying to find a comfortable position. It didn't fool him for a minute. She refused his help and moved her injured leg to a different angle. "I'll sure be glad to get out of this bed."

"They say the infection's clearing. Your white cell count was normal. That's good news."

"Yeah, I don't think I can take another week in here. I don't know how you keep it up, sitting here everyday."

"Are you getting tired of seeing me?"

She tried shifting her pillow with her one good arm and had to give up and let him help her. "I'll just be so fucking glad to get out of this!" She closed her eyes and took a deep breath.

"What do you really want to say, kiddo?" She didn't know why he'd picked that nickname. It sort of felt good, but she was so aggravated she felt like picking a fight.

"I feel like kicking something, or screaming at someone, but I don't want to fight with you. Do you think you have to come every day to please me? I really don't want you to get tired of seeing me so messed up."

"Yes," he responded, "I do get tired of being here, but I can't imagine putting up with all the casts, IV's, nurses every four hours like you do. At least I get away once in a while. But it comes down to this." He took her chin and looked into her eyes. "I never get tired of seeing you."

All she could do was nod. He let go of her chin. "Now I want to hear about this tall, dark and handsome Navajo you dated."

She released his hand and covered her eyes. From behind her hand she whispered, "He didn't want to have anything to do with me after summer break. He found out about Carla and all the lies she told about me."

He wouldn't have heard her if he hadn't still been leaning in close. Her hand shook and tears appeared on her cheeks. He took her head in his hands and kissed her forehead. "I am so sorry, Liliana."

He continued to hold her. She could tell he was listening to her breathing. Purposely, she took some deep breaths and let go of the tension. This was old anger. Indra had been there to help her through it. It was just so damned embarrassing to have another tragedy to tell Terry.

Finally, she uncovered her eyes and asked him. "When are you going to get tired of hearing about all of my troubles?"

"Never." His pale, hazel eyes looked over every inch of her face. She wanted to hide from his gaze.

He sighed and leaned back, taking her hand in his own. "You have had two weeks of hell, and still you make your family laugh even when you complain. You have a brain so shining and brilliant that it amazes me every time we talk. You're interested in everyone else's problems more than your own. You have already accomplished so much. At twenty you have a seat waiting for you in medical school. You finished high school two years early. You have accomplished so much. I can't conceive of calling any of that trouble." He looked down at her hands, because he couldn't bear to see more tears for just a moment. "You have terrible memories and they will rise up sometimes and you might have setbacks because of them, but believe that they will never scare me away. I know who I am, at my age sometimes that happens. I am stubborn, which is how we met, so I can't be too sorry about that." He paused to wipe her tears away.

"You sure looked like coyote bait that day," she said.

"And what do I look like now?" He was smiling, but his eyes were serious.

Sobbing threatened, so she said what her heart wanted her to say before she lost it. "You look like the most beautiful thing in my life. I love how you look, even when you look like coyote bait. I love who you are and I love that by some strange miracle you are here for me." Then it hit, the ugly cry: sobbing, shaking, and snotty.

He got on the bed on his side, slipped one arm under her arm cast and the other behind her back, hugged her tightly and kissed her tears, then her mouth. She wrapped her free arm around his back and held on. After a long, deep kiss, she put her face in his neck and held him. For a few seconds she opened her eyes and saw Denise at the door, checking on her. When their eyes met, the wily redhead gave her a thumbs up and stepped out of view. She closed her eyes and let herself feel him and smell him.

Chapter 13

A Very Different Life

Four days later, Dr. Berger told them that Liliana's chest x-ray had cleared, but more importantly Dr. Smith decided the infection in her leg had cleared enough for Liliana to go to an intermediate care facility or home with her grandfather. The infection in her leg would take time to clear completely, but she could get intravenous antibiotics, bathing help and wound dressing changes at home through the local home nursing service. Frank was worried about Liliana having unsupervised time since she was still having panic attacks, but the family promised to hire someone to be there so that if everyone was busy, someone would be on hand. Liliana watched the negotiations with some trepidation. She wanted to go home; she was desperate to get out of medical facilities. She put on her best coping face, despite hating the idea that she would still be dependent, and was very glad when she was discharged home.

Still, she was supposed to spend most of her time in bed, since the leg was still unstable. She was able to use an electric wheel chair with the bad leg supported straight outward like a battering ram when she needed mobility. Crutches were still a dream of her future. When she moved in with her grandfather they decided to put her in the front room that was her grandmother's pottery studio.

They needed that room, because of its proximity to the front door and large size, which was needed for the complicated hospital bed equipped for pulleys, as well as IV stands and the cabinets and tables her medications and supplies needed for her treatments by the visiting nurse and physical therapist. Jim had suffered in silence. When Liliana asked Donna, she told Liliana about the long walks he took as the construction was under way. The loss of the place that was special to his beloved of more than sixty years hit him hard. Liliana could see he was hiding his negative feelings, because he did very much want Liliana to live with them.

On the day Liliana was finally released and installed in her new prison, as she called it, she felt good to be back in the home she had before the motel became her home. However it still felt strange not having Carla's music, smoke and foul language around.

Terry was worried about all the personal, legal and financial arrangements that required his presence in Amarillo. So, once Liliana was settled, he returned to Amarillo for two weeks. They had saved his father's house for him to go through. He called every day, sometimes twice and she'd call at night. She hoped it wasn't too much for him, but she wasn't able to stop herself. In order to keep the nightmares in control and her anxiety about Terry manageable, she finally decided to accept Valium as a temporary addition to her life. At least it kept her out of the hospital.

It was so hard. When she wasn't talking to him, he was all she thought about and all the reasons they wouldn't work out. Then he'd be on the phone and her brain would turn to mush, refusing to think about how it couldn't work. Then there was Carla's funeral that she had scheduled for after his return. She wasn't ready to deal with it yet. The idea of putting together a eulogy was overwhelming. Maybe time would help.

Her grandfather hired a retired nurse to help her during the day, as he had promised. He was busy with tribal business, and Donna had to go back to work. The nurse quit after a week. Liliana announced she was perfectly able to take care of herself, and tried to prove it to Donna by getting up on her right leg, but the dressings on the fractured leg started to slip and there was so much pain she was forced back onto the bed.

After a call to a mutual friend, Donna discovered that the usually kind woman hadn't approved of Liliana's grandmother, Carla, not unexpectedly, and Liliana had sensed her true feelings. Angelo was still on summer break and could help Liliana with fetching and carrying things, but she needed a lot more help. Donna called Dr. Karnes who had a suggestion for someone who was immediately available and could spend more time with her than the usual nursing visits.

The next day Angelo was destroying a distracted Liliana at checkers when someone knocked at the door.

"I'm coming," he called out and turned and pointed at Liliana. "Don't you dare move any of my pieces."

"I won't, but I can't speak for Grandma's spirit. She wants me to win."

He frowned, knowing she was kidding. He sent her a glare and went to get the door. He and a tall, solidly built, young woman arrived at the door to catch Liliana rearranging all the pieces.

"Hey, I was winning. You're cheating! I'm not playing checkers with you anymore." He left the room complaining about how Liliana could be such a turd.

Liliana looked over the young woman who appeared to be her age, then saw the badge she wore identifying herself as a visiting LPN.

"Julia! How did you get so tall?"

Julia set her bag down on the chair by the door and went to take Liliana's hand. "Liliana, I've missed you so much since we moved to Albuquerque."

"Yeah. Me, too. I didn't have your address and I didn't think your mom would have wanted me writing anyway." She squeezed the hand of the girl who had been her only friend in grades 1-3. Julia's face was round and soft, a little darker than Liliana with light brown hair in a ponytail. Her eyes were dark brown, small and sat deep over her round cheeks. Julia was one of the most loyal people Liliana had ever known. One day Carla angrily came to pick her up and forbade further visits. The girls still managed to talk at school, until the fourth grade when her father found a job in Albuquerque.

"I saw them rescue you on the news. It was awful. You look so much better."

"Yeah, but I'm going nuts with all this stuff. I can't even piss without help. I see you are an LPN now. Are you here in an official capacity?"

"Yes, of course." Julia responded with exaggerated professionalism. As children they had played real doctor and nurse and wrapped Julia's little brother in bandages and wheeled him around in the wheel barrow. "I have been officially assigned as your full time aide."

Liliana laughed. "They did you bad, girl. I am the worst patient in the world."

"Yes. I fully expect to have some difficulty, but I'm sure we can make some compromises." She started giggling. "It's so good to see you. Is there anything you need right now?"

"Why don't you get a couple of sodas and some cookies from the kitchen and we'll catch up. Angelo, show Julia where the kitchen is."

"That's okay. I can find it."

Liliana was grateful for Julia, but she still resented being immobilized. They wouldn't let her drive a car, which she actually knew was impossible, but she complained anyway and received a number of rolled eyes, snorts and sarcastic laughs in return. Mike had offered to get her a small, souped-up tractor with a platform to keep her leg elevated, but Donna put her foot down. So Mike, in secret, researched what kind of modifications it would take for her to drive once her leg was stable.

The cast on her left arm would be on for at least another four weeks. The left calf was more worrisome. The shattered bones, having penetrated the skin, had gotten infected and once infection invaded the bones it took a long time to clear. She'd gone through a second operation to take a vein from her good leg and graft it onto the left one to improve the circulation, both to help heal the infection and to prepare for the beginning of the bone graft surgeries to replace the shards of bone they had to remove in the first operation and to stabilize the leg with steel plates and screws. All of this would take time. Dr. Smith, her orthopedist, told her it could be six months, possibly more. She had to see him, or Dr. Karnes once a week to make sure her casts were holding up. They both knew how restless she got. She received IV antibiotics twice a day, so, at first Julia or one of her associates was there all day.

On her third trip into Albuquerque, sitting on the back bench seat of her grandfather's large cab truck, her left leg cast extended out in front of her. Liliana struggled to settle the pillow comfortably between her back and the door's armrest and decided it was time to broaden their conversation past the weather, village gossip and council news. He thought he was safe in the driver's seat where she couldn't see his face, but she was good at interpreting voices.

So, having made up her mind, once they were on the road she allowed some time for quiet, and then took a breath and started. "You know, Grandpa, I never heard the story of how you and Grandma got together." Whoops, she'd almost said hooked up, a phrase he hated for its blatant reference to "modern promiscuity."

"Sure you have. You know we lived on the same street all our lives."

"I know that part, but I kind of need your help." This wasn't an exaggeration; she'd never shared a falling in love experience since she had no close school friends. Her semester with her one boyfriend would never count since it was too painful to remember. Other than glimpses of Donna during her marriage, and her grandparents after fifty years of marriage, all she had was what she learned while living with Carla. She had no idea how to act with Terry. Donna had told her it was too soon after her divorce, two years before, to talk about falling in love. Donna also wanted to have enough time to tell the story all at once, and, for now she was too busy with her job, Angelo, keeping the house running, and managing Liliana's needs.

"Why do you need my help?"

"Honestly, Grandpa, I don't know what I'm doing with Terry." She took a deep breath. She'd discussed her confusion with Julia, Frank and Peter, but she wanted as many real life stories as she could find. Liliana needed to know if it was it normal to get lost in his eyes, or to want to touch him every minute of the day, even if it was just his littlest finger touching hers. "When did you know you loved Grandma?"

"I thought you wanted to know how, not when. That's starting at the end of the story."

She smiled, and was almost caught when he glanced back over his shoulder. "I want to hear the whole story."

"Well, that could take a long time. Can you stay awake that long?"

"Yeah. I'm not tired at all today."

"If you say so. Okay. Well, you know we lived three houses apart all are lives." He paused.

"Yup." He was going to tell the tale properly, she realized. From beginning to end, the way Pueblo legends were taught.

"Well, what most people don't remember now is that when her family moved in our fathers got into a big fight because Dad thought her father was flirting too much with my mother . . ." She settled in for the first part of the story that she already knew.

Jim and Dolores played with the crowd of neighborhood kids during very hard times, too young to understand what was going on in the Pueblo community. Both spent years in forced attendance at gender segregated boarding schools with Native Americans from other tribes, so they only had school holidays to see each other. Jim explained how the government had a project to force the assimilation of Native American children into the dominant culture of the USA, denigrating the millennia their own cultures had developed on the once isolated continent. They were only allowed to speak English, which actually helped some of them communicate with other children since they were torn from different tribes who spoke different languages.

Liliana had to wait for the trip back to hear the part of the story she wanted to hear now. Once they were on their way back, he waited for her to ask before continuing the story.

"Okay so you were both away a lot until she was thirteen and you were fifteen. What happened once you were back home for good?"

"Well," he sipped the coke he'd bought at the hospital. "You know, we had both changed a lot when we got back. We barely spoke our native tongue anymore and at school they taught us that white men were always right and our ways were no good. It kept us from being comfortable with our families, but it gave us something in common. We got home at the same time, since they took her when she was two years younger than me."

He paused, remembering, or hesitating. "There was a big powwow close by that first summer and our families went together, since one of her father's horses had gone lame. We were in the back of my daddy's wagon with our mothers and all us kids and their other horse to help pull the load. No one noticed that I sat down next to her. When the wagon hit a rock, I would bump into her. One time she landed in my lap. She jumped off right away; her face was very red. My sister started laughing, because my face was very red, too. My mother saw then how close we were and moved us to opposite sides. I could see Dolores was as disappointed as I was.

"So after that I tried to stand or sit or walk next to her whenever I got a chance. Most of the time, we didn't even talk. Then one day, I held her hand. She looked at me and her eyes were shining. It was late, cooling off from a hot day. She told me she wasn't sure I liked her because I never talked to her. I was surprised. I thought she knew how I felt. So I asked her if she liked me, because she never talked to me either. She just smiled and looked down at our hands.

"I was working on my father's farm a lot and she was busy making pottery. I think our parents tried to keep us busy, but I don't think they had any problem with us choosing each other. A year later, I asked her to marry me and she said yes."

Typical, Liliana thought, *he leaves out the best part.* "You got married pretty young."

"Everybody did in those days. There wasn't much more school there for us. Later on I went back to school and my parents helped us out."

"How long after you held hands did you kiss her the first time?"

"Liliana!"

"Okay. It was different then. How did it feel to be next to her?"

"Two minutes."

"Two minutes, what? Oh, you kissed her just two minutes after you held hands. Grandpa, I didn't know you were such a . . ."

"I was just a regular guy. But she was special. You have her big eyes and long lashes. She did what her mother said and was a good girl and she liked to laugh. Sometimes I'd be at our dinner table and I'd hear her laugh all the way from her house. My sister said I was making it up, she hadn't heard a thing. Then I'd ask Dolores and she'd tell me what happened and it would make me laugh every time."

"And it felt wonderful and terrible at the same time."

"What did?"

"Liliana, don't you remember your own question?"

"Oh yeah. That's how it felt to be next to her. Why? How?"

She caught the corner of a smile as he turned his head to check the rear view mirror, which she avoided looking at.

"Because I wanted to hold her all the time and I was afraid she wanted to, too, and I knew we'd get in big trouble if we went too far. That was what the white man taught us. To be ashamed of what we felt. We could have married any time, with our families' permission, if we wanted, but I wanted to finish the little house my dad helped me build next to his house, before we started making babies. I wanted to be independent and a good husband." Then he was silent, lost in memories.

She nodded; that was about all she had expected to get from her grandfather. It was good to hear that someone else had felt as confused as she did, but it was different. She knew older men married younger women everywhere, but she and Terry came from such different backgrounds. There was a chance that after being apart he would realize that she was broken inside and would be a person he could not love.

"You know. Sometimes things just happen." He turned her way for a glance. "Nobody knows the future. I was lucky to have Dolores."

She felt her face go red. She wanted Terry so much it hurt, but that was not a granddaughter to grandfather conversation. Aunt Donna seemed to understand even if they hadn't had a sit-down talk. She looked down at her broken leg and hated it for the way it kept them apart, but then she was glad, because maybe she would have moved too fast if it weren't there to slow her down. Lots of people seemed to think that having sex right away was okay, but she was different. Everyone knew she'd been raised by Carla, and Joe and they could easily believe that she acted like Carla. Somehow she needed to find a place to be safe in this world and free of shame. She couldn't bear to break in to any more pieces. She must find a way to trust him, or leave if he was not to be trusted with her heart. God, how she wished he hadn't left.

As it turned out she was in a session with Dr. Karnes when Terry arrived in Laguna after his two weeks in Amarillo. She couldn't concentrate on the conversation, too nervous with the anticipation of seeing Terry as she sat in Dr. Karnes office, which was barely big enough for a big comfy chair, his desk and two large bookcases and her human-powered wheel chair. He liked pictures of old Laguna and had hung a mix of paintings and authentic turn of the century, nineteen to twentieth, framed photographs. Half way into the session she realized she was answering questions he wouldn't have dared asked if she wasn't so distracted.

"Okay, I'm on to you now." She stated.

"I have no idea what you're talking about," he said as he calmly made a note in her chart.

"What are you writing down?"

"Just my new record for the longest time we've ever had a session that would be typical for any other typical person."

"Are you saying I'm weird, in Deep South polite words?"

"Bless your heart, Dear, what do you mean?"

"You took advantage of my distracted state. That is not fair."

"How else am I supposed to get a straight answer?"

"I tell you the truth."

"Yes, but rarely all of it at one time."

"When did you figure that out?"

"You have been outsmarting me since you were nine."

"It took you that long to figure it out?"

"Don't pretend that you knew that you were doing it. I know it was how you had learned to cope with your world."

"Who's pretending? Anyway, I don't want to be inside any more. When's Grandpa picking me up?"

"Not for half-an-hour. What's the rush?"

She pushed her empty snack table out of the way. "I need to get out of here. Let's go outside and talk, if you insist."

"You know what happens if the nurses see me."

"We need to build you a secret exit. An escape tunnel."

"Tell me what's up."

"I can't. I don't know."

He waited, while she rubbed her face with her free hand. Then she took off her earrings and put them back on. Then she started picking at loose bits of her arm cast.

"I don't believe that you can't take this thing off if I promise to be careful."

He watched her, but she didn't return his gaze, for several minutes.

"How do I know?" she finally asked.

"That he won't hurt you?"

"That he won't just stick around just because he's worried about hurting me."

"He's too good to hurt you, and you don't deserve it."

She let her head fall back and looked at the ceiling.

"Are you counting ceiling tiles?"

"That was a long time ago . . . No. I just wish I knew."

"No one knows, Liliana. You have to decide if your heart can trust."

She turned to look at him. "You're lucky to have Peter."

"Yes, I am very lucky, but it's not just luck and trust. It's a lot of work sometimes."

"Even in the beginning?"

"Especially in the beginning." He stood up. "Come on, I'll walk you to the door and you can pace outside."

"Three steps."

"I'd bet on one step before a nurse grabs me."

"How much?"

"A nickel."

She snorted, "Cheapskate."

"Yup." He managed to make it to the main door and let her out into the blistering July heat when a nurse caught up with him. "I'll see you later."

"Thanks for helping him move in."

"It would have been impossible to keep Peter from arranging a move in and where Peter goes, I go." He kissed her on the forehead. "I'm getting out of this heat. Have a good reunion."

She looked up and he saw the anxiety in her eyes. "I hope so."

He patted her shoulder, waved at her grandfather as he drove up and disappeared inside.

With the help of Liliana's friends and family as well as a few neighbors, Terry had begun moving in the truckload of boxes and the table he'd brought from Texas. He had let professional movers move the furniture he wanted from his house in Farmington and the few pieces of his mother's from his parent's home. Those pieces wouldn't arrive for several days.

With special permission from the Pueblo council, Terry had arranged to rent the Jim Hunt's family home on the same block. Jim had helped with the arrangements after showing Terry the empty house while Liliana was still in the hospital. He was glad to get the place right away; he was weary of sleeping in hotels and couldn't decide if he should stay in

Albuquerque where he was most likely to find a job, or move to Grants to be close to Liliana.

Liliana found it impossible to sit still in the back seat of her grandfather's truck. He watched her in the rearview mirror as she chewed her fingernails. He was worried that she was going to get her heart broken. He hoped the Texan didn't hurt her because then he would have to help pick up the pieces when he hadn't had time to learn all the pieces of her and where they would scatter. Donna had phoned that Terry was busy moving in and would join them for dinner. Jim decided Liliana couldn't wait. He knew he was right when he arrived early to pick her up and she was already outside. So he pulled up in front of Terry's new home whether or not Terry was ready for company.

Terry stepped out the door of the traditional flat-topped adobe house with hope in his eyes as Jim drove up. When he met Jim's eyes, Terry gave him a big smile and looked for Liliana who had scrunched down in the seat in a sudden fit of terror. He walked around to her side of the truck and looked inside. Jim put his arm on the seat and turned so he could watch her reaction. He saw the fear and hope in her eyes and nearly wept. He had already seen her suffer too much; it hurt to see fear in her eyes. She turned to look at Terry and her eyes began to shine, then she was smiling and crying. Jim could only shake his head. He knew they had spent hours on the phone yesterday, yet she was still filled with doubt. He might have to clean his hunting rifle. If this Texan hurt his granddaughter, he would kill him.

She didn't know what to do, she wanted to be in his arms, but extricating her encumbered body from the small back seat was no easy task. She leaned forward so he could open the door, keeping her eyes on his all the while. She saw his joy at seeing her. Finally, actually only seconds later, he took her face in his hands and kissed her. She felt the heat of the kiss travel down through every cell of her body, but all she could do was kiss him back as hard as she could, since her good arm was supporting her weight. He put his cheek to hers, the easiest way to hug, *damn the casts*, and then kissed her again. She wanted him to kiss her just like that forever.

Somewhere else in her mind she heard her grandfather sigh with relief. He got her wheelchair out of the back and set it next to Terry. Terry was supporting more of her weight as she leaned to get closer to him, then he lifted her, still kissing her, as her grandfather supported her leg and together they sat her in the chair. Once her right arm was free she wrapped it around his shoulders. He knelt down next to her, as lost in her as she was in him, while her grandfather strapped her leg in place on its support.

A couple of wolf whistles went up and Jake called out from the door, "Are you guys going to come up for air any time soon?"

Peter added with a laugh, "That's why Liliana took that swimming class. She was practicing for the long-kiss event at the Olympics."

Liliana felt Terry's laugh, finally realized that a lot of people were watching them, and then buried her face in his chest, embarrassed.

"How soon can you get them married?" young Angelo added. "I don't think they can wait much longer."

"Angelo!" Donna scolded and slapped his arm, then brushed away her tears. "Come inside and see, Liliana. We got a lot done."

Terry took her hand and stood. "Yeah, I had a lot of help. Let me show you." He unlocked the wheels and pushed her into the small house. She held his wrist as he pushed her into the cool darkness of the square adobe house that stood right up against a road that was more of an alley so it wasn't paved.

The small living room was painted pale pink and was empty except for a rug in front of the door that Liliana recognized as one of Donna's. Shelves from previous owners lined two of the walls, three shelves to a wall. On top of the highest shelf closest to the front window lay a huge, silver, long-haired cat with big yellow eyes. He lounged with his rear legs hanging half off the shelf, supervising all that went on around him. When Liliana saw him, she sent him the slow, welcoming blink. The cat returned the blink and waited until she looked away to lazily jump down then jump onto her lap. She stroked the top of his head and back, letting go of Terry for that moment. Just petting that cat did wonders in calming her leaping heart.

"How you doin,' you old Don Juan? This is Fred's cat," she explained to Terry. "Fred lived here until he died of AIDS. The neighbors have been feeding this old guy. He's too fat to be living off the rabbits he catches. Let's see the kitchen."

It was time to get moving. The weight of the cat was hurting her leg but she wouldn't admit it. As she expected, when the chair moved the cat gave an annoyed yeow and jumped to the ground.

"He must have just showed up. I didn't see him before. What's his name?" Terry asked.

Peter laughed, "Freddy called him Girlfriend Cat Tail, which confused the whole neighborhood. The complaint is that he is not two-gendered like Freddy, so why would he call him that? Clearly, Fred had his own point of view."

Terry laughed and pushed Liliana forward, "Donna's been busy here in the kitchen. I rescued most of the cooking gear from my dad's house. I have my mom's china boxed up over there and this is the kitchen table from the house."

Liliana looked around, "Something's different."

"See, I told you she'd notice," Angelo said. "When Freddie was stuck in the wheel chair, they widened the doors so he could get around with the chair and added some other stuff. You didn't see it, because he died a month later while you were at school. Come and see the bathroom. It's really cool. They added more stuff for you. It's as good as the stuff we have."

There was a large, walk-in tub with safety hand rails and the temporary bars on the side of the toilet and sink. "This must have cost a fortune. Who paid for the fancy tub?" She turned to her grandfather, he nodded.

"He suffered for a long time." Jim said.

"What about . . . ," Angelo started, and then stopped suddenly.

Liliana turned to see Donna's hand on his head. "Spit it out, Angelo."

Donna looked at the ceiling. Angelo continued, "We just thought you might want to spend a lot of time here, since you been talking to him all the time on the phone. So Julia helped us pick out what kind of handle bars you might need."

Liliana covered her eyes, hiding her heated face. No one would understand how different this moment was from anything she had ever experienced in her years with Carla, or had expected ever to experience in her life. She didn't know if she was supposed to laugh, or reprimand Angelo. She finally looked up to see Terry's smile. He started laughing when he saw her look.

"Congratulations, you now have a family," he said. Jake and his two friends laughed. Donna and Jim looked at each other and shrugged. They had resisted the idea when Julia proposed the changes, a bar hanging from the ceiling to help her transferring from the wheel chair to the toilet and one over the bed, thinking that Liliana might feel like they were pushing her into a relationship before she was ready.

Peter explained. "Most of this was already here for Freddy. We just polished it up and added a few things for you. Like Angelo said, we figured to make you comfortable when you came to visit."

"Had it been that long since I saw Freddy? I was too involved in myself to come and see him. I would have liked to see him once more at least."

"Don't worry, Sweetie," Peter leaned down to kiss her cheek. "You visited him when he was in the hospital. He knew you were working hard and he wasn't himself in the last months. He got a fungal infection in his brain."

"Freddy used to baby-sit me when I lived with Grandma and Grandpa." She looked up at Terry. "I'm glad you picked this house."

"I was going to live close, anyway. This place turned out to be empty and perfect, since we don't know how soon you'll be able to go to crutches."

"Look," Angelo pointed, excitedly, "the tub has water jets. Can I come over and use it?" He looked at Liliana.

"Ask Terry; it's his house."

"I already did. He said I could if you didn't mind."

"Why don't we head home for lunch?" her grandfather interrupted, to her relief. "This old man gets grouchy when he misses a meal. And Liliana needs a nap. Look at her, she's worn out; it's been a long day. Come on, girl, he's coming for dinner. Let him finish with his house."

She looked up at her grandfather, intending to rebel. Then she realized that it wasn't just the cat that made her leg hurt. It was time for her pain meds and she was tired. She avoided Terry's eyes, not sure how he would take her disappointment. *Too needy*, she reminded herself, *I can't be too needy. Nobody likes clingy, needy partners.*

Donna added, before Liliana responded. "Anyway, it's almost time for the nurse's visit. You should eat before she gives you all that medicine."

Liliana resented them telling her what to do and did not want to leave. Terry stooped down to kiss her, again. "I'll be over in no time. Go rest. I've got plenty of help. If we do it all wrong you can tell me later."

"Yes," she agreed reluctantly, "be prepared for a thorough inspection."

"Yes, Ma'am," he replied.

Her grandfather patted Terry's shoulder and took control of the chair. Goodbyes followed her out the door.

Terry had found an opportunity to volunteer at the Laguna Acoma High School in the math, auto repair and shop classes. So it made easier to live nearby and he wouldn't get bored. Liliana seemed glad; he hoped she continued to be glad that he was living so close.

He used his sleeve to wipe the sweat from his forehead as he watched her wheel away. When she looked back, he blew her a kiss, triggering a raucous laugh from his girl. She was still giggling as she passed from his view.

Later, during dinner, he realized how comfortable he was in the Hunt home. The food was good and his hosts were intelligent, thoughtful people. Occasionally he caught either Donna or Jim watching him. He knew had a lot to prove to them. Just because his father was successful, didn't mean he would be. It would probably take years for Liliana's grandfather to trust that he would provide for Liliana in all the ways she needed him. His situation when he first met Donna would not be reassuring, a dusty Texan, broke and stranded, definitely as the result of a series of bad decisions. Liliana would be the one to decide; if she wanted him he would be there for her.

After dinner, she insisted on seeing the changes Peter, who had skipped dinner to keep working on arranging the house, had made. So she drove her electric wheel chair as he walked alongside, enjoying the peaceful evening away from the noise and lights of the city. The stars were so much brighter out here. He laid his hand on Liliana's shoulder, and she looked up, smiling.

"It's so peaceful here. I think I'm going to like it."

"Grandpa makes sure it is. He doesn't put up with noisy parties in his neighborhood."

"Yes, I can't imagine anyone facing him down."

"Yeah, he's definitely got the power eyes down, but I think that the people who come to live near him like quiet. The noisy kids live a couple of streets away. And everyone respects him. He helps them when they need to get something done."

"How have you been getting along since you settled in?"

"It's so much better than the hospital, I can't complain."

"I keep secrets, well. Go ahead and complain."

"So you're trustworthy?" he nodded in response. "Well, we have to use headphones and keep our voices down when we play video games in my room. And sometimes he stops by my room and I know he's missing Grandma's things. He doesn't bring up Carla at all, but I don't mind that."

"He drives you in for your appointments?"

"Most of the time."

"You must talk then."

"Yeah. I talk a lot and sometimes I can drag a story out of him. I got him to tell me about my grandmother today. They were teenage sweethearts. Things were so different back then."

The story was something she could talk about without feeling like she was babbling, while her mind wandered, no, it struck out in one direction and one only. A direction confused by many possibilities. When they opened the door they found Frank and Peter cleaning inside the last of the empty kitchen cabinets. Frank turned to Peter and said, "I told you we should have left. Sorry, Liliana, once Peter gets going he can't quit until everything is perfect."

Peter came over and kissed her cheek. "Did you have a good nap, Sweetie?"

"I rested some. I wanted to see the results of your decorating skills."

She looked around. A sofa covered with a vibrant red cover had appeared and above it hung an abstract painting done in reds and black;

"Fortitude," was its name. She had complemented Peter on the painting many times. A large Navajo rug lay in front of the sofa. Next to the sofa stood a three foot high ceramic sculpture of a Pueblo woman dressed traditionally, holding a ceramic pot. Pouring out of the pot was an abundance of a tiny leafed plant that made a solid, draping mass with fronds that hung to the floor.

"Oh, Peter, this is your stuff," Liliana exclaimed.

"Oh, it's just a loan, until you guys, I mean Terry, can pick up stuff he likes. It was so plain and drab. I couldn't stand it."

"Thank you, Peter." Terry added. "It is definitely more cheerful."

Frank emptied the bucket of dirty water in the sink, saying, "Peter is a colorful soul; he just cannot bear drab. We'll leave you two to explore the house. Now," he took Peter's arm firmly, "we'll pick up the dinner Donna promised us, and head home."

After hugs all around and Peter's promise to return with curtains he'd recently changed out when he repainted their house. When they were gone, Liliana wheeled through all the rooms, noting that the bed was queen-sized with a colorful tie-dyed bedspread with matching shams scattered amongst many pillows. The television sat on a plywood board supported by cinder blocks, with separate speakers on either side. She looked over her shoulder to tell Terry that she'd go with him to shop for furniture, but lost her words when she saw his eyes. Her body responded immediately to the heat in his expression.

He leaned down, lifted her chin with one hand and kissed her for a long time, but still not long enough. "Finally, I have you all to myself," he whispered. She wrapped her arm around him and he picked her up and laid her carefully on the bed and made sure her leg was in a comfortable position. He plopped down next to her. "Now I get to show off my new television." He pointed a remote at the large flat screen, but nothing happened. The disappointment that touched her heart in that fleeting moment disappeared as she realized he was kidding.

"I guess you forgot to plug it in."

"I guess I did." He set down the remote and leaned over to kiss her again. Gently, he held her close, kissing her and running his hands down her back and her hips. He propped himself on his elbow and pushed her hair back from her face. "I keep expecting Denise to show up at the door."

"I suspect she had a spy camera set up with her cell phone."

"I like this better."

"Me, too." She pulled his head down to kiss him, again. Her body burned at his touch. She wanted him to touch her all over, to feel this burn on every inch of her body. Pressing herself against him as much as she could with her left arm strapped to her chest and her leg weighed down with the full length cast. She slipped her left arm out of the sling and watched his eyes as he looked down to see her breasts as he opened her front opening bra, then he looked up with a wicked look. "You have too many clothes on."

"Watch out for glass houses."

He smiled, sat up and took off his shirt. He was so pale and pink under his shirt, it caught her by surprise, which immediately transformed to lust as she stroked his chest. Then he finished unbuttoning her blouse, pushed her bra to the sides, then looked at her generous, copper-brown breasts. He leaned forward to take a dark nipple in his mouth. She trembled with desire, and pushed the automatic shame into the closet in the very back of the house that was her mind. He unbuttoned her pants as she teased his pink, hard nipples. She felt his erection pressed against her hip as he rocked his hips against her. Fire erupted in the sweet area between her legs as he reached down inside her pants and stroked her clitoris; she moaned and arched against him. He reached into her vagina, and then looked up, gentle concern in his eyes.

"You're a virgin." He kissed her, still stroking her. His voice was husky with desire "So I don't have to be jealous of Tall, Dark and Handsome."

"You never did."

"I love you, Liliana." He pressed himself against her and kissed her again, while stroking around her hot, wet vagina, his palm rubbing her clitoris with every stroke. She trembled with desire. "Are you sure you're ready for this? I don't want to hurt you."

"I'm ready; please don't stop." Then it was too much, her eyes closed as her orgasm overtook her, opening her wide then clamping down on the gifted digit. She struggled to open his pants with one hand, succeeded, and then got shy.

"I've wanted you for so long, but I can wait. I don't want to hurt you."

She pulled his head down. "Don't you dare stop now."

He began to undress her. Their eyes were locked, drinking in each other's passion. He smiled as he found the Velcro strips built into her shirt and pants to make it easier for her to change.

"What?"

"This sound," he separated a strip of Velcro with a flourish, "reminds me of the stripper at my last birthday party." He licked his lips then kissed her again, his tongue teasing hers in a delicate wrestling match. He looked down her nude body as he pulled back to remove the rest of his clothes. Her blush traveled to her toes, as she watched him undress.

He was lean and somewhat muscular. A patch of light brown hair spread between and around his nipples, and then traveled in a line to meet the thicker patch of brown hair above his erect penis. The expression in the sea foam colored eyes she'd fallen in love with at first sight as they took in every inch of her body was all she could have hoped for. For a millisecond, she had to work on chasing old memories into their closet and focus on the moment she'd dreamed of for so long.

Gently, he pulled the bedspread and top sheet from underneath her in steps as he gradually moved her right leg to the side and lay on top of her. The feeling of her bare breasts against his chest took her to another level. They kissed longer as he rocked and rubbed himself against her hot place. He squeezed and stroked her breast while he held her close with his other hand. She held his neck, sometimes running her fingers through his hair. With a sudden surge of desire, she pulled his hair. "I want you inside me."

He looked into her eyes and saw no doubts or fears. He lifted his hips letting his penis rub against her clitoris and labia, passing over the opening to her vagina several times. She nearly cried out with desire. Finally he firmly thrust himself inside of her. There was some pain, but it was forgotten as they panted together in rhythmic passion with his thrusting hips. With each thrust, she lifted her hips to meet him. Her right leg wrapped around his hip.

It was awkward with the cast; fortunately there was just enough room for his slender hips. The pain in her leg integrated as just another sensation adding to the others as she felt her insides try to pull him farther inside of her. Then her body exploded, her passion rushed from her groin arriving all at once to her head, her toes, and her fingertips.

His thrusts intensified, deepened and came faster as they reached their apex together. With one final thrust, he held himself against her. She held his buttocks with her hand and leg, keeping him there as a series of aftershocks ricocheted through her body. Gradually, he relaxed, letting himself lie on her, but still supporting most of his weight on his elbows, conscious of her half-healed broken ribs, his face buried in her neck, his hot breath tickling her neck.

Finally, he gently pulled away and lay next to her. If her leg and ribs hadn't been hurting she would have kept him on top of her forever. She took his hand and laid it across her face, taking in her smell from his hand. He gently brushed her eyebrows, then her cheeks, and then he kissed her slow and softly.

"Will you stay the night?"

"Man that is a hard one," she replied.

"I know, but will you stay the night?"

She pushed his hand away, laughing, and then tried to push herself up on the pillows. He took charge, arranged the many pillows into a nest for both their heads, and then pulled her up until she was half-seated. She pulled the sheet up to her shoulders. He slid in next to her.

"It's all right. It won't be forever. Once you're independent you will forget the hard, I mean, difficult parts."

She tried to bring back the smile and chase away the frustration. "I don't know what to do. I want to stay here with you, but I don't want Grandpa to lose what respect he has for me. I have to see how they react to this evening. And I'm a lot of trouble to take care of right now. Julia comes in early for my bath and my IV medicines." She looked down at the IV port taped down on her right arm. She'd forgotten all about it. Fortunately, it was taped down well. Suddenly she panicked, "Oh no, we didn't use protection!"

His finger on her lips stopped her. "Remember when I told you I couldn't give my wife a baby, well it's been the same with other women I dated. The doctors said I was sterile, low count and abnormal sperm, so it would be a miracle. But sometimes miracles happen at the most inconvenient times," he said dryly. She smiled, loving every word he said. "Since I have a few healthy swimmers, I'll get supplies tomorrow. I think the odds are good for tonight."

Shyly she added, "I just finished my monthly so I shouldn't be ovulating. And I guess we should have discussed this before. Have you been tested for hepatitis and HIV?"

"You are the first to ever ask that. Good for you."

""It's kind of hard not to think about it here. You didn't know Freddy. He was an angel.""

""Bless him for being your friend."" He paused, "Yes I was tested six months ago and no risks since then. And I'm not going to tell you why I got tested today. Okay?""

She smiled, ""That's better. I don't want to hear about anyone else right now.""

""In any case, I shouldn't have laid the decision on how we manage sleeping arrangements on you alone. I want you here, but this isn't the right time. I know that. This is a small community and you need to feel like they accept you, so you can live here in peace."

She closed her eyes, the bad memories, the shame, threatened to steal the joy of this moment away from her. She felt his hand stroke her forehead and his lips kiss her eyes.

"So," he continued, "we will have to pretend to be teenagers sneaking around their parents. I think that's a Liliana they can accept. You never know, it might add a little spice."

"I don't think I can handle anymore spice."

"Oh, my dear, this is just the beginning," again he gave her his wicked look. "There are some advantages to sleeping with an older, more experienced man."

She would have thought she couldn't blush any hotter. She stroked his hand, "You're right. They'll assume we're . . . making love, but sneaking around might let them know I respect my grandfather's reputation. How stupid is that?"

"Who knows? We might be making too much out of this, but I'd rather be careful, for now. Once they get to know me, maybe they'll stop calling me a dirty old man."

"Who said that?" she snapped.

"Peter," he laughed.

With a sidelong look she relaxed. "The next time I see him I'm going to pull out all the chest hairs he has, one by one."

Terry slipped his arm under her neck, so her head rested on his shoulder. He aimed the remote at the TV and music started.

"Julio Iglesias?"

"Yeah. He's even older than me, but he sings a lot about love and romance."

"I like some of his stuff. Carla liked him, but she only played country western."

"I thought it would be relaxing." His eyes were serious. "Did I rush you? All I could think about since I arrived in Albuquerque was getting a place where we could be alone. Waiting this afternoon and through dinner was killing me. Every time I had a lustful thought, I'd look up to see your grandfather watching me. We spent the whole evening eying each other." She laughed.

"Don't worry. You got it right, Old Man. I would have come and raped you in the middle of the night if you hadn't brought me over."

"You will never have to rape me, Native Warrior. I will always surrender at the first sign of a threat."

"So . . . I need to go back."

"Yeah, it's getting late."

"I don't want to."

"I don't want you to, but it's after ten. I don't want Jim to come with a shotgun to rescue his granddaughter. Let me help you get ready."

He brought a basin of water, soap and a washcloth and gave her gentle, thorough sponge bath. She hadn't considered the odors that clung to a body after satisfying sex. Her grandfather would know them, she was sure. Then he dressed her and sat her in her chair and brushed her hair.

He knelt in front of her and kissed her. "Do you believe me when I say I love you?"

She looked down, again shy. "Yes, of course I do."

He waited. She was confused at his waiting silence, and then realized what he was waiting for. She looked up and saw understanding. Pulling his face close she whispered in his ear, "I love you, too. I can't say it too loud. The wicked spirit that haunts me might take you away."

Silently, he pressed his cheek against hers, and then stood up. She started the chair moving forward and he walked her home.

When she arrived, her grandfather opened the door for her before she touched it. "Well, did Peter do a good job?"

"Yes. The white glove inspection was a success. I give him five stars."

∞

Jim smiled and stepped aside to let her in. Terry wished him goodnight, but he just nodded in return. The guilt in his granddaughter's eyes worried him, but he was grateful that she was happy. Now he would have to wait to see how she processed all these new feelings. Frank had warned him that, although Terry would be good for Liliana, she had many emotional earthquakes in store as old memories were triggered by the happiness she'd found. He was glad Liliana had given Frank permission to speak to him. He was blessed that Liliana trusted him with all her secrets.

∞

Donna arrived to help Liliana into bed. She shut the door behind her as Liliana began the struggle of removing her blouse. Donna smelled the fresh soap and saw the curling fringe of wet, short hairs that surrounded her face. She wanted to respect her niece's privacy, but a combination of curiosity, joy, and her worry about the twist Liliana's history would put on this memory made her ask, even though she saw the look of dread in Liliana's eyes.

"Yes, I'm going to ask. Tell me how it went. I want every detail."

"Aunt Donna, this is too much."

"Okay, too soon. This is the first time you guys have been alone together after everything that's happened. I see the way he looks at you and you look at him. I get hot just being around you two."

Liliana giggled, and then looked up with tears in her eyes. Donna hugged her. "So it was scary. It's always scary. We would all breed like rabbits as soon as we reached puberty if it wasn't scary."

Liliana took her hand and said, "I can't even describe how awesome he is. I don't deserve anyone so perfect."

Donna leaned back. "Number two: no man is perfect. Number one: you deserve everything wonderful." *Oh, dear Lord, don't let him break her heart.* "So, can you talk about it tonight?"

Liliana shook her head.

"Will you tell me soon?"

Liliana shrugged.

"Well, that's not a 'no.' I'll just have to wait." She handed Liliana her pain meds and Valium and pulled the blankets up to Liliana's neck. "Try to get some sleep. Call me if you need anything." She placed the remotes to the TV, lights, and the intercom to her room next to Liliana, kissed her cheek and left. Liliana took the pain meds and left the Valium.

She's cold, her leg feels like it's being ripped into pieces, her ribs and her arm send jabbing pain with the slightest movement. A glimmer of light from one highway halogen lamp splashes eerily on the water in the truck, reflecting off the chrome and the mirror. Her throat burns, her sunburned eyes feel dry and swollen. Her right hand comes up to wipe the goop that clings to her eyelashes and she glances up to the rearview mirror and Joe's there in the mirror, a knife in his hand. He's behind her. But how can he be? There's no backseat. His smell fills her nostrils. She's trapped. She's lost her knife. She struggles to get free and screams with pain and fear . . .

The horrific scream pulled Donna out of her bed before she was awake. She rushed to Liliana's room to find Liliana thrashing in the bed, trying to rip the cast off her left arm with her teeth and nails. As soon as Donna reached the bed the lights turned on and she glanced back to see her father in the doorway, eyes wide, his hair standing on end.

"He's here! He's here! I'm stuck! Get me out! Help me! He's going to kill me! Momma help me! MOMMA . . ." Liliana screamed. When Donna tried to hold her right arm, Liliana struck out. "Noo, don't touch me!"

"Liliana, it's your aunt. You're okay. You're safe. Wake up, Sweetheart. Please, wake up. You're safe."

Still struggling, Liliana's eyes opened. They were wide and wild, her pupils dilated in fear. Panicked, she looked frantically around her. Donna took her face in her hands while her father held tightly to Liliana's right hand. "Look at me, Liliana. It's me. You're safe."

Angelo's sleepy voice came from the doorway. "What's going on, Mom?"

His grandfather answered, "Get the pills that say diazepam. Then set up the nebulizer for a treatment. Call Dr. Karnes."

Gradually, Liliana's eyes began to focus on Donna's. "He was here. He was in the truck's mirror. He's in the mirrors. He's going to get me." Her voice and body shook with panic.

Angelo handed Jim the pills and a glass of water. Liliana was startled by the movement then recognized Angelo. Her panic began to change to confusion.

"Here, Baby, take this pill. It will help your breathing." Liliana shook her head. "Please take it. It's safe. If you don't take it you might have to go to the hospital."

Liliana's eyes widened, and then she took the pill and spilled half the water as she tried to drink with trembling hands. Soon afterward Angelo set the steam spouting nebulizer on the bed. "What do I tell the doctor?" he asked.

Donna held Liliana's head against her chest, kissing the top of her head. "It's okay, son, I'll call him."

As Liliana's panic receded, she started to cry, sobbing into Donna's arms. "I want my momma. Why did she leave me? He was there! He came after me."

"It's okay, Liliana. It was a bad dream. He's gone. He can't get you anymore. You're safe." She looked up to her father and nodded. He went to get the phone. As he passed the door, someone knocked. Unsurprised, he let Terry in. Donna could hear them in the hall.

"Sleep walking, eh?" he asked. Terry's eyes were nearly as wide as Liliana's were.

"I'm sorry. I was walking around the neighborhood. I couldn't sleep. I heard her scream, can I come in?"

"Sure, go on in. I'm going to call Frank."

"This is still happening. Has it been as bad as in the hospital?"

"No. This is the worst since she got here. Go, go on in." He turned toward the living room while Terry quietly stepped up to her bed.

Liliana's face was buried in Donna's chest, holding the blue tube from the nebulizer in her teeth as she cried and wheezed. He touched Donna's shoulder and she nodded without looking up, her cheek pressed against the top of Liliana's head.

Angelo stood next to her making sure the nebulizer didn't tip over. "She had a bad dream. She saw him in a mirror. Hold this." Terry held the machine while Angelo left and returned with a hand mirror. He held the mirror out to Liliana. "Look, Liliana. See it's safe. He's not in the mirror. Look, he's not there."

He held the mirror in front of her face. She looked up to see her reflection in mirror. "No!" she yelled, and struck the mirror from his hand. Angelo stepped back, shocked.

"I'm sorry. I was just trying to help." Angelo struggled to hold back his tears.

"It's okay, Angelo. She's still in shock. You had a good idea." Terry gave him a hug, and then moved in as Donna made room for him next to Liliana. She hugged Angelo.

"It was a very good idea, Hijo. It's okay. Why don't you ask your grandpa if Dr. Karnes is going to come over?"

Angelo nodded and slowly turned to leave, his worried eyes on his cousin. Donna brushed his hair off his face and gently nudged him on his way.

She turned to see that Terry had wrapped his arms around Liliana with his head pressed to hers. Liliana was no longer shaking and was holding on to him with her good arm. Donna sat at the foot of the bed, counting Liliana's respirations. Her breathing was slowing down and the wheezing wasn't as bad. She checked Liliana's fingertips, wanting to see her lips, but not willing to disturb her as she calmed down. She squeezed Terry's shoulder and left to tell her father that they might not need the doctor.

When she got to the kitchen, Dr. Karnes had just gotten to the phone. Her father handed her the phone, placed his elbows on the table and covered his face. She rubbed his shoulders as she took the phone.

"This is Dr. Karnes."

"I'm sorry to wake you, but Liliana's had a bad panic attack."

"That's okay. I'm in the ER stitching up a kid. What happened?"

Donna described the incident, and gave him her rate of breathing, her color and how she sounded.

"It sounds like you're managing okay. Do you want me to stop by?"

"I think we can manage this time." She took a deep breath.

"Good. I'll call when I finish here to make sure she's stable before I leave. Is that okay? Are you comfortable managing this."

"Yes, we're okay. That's great, Doctor. I'll talk to you then." She hung up and turned to hug her father and son together. "We knew this was coming. She's been doing too well so soon after everything that's happened. It's good that Terry's here."

Jim nodded doubtfully. She went to stand in the hall to see how Liliana was doing without interfering. If Terry wanted a life with Liliana, he would have to learn to handle the results of all the trauma Liliana had suffered. She hoped he was up to it.

Terry knew Liliana was keeping a secret, a secret that could only hurt her. He'd seen it in the way she avoided mirrors. She'd let her hair grow out without Adela to cut it, and he had watched her apply mascara without her reflection to guide her. His wife had not been very vain, but she checked her reflection whenever a mirror was near.

He remembered Carla's cruelty when she told him that Liliana looked just like Joe and Liliana still believed that everyone thought she looked like Joe. He had tried to help indirectly, by telling her how much she looked like Donna and the pictures of her mother, Susana. Liliana would shrug, smile and kiss him and then look away with troubled eyes, if she was in a good mood. He didn't try to bring up the subject when her eyes were filled with dark clouds.

As horrible as the dream must have been, Terry feared Liliana's bigger problem was what lay behind that dream. Liliana saw Joe in her own reflection, and seemed to hate her image, or herself, as much she hated him. Her dream about Joe being in the truck was terrible by itself, but it presented with his image in a mirror. There was a link Liliana might partially understand, and fear; the only solution was to bring the secret out and so far she had seemed too fragile to handle it.

He couldn't escape his own guilt; he was sure that her first sexual experience, even though it was with someone she loved, had triggered the dream. Not that he could have waited. It was hard enough for him to manage his own desire, but he had felt her burning for him in her voice, her glance, her touch. Every time he let an opportunity pass to do more than kiss, believing that it would be too soon, he could see the self-doubt growing in her eyes. She needed to believe; he needed her to believe in the depth of his love.

Thinking it through as they sat holding onto each other as her trembling slowly calmed, he decided that it was good news that she had made it through this attack without having to go to the emergency room.

"When I was little one time I asked Carla why she didn't have any pictures of me in the apartment."

"What did she say?"

"She said, 'Why do I need pictures of you? All I have to do is look at Joe to see you.'"

"Liliana, you don't look like Joe." He waited.

Then finally, "Yeah," she responded in a disbelieving voice.

He felt the tension in her shoulders. He wanted to see her face, but she held on tight, her face buried in his chest.

"What are you thinking, Liliana? Talk to me."

She pushed away, shrugging off his hands and turned away from him. He reached for her chin; she pushed his hand away angrily.

"It was just a bad dream. Why does everyone want to get all psychoanalytical on me? I would be like anyone else of I didn't have asthma." She'd managed to twist around to where her hunched over back was all he could see.

"It's not just the asthma, Liliana. You know that. The accident alone would have traumatized anyone. You have good reasons to have PTSD, even if Carla and Joe had never been in your life. I know Frank has discussed group therapy with you."

"I already tried that last year. A bunch of whiners. I don't need them." She twisted around to face him. She was angry. "I can handle this on my own if all you guys would just leave me alone once in a while. God, I can't do anything alone!" She turned away, rubbing her face. "I don't think this is going to work out. I'm not ready for a relationship and I know you don't want a train wreck. Just leave me alone, will you!"

Donna stepped in behind Terry. "Liliana," Donna said gently, "we want to help you. You don't have to do this on your own. Tell us where it hurts. Maybe together we can make it better."

Liliana shook her head. "Just go away and leave me alone! I just need some time alone!" Her voice was shrill with anger.

Terry closed his eyes as the pain in her voice stabbed at his heart. She couldn't accept help right now. She couldn't tell them what hurt. He was frustrated even though he understood her reaction. It was the fear that if you took one more step toward your pain that all the things you struggled to manage would break through and wipe you out. In addition she feared that if she was too much trouble they would give up on her. He had gone through a similar state of mind as he decided that divorce was the only option for his miserable marriage. It was a state of all or nothing, misery or total destruction. There was no place to maneuver from that place. All you could do was freeze and hope the chaos settled on its own, or leave. Terry wasn't sure he had the patience to help her through that storm. He knew he wasn't a saint; he had a temper of his own. Yet at this moment he was not angry; he just hurt and he could not leave her.

"I'll be outside if you need me." He took Donna's arm, led her out of the bedroom and pulled the door nearly shut, giving Liliana the space she'd requested. In the hall, Donna looked like she wanted to talk, but he shook his head and stepped outside shutting the front door behind him. Out of the corner of his eye, he could see Donna peeking at him through the living room curtains, making sure he wouldn't turn and ask for her help.

He walked around the house to the garden in the back yard. The sun was cautiously sending orange tendrils over the horizon, testing the sky to see if it was ready for the day. It was light enough to see that the corn would be ready to pick soon; there were chilies that were ready to pick. He didn't know anything about growing beans, but they looked ready to him. Pale pink, blue and white morning glories cautiously relaxed their petals to the gentle morning light, letting bees probe their depths, but ready to close them again when the sun was too bright and too hot.

He touched the soft petals. They were like Liliana: fragile, yet able to grow almost anywhere, closing their colorful sex to protect it from being traumatized by too much light. A few bees were getting an early start. When one bee couldn't get inside the morning glory blossom it had picked, it settled for the busty, brilliant zinnia brazenly competing for its attention.

Sometimes Liliana was the zinnia, confident, in your face. Then she would be the morning glory, opening for a while, and then closing up tight when it got dangerous.

Damn, he could have waited, he wished again, but it was one of those situations: damned if you do; damned if you don't. He could feel Liliana's pain through the phone the entire time he was gone. She was afraid he would leave her, but paradoxically, she was more afraid that he would leave *because* she was so afraid he would leave. Carla had taught her to fear needing anyone; so she struggled to hide her need. If he hadn't made the decision to consummate their love, she would have believed he didn't love her. However, just the fact that she had needed the reassurance the love-making gave her made her ashamed. He wished he could love that shame away.

He'd not yet told her about his second love, because he didn't want her to think he was comparing her to the woman who lived in Albuquerque, too close for comfort. He loved Liliana more than he'd ever loved anyone, but Liliana would be angry and insecure, when she found out he had waited to tell her.

Alex was a slightly older woman who lived a solitary life believing she was unlovable. They were together for a year. During that time, she shared all her childhood pain with him. Because she was older and had years of therapy under her belt, she was aware of her unearned guilt and the behaviors it triggered. He learned a lot from her. When she was ready to move on, deciding she really did prefer to live alone, and wasn't lonely anymore, he accepted her decision. He stayed away for a few months, and then they were able to be friends. Occasionally, he wondered if Alex could help Liliana. She could, if she hadn't been his lover.

His eyes had strayed to Mount Taylor while he remembered. Sunlight sat on the mountain top and snuck down its slopes. He turned away to walk to the small, empty barn and corral. Something touched his calf and he looked down to see Girlfriend loving his leg, rubbing his face on his jeans. He stooped down to pet him. In response, Girlfriend closed his eyes and lifted his chin to be scratched, revealing with his extended, vulnerable neck his willingness to trust a relative stranger.

"Why do we like to hurt each other so much, Girlfriend? Where does all that meanness come from?"

He reached under the hefty cat's belly and lifted him to his shoulder. Girlfriend allowed one short hug, then climbed over his shoulder and sprang away from his back. He then sat down to settle his disarranged fur, indicating that humans would be okay if they weren't such a bother. Then he stared expectantly at Terry. When the screen door opened, he raced over and did a happy dance around Jim's legs as Jim filled a dish with cat food. Girlfriend dove in, immediately losing interest in the human that fed him.

Jim joined Terry in his walk to the barn. "Where are you headed, son?"

Terry smiled sadly, "I thought I might visit old Paint."

"Yeah. Since Liliana's been hurt she hasn't paid much attention to old Paint. Or maybe it's because her mind is full of something else."

Terry sighed. "I hate to see her hurting. Carla filled her head with so much garbage, but she loved her anyway. I think she's ashamed to grieve for Carla, or maybe she's just confused."

"And guilty."

"For what?" Terry snapped, and then took a breath. "Sorry. You mean guilty for being loved when Carla never was."

"Yup." Jim kicked a rock and watched it skip away. "How long are you going to give her? I assume you have a plan."

"I wish I did. Her life has been turned upside down. She can't work off the negative energy like she's used to doing. And she's too damned independent to accept help easily. It's getting to her."

"She has an appointment with the infection specialist tomorrow. Frank called in to push them a little; that's why this appointment is so soon. He'll decide if they can do the next surgery now. She hasn't given the medical school an answer yet if she's going to start next month or next year." Jim leaned on the corral fence and watched the edge of the sun grab the edge of the horizon, pulling itself upward, ready to bake everything that braved its presence.

"Why?" Jim asked, looking into Terry's eyes when they turned to him in confusion. Jim started walking and Terry followed.

"Why hasn't she notified the school?"

Jim shook his head. "Why do you care so much? From the first time I met you up to now, you have been filled up with her. Like that," Jim snapped his fingers, "she picked you up on the freeway. She took you to see her crazy grandmother. You stayed with her in that wino motel. A stinking drunk tried to steal your wallet. Then she took off from your ranch leaving you to get arrested by the FBI." He shook his head. "Man, I would have headed for the hills after meeting Carla, much less stick around after getting arrested. Donna thinks it happened when you rescued her, but you were hers way before that." He turned to look at him, and then looked down at his boots. "I wonder why, but then I see her crazy for you. She's had a few dates and that semester with that Navajo kid. Donna told me about them, but it's never been like this for her, which might not mean anything since she never really had a chance with Carla around. Anyway, Donna said she was already crazy for you when she brought you to the house. What, less than an hour after you guys met? Why? I know I loved my wife, but we knew each other since she was born. Donna didn't decide on her husband until she knew him six months . . . It's just crazy."

Terry tried to answer the first question, and then realized that Liliana's grandfather was just working through his own thoughts. Then the old man stopped and turned to face Terry with his fists on his hips. "I think I'm glad you're here to help, but she would go through this stuff if she never met you, and we would help her and, with God's blessing, she would eventually get better. Why are you here?" His head was tilted to one side, his eyes focused on Terry's eyes.

Terry had to look away. "I'm sorry. I can't explain it. I can make a list of all the things I love about her, but I don't know why it adds up the way it does."

"You were married for eight years."

"Yeah."

"What happened?"

"Oh, I don't know . . ." Jim snorted, sounding just like Liliana. Terry smiled sadly and continued, "Okay, I think I loved her looks and her energy, but there was never a deep link. She said she wanted kids, but, now she's been married six years with a man that can give her kids and she doesn't want any. She liked expensive toys and I wasn't ambitious enough. The more she had, the more superficial she got. Then it was over."

"You're sterile? Does Liliana know?"

"She knows, but she brushes it aside and says if she ever wants kids there's a lot of reservation orphans. I don't know if it doesn't matter or if she doesn't want to think about it. We'll talk about it again when things have settled down a bit. It still feels like I'm on an out-of-control railroad train when I'm around her."

Jim laughed. "If you think that's going to change, you don't know Liliana."

"Yeah. She's been tied down with the casts so long, I forgot how she never stops moving."

"Yup. She managed all of her families, graduated two years early from high school and already finished college and she turns just 21 in a week. She's a high energy girl."

"Next week? We never talked about birthdays. Are we . . ." He turned when he heard Donna call for him. He jogged back to the door.

"She's asking for you."

"Thanks."

$$\infty$$

Donna smiled as her dad passed by her. "Did you get your answer?"

"Heck, he knows less than I do about what's going on."

"How can love work any other way? It's a blessing, not a strategy."

"How's our girl?"

"She's crying."

He nodded, "Good. Tears can wash away a lot of pain."

"At least she's not keeping it all locked up in that closet of hers. It must be getting crowded in there."

"Closet?"

"That's what she calls the place for stuff she doesn't want to think about. She told me about it years ago. I'd forgotten until today."

∞

Oh, God, oh God, oh God, he's going to hate me. I'm so damn weak and mean. Why do I say those things? I hate it all. Most of all, I hate him seeing me like this. I don't want to be carried around and have pillows fluffed. They are driving me crazy! I have to stop being such a whiner. Nobody loves people who cry all the time.

She had been sobbing all out since he left the room. Her eyes and throat ached, but her tears dried as she realized that she was repeating Carla's words: "Stop crying, nobody likes crybabies. Susana told me you were always whining and I wouldn't like taking care of you. That's why she never let me baby-sit. She thought you would drive me crazy. She loved me more than you." She had to unwind that tape and throw it into the bonfire in her mind, but right now it was stuck on play.

How could she miss Carla? Why did her heart ache when she realized her grandmother was dead? No one liked Carla, except maybe Eddie. It was like he was infected with Carla. Carla treated him like shit and he kept coming around anyway. Liliana remembered Eddie throwing the ball in a slow, round curve so little Liliana had plenty of time to catch it. Then he'd patiently fetch it from the street after she missed. She must have been seven years old.

But she could only blame herself for acting like a bitch to Terry. Tears had come to his eyes when she yelled at him. *Oh, please, God, let him forgive me, again.*

Liliana had managed to scoot herself back so she could lean on the headboard. As she checked the places she'd torn the cast; she was surprised to see a river of tears pouring onto it. A deep sob pushed its way out of her chest. She covered her face with a pillow.

"Shall we name this pillow the snot pillow?" Her shoulders started shaking as she laughed and cried with relief at the sound of Terry's voice. Sometimes, he managed to make her feel better with just the right words. Okay, sometimes he missed. Liliana lowered the pillow to see him open a new box of tissues and replace the empty one at her side. He swept the pile of used tissues into the trash can without hesitation.

"You even put up with my snot. You put up with me when I am being a snot. Why?"

He set the trash can down, put his hands on his hips and tilted his head to one side, just like her grandpa did, she giggled, just a little hysterical. With a wry smile he leaned over and kissed her red, swollen lips. Then he climbed on the bed to sit next to her.

"You're grandpa just asked me the same thing. What's with why? I can't write out the series of chemical reactions, or the names of the pheromones, or the theory of human attraction. I just love you."

"Maybe we could write it up and get a grant to research the issue." The words were light, but her voice was heavy with grief. He pushed his arm over the pillows so he could hold her shoulders. Then he pressed his head against hers.

"Okay. You can't tell me what's hurting. I'll start guessing and you can start crying again when I've hit the spot."

"You are so wise, or is it wise-ass?"

"You're not going to get out of this by ridiculing me." He leaned forward to make sure the door was shut. "Here we go. Number one: I was such a lousy lover that you are weeping with disappointment."

She snorted and punched his leg.

"Ow, be careful. I was ravaged by a wild, beautiful woman just hours ago. Number two: You'd rather have your arm and leg cut off than have to put up with the casts one minute longer."

She moaned. "That one is almost true."

She waited, "Well what's number three?"

He had his eyes closed as if concentrating. "I'm trying to decide which one of the dozens of possibilities is number three. This is it. Number three: You miss Carla desperately and either A: hate yourself for missing her; B: think you're stupid for being gullible enough to love her; C: you think you need a straight jacket, because you'd have to be crazy to miss all the shit she put you through."

He reached around with his right arm and leaned in to hug her close as she heaved with deep sobs. She started trying to get her right arm free, so he brought the tissue box to her lap, pulled out three and began wiping her nose. "I think this is too much for tissues. We may have to resort to the snot pillow." She pushed her face into his chest, still shaking with hard sobs. "I guess a snot shirt will work just fine." She felt his deep sigh as he held on to her.

She heard Donna open the door quietly and set up the nebulizer. Liliana tried to control her resentment at the fate that had given her asthma. It was hard to breathe and cry at the same time, but she could deal. Donna set the machine on the bed, plugged it in, and then left, shutting the door firmly behind her.

"I wonder if she was listening when you agreed that I was a lousy lover. My reputation will be ruined."

"Didmmmmt"

"What did you say?"

"Did not!"

"Oh, I guess I misunderstood. I know I've cried right after sex, but usually I'm alone." He paused. "Actually, some women have complained, but no one has actually cried."

"What other women?" she mumbled into his shirt between sobs.

"There have been so many I can't possibly remember them all."

She tried to take a deep breath to produce a sharp retort, but could only start crying again.

He stroked her hair, and then began combing it with his fingers. In the nearly dark room, her hair looked jet black, the red tips a brilliant complement to the black. He wondered how she'd managed to get a bright red over the black. Adela had probably done it for her. Then he wondered if she planned to let it grow out. He had a wicked thought. No, it was too soon. It would wait for another day, but maybe he could nudge her forward on the issue that worried him most.

He brushed her hair back from her forehead and kissed the dark pink scar from the accident. To hell with it. She'd managed the rest and he wasn't afraid of her getting mad at him if he blew it. He took a thick strand of hair and stretched it out.

"I guess I'm going to have to learn to fix your hair since Adela's not here and you won't look into a mirror."

He felt her shoulders tense up. "I guess I'm too much of a freak for you," she responded angrily, but she didn't push him away.

Well, he'd gone too far. "I'm sorry, I crossed the line," he kissed her head. "This really worries me, Liliana. Can I tell you why?"

"No."

Okay. He'd have to keep worrying. When he didn't push the topic after several minutes she started to relax.

"Did you know that your grandpa feeds Girlfriend?"

"He doesn't like cats."

"Well, Girlfriend certainly likes him."

She pulled back to lean on the pillows and started wiping her face with the tissues. Terry got a wet washcloth. She reached for it, but he wanted to clean her face for her. She looked annoyed when he pushed her hand away and gently started wiping her forehead, but she put up with it.

"Grandpa liked Freddy when he was little. Then he started letting his feminine side out and Grandpa figured out that he was gay. It wasn't 'til Freddy's family got tired of taking care of him that Grandpa accepted who he was and started helping him. Donna told me Grandpa was the one who fixed up the house for Freddy, then it turned out to be useful for you and me."

"I don't think your grandfather is sure about me, yet." He waited for a jibe at white men, but, when she finally spoke, she was serious.

"Sometimes Carla and I made cookies together. I don't think we ever got a whole batch. She'd either get bored in the middle, forget and burn half of them, or one of her friends would show up. It would be fun for a little while. It was pretty rare when I was little and disappeared about three years ago. Since then she would work herself into raging tantrums, because I was spending so much time in Albuquerque. She never admitted she missed me."

"She wanted you so much she fought the world to keep you with her. What did she have without you? Maybe, in some broken way she loved you, but she was too wrecked to be able to show it or even know it. You took care of her, Liliana Hunt. She would have come to a bad end a long time ago if she hadn't had to fight for you and if you hadn't tried to keep her healthy."

"Yeah, sometimes it was like she lived for the fight. She acted like it was because she wanted to show everyone that she could keep me no matter what she did. It made her feel powerful."

"So you made cookies together. What were some other good times?" He folded the washcloth and tossed it onto the rug. Then he settled in next to her. He began to think she wasn't going to answer.

"She'd take me to the bar with her and I'd get a Shirley Temple with lots of cherries. Her friends would say how cute I was."

"What did she say then?"

"Sometimes it was the 'this is my pride and joy' rap, or she'd tell them about how much I looked like Joe."

She jumped when the alarm clock went off. "I hate that thing," she sighed. "Julia will be here soon. It smells like Donna made coffee, could you bring me some."

Well, we got further than I thought we would. It would take time. "It does smell good. Is there any of her bread left?"

"I don't know. Frank and Peter might have swiped the last of it."

He stood at the door looking at her. She'd cried so much her voice was hoarse. "Last night was wonderful. Please, don't feel bad. Just because you're older doesn't mean you're responsible for everything. I'm an adult. I know what I want." She looked up to meet his eyes.

He smiled, "Yes and you'll be one year older next week."

Her forehead creased, "It is? Damn, I forgot all about it."

"I bet Peter didn't."

"Don't you dare remind him!" Terry smirked and she threw a pillow at him.

Chapter 14

From Beyond the Grave

Another month of antibiotics, at least, the doctor had said. Jim, Terry and Liliana were in the large cab truck Terry's father had left him, driving home from her visit with the infectious disease specialist in Albuquerque. They had Liliana cocooned with pillows that she pushed away in frustration. She really wanted to rip the pillows to pieces. Terry had offered to take her to a swanky restaurant for lunch, but now she wasn't in the mood.

After getting the verdict, they had stopped by the administration office of the University Medical School to notify them that she couldn't start in August. Everyone was so sympathetic that all she wanted to do was punch the next sympathetic face. If it was just the antibiotics there would be no problem, but the surgery would come at the beginning of the semester. It looked like they were going to have to put an external extender brace with the bone grafts to be sure the bones came out the right length. When she complained, her orthopedist told her she should have been in traction for weeks longer, but they were worried about her anxiety attacks and asthma. She thanked him for being truthful, as she fought back the rage at her weakness. She would have clinical and laboratory classes that she couldn't manage with one leg sticking straight out. She had a sneaky feeling that Doctor Frank had talked to Dr. Kauffman about her PTSD. Dr. Kauffman had seemed a little relieved when he heard her decision. It would take time to plan Frank's murder, but first she had to prove he was guilty.

If she allowed herself to face the truth, she couldn't blame this on anyone else. It was her own fault. No one else had driven her off the road. She didn't even want to talk to Terry, who, unlike her grandfather, expected her to talk about what was going on in her head. Right now everything was dismal; she wanted to drive off a cliff and leave it all behind, but she sure wasn't going to tell Terry that. He'd have Doctor Frank, Jake and Peter help him stand 24 hour watch on her. She was ready to start school. She needed to start school. It was the only thing that kept her head from exploding.

She watched the back of Terry's head, needing a target for her anger. He hadn't brought up her temper tantrum after her dream two nights ago. She hated it when someone had something on her. It kept her on edge, waiting for payback. Carla had been the most predictable, but she was getting good at predicting her aunt and grandfather. Terry hadn't revealed his payback yet. She knew he had one, everybody did: an indirect criticism, a forgotten favor, telling her teachers that she was a slut.

To top it off Dr. Kauffman had other news to pass on. He spoke to her alone to tell her that someone had sent in a copy of her juvenile record from Grants. He knew about what Carla had done to sabotage her granddaughter's success at school and had agreed to keep it secret. The only living person she knew that would go to so much trouble to get her payback was Joe's widow, Lorraine. It had to be her. If it was Lorraine, that bitch would find out what real payback was.

Dr. Kauffman reassured her that once she told the story to the committee, the problem would disappear, but she didn't want to talk about it. She just wanted to erase Carla from her memory and start her life all over.

Terry helped her into her electric wheel chair without a word. He'd installed an electric lift on his truck so she could take the heavy chair with them. Once she was home, she went to her room and shut the door. It would be so much easier, as she had so clearly told him, if it wasn't for her asthma no one would fuss when she got upset. Her episodes in the hospital had scared her family stupid. If it wasn't for Dr. Karnes' reassurances, they would have put cameras in her room and surveillance on her chair, so they could reassure themselves that she was okay every minute of the day.

∞

Peter stopped by to learn the verdict on her infection. When he walked in the door he saw three worried people sitting in the kitchen. The object of their worry locked away in her room.

"Okay, so who died?"

Terry looked up, annoyed. Donna punched Peter's arm.

"Well, tell me. What did the doctor say?"

Jim answered. "Her blood cultures came out positive. She's still got the infection. She has to wait for the surgery. She decided to delay entering the medical school at least until January."

"So she's mad. But she knew this could happen. What's this Big Deal? You all look like the world is ending."

Donna set a mug of tea in front of a chair. Peter sat down and picked up the mug. "You guys have been spoiled. You've never seen a really mad Liliana. I could tell you some stories. So could Jake and Frank. She can be a real brat."

"Dr. Kauffman told her something that set her off. She won't tell us what he said," Jim replied.

"Ever since her sidebar with Dr. Kauffman," Terry added, ""she's been sparking electricity. All I get is yes and no answers or silence. When I tried to ask her about her plans for school, she told me to "cut the unnecessary verbiage." I figured it was time to leave her alone for a while."

Peter rubbed Terry's shoulder, ""So she told you to shut up. You should hear some of the things she's told me to do, most of them physically impossible."" He leaned forward and caught a trace of a smile on Terry's face. "If she's so mad that she's turned you all upside down, you know it has to be Carla."

"But what can Carla do from the other side?" Donna worried.

"Oh, you didn't know Carla very well, did you? Have you heard about any crops dying, cows going dry or husbands going mad?"

"Peterrrr. She wasn't a witch and she's definitely dead," Donna protested. Peter just raised his eyebrows.

"Where's Girlfriend? When afraid of claws, bring your own."

Donna shook her head. Peter was incorrigible. "He's on the patio."

Peter took a sip of tea then stood up purposely and went to fetch the cat. "Come on, Girlfriend. A child has fallen in the well and we have to rescue her."

With the cat on his shoulder he knocked on Liliana's door and opened it immediately. "Oh, doom and gloom, Sweet Thing. You have everybody scared to death . . . My, my, such language. Do you kiss Mr. Handsome with that mouth?" The door shut and they heard no more.

Terry rubbed his eyes. "I think I'll head home. I got an offer on the house today. I have to contact the realtor to see if the buyers were approved by the bank. Call me. No, never mind. She knows where I am, if she wants to talk."

"She really hurt his feelings," Donna said after he left.

"It wasn't pretty," her father replied. "She yelled at me, too."

Donna smiled at his exaggerated whine and kissed his head. "You poor thing. Do you have a special request for supper?"

"Yes, lamb chili and fried bread."

"You are so predictable. You have to go to the store for the lamb, and..."

A loud crash came from the room. Jim stood up, alarmed. Peter called out, "It's okay. No war wounds . . . yet."

Peter stood against the door, out of her way as Liliana maneuvered the compact, electric wheel chair to pace back and forth in the small room. The crash was a result of her extended leg knocking over a small table by her bed. When he tried to retrieve it she snapped, "Just leave it there, dammit. You don't have to pick up after me."

"Yes, ma'am," Peter said, exaggerating his alarm to match her rage. Raised by a bipolar mother, he had early training in working with bad tempers.

"I'll kill her. That stupid bitch. Why didn't she croak along with the other two?"

"I put in *my* request," Peter replied. "But God wasn't listening. Anyway, you don't know for sure that it was her. Carla's had lots of enemies who resent your success."

"Nah. It was Lorraine. Carla was at her house all that last night. She had a copy of the police report and it's not in the box of papers you brought me. Lorraine did her dirty work."

"You said Dr. Kauffman told you it would be fine. Except for that your record is clean and your school reports are perfect."

"You forgot that she accused me of murder last month. The FBI came for me, Peter. Anyway, I know I'll get in. It's just that now the gossip will spread all over the school, again! I just wanted a fresh start."

"But for them it will just be rumor. None of them know Carla." he paused. ""Have you thought about going out of state? Mr. Moneypockets would fund you."

"Don't call him that! Anyway, how long is he going to stick around? Every time I turn around more shit falls from the sky. Eventually, he'll figure out what I am and give up."

"What are you that's so terrible?" He sat on the bed petting the cat that ignored anything that didn't include him. Despite the noisy crash, Girlfriend was calmly purring. "To me you're just another beautiful genius."

She snorted. "Right. I'm a train wreck. Everything is wrong. I don't know how to act with regular people. I hate these casts. I hate that bed. I hate everything."

"Sounds like you hate yourself, Liliana," he said quietly.

"How can anyone love me when I hate myself?"

"You'd be surprised. I hated me when I met Frank."

"Frank's a saint."

"And Terry's not? Girl, he put your grandmother to bed and got out unscathed."

"Unscathed, huh?" Liliana sent him a skeptical glare.

"Yes, it's my new word for the week. I have to use it five more times."

She leaned her arm on the small table in front of the window and rubbed her forehead. "I get so tired; I just want it to end."

Peter pulled over a stool to sit next to her and rub her back, while he unobtrusively took inventory of all the medications in the room. "I would miss you too much, Sweetie. You can't let it end."

He pulled a huge pink handkerchief from his back pocket and gave it to her. She covered her face, catching all the tears. "Another snotty day."

"Oh, do you mean real snot, or how you treated Terry and Jim?"

"He's not going to keep on forgiving me," she choked.

"Maybe not. But I think he still has lots more forgiving left in his heart."

After some time behind the pink hanky, Peter heard a mumbled, "No chocolate."

"Oh, nooo," he responded in mock distress. "I have a new recipe. You'll like this one, I promise. Please, please, please. There has to be chocolate cake."

"Then you'll have to make two."

"I can deal. That's cool. Vanilla with raspberry frosting."

"As long as it's not chocolate."

Terry picked out a colorful shirt from his closet and threw it on the bed. Peter said the theme for Liliana's birthday was Hawaii and offered Terry one of his shirts, but this shirt would do. It was a gag present from his first wife, the message that accompanied it was angry since his employers had unexpectedly canceled his vacation due to some emergency he couldn't even remember now. The shirt was supposed to be a thank-you-for-finally-taking-a-vacation-with-me to Hawaii gift, but it had turned into a remember-what-we-could-have-had gift. All he had from that painful, drawn out destruction of their vows of marriage was this shirt that he found in his luggage with a card attached. His gut had wrenched when he found it as he finally unpacked his clothes in his new apartment six years ago, but he kept it as a reminder of the mistakes he'd made. In the shirt he imbedded a vow to protect himself, to tell himself the truth at all times and to remember that fairy tales were just stories.

Liliana came over to apologize for being a jerk after her visit with Peter. He understood her rage, but it hurt when she locked him out. When he asked her why, she just cried. They'd made superficial small talk after he accepted her apology and she calmed down. Then she went home with the real issue unresolved. He hated making her cry so he dropped it. Maybe he was wrong. He thought he knew the root of her problem, but maybe it was something else. If she couldn't trust him with her pain, then there wasn't much of a future for their relationship.

Everyone in the Hunt home was trying to recover from Carla's attack from the grave. Jim and Frank went to confront Lorraine. She admitted that Carla had given her the report to send to the medical school to make sure that Liliana paid for murdering Joe. Lorraine insisted that Liliana was so smart she had found a way to kill Joe that no one could figure out in response to the argument that Liliana was not a suspect. She laughed at their anger. There was nothing they could do. It was a true report; no slander or libel was involved on Lorraine's part.

Worst of all, it was clear that Liliana couldn't let it go. She tried to smile and talk, but would lapse into brooding silences. Donna worried that Liliana was close to giving up. Even though Terry knew Liliana would never give up, he prayed that she had the reserves to get past this with him at her side. She would never give up, but she could become self-destructive enough to drive him away. It didn't help that the Fowler crime had heated up in the press as the widows fought over the substantial inheritance. The news services retold the story of the murders over and over, making a sensation out of the current battle over the Fowler fortune.

Locally, some were blaming Liliana for the murder/suicide of the two policemen. He'd seen the looks for himself when he took her with him to get groceries one afternoon. He just couldn't understand how so many normally, kind, rational people could justify blaming the victim for the results of their victimization. It wore him out.

If he could be sure his life would work out with Liliana, he would be happy. He had been happy that night. They'd both been happy. Then her demons attacked in her sleep. Then the damn infection didn't clear, so she couldn't see a future with her independence restored any time soon. Then came Carla's ambush from the grave.

They weren't talking as easily as they did before. He was trying to act the same with her as he had before they had sex. He thought that he was doing all right, but he was sure she was feeling ashamed. With the roller coaster of her life, the deaths, accusations, the long day in the wrecked truck, broken and dying alone and hopeless, there wasn't any emotional space left to heal and decide together what had changed after their night of intimacy. He still believed they had a good thing, but it was beginning to look like he was wrong.

∞

Liliana was terrified that he was beginning to dislike her and it was all her fault. She didn't know what to do. He was going to leave her, but she couldn't be better for him. Her rage consumed her. It filled her mind day and night. She had let down her barriers long enough to cry for Carla and BAM! Carla struck again. She should have known that she wouldn't be able to get through medical school without Carla fucking it up. Lord, how she hated being this angry.

She knew she had a staunch ally in Dr. Kauffman and she knew Frank would fight tooth and nail to fix the problem. However, spreading secrets, gossip and stupid, judging humans couldn't be avoided; they had afflicted Liliana all her life.

Terry hadn't called yet. The guests would start arriving soon for the patio barbecue Jim and Peter had been working on all day. They had a spitted lamb, turning, roasting. She could smell it and it made her feel sick. Today, and maybe forever she was going veggie. Death was too heavy on her mind to deal with the idea of a spitted lamb. It used to be her favorite activity, helping to baste the slowly browning carcass. Carcass, what a great word for the uncertain appetite.

So she was officially twenty-one years old today. And her mom and dad had died sixteen years ago tomorrow. *Thank you, Carla*, she muttered bitterly. Other kids turning twenty-one would be toasting with their first legal drinks. She hadn't decided what she wanted to do. Grandpa and Aunt Donna had the occasional drink, but she didn't think they'd be too happy if she decided to have a drink or two or ten. She had had a few beers at University related parties, but the idea of drinking until she was stupid had never appealed to her until today.

She heard his steps on the gravel, despite the music that filled her room, Julio Iglesias. A morning of meditation hadn't helped her nerves. She took a deep cleansing breath and hoped the music would make him smile. She hoped it would make him happy. Jim had bought her three Spanish romantic CD's the same day she asked for them. She didn't tell him why she'd made this uncharacteristic choice in theme music. Peter, with his music by Izzy, didn't protest; he simply changed the theme of the party to the Philippines where they had tropical islands and spoke Spanish.

Liliana met Terry at the door and burst into laughter when she saw him. He was wearing a brilliant purple shirt with many garish toucans coupled in suggestive positions. "Hi," she choked out.

He smiled, "Hi."

"Can you do me a favor?"

"Sure."

"Can you do a three-sixty so I can get the whole effect?"

He shrugged, raised his arms slightly and turned around slowly until he faced her again. Hoots of laughter bounced off the walls from Peter and Frank standing in the hall behind her.

"Wow, Julio Iglesias and nasty toucans. You guys are definitely trying to communicate something. Let's see could it . . ." Frank grabbed Peter's arm and dragged him away before he could finish his theory.

"Wow," came from Angelo who had come in from outside to see what he was missing. "That is some shirt. What are those birds doing?"

"Nothing more than you'd see on a PBS program about birds," Terry responded, embarrassed that he had forgotten that children would be there. It was too late to change now.

"Yeah, but these birds look like they've made it into a team sport."

Donna came, cocked her head at the shirt and dragged Angelo off to the patio as he protested that he could see the same thing on PBS. She called out that there was Sangria punch when they were ready.

"I like the music," Terry said as he leaned down to kiss her. She counted the twenty seconds, described by experts on talk shows as the minimum a kiss should last to be counted as real affection.

"I'm not too sure about the shirt. Where did you find it?"

"It was a gift. This is the first time I've worn it."

"And today was the day."

"Yup."

Her lips twisted in a wry smile. "I can live with it."

"Will you?"

251

She met his eyes and saw the sadness that was all her fault. "Of course, remember I was the first to invite you to live with me."

"Yes, but could I opt out on the hogan? I like my hot showers."

"Spoiled white man."

"To the bone."

They arrived at the patio smiling for the moment. Mike and Adela and their families, Emmy and Eddie, Jake and his wife and kid, Julia her husband and baby girl, and, a surprise for Liliana, Denise with her husband, all were there.

"Denise, wow! You came all the way out here."

"Anything for a good party. This is Paul, my hubby. I left the kids with Grandma."

"They wouldn't let me help," Liliana complained as she examined Paul. He was tall, dark-haired, with a pleasing face and great build, a typical good-looking fireman.

Denise looked down at the leg critically. "Well, carrying that battering ram around, they might have been worried that you would . . . no, no, that they might accidentally run into it and hurt you."

"Nah. They wanted me out of the way in case I knocked everything over." She went on to make sure Denise and Paul were introduced to everyone. Terry brought Liliana a glass of sangria with a little red umbrella stuck into a slice of orange.

"Sorry, this is virgin sangria. The doc said you might have a reaction with the medications you're on."

"Traitor," she said loud enough for Frank to turn around. He shook his finger at her with a semi-serious frown.

A few neighbors that she knew arrived as Peter announced that the lamb was ready, and began slicing pieces onto paper plates held eagerly in front of him. Liliana took a veggie burger instead. She glanced up as Donna brought her a scoop of potato salad. "What did Peter decide on for the not-chocolate cake?"

"He made a pineapple upside down cake."

"Perfect."

"And I made a couple of lemon meringue pies."

"Sweet!"

"That's the word." Donna glanced up at Terry. He was quieter than usual. Liliana watched Donna's worried look and Terry's smile as he took a bite of the fried bread stuffed with lamb and red chili.

As guests slipped away hours later, Liliana couldn't find an excuse to leave with Terry. Finally, after helping Donna and Jim clean up, Frank and Peter kissed Liliana goodbye. It was only nine o'clock, so Terry sat on the sofa not talking much to Liliana who remained close by. Donna, Angelo and Jim came into the living room to relax in front of the TV before heading off to bed. Perfectly normal.

Soon after the first program started, Liliana announced that she was going to wheel around the block since the night was cool and clear. Terry smiled and joined her, trying to appear casual. Before they left, Angelo asked if they were going to her parents' graves the next day as they usually did on the anniversary of their death. She nodded and wheeled through the door Terry held open for her.

"You have great friends and family," Terry commented.

"Yeah. They're good people. I didn't realize how many there were. They've had to put up with a lot because of me."

They made their way down the path, holding hands, until the reached the small barn. Although Paint was a calm animal, she had learned to restrain her temper around him since the horse was so sensitive to human moods. Yet she hadn't been able to do the same for the man she loved.

"I'm sorry I've been such a bitch."

"You already apologized and I have forgiven you."

"Yeah, but it still affects us."

"We're only human."

She took a deep breath. "Okay, I'll talk about the mirror thing."

He turned to lean on the rail of the corral, looking at the framed, stuccoed houses on the other side with the clouded sky and the blurred bright spot that was the sun sitting on the horizon for one last look before it left for the night. "What part do you want to talk about?"

"You started it. What do you want to know?" Oops, too late to bite her tongue.

He turned around to face her, leaning his back on the rail. "I want to know what I can do to help you, because I love you and I hate that this causes you so much pain."

"I've never talked about it. No one's ever asked."

"Maybe you hid it too well, or maybe they didn't want you to be hurt by their questions."

"I don't know what to do about it. He's in every mirror and I hate him so much the sight of him makes me sick."

Terry went for the stool from inside the barn and set it in front of her. He sat down and took her hands in his. "I see two directions you can take. One is very difficult; the other might be doable." He caught her eyes with his. "You can forgive him, which I don't know if I can do and I never knew him. Or you can believe that people see what they want to see and you know that Carla was a bitter woman, and jealous that you had people who wanted to be with you. You might have some of Joe's features, I don't know for sure. Even if you do, they originated in his mother, who is the sweetest woman in the world."

Inside she felt the first brush of a cleansing breeze. She was able to give Terry a small smile and nodded.

"Okay," he continued, "maybe you should examine the faces of all the people whose genes you carry and see where the different parts of you come from."

"In a mirror?"

"Yes, a mirror, or photos. Eventually, you need to face that mirror."

"I might, but that would take a long time." Her hands were trembling in his. She tried to stop it, but it only got worse.

He squeezed her hands and kissed them. "There's no rush. It's the start that's important."

She closed her eyes and leaned her head back. She wanted to yell at him and at the same time she knew it was fate she wanted to hurt, but it was untouchable. "Okay. I'll pull out my pictures of everyone and start tomorrow. I want today to end with happy thoughts."

"All right. We can start it together tomorrow."

"I don't know. I don't want you to…"

"You can yell at me and call me names while we work on this. Don't be afraid. I can take it as long as you share it with me." She could feel his eyes watching her. She finally opened her eyes to see him smiling. "I was just wondering," he leaned close and whispered, "if you would be interested in a birthday bang."

She wanted to laugh, but she couldn't because she was kissing him. It was really hard to do two things at once.

∞

Liliana slept very well considering what she had agreed to start that morning. When she awoke she realized that it was going to be a long, emotional day. She had promised to try to repair a part of her that had been broken for as long as she could remember. It didn't feel like a good day to start the painful process. Logically, she knew that phobias could be conquered; she even knew the therapeutic method. As stubborn as she was, she had wanted to be rid of the problem and tried on her own to cure it, but had so far failed. Now she felt coerced, face the mirror or lose Terry. It was still early in the day. Maybe she could talk Angelo into helping her get to her new van for a test drive. She would drop him off at the community center and head for Mexico. She looked at the cursed leg, the reminder of her last cave-in to panic. This time she was in no shape to run anywhere.

Her fear of mirrors confounded her. If it was the image of Joe, why hadn't she ever panicked when she saw the turd in person; she saw the disgusting drunk nearly every day she was at Carla's. The sight of him made her want to puke, but it didn't terrify her. Seeing him in her mirror image was the only thing she had come up with to explain her phobia.

It would be worse now that she had said and done things that made her more like him. Before that day, maybe she could have made it past this hurdle, but now she knew she was the child raised by Joe and Carla. Only such an evil person could have said those things and left Carla to die. She had found the evil parts of them she carried within her.

Time passed so slowly until it was close to time for Julia to arrive. Terry was supposed to arrive an hour later for breakfast. A confluence of community meetings and school registration left the house to the three of them for the morning. She needed a plan. She had to get past this without revealing the part of her that would send him away forever. She focused on her closet in her mind and carefully packaged the memories of that morning in one box, then that box in a larger box. When her boxes numbered twenty, each with its own passkey, she closed the closet door and locked it. Then she let her mind drift back to her room and found Julia already there setting up the bathroom.

"Well, good morning, sleepyhead," Julia greeted her cheerfully. "This is the first time I caught you sleeping. You look sweet when you sleep."

"And a grouch when I'm awake."

"It's okay to be grouchy sometimes, but I've never seen you as grouchy as my dad is in the morning."

If she"d had her gun by her side Liliana would have shot her for the crime of too much cheerfulness. "So how's the baby. Everyone loved her yesterday."

"She slept so well after they wore her out. Have you and Terry talked about having kids? I know you'll probably want to wait 'til you've finished medical school."

"Terry can't make any babies. He's infertile. So, I guess when we're ready we'll go shopping for one."

"I didn't know. I'm so sorry. You never did want kids when we played house. Do you remember?"

"I still can't imagine having all that responsibility. So Terry and I have one less thing to worry about."

"You're nervous about today, aren't you?"

"Don't tell me he called you?"

"Yes. He wanted me to bring the pictures of us playing together."

"I don't remember any pictures."

Julia sat on the edge of the bed. "It was the day Carla came to get you. You prob'ly forgot. My mom took pictures of us dressing up. Carla was mean; that's probably why you don't remember."

"Carla was always Carla. Can I see the pictures?"

Julia grimaced guiltily, "I wasn't supposed to tell you, oops. He wanted to pick out the pictures."

"And what makes him the boss of me?" Liliana complained as she scooted on to the chair with Julia supporting her leg and Julia began undressing her.

Julia tried distracting Liliana, sometimes it worked, sometimes it didn't. "Why don't we get the bath done so you can be ready when he gets here, then we can relax and look at pictures?"

"Okay, I'll let it pass this time. I can't do much if I don't have you to put on my underwear."

"Yes, I know. The next time you'll fire me."

"You know it, girl."

∞

Julia wished there was less anger in Liliana's voice. This was going to be a difficult day for her. When Terry called asking if she had any pictures of Liliana when she was little, she knew what he was after. Julia thought it was strange that Liliana made her cover the mirror with a towel while she bathed. Clearly avoiding the truth, Liliana made her laugh with stories about her Pueblo grandmother showing up in the mirrors to haunt her, but Julia knew Liliana didn't believe in ghosts. She had told the previous nurse the same stories. The woman finally lost her nerve at the idea of ghosts haunting Liliana.

The nurse had sworn Julia to secrecy, since Liliana had threatened to send the ghost to her house if she told the family why she left. Liliana could definitely be a brat. In truth, Julia didn't like the woman. She had spent the rest of the orienting session telling stories she had heard about Carla and Joe, and fishing for any new stories Julia knew.

Julia kept Liliana busy with exercises after the bath until Terry arrived. She opened the door and he came in with a briefcase. He kissed Liliana and set the case on the bed. "First your arm brace." Julia announced.

"I get the cast off and he makes me wear that thing," Liliana complained while Julia laced the metal reinforced leather brace to her left arm and thumb.

"Did you know that he had that made special for you?" Terry commented as he watched. "He knew that the casts would drive you nuts."

"Oh, he's so kind," Liliana responded trying to sound sarcastic. She already owed her doctor too much.

"I hope you have many patients like yourself to take care of," Julia said.

"And I'll deserve every one. So how many extra mirrors did you bring?"

"Are you planning on breaking mirrors?" He looked tired and worried to Julia. He was looking forward to this about as much as Liliana was.

"Hey, it's not my fault that they break when my face appears."

He gave her a sidelong look. "Okay. Today will be a short experiment. First let's get all the pictures together. Donna left her collection on the dining room table."

Julia opened her bag to get the photos when she discovered another packet. "Oh, no, I forgot."

"What?" Liliana snapped. Julia put her hand on her hip and tilted her head, waiting. "Okay, I'm sorry. What did you forget, Julia dear?"

Julia pursed her lips at the lack of sincerity. "I forgot that we have to change the dressing on your leg and take cultures," she held up the package. "We should get it over with while I have Terry to help. Angelo is just a little too curious about wounds and broken bones."

Terry lifted the cast so Julia could unwrap the stretch bandages. Then he laid the leg down and Julia opened the cast removing the top half. Liliana started to push herself up on her hands, but Julia moved her left arm to her chest and placed her right hand on the overhead bar. Julia then returned to removing the old bandages as Terry held the leg above and below the break.

"It feels more together than in the hospital," he said as he looked at the wide lightening shaped scar and where, because of the infection, they let it heal from the bottom up, instead of closing it. "I don't see any pus. That's a good sign."

"We can hope," Julia said as she swabbed the sight of the infection and replaced the covering over the swab.

Julia started washing the leg around the wound, and Liliana let herself fall back. "They're just going to have to break it again to make it straight. Why another test so soon after the last one?"

"I don't know; maybe it's wishful thinking." Julia said as she and Terry shared a look over their work while Liliana lay with her right arm over her eyes. She was feeling down and trying to cover it with anger.

Terry asked, "When are you going to the cemetery?"

"After lunch. Donna and Angelo will finish with his school registration this morning and Grandpa only has morning meetings."

"We have a lot of pictures to go through. Grandma Emmy brought me all her pictures when Adela brought her."

"But she's gone back. I wanted to look at them with her."

"I'm sure you'll have another chance. Anyway that's probably all we'll have time to do today."

She took a deep breath. "You don't have to baby me you know."

"No I don't. You are Superwoman. But it's already a hard day."

"They died a long time ago, Terry. I barely remember them."

"I don't believe that. You've told me detailed stories about them."

"I don't want to argue."

He saw her peeking under her arm as he pressed his lips together, holding back his retort. They could fight when she wasn't so vulnerable, her shattered leg open to the air. He looked into her eyes and she covered them again, reassured that he wasn't going to leave her that very minute. Once the leg was clean, the wound redressed and the cast replaced, they moved to the dining room. Three large albums lay on the table.

Liliana said, "I've seen these pictures before."

"Donna said we could pick some out and I'll copy them so you can have your own collection. I brought a photo box until we see if you want to put them in an album. We should look at Julia's pictures first so she can go home for lunch."

"Yeah, maybe I'll remember the first half of that day when I see the pictures."

"What happened the second half of the day?"

"Carla beat me with a belt then locked me in the closet until the next morning." Terry's eyes closed involuntarily. Liliana avoided looking at him. "I finally got big enough to break the door. Then I got big enough to run away until she got drunk and forgot. Then she learned which words hurt worse than belts and closets." He had to learn what he was starting with the mirrors. There was a lot that was worse. Julia watched them, concern in her eyes.

By the time Donna and Angelo returned Julia had gone home, leaving behind pictures that made Liliana cry as she remembered the small joys that Carla had stomped from her mind. They were going through Donna's collection since Liliana could tell the stories behind the pictures of her with her parents and grandparents when she was little. They already had a generous stack of pictures set aside and they hadn't been through Emmy's yet. With the pressure of facing the mirror postponed, Liliana relaxed with Terry, while he made lunch for her family.

Angelo joined in the picture stories pointing out the pictures of him growing up. Jim arrived within the hour and they sat down to the chicken salad sandwiches and coleslaw Terry had made. It was clear Liliana had been crying, so the mood was quiet. Afterward they climbed into Terry's larger truck, Liliana sitting in the back with her leg across Angelo's lap, and drove to the pueblo cemetery. Donna laid Liliana's flowers on their graves and wiped down the gravestones with Angelo's help. Donna and Jim prayed while they touched the gravestones.

Terry watched the dry wind kick up dust in the dry cemetery and blow it toward the old Spanish mission. Grey, buffalo grass held most of the dirt down and some cactus, sage and mesquite bushes had taken root scattered amongst the small stone crosses and headstones. It was a very different place from the well-watered lawns at the cemetery where his father, mother and brother lay.

He waited until Liliana tried to turn her chair away and then he pushed her to the car. Angelo came with them, but Jim and Donna stayed. It was over an hour by the time they returned home. It might have happened years ago, but it was clear Jim's grief for his son was still fresh. As he watched them during their quiet evening in front of the television, Terry realized that Liliana's uncle, a lawyer living in Albuquerque, hadn't come to Liliana's birthday party.

During his evening walk with Liliana, he asked why her Uncle Tony hadn't come to her birthday party. She didn't answer until they reached Old Paint's corral, as it would always be to him since she first named it for him.

"Tony was the one who tried the hardest to keep my dad from marrying my mom. His friends at school were harassing him about his brother's choice in women, and Grandpa was so angry. Tony and my dad had just had an argument, again, when Mom and Dad accepted Carla's invitation to dinner at the restaurant that was part of the new casino on the day after my birthday. Have you noticed how high on the hill it sits?" She laid her head back to look up at the moon. "Tony got worried when they didn't get home to pick me up. He went looking and found them dead at the bottom of the hill, Mom's old Pinto smashed into the cement that separated the ramp to the highway entrance. My dad didn't have a seatbelt on and his head was nearly cut off by the windshield. Tony hasn't looked at me since."

Terry was sitting on the stool from the barn holding her hand. "So, have you had enough yet?" She asked with bitter resignation. The shit just kept falling from her life onto Terry's head. He kissed her, but she didn't believe the kiss. "I'm tired tonight," she said, "I think I'll crash early."

He stood as she turned her chair around. He was quiet as he said goodnight after lifting her onto her bed and handing her the pajama's that Donna would help her with. "I'll come by tomorrow and take you for a ride. A trip to the mountains would be good. What do you say to a picnic? I haven't explored Mt. Taylor yet."

"That will be great," she gave him a smile of relief and they kissed goodnight.

While Donna helped her change clothes, she asked her, "Liliana, can you do one thing for me? It's important."

Liliana closed her eyes and leaned back against the head board as she unlaced her arm brace for the night. "What?" she asked suspiciously.

"I want you to look in the mirror and tell me what you see."

"I can't today. Maybe tomorrow."

"You know we love you."

"Yeah. I know. I love you back."

Donna hugged her goodnight and left the mirror on the bedside table next to the box of photos. Liliana eyed the mirror with more disquiet than she would a rattlesnake. At least you knew that a rattlesnake would leave you alone if you left it alone. Mirrors snuck up behind you and scared the piss out of you. It happened constantly at the University. Those in charge of bathrooms were so fond of mirrors that, if she wasn't careful, she would turn around and wet her pants in fear. She had managed to hide this weakness by carrying extra clothes to school and learning a few bathrooms well enough to negotiate them with her eyes closed. Terry was too smart to deceive and she'd let him too far into her world. She wanted him in her life; she just couldn't deal with mirrors.

Her hand shook as it reached for the mirror and turned it face down. Then she picked up the box of photos. She laid out the photos of her from Donna's collection, which she hadn't realized did not include her mother's pictures. There had to be lots of them, even though her parents were too poor to indulge in a lot of film developing. She would ask Donna if she had ever seen them. As she laid out Julia's pictures, she remembered the day Carla came for her. What Julia didn't mention was that her mother had called Carla and taken pictures because of the foul language and "nasty" things Liliana was miming while she played house. So the punishment was harsh and Carla saved the worst of the pictures. Fortunately, Liliana was able to find and destroy those pictures.

She laid pictures of her as a child out and arranged them next to family at the same age. Then she pulled out her driver's license and, for the first time, looked at the picture. She surrounded it the same way. She dragged her backpack from under the bed and arranged the pictures on paper, taping them down. She pulled out her sketchbook, her secret pleasure and she started drawing from the pictures, overlaying her photographed face with family faces. Finally, she drew Carla and then Joe, for the first time. Then she drew Terry, stared at it a long time, hope warring with despair until she finally fell asleep.

Donna tried to sleep, but only dozed fitfully waiting for Liliana's cry for help. Liliana was too independent to let anyone make her resolve a problem on their timetable. Donna knew that Liliana understood the message of the mirror she had left beside her. Liliana had given Terry too much power, because he was so important to her. He wanted the best for her, and he was right, but Liliana needed to manage her problems herself, when she was ready, not with the threat of losing the one she loved hanging over her head. It was how she had survived with Carla. That was a skill that she could hold on to; it would serve her far more reliably than the love of another person. A gentle push from a not so vital person in her life might get her past it with her self-reliance intact.

But finally Donna couldn't wait any longer. Just before dawn she gave in and as quietly as she could she opened the door to Liliana's room and saw her sleeping propped on a pile of pillows with pages of photo collages strewn across the bed. Most surprising were the pictures she had drawn of Carla and Joe on the floor beside the bed and a drawing of Terry that she held in her hand.

Donna picked up the sketchbook and sat down to look at all the sketches by the dawn light. The thick book was full of sketches, some buildings, some crowds, but mostly studies of different faces. Mixed in were life drawings that looked like a class atmosphere. As the sky and room brightened she studied more detail and discovered that in most of the scenes of multiple people on campus, in a park, eating lunch, there would be very small pictures of Carla and Joe amongst the strangers. The faces were so small and stylized that it could have been that those were familiar faces and in drawing faces from a distance, Liliana had drawn on that knowledge base.

"Aunt Donna?" Liliana's voice was questioning in the way of someone unwillingly waking from deep sleep.

"Liliana, these are beautiful. I can't imagine where you found the time with everything you were doing. Did you take classes?"

Liliana rubbed her eyes with her left hand then looked at it with confusion. "Um, yeah. Sort of." She shifted so she could see Donna. She wasn't ready to get up. "I took some open classes they have for the art students to practice. Those are the nude life drawings. I never had the guts to ask someone to pose for me."

"Of course, I shouldn't be surprised. Am I going to find out next that you are already a super scientist working in secret for the government?"

"Well, if I told you I'd have to kill you."

"Of course." Donna felt pride filling her heart. "You are so special. Do you want me to put these away?"

"Actually, do you still have that cork board that used to hang in the kitchen? I'd like to hang some of these others." She stacked the collages together.

"I know it's around here some place. Do you want a snack? I bought bearclaws and donuts yesterday."

"Bearclaws! I haven't had one of those in ages. Can you make some coffee, too, please?"

"Of course," she said as she stood up cheerfully. She laid the sketchbook on the bed and went off to the kitchen.

Liliana covered her eyes with her forearm as the reactions arrived in waves: anxiety, surprise, pleasure and most of all fear of what would next be expected of her. She had stepped forward on a course she had set for herself the last time she had to change clothes after a mirror caught her by surprise and she was late for class. She had been drawing before, but it had a different purpose after that incident. A purpose she never directly thought about. The only kind of plan she could manage was like a leaf falling from a tree floating on the wind. It would have to touch ground eventually, but the slightest breeze moved it in a different direction. It had no purpose, an unknown fate. Even after it landed, another gust could return it to the air, no ground, no ties, and no final decisions. It could land in the water and float to the desert or on a road to be crushed by a car. Or it could land on fertile ground and add its essence to the cycle of life.

Drawing improved her knowledge of faces and helped her think about what would be the worst thing a mirror could do to her if she wasn't in front of people from whom she had to hide her fear.

The smell of coffee woke her from a doze. When she heard cups being moved, she cleared up her papers, set them on the table and dropped the backpack to the floor. Donna came in with the bed tray loaded with warm bearclaws and coffee with lots of cream and sugar. Liliana pulled herself up using the bar and arranged her own pillows, then Donna sat the tray over her lap and took her plate and cup and sat down, ready to chat.

Liliana bit into the sweet, cream cheesy pastry then washed it down with the sweet coffee. A satisfied "mmm" escaped her lips. She watched Donna wait for her to pick the topic. At this moment, Liliana needed a break from her troubles. With wry humor she asked, "When do you think we can get another horse?" She knew Angelo had been working this angle all summer.

Donna choked on her coffee. "Liliana, when you change subjects the next direction is like . . . like falling off a horse."

"Angelo really wants a horse. We could share one so it wouldn't cost as much to buy two."

A small laugh escaped Donna. "Well, for one thing we would have to repair the barn, which Dad was thinking of tearing down, and the corral. We'd need to run waterlines to the trough and the cost of feed has skyrocketed."

"Aha, so you did check it out."

"Yes, Angelo has been asking for a while. It's expensive and a lot of work and you won't be here much once school starts."

"I guess I'll have to wait until I'm a rich doctor."

"I agree. By that time Angelo will be old enough to take care of it when you're busy."

It was strangely disconcerting to be planning a future that had some chance of actually happening. For so long, especially since the accident, she had struggled to have faith that one day would follow the next. "Then you're going to have to find a way to keep Grandpa from tearing down the barn."

Liliana looked past Donna when Jim appeared at her door. "Keep Grandpa from tearing down what? And why didn't anybody bring *me* coffee in bed?" He was wearing his glad grumpy face. "And what are you two doing up at this hour? I'm usually the first one up in this house."

"Donna decided to visit. Pull up a chair, Gramps, there's another pastry and I'll share my coffee with you."

"No, no. You like it too sweet. I'll get my own coffee." He returned with his black coffee and a plate of glazed donuts. Once he settled in a chair, the debate over the horse continued, then Angelo woke up to the word "horse" and joined them for donuts, sitting on the bed, swinging his legs as he added his opinion to the debate.

Finally, Jim stood up. "We'll just wait and see. I'd like to put a crop on that ground, but I'll wait to tear down the barn. When you finish all that school, we'll see if you find any time for a horse.

There was a knock at the door and Angelo went to let Terry in. He clearly hadn't slept well, but seemed cheered to see the good-humored bedroom powwow.

Angelo offered him donuts, and exclaimed, "Guess what? When Liliana is a rich doctor she's going to get a horse and let me take care of it.

Liliana do they let you skip years in medical school like you did in school here?"

"Nope. It's four years after I start, if everything goes right."

"I hope it goes fast," Angelo said, trying to cheer himself up.

"It sounds like a great idea," Terry added. "I could help Angelo rebuild the barn."

"Me! I don't know how . . ." He stopped, realizing he was about to jeopardize his chances. "That would be great. I always wanted to learn how to build a barn." Everyone laughed and Donna pulled him into a hug.

"Well, I don't know about you guys, but I have meetings this morning. I think it's time we all got dressed." Jim said with a warning look at Angelo. The boy left with Jim and Donna when he really wanted to talk Terry into buying him a horse. A moment later he returned with coffee for Terry.

He whispered in Terry's ear, "Maybe you could loan me the money for a horse and I'd pay you back."

"Sorry, son, that is your mother's decision, not mine."

With a twist of his lips and a posture filled with exaggerated disappointment, he turned and left. Terry took the chair nearest to Liliana after her good morning kiss. He looked optimistic, but wary. He saw the stacks of pictures and the open sketchbook Angelo had been examining.

"You've already had a busy morning. How did you sleep?"

"I was up most of the night. Donna was checking on me when I woke up and we started talking."

"About horses?"

"It seemed the safest second topic."

He nodded. Liliana set her cup and plate on the side table and folded the bed tray and set it beside the bed. She patted the bed beside her and scooted over. Terry held his donut in his mouth and carefully balanced his hot coffee as he lay down next to her. She took his coffee so he could eat. "Maybe we could take a little nap. You look like you didn't sleep, either. Julia's not coming until this afternoon."

He finished his donut and set his coffee aside, turned onto his side with his arm over her stomach. "You seem to be feeling better."

"Yeah. I did a lot of thinking, but right now I'm still tired."

"Me too." He snuggled his head into her neck. She held his left hand in her right hand. Soon they were both asleep. In passing, Donna saw them sleeping and shut the door. Liliana heard the door shut, then relaxed into deep, restful sleep.

They woke looking into each other's eyes when Julia knocked on the door. "We missed lunch," Liliana complained as he opened the door.

Julia smiled, unsurprised to find Terry there. "I'm sorry," she said, "I'm early. My mom wanted to talk to you. It's her lunch hour and her evenings are full all week. I thought you'd be dressed so I didn't call first, sorry."

"We took a nap. It's okay, Julia. I've gotten used to having visitors while I'm in my pajamas."

Julia smiled uncomfortably, "All right. I'll go tell her it's okay."

Terry turned to her, question in his eyes. She shrugged. "Her mom is a big shot in the community. She's on the multi-tribal school council."

"Should I leave?" Liliana could tell he suspected the visit had something to do with the pictures and what Carla had done to Liliana that day. He was worried, a look that had become too much a part of him recently.

"Sit down here," she patted the bed. "I don't want to have to repeat it all later. Now you can tell Grandpa and Donna for me."

"Always thinking," he smiled.

"Learned from experience."

She grabbed the bar to scoot back as Terry arranged her pillows and then tried to straighten his sleep wrinkled hair and shirt. He turned to smile as Julia tapped lightly on the door frame. "This is my mother, Anita Beltran. Mom this is Terry Prentice and you remember Liliana Hunt."

The short woman with curly, bouffant styled light-brown hair and a trim figure in a tailored jacket, skirt and practical heels. Liliana smiled, but didn't trust this woman. She knew that Anita had been working on her grandfather to approve a social center for teens. Liliana suspected Anita wanted Liliana to forgive and forget the past. She was there to make sure Liliana didn't mention the incident to her influential grandfather.

"How are you, Liliana? You look well considering what you have been through."

"I am well, thank you Mrs. Beltran. It's been years since I saw you last." She presented a huge, fake smile and shook hands with the woman while ignoring Terry's discomfort. Liliana had no intention of making this easy for Mrs. Beltran, despite her love for Julia. "Terry, would you bring a more comfortable chair from the living room."

Once she was settled, Mrs. Beltran said, "Julia told me you've been looking for your childhood memories in pictures."

Liliana smiled and nodded. Mrs. Beltran seemed tense. "You were a good girl, Liliana, but the life you lived at home would show up when you played. That is perfectly normal, but I didn't know that then. In those days, I believed those things were passed in the blood. I worried about Julia; I didn't want her to start acting in ways that would attract negative attention. I called Carla to protect my child, instead of teaching you what was right. I am so sorry. I knew she was hard on you, but I never thought she would hurt you like that."

Liliana's face was calm as glass. She knew Terry sensed her simmering anger, but she was glad he didn't interfere. "All that is in the past, Mrs. Beltran. Right now I'm just trying to figure out my present. Thank you for the apology."

Mrs. Beltran waited for more and seemed unsure what to say. Her visit was an impulse she hadn't thought out, Liliana surmised. The woman, thanks to her daughter's professionalism, didn't really know anything about what Liliana was going through.

"I watched the rescue on the news. That must have been terrible. You were so lucky that your fiancé found you."

"Yes, I was."

"Do you know how long it will be before your leg heals?"

"Only the spirits know, Mrs. Beltran. Carla put so many curses on me it's hard to keep track of them."

"She was a troubled woman."

"Yes. Trouble is the word." Liliana replied flatly. Terry sighed and leaned back on the headboard next to her. Liliana could keep this up for hours if her target failed to recognize the game, but he had succeeded in distracting the woman's attention with his movement. Her eyes narrowed as she realized this was not the needy child that would do anything for affection.

"Well," she said as she stood up, "I'll leave you to your lunch. I hope you forgive me some day."

"You have a real good day, Mrs. Beltran," was Liliana's only reply.

Julia gave a small wave as she left to take her mother home.

"Why did you give her such a hard time?" Terry asked.

"Carla acted like Carla and offended her, so Mrs. Beltran spread that story all over town to get even."

"Then she deserved worse," he responded. "Now tell me when you started drawing; these are great." He started leafing through her sketchbook. "You've drawn yourself and Joe. Do you still believe Carla?"

"No. I mean I do have some of his features, he was my great-grandfather, but I'm different. Mostly I look like my dad and mom."

"Have you tried the mirror again?"

"No. I can't." Her hands clenched in her lap. "I thought I knew why, but I was wrong. I just can't do it." She looked into his worried eyes. "Are you mad?"

He laid the book down. "Why should I be angry?" He hugged her. "None of this is your fault."

"Are you getting tired of all this shit?" she whispered in his ear.

"I'm just worried about you. It wears me out; I can't deny it. But all I want is to be with you, despite all the troubles." He nuzzled her neck, taking in her scent. "I want to help you work this out."

"Can we skip it for a while? I can manage it. Please, don't worry."

Julia returned, her face red with shame. "I'm so sorry, Liliana. I made her tell me why you were still mad. She won't apologize again. She says one apology should cover the whole situation."

Liliana let go of Terry and put her arms out. They embraced. Liliana said, "Have you ever heard the apology, 'I'm sorry for whatever I did to hurt you?'"

"Yeah. A lot of people use that bullshit line."

"Oh, Julia! Such language." Julia's sunny smile returned. "Nobody really wants to admit to being evil, so they hope that a vague, blanket apology will throw dust over their crime, just in case you don't remember every thing they did to you."

"Did Carla ever apologize to you?" Terry looked from Julia to see Liliana's reaction.

Liliana returned his look. "They both did when I challenged them about minor stuff in public. When we got home, I got smacked. They only had worthless, spineless, guilty words."

Terry smiled, warming her all over. He was proud and would remember those wise words later and compare his own experiences. She smiled back, trying to disguise her very warm, but confused, response. He raised his eyebrows and quickly turned his chin toward his house. Liliana blushed then heard Julia's laugh.

"I think you guys should move in together. I can come over there just as easy."

"We decided that while this leg is so weak I'd be too much for one person. Once they've put in the braces and screws to stabilize the bones, I'll be able to use crutches sometimes."

"Well," Julia changed the subject, "let's get the work out of the way and then I want to look at all your pictures."

The rest of the day passed easily for Liliana. It was a relief that Terry had so easily agreed to give her time to work out the mirror issue. To tell the truth, she was confused. She had been sure that her mirror phobia, eisoptrophobia—the fear of mirrors or one's image in a mirror, she'd looked it up, was a result of Carla's mean comparisons. Maybe an image in a mirror had a more powerful impact than the real person or a photograph. Liliana finally decided that logic was not going to work for this situation. The pressure she put on herself added to Terry's well-intentioned encouragement. To be lost in the bliss she felt when she was with Terry was all she wanted; she was terrified to lose it. However when he mentioned mirrors her head and chest hurt with a memory she couldn't identify and with the fear that Terry would give up on her. She knew he could feel her tension; sometimes she felt like exploding and it was getting worse. She managed to joke and tease, putting on the face she'd used for so many years, but she felt a bigger break coming. Her work with the photos and drawings managed to ease Terry's worry enough so that he didn't push the mirror issue, but she knew the black reflection of fear waited for her on the horizon.

Finally, the doctors agreed the infection was cleared and they set a date for her surgery. If only they had been able to take her the same day. She should feel privileged that she only had to wait for a week. Once the surgery was done, she would be able to walk with crutches. That is, if once they got inside they saw the bones healing as straight as they appeared to be healing on the x-rays. Although straight, they were still weak and it could take a lot longer for the missing bone fragments to fill in around and through the grafts. *Oh, heaven, to be out of the wheelchair, finally.*

Terry hosted his housewarming the weekend after the doctor's visit. It was good to have a noisy room filled with her friends to celebrate the good news and distract her from the tension building inside her over his decision to return to Farmington. He couldn't find anyone to manage the work on his house and there weren't any financially viable offers on it in its "as is" condition. Once she was settled after her operation, he would leave. He had spent hours on the phone getting various contractors to agree to the most efficient timetable. He hoped to finish in two weeks by having someone working seven days a week, which meant that he wouldn't be able to come home for weekends. However, he knew how construction worked; he would be lucky to finish in a month. She dreaded every hour he would be gone.

Now that Julia was only visiting three times a week, Liliana had taken the opportunity to spend whole nights with Terry. Only Angelo commented with what he thought was a worldly wink at Terry the day after their first night. She was glad that no one asked for explanations, or seemed disturbed by her decision. Even so, shame plagued her and she often had trouble meeting the eyes of her family. However it wasn't enough to counteract how good it felt to spend more time with him.

The week passed too fast. Liliana managed to limit her arguments with Terry to one, plus a couple of spats that didn't deserve notice. The day of the surgery arrived, and, because they used spinal anesthesia, she was able to watch the surgery. There were no surprises since she'd researched the procedure. They took time to remove most of the thick scar tissue and leave a thin, lightning strike shaped incision in its place. She was disappointed that she couldn't actually see the bone work close up, but she saw the screws and plates that went in and the metal braces surrounding her leg on the outside. She was able to return home the next morning and spent the next three nights at Terry's house.

It felt natural to sleep with him although Liliana didn't sleep as deeply with the random movements of another sleeping body and the pain in her leg disturbing her. The level of pain after the surgery surprised her. So she had decided, despite her constant fear of addiction, to take their advice and use as much of the pain medicine she needed in the beginning, because research had shown that post surgical pain resolved sooner if adequately treated and resulted in fewer cases of chronic pain and/or addiction. The result was that she remembered more of her dreams and many of them were strange. Mirrors appeared in strange shapes, often appearing at the edges of whatever dream she was having, leaving her disquieted.

Two days before he was to leave they went to picnic on Mount Taylor. She managed a short hike on a level trail using her crutches and was completely exhausted having been inactive for so many weeks. Fortunately, she made it to the level clearing next to a stream that she knew. There were only a few rocks and soft grass. A stone fire circle was in place, but the fire danger was too high after the unusually hot, dry spring and summer. Terry laid out the plaid wool blanket, and a basket filled with left over fried chicken, potato salad and cold beer. It was pleasant lying on the blanket, her head spinning just a little from her half bottle of beer. The pine trees rose straight up above her seeming to touch the sky. The stream was small and rocky, and gurgled pleasantly as it carried the clear, cold water down the mountain.

"So, when are you going to visit Adela?" Terry asked, resting on one side, his head on his hand.

"Lourdes' birthday is next Saturday; she'll be thirteen. She wants to ride up to Sandia Crest on the Tram. I'll go over on Friday and spend the afternoon alone with Grandma Emmy. Thank you for renting the van Uncle Mike found for me."

"I thought you deserved some independence after such a long prison sentence."

"A prison with some definite perks. Like my own chauffeur and masseur."

"Glad to provide a service, ma'am."

"I think you deserve a generous tip," she said as she pulled his face down for a long kiss. His hands had just managed to open her blouse when they heard the noise of a family chattering as they approached along the trail. She buttoned up quickly and sat up, guiltily. Terry laughed. She poked his ribs; it annoyed her that he was entertained by her shyness.

"What happened to my tip?" he asked just after the family passed.

"I'm afraid you're going to have to wait until we get home for any special tips." He pulled her down to lie beside him and they spent time discussing little things, then they both dozed off. When they woke the sky was cloudy, threatening to rain. Terry helped Liliana to her feet and then lifted the pack to his shoulder. It was a slow walk back to the truck since she was tired from the exertion early in the day. It was raining by the time they reached his house.

"So," he asked, distracting her from a story about Eddie Chee's visit and his exuberant competition with Angelo on the video games despite losing every game. "When do I get my reward?"

"I've been thinking about that. You've been very good today, so . . ."

"I can be even better," he said, moving his hand up her leg. She leaned over at the stop sign and kissed him until headlights appeared in the rear window. He pulled up in front of his door and they got lost in their kisses. He pulled back and kissed her forehead, "You know there's a very comfortable bed about thirty feet from here."

"It's too far."

He laughed, pulled away from her, went around to her door and took her in his arms. "Then I'll carry you. I like beds."

When they reached the door, she unlocked it. Once inside, he waited for her to turn on the light. "No lights. That way I can pretend we're still outside."

"Hmmm, with a herd of children coming up the path."

"No, no interruptions in our special place outside." There was just enough light from the window to find the bedroom where he eased her onto the bed, gliding on top of her, both of them frantically unbuttoning and pulling off each other's clothes. Liliana turned her head as he kissed her neck, and screamed.

"He's here. How can he be here? Where did he come from? Help me, please." She started pushing Terry off of her so she could get away from the terrifying image.

"What's wrong," Terry held on to her trembling body to keep her from hurting herself in her panic to flee. "There's no one here." Then he saw vague, dark shapes moving on the wall beside the bed and kicked himself. "I'm so sorry," he said as he reached for the bedside lamp, holding her trembling body against him. "I forgot to tell you they were going to deliver the dresser today. My neighbor must have let them in. I told them to leave the mirror in its box. It's just a mirror on a dresser, Liliana. I'm so sorry, Liliana. It was a mistake. We're alone. You're safe."

"I remember," she sobbed. Then she cried for a long time. He wrapped his arms around her and waited patiently. Slowly, the sobbing eased, and then stopped, and then she was quiet, still holding on tightly. Eventually, she leaned back and let go. He kissed her and draped a sheet over the mirror.

"I hadn't been with Carla for very long. I still had the mirror on my dresser in my bedroom. It faced the door. It was on one side of the bed so that when I lay on my side I saw the door's reflection. I think I was having a bad dream. I woke up groggy. I wasn't sure if I was asleep or awake. Joe was standing over me with a big knife. The hall light was on behind him, but I knew it was him in the mirror. Then Carla came in the room screaming at him in Spanish. I didn't speak Spanish then. She dragged him away and shut the door. She must not have known I was awake. I couldn't move for the longest time. My arms and legs couldn't move. Then I started shaking. I took my pillow and blankets and slept under the bed that night and for a long time afterward. I started to see Joe coming to kill me in every mirror. I forgot the actual episode. I forgot about the night Joe was going to kill me. After that every time I saw a mirror, his face and the knife would be in it and I'd panic. I don't know when I stopped seeing the details . . . I never told anyone."

She sat back against the wall, holding onto his hands.

"Did you ever find out why Joe wanted to kill you?"

Liliana shook her head, and then reached for a tissue. "Yet another snotty day." She wiped her nose again. She looked so weary, her eyes nearly swollen shut, her nose and lips raw and red. His heart was breaking as he imagined the fear she had carried for so long. He saw her eyes slide toward the covered mirror, then quickly away again.

"Joe and Carla used to fight all night when they heard about someone accusing them of killing my parents. They used Spanish, but I heard them say my parent's names. I used to leave noisy toys on the floor between my bed and the door at night. Carla slept late, so I had time to put them away so I wouldn't get hit for having a messy room. It worked; I don't know how many times Joe would leave after noise from stepping on something, or yell if he hurt his foot on a toy. He was too stupid or drunk to figure out that he could make a path with a broom. Carla slept lighter for a long time and would scream at him when the noise or his yell woke her." She sighed. "Anyway, for a long time every time I passed by him, he'd glare at me. It made him even uglier. I got Aunt Donna to start teaching me Spanish when I got to visit. By the time I understood enough Spanish, they had stopped talking about it. Maybe he thought that I knew something, or had heard them talking about it. Maybe he just wanted Carla to himself."

Terry climbed over her to sit on the other side.

"Could you uncover the mirror?" She closed her eyes and waited. When he was back at her side, she sat on the side of the bed and lifted her face. Terry knelt behind her, his hands on her shoulders. She opened her eyes and smiled at him in the mirror. Joe was gone. The fear was gone. Terry pulled her down and kissed her most thoroughly, in the light, their reflection in the mirror.

Terry woke to sunlight in his eyes. He heard Liliana hopping around the kitchen and smelled the coffee and bacon. He pulled on his boxers and stepped quietly to the kitchen door. It was a galley kitchen with a window at the far end. Liliana, outlined by the light from the setting sun, stood with one crutch, flipping bacon in the fry pan.

"So, does this mean I was going to get breakfast, I mean dinner, in bed for a change?"

"I heard you coming. You need practice before you can sneak up on an Indian." She looked up, her white teeth revealed by her grin in the shadows that hid her face. He flipped the kitchen light on and saw she was indeed smiling, lips, cheeks, even her eyes participated. "And," she continued, "you only get to eat in bed if you want soda and sandwiches. *That* I can carry."

"I think I'll take it in the kitchen with coffee and plates of eggs and bacon." He hugged her from behind. She leaned back against him and turned to give him a kiss. A loud pop from the bacon made him step back. "Since you have my robe, maybe I'll put a shirt and pants on first."

"Donna gave me a lacy apron."

"Sure," he said, grabbing the apron from the hook on the door. "I'll just have to remember not to turn around."

"Keeps you on your toes." She whistled when he turned to put bread in the toaster. "And I get a better view." He shook his butt at her.

Sitting at the small kitchen table, Liliana watched him eat as she chewed a piece of bacon. "I wish you didn't have to leave."

"Me, too, but I harassed and threatened so many people to get the work scheduled, if I don't show they'll hunt me down."

She knew he needed to finish this task, but she had missed him so much the two weeks he was in Amarillo, she didn't know if she could bear a longer separation. The only two offers on his house had fallen through when the bank refused the loans. His realtor suggested some repairs and upgrades to the house to attract some more financially solvent customers. She didn't want him to go, but he needed to tie off the loose ends of his life there. It would take some time, a couple of weeks or so.

"I'll call a lot and if it gets to be too long, you can come up and visit. Then I can show you off to my friends."

Liliana smiled, but she was unbearably sad inside. The pain in her leg made travel miserable. They had talked and made love most of the night. Finally remembering the source of her phobia had nearly erased her fear. She still checked the mirror before she entered the room; that habit would take awhile to disappear, if it ever did.

So he was going. No matter how hard she tried, she couldn't believe that he would come back. She didn't say it. He would just reassure her, and she was sure he was sincere, but instinct for self preservation kept warning her to hold back. She still didn't understand why he would want to come back to a disaster like her.

After he left, the days dragged by. She wished she had scheduled classes, but she had wanted to be free when he got back. As the fourteenth day approached, he told her the work was behind schedule; of course they had known the work would probably stretch out. Still she worried that he was giving her time to find her own life. She didn't want to impose herself on him more than he wanted, so she didn't hang onto the phone like she wanted to, or call him every hour of the day like she wanted. They were miserable apart, but neither one would complain.

Worried that she was abnormally attached to him, she tried not to complain. She didn't mention the nightmares that tormented her every other night. Deep inside, she knew that once their life was stable that separations would not be so devastating. If it ever did stabilize. It didn't help to think positive thoughts this time. The separation came too soon after their special days together.

It seemed to her that while Terry was in Farmington he was looking for excuses not to come back. Her heart ached when she thought about him. If she woke up dreaming about him, she'd try to stay asleep to recapture the dream. After he called, she'd spend her time lost in memories of their short time together. Her grandfather sat down to tell her about how this white man was too old for her and didn't really understand their ways. She told him that she hadn't really been raised in Indian ways, so it didn't matter, but she didn't have the conviction to declare that she knew Terry loved her.

James Hunt watched his granddaughter suffer. She resisted any suggestion that she join Terry since she would only get in his way. He understood her persistent insecurity and although he understood there would be problems with an older man from a different culture, he also knew that once the heart was given, it could only be returned broken. One day the sadness in her eyes was too much for him. He got in his truck and drove to Farmington.

Jim found Terry's address with his dad's silver and black Ford truck parked in front of the small unremarkable frame house Terry could not sell. He parked in front of it. After no one answered his knock on the door, he headed for the sound of water running in the back yard. He came around the corner to see Terry sitting on the steps, hunched over, listlessly waving a stream of water from the hose over some half-dead rose bushes. Jim stood for several minutes, watching him, waiting for Terry to realize he was being watched, but Terry was lost in thought.

Once Terry arrived at the house, he had no energy for the work that needed doing. Workers came and he supervised, uninterested. He realized how listless his life in Farmington was and felt himself sliding back into that pattern. He would look through pictures of his marriage and the life he had shared with his wife, which reminded him of the painful divorce. Terry began to think that maybe he had committed himself to Liliana too soon. He didn't want to hold her back in her new life and all of its possibilities. Without Carla she had a chance for a real life and friends, and love with someone closer to her own age. When he looked in the mirror, all he saw were his wrinkles and grey hairs, and he began to doubt that she would continue to love him once she'd healed from her past. It wouldn't be right to saddle a bright, young girl with an old man with so much baggage.

Too far away to touch her skin and look into her eyes, he had to rely on what he heard in her voice to know how she felt and he could tell she was holding back. He knew she cared for him, but he had also seen her pain and need. If they weren't tied together by so many tragedies, she could heal and fulfill her potential and become the bright, independent star she could be. She wouldn't need him when she'd finished healing. Then all their differences could break their bond to each other. He wasn't sure he could go through that again.

He'd already sown his wild oats and was on his way to settling into middle age. A young man could offer her decades more of love than he could. A young man could give her the youth that had been stolen away by her disastrous life. She needed to learn to be young, to make silly youthful mistakes, and to have adventures.

Liliana deserved so much more than he could give her. He wanted to talk about it on the phone, but he was afraid to hurt her. During his nights alone in his empty house, he began to believe that she clung to an idea of him that was more than he could live up to. He would drive out of the city and walk into the wild to watch the sunset and throw rocks at the horizon. He hurt. He was afraid. He wanted the best for her, and he wasn't it. He spent his time between their phone calls staring into space, listlessly listening to every excuse his contractors gave him for why they needed more time. As his roses died despite the care he gave them, he began to believe that he couldn't do anything right. He knew that if he gave her enough time, she would find someone more suited to her needs.

Jim kicked some gravel and Terry turned slowly toward the sound, and then stood up in surprise with a smile and an open hand. "Well, Jim Hunt, I never expected to see you up here. What brings you to Farmington?"

Jim shook his hand, and looked into eyes that were too sad to be touched by the friendly smile. He had to decide if he was he going to be polite, or if he was going to get right to the point. Well, this was just a white man and polite conversation before bringing up the point of his visit would probably be wasted on him. Jim came to the point.

"What are you doing sitting up here watering dead flowers, while my granddaughter cries for you in her heart? You keep calling, so you remember her. Why are you torturing her? She doesn't know if you care, or if you don't know how to tell her that you don't care. Get up off your butt and make a decision, boy."

Terry stepped back in surprise. Initially defensive and angry, his eyes then filled with tears and he turned away.

"I don't know which is worse, a white man who thinks he knows everything, or a white man who doesn't know his ass from his elbow." Jim stood, a hand on each hip, waiting for Terry to decide if he was going to hit him. When he saw Terry's shoulders shaking, he worried that he'd pushed too hard. After all, the man had recently lost his own father. He kicked himself for coming on too strong and started to reach out to touch Terry's shoulder and apologize. Then he heard the laughter, and stepped back, smiling in satisfaction. There were advantages to being an old man. He didn't have to worry too much about getting hit for being obnoxious.

Terry had one hand holding the hose and the other over his eyes. He turned around slowly and dropped his hand to cover his mouth as he laughed. "For a minute there, you sounded just like my dad." Then he stood there laughing, shaking his head.

"I'm sorry about your dad, Friend, but you have to decide what you're going to do about my girl. Nothing I do is working. Do you want her, or not? Who cares if this house sells? Give it to the homeless or something. You're a cajillionaire. You can do what you want. Do you want to come home, or not?" Now that he had Terry's attention, he became serious.

Sadness bloomed across Terry's face, but didn't erupt into tears. "I thought you didn't approve."

"I don't, but I don't have any say in this. She already gave her heart to you. She didn't ask me first. I try talking to her, but she just gets quiet." He walked over to sit on the steps next to Terry, taking the hose, aiming it expertly at the bases of the rose bushes. "She's having bad nightmares. Thank God, her asthma's been better. Finally, we got her to spend some time with Frank, again." He glanced over to Terry, waiting for the invitation to continue.

"Is he helping?" Terry asked as he went inside. He came out with two cold beers and sat down on the step, handing one to Jim.

"I don't know. I wake up and hear her machine going." Terry nodded. "But she won't talk about it. Liliana has your picture taped to every mirror. It scares away the monsters, she says." He shook his head sadly, and pushed his cowboy head back to scratch his head. "I thought it was my fault for thinking she looked like Joe, but she told us what she remembered. If that old SOB hadn't died on his own, I'd be in prison for killing him." He turned to face Terry, "She knows you're afraid to love her."

Terry looked over and Jim held him with his eyes looking for hope for Liliana. Then Jim looked away and took a long drink of his beer.

Terry kicked a rock and sighed. "I don't want to hurt her any more. I love her, but it happened so fast and there was so much going on. What if it doesn't work?"

"And you're almost old enough to be her father. And you're white and from Texas of all places. And she met you when you were dying on the side of the highway because you were so stubborn you drove an old truck that left you stranded on the hottest day of the year." Jim paused, "And you don't know the first damn thing about taking care of roses."

He stood up and picked up a pair of clippers from the top step. He turned down the water to a drip and laid the hose on the ground, letting the water soak into the ground, and began pruning off dead and diseased branches from the nearest bush. "You gotta cut off all the sick parts, so the bush can use its energy to make beautiful flowers. It's the same with family. Sometimes you have to cut away all the sick feelings they gave you so you can learn to live a good life. The rose can look forward to making beautiful flowers. That's all it has to do. Liliana can't see anything to look forward to without you. Sure she'll be a great doctor whatever you decide to do, but she won't be happy. She needs help cutting away the sick parts they left her with. I was part of the problem, so I can only do so much to help her. I don't think a boy her age would know enough to help her either."

He grunted as he reached for a low branch. Terry got another set of clippers and started on another bush. Jim explained which branches looked sick, told him about cutting dead flowers back to the first stem with five leaves. They worked in silence for the most part with only an occasional question and answer about caring for roses. After finishing the row of six bushes, Terry asked, "You interested in getting some supper?"

"Sure," Jim said. "Do you know any place we can get some Navajo tacos?"

Terry nodded, "I know just the place."

"We'll take my truck," the old man said as he walked away. Terry chuckled and followed him. Age didn't always bring wisdom, Jim thought, but this was a wise young man. Terry had had his share of suffering; he would be able to help Liliana. Now all Jim had to do was get him back to Laguna.

After finishing dinner, they sat drinking coffee in the old fashioned diner and Jim waited for an answer. He knew Terry was wrestling with himself. Jim made himself comfortable, leaning in the corner of the booth, with one arm over the back of the red, plastic padded bench.

Occasional trucks passed on the narrow, dusty, paved road outside the window beside them. He watched the trucks, he watched the pretty, young Navajo waitress behind the counter. He sipped his coffee, and the silences became longer as they ran out of things they felt like talking about. After a particularly long silence, Jim asked, "So you met Carla. What did you think of her?"

Terry looked up at Jim's face before he spoke. He looked down at his cup as he answered, seemingly reluctant to discuss an unpleasant topic. "She was a terrible, sad case. She kept trying to seduce me. We didn't spend much time there; it was awful. I never saw her again."

"Liliana never talks about that day. Do you know what happened when she went back the next morning?"

"Yes. She told Carla the brutal truth in brutal language. Carla picked up a heavy lamp, threatening to kill Lili, but then she tripped and hit her head on the base of the lamp. It looked like it was just a scrape and Carla was awake, so she left. She feels terrible for what she said and she's afraid she's indirectly responsible for Carla's death," he paused. "She's a good kid, despite her time with Carla. Ben and Susana were good parents."

To Jim it sounded like Terry was trying to convince himself. "So tell me the truth. Do you think that she will turn into Carla as she gets older?"

Terry looked startled. Then he thought for a moment and looked surprised at himself. "Sorry. I can't say the idea hasn't occurred to me. But the better I get to know her, the more I realize that will never happen. She's not only smart, she's wise. And, she has a lot of good people to help her."

Jim watched the waitress approach and held out his cup for another refill. This white man had better hurry up and decide, or he was going to spend the next month in the bathroom. He slid a glance over to Terry as he sipped the hot, black coffee. "My time on this world is short. She'll have a better chance if she has you. She already loves you. If you leave, she'll have to heal. If she succeeds in healing then she'll have to start looking for someone to love her. You know how hard that is, especially after all the publicity in Grants and especially for a female doctor. She has secrets that will scare away anyone who hasn't seen how strong and good she is despite everything that has happened to her. Believe me, her tantrums are nothing compared to what I've seen in girls her age without so many problems."

"Her tantrums don't bother me," he smiled. "The more tantrums, the more making up we get to do."

Jim gave him a warning glare.

Terry watched the old man, and his eyes revealed that he knew what Jim was doing. Still, the doubts and the memories of all Liliana had suffered held him back. He stared at the coffee grounds settled at the bottom of his cup wishing that the grounds would foretell his future. Jim moved and he looked up. Jim had both elbows on the table and was leaning forward.

"Okay. This is too hard to decide right here and right now. Come with me to Laguna. Then you can ask Liliana what she really wants. Face to face. It's too easy to hide on the telephone. Come now, or come for Frank's birthday on Saturday, four days, if you want an excuse, or more time. Peter cooks enough for the whole Pueblo."

Terry finally nodded. "Okay. I'll come for the party and turn the house over to the homeless projects." He was done with the whole thing and had already considered that option. He needed a day or two to set it up.

"Good. Now I have to recycle some of this coffee and get on the road home."

"Stay the night. That's a dangerous highway at night."

Jim agreed. As Terry watched him walk away, he felt good about his decision.

When Jim called home, Liliana watched the phone with eyes filled with dread as Donna spoke to her father. She knew that her grandfather had gone to Farmington and she knew why, and it scared her. She stood watching her aunt as she hung up the phone. Donna turned and smiled.

"Terry's going to come for Frank's party whether or not the house sells," she said, as Liliana's face crumpled into tears. This was the first time she'd cried over Terry in front of Donna. Donna hugged her, "Sometimes men can be so stupid."

It was four days until the party. Liliana wasn't sure if she wanted it to go faster or slower. She couldn't sit still. She went to Albuquerque to visit, and went to Mike's house for dinner, and went to the school to talk about starting in January and managed to wear Angelo out playing video games. Yet, every time she turned around, her mind would wander off to swim in the sea-foam-colored eyes, stroke the sandy hair and watch the bowlegged walk of a man who'd grown up riding horses.

One night, after spending the day in the garden, Liliana lay in bed thinking about Terry. She was going over all the times they had been together, trying to figure out how he felt. She was afraid that she had been too pushy, which reminded her of Carla's embarrassing behavior when she met Terry. Then, the night before Terry was due, Liliana thought about how he had looked when she finally told him about going back to the motel that morning, which led her to the awful things she'd said to her grandma, and how she'd left her on the floor to die. It didn't matter that she hadn't thought that the injury was that bad. He told her he was angry at Carla for causing her pain even in her death, but she couldn't understand how he could love someone who had done such awful things. The tears started and the bile of guilt rose in her throat. She missed him so much, and, dammit, she missed Carla. She started coughing and used the nebulizer, but it didn't help. She cried, and coughed, and couldn't breathe.

Before she knew it, her grandfather was at her side holding the blue tube and hugging her, while he called to Donna. It wasn't long before Liliana was in the ER. Frank was waiting and the nurses had IV's, a nebulizer and oxygen flowing. Finally she stopped coughing, but kept on crying, hating herself. Eventually the Valium took effect, her breathing cleared and she dozed off.

The minute Donna finished calling for the ambulance, she called Terry.

"Do you think I should come down right away?" he asked.

"Of course, you idiot! Get your butt down here. Sometimes I wonder why God skipped all the men when he was handing out the brains. Between you and my dad, I just don't know. She wants to see you, for

Heaven's sake. Haven't you been listening to what she's been telling you?"

"I'm sorry. I really am. I didn't want to hurt her more if things didn't work out."

"What do you mean if things didn't work out? How are things supposed to work out with you up in Farmington? She knows life has no guarantees. She just wants a chance. Can you give her that? Can you give her a chance? Do you care for her?"

"Yes. Yes and yes. I care for her a lot."

"Then get on a plane and come now, call us with your arrival time and we'll pick you up."

"Okay. I'm coming. I'll call you when I find someone to fly me in."

"Good," she said. "I'll see you soon. Mike says your truck is ready and to have your checkbook ready when you show your face."

She heard tears in his laughter as he said goodbye.

Liliana was running, but she couldn't get away. Her legs were too short. Carla was chasing her, threatening her with a huge lamp held high over her head. Joe was in the bedroom mirror, waving a knife. She crawled under her bed into the darkest corner. Carla was drunk and screaming. Liliana had seen her with Joe. It was her fault, because she wasn't supposed to be home. She covered her ears and squeezed her eyes shut, praying to her Mommy to make Carla go away. Then she heard a man. She thought it was Joe, but it wasn't. He was trying to pull Carla away. It was Eddie Chee. He was telling Carla to leave Liliana alone. Liliana had seen him lying next to the wall of the motel, an empty bottle in his hand. She'd thought he was passed out. Carla's screaming must have awakened him.

She covered her ears again and wished herself away. Then she was in her daddy's truck, but it couldn't be her daddy's truck; that truck drowned in a big arroyo. She was looking back at the motel from inside the truck with eyes blurred with tears and a foul taste in her mouth from the ugly words she'd screamed at Carla. Eddie Chee was standing beside the maintenance room. He looked at her, and then he went into the apartment. She gunned the truck and drove away to find the kind eyes she already loved, the reason she'd finally had the guts to tell her grandmother what she thought of her.

Gradually she awakened from the disturbing dream, dream thoughts mixing with awake thoughts. Her eyes were still closed as a waking memory reminded her of how mortified and furious she'd been when Carla went after Terry that first day. That was why he didn't come back from Farmington. He thought she would turn out like Carla. She didn't want to open her eyes. She didn't want to wake up and learn that he hadn't come home again. Then she felt his caress on her face and opened her eyes to see him leaning over her. She touched the little bags under his eyes that made them look so sweet and pulled him down for a long loving kiss.

"Liliana Hunt, will you marry me?"

Tears ran down her face. She could only nod, and hold him with both arms pulling him to lie beside her on the bed.

Her joy at his return was not enough for her to share her new realization. Somehow Eddie Chee had ended her problems with Carla. Eddie, her long-suffering knight with the shining bottle, had finished it, thereby freeing her of the curse of the wicked witch. It would be their secret forever.

She felt Terry's eyes on her as she sent that knowledge to her secret place. The peace it gave her to know for sure that she hadn't left Carla to die from her fall, let her finally open another door to Terry. The last big door that stood in the way of their love.

"Do you think I'll turn into Carla?"

He cupped her cheek as the grim expression crossed her face and answered the question in her eyes. "You will never be like Carla, but she will always be a part of you. She raised you for most of your life. You have no choice."

"So you'll tell me if I start acting like her."

"How would I know? I knew her for half an hour at most. I promise I will never judge you. You are you; you didn't get to choose where the bits and pieces of you came from. You are my woman, now, Liliana. I would be happy to share my hogan with you."

She joked, through the tears. "Yeah right. A hogan with a Jacuzzi."

"This white man needs his comforts."

He brushed her hair back from her sweaty forehead. Once again she got lost in his sea foam colored eyes.

Chapter 15

The Story of Carla
According to Edward Chee

Then, one day during spring break, Eddie Chee called. "How you doin,' chica?"

"Okay, I guess."

"How's the leg doing?"

"Great. I'm out of the braces and I only need the cane when I get tired."

"It's been kinda chilly; how's your grandpa's arthritis holding up?"

"You know him, he won't admit that he's hurting, but he doesn't seem to be limping very much."

"Good." In the silence that followed, Liliana knew he had something on his mind.

"So, what's up Uncle Ed?"

"Well, I've been thinking that it's been a long time since I visited the spirits in the Canyon. They might think I don't love 'em anymore."

Liliana nodded. "Well, I'm free this week; I'm caught up on my homework, and I have a nice new used truck. We should take a road trip."

Acting like it was all her idea, Eddie said, "Hey, that is a good plan. We should get an ATV. I'll get permission from the tribe. The walk would be too long for your leg."

"My truck is four-wheel-drive; it'll get us there. I'll bring lunch, you bring dessert."

"Maybe we can leave at three in the morning so we can see the sunrise."

"That sounds great. Where will you be?"

"Pick me up at my sister's house."

She marveled at how much Eddie Chee had changed since Carla died. He'd stopped drinking. His color was better and he was always clean and neatly dressed. On the way to Canyon de Chelle they chatted about the time they had spent together as she grew up. He had taught her how to play hopscotch and swung a rope tied to a faucet on one end so she could learn to jump rope. He knew she couldn't have any friends while she lived with Carla, so he had been her friend.

As they chatted, she remembered how Eddie had tried to protect her from Carla and her suspicions of how he might have ended her suffering in Carla's care. She remembered his kind face, waiting with everyone in the hospital when she was sick last summer. Old Eddie had always been her friend. Now she could keep his secret and her silence. He didn't need to be reminded of that dark day. It wasn't her dark dream anymore. It was acknowledgment of a gift.

Putting those thoughts away, she made up her mind to enjoy her visit to the Navajo badlands and the ancient, deserted ruins in Canyon de Chelle. When they finally reached the end of the highway, Eddie directed her to a cousin who had horses. It was a special surprise to be able to ride a horse, instead of driving a noisy vehicle, to the high cliff that looked down on the revered valley. As she rode she listened to the early dawn noises of birds and small animals scurrying, the horses hooves striking the hard ground, the squeak of the saddles. She smelled the arid earth, sage and mesquite, and horse, and watched the drapes of turquoise and orange colored clouds change shapes in the sky.

Once they were on the cliff, they laid out the blanket and their breakfast. Eddie took a deep breath of mountain air and asked, "So is everything all arranged?"

Liliana blew out her lung full of fresh air suddenly, "Yeah. I still don't believe it's going to happen."

"It's going to be at your grandfather's house?"

"Yeah. Aunt Donna wanted a Catholic ceremony, but neither of us is baptized Catholic. She invited her priest to the party to bless our union."

"Is Donna doing all the cooking?"

She laughed. "Are you kidding? She's got my days planned for weeks before. I'll land out cooking as much as she does. And you know we won't be able to keep Peter out of the kitchen." She paused, "I guess Adela, Emmy, Mike's wife, Jake and Jake's wives are bringing stuff. Oh well, everyone is helping."

"Will there be a lot of people there?"

"Nah, just us."

"Just us?"

"Well, you and your sister's family, and Grandpa, Donna and Tony and his family, Grandma Emmy, Mike and Adela and their families, Dr. Karnes and Peter, of course." She turned to Eddie to see that he was now counting on his toes, having used up his fingers. He flashed a goofy smile. Her eyebrows creased as if she just realized how many people were coming. "Oh, and Grandpa is inviting his friends, probably all of the tribal council. Then there's Terry's friends and family coming from Amarillo."

"And . . ." he asked.

"Well Jake, and Gerry and their families and maybe some of my dad's other friends."

"Uh huh?"

"Maybe Dr. Berger and Dr. Palley and Dr. Kauffman and their families."

"Any more?"

"Geez, Eddie. My step-granddad is bringing his family from California. Can you believe it?"

"Yeah. I always liked him. It was a good thing Carla was shit-faced when she shot him . . . or he'd be a California corpsicle."

"Yeah."

"And your friend?"

She laughed, "Of course, he'll be there. He's the groom."

"Are you sure?"

Liliana looked far into the distance, and said quietly, "Yes, I'm sure." She turned to Eddie with a shy smile. "You can sit in the front row so you can trip him if he tries to make a run for it at the last minute."

Eddie nodded firmly. "I'll be there."

He took her chin in his hand and said, "Now I have to tell you the story of Carla."

Liliana tensed, but, because she knew that Eddie would never hurt her, she didn't panic.

Eddie gave her his lopsided smile, then took a deep breath with his hands on his knees and began the story, his round face peaceful, but his eyes revealing some of the torture he had lived with for so long.

"Joe Yazzie was young when he fell in love with the prettiest Spanish girl in Grants, Carla's mom. Since he was already a bad guy, her father tried to chase him away. But he stuck around and got her pregnant. He thought her traditional father would allow the marriage, but he was wrong. Anna's father saw the evil in Joe and refused to let her marry him.

"Anna had Joe in her blood and didn't want to give the baby up. But they made her. Then her father married her to a friend of his, Billy Fredrichs. It never worked. Then it turned out the hubby couldn't give her any more babies, so she got mad and they both began to drink. She went to court and eventually got her baby back. Carla was two, a very hard time for a baby to lose the only parents she knew.

"Carla thought her mom's first husband was her father. Then Joe told her different one night when they were drunk and beating each other up. This was before your mom died. Billy was good with money. You know he built the motel. Anna died from her alcohol poisoning when Carla was five years old. I never learned why she had to drink so much. Her step-daddy kept drinking and died after being stabbed in a fight at the bar. Her grandfather moved in since Carla was only ten and he ran the motel after that. Carla grew up to be the prettiest girl in town just like her momma. It didn't matter; she didn't care about herself. I think her step-dad did that to her. He never wanted to get her back and then he was stuck raising her alone.

"By the time Carla reached junior high, Joe was drinking a lot and lived here and there. Carla and I were in classes together. I always had a crush on her, but I was just a scrawny kid. One day Joe was drunk, hanging around after school let out and he saw Carla. She was just thirteen and he was still a good-looking sum-bitch. He pretended to love her, but he never loved nobody. He just hung out by the school with his latest fast car to watch little girls' panties. He never had a place to sleep, but he always had a fast car. He killed a couple of people driving drunk, but nobody did anything.

"Carla's granddad tried to keep her away from Joe," he shook his head, eyes filled with old, worn out grief, "but Joe was all she wanted. He was good at tricking girls." Eddie took a deep breath, "I tried to tell her I loved her but it didn't help. Joe had got under her skin, but he had other troubles at the time."

"Carla told me that Joe swore later on that she wasn't his daughter. He said he was lying that night when they were fighting. After that Carla didn't believe anything he said. Sometimes she thought he was her father and she'd get drunk from the shame. Susana heard all of this. Carla used to tell me anything when she was drunk and Susana would talk to me sometimes. She asked me if she should let herself love Ben. I told her Ben might be her only hope."

Liliana put her arm around his shoulders. She'd always known that Eddie had loved Carla; she now knew he'd helped her mom. He patted her hand, but continued to scan the rugged valleys below them as he told his story.

"Anyway, Joe got another girl pregnant. That time he got a shotgun wedding. She was a cousin of mine, Lorraine. Carla made me take her to the wedding. Carla got really drunk there and started to call Lorraine bad names. They threw us out, but Carla didn't want to go home. We kept drinking and after a while she started calling me Joe. I let her, because she let me touch her if I was Joe." He looked down in shame. "Anyway, she turned up pregnant, but she always thought it was Joe that night, and I couldn't tell her the truth."

Liliana's brows came together and she leaned forward to see his face. "Are you saying that you are my grandpa, not Joe?"

He nodded, looking down at his boots.

"How can you be sure?"

When he heard in her voice that this was a good story for her, he smiled and looked up to see her surprised eyes. He smiled and touched the deep dimple on his left cheek, then poked her in the ribs to make her laugh. Then he touched the dimple on her cheek. After a moment of surprise and disbelief, tears welled up in her eyes and she hugged him.

He patted her knee and said, "There's more. I'm sorry."

Liliana remembered the wink Eddie had given her the first time she saw him after Carla died. She didn't want to hear this secret. "No, don't tell me. I don't want to know."

"It's okay, kiddo." She smiled, Terry had been the first to call her that. "It's not as bad as you think, that's why I have to tell you." He cocked his head forward to show her his teary-eyed smile. "But it will still be a secret. You can tell Terry, but that's all. A wife shouldn't keep secrets from her husband."

Liliana's eyes filled with tears. Because of his doomed love for Carla, Edward Chee had never even looked at another woman. Now he had no one. "Did you tell Mommy that you were her dad?"

"I wanted to, but I was afraid Carla would find out." A huge sigh escaped. "I wish I told her. Then she was gone." He brushed tears away. "So . . . on the day Carla died, I heard you fighting with her. I worried about you, but I was glad you told her that she broke your heart."

"I didn't say that."

"Yes you did; you just didn't know it." His arm sneaked around her waist. "I went in after you left. I heard her fall and I was worried. When I got to the living room she was bending over to pick up the lamp. There was a little blood on her forehead. She saw me and then she stood up with the heavy lamp in her hands. She started yelling about how awful you were and the awful things you told her, like she always did, but this time it was too much. I saw how you looked at your Texan. I knew Carla would find a way to wreck it and there was nothing I could do.

"I told her you were a good kid and she was a terrible person. I reminded her of the bad things she did to you and many other people. She started screaming and I yelled back. I told her it was good that you finally told her the truth and that she was going to Hell for killing Susana and Ben." He began to tremble, so Liliana hugged him tighter. "She lifted the lamp over her head to hit me with it, but it was too heavy and she was too weak, or drunk. She fell backward and the bottom of the lamp fell on her head. There was a lot of blood." He blew out another deep breath.

"I tried finding her heartbeat, but there wasn't one. I swear there was no heartbeat. When I found out Carla was still alive all that day, I figured that she had given her heart to a witch that was why she was so evil and powerful. How could she be alive without a heartbeat? Since I thought she was already dead, I didn't call an ambulance. You needed time to get away; I knew the police would stop you. I went back to the maintenance room and pretended I never left it. I knew people had seen me there, so disappearing would have looked suspicious. I pretended to be really drunk when the cops finally came and I told them I heard someone else arguing with her. They believed me, because I was just a drunk. Why would I kill the woman who gave me booze when I wanted it?"

"Then I saw the ghosts kill Joe that night, so after a while I figured maybe it was the ghosts who tricked me into thinking that Carla was dead. It scared the crap out of me. I know the cops won't believe me that it was an accident, so it has to be a secret. They would stick this old wino in jail forever, just because. Carla's gone; I want a life now, not prison."

Liliana was crying and soon her Grandpa Eddie was crying, too. "I will never tell anyone, except maybe Terry. You didn't do anything wrong. You saved me more than anyone. I don't know if I would be a true person if you hadn't been there to show me how someone loves a child. I love you Grandpa Ed." He just cried and held her.

"Wait, there's one more thing." He turned to dig in his backpack. She watched him, wondering. Finally, he pulled out a thick manila envelop and handed it to her. She opened it slowly and pulled out a thick pile of photographs of her mother, father and herself from when she was brand new to when she was a tiny little girl. She started crying as Ed hugged her and she looked through the lost photos.

"Where? How?"

"Carla had a hiding place that she left open one day when I was there. There was a lot of money in there, too. I left that with your grandpa to keep safe until we talked."

She didn't know what to say. This was the crowning gift in a year of amazing troubles, triumphs and love. Tears continued to stream down her cheeks. Ed brushed them away and kissed her cheek.

Eddie Chee had always had a special place in her heart. He had always tried to be around to take care of his grandchild the best he could.

She knew he had called Jake on Carla many times when it was really bad and he had suffered with having to watch Joe and Carla's dance of self-loathing for so many years. Now Liliana had another good grandfather and Edward Chee had the comfort of knowing she didn't blame him for anything, and that she loved him.

As the realization that she was free of Carla, the shame of incest, and the guilt of letting her grandmother die, took hold, she saw a smoky, black spider web float away from her, dissipate and fade away in the bright sunlight. Her freed spirit turned toward the joyful life that awaited her.

Author's Biography

Although Mary R. Gutierrez has written short stories and books most of her life, this is the first book she has published. She is a retired Family Practice Physician, who was born and mostly raised in New Mexico and now lives in Denver, Colorado. She completed a Bachelor of Science degree in Psychology with honors and graduated from the University of New Mexico Medical School. She then moved to Massachusetts to complete her residency in Family Practice, taught there for two years then moved to Colorado.

Her studies and practice focused on women's rights, family dynamics, sexual abuse, domestic violence and caring for underserved populations, homeless families, immigrants, and addicts. Through the years she has learned there is no ""type"" of person who abuses and abusers are the best at denying the damage they do. Families are always complex, but the interactions of abused, or the mix of abused and not abused children, is nearly an impossible tangle.

She married and divorced young, then worked her way through college. After returning to the Southwest, she worked with the underserved at Denver Community Health Clinic until physically incapacitated to work by Fibromyalgia. A sexual abuse survivor herself, depression complicated her illness. She is a fan of literary books that explore families as well as the more abstract approach to human dynamics in the fantasy and science fiction genres. Other interests include painting in watercolor and pastels, and learning to sing and play the guitar. Her living companions are her cats, a chubby female, shorthair tortie rescue, and a red, short-haired tabby male, a delightful fellow that adopted her.

Summary

On a hot June day, Liliana, a brilliant, young woman of Native American, Hispanic and Anglo-Saxon heritage is irresistibly drawn to a cowboy despondently leaning on his truck on the side of the highway as she drives home to Grants.

"Reflections of Love and Loathing" takes place in New Mexico, where Liliana loses her loving parents when she is five. Secret resources enable her abusive, alcoholic grandmother, Carla, to keep her; so Liliana is forced to live with the persistent stalking of a serial pedophile, Joe, who is her great-grandfather.

When Terry sees her recklessly cross the highway to come to his aid, he begins the wild ride into Liliana's life. After meeting Carla and Joe, he has his doubts about being with Liliana, but soon he realizes that love binds him to her. After driving Terry to his destination in Texas, Liliana learns that Carla has accused her of killing Joe and flees in panic. She wakes to find herself broken and alone; her truck wrecked in a deep arroyo. Only her love for Terry gives her the strength to fight for survival in the flashflood that threatens to finish her off and only Terry's mysterious link to her allows him to find and rescue her.

While she lies broken in the hospital, Terry learns of the perversions and misuse of power that maintained multigenerational sexual abuse that destroyed the lives of three generations of women and dominated Liliana's life with Carla.

Then begins Liliana's true challenge. As her body heals, she will have to rise above the emotional damage caused by Carla and the nightmare mirror image of Joe that tempts her to drive Terry away rather than face her fears and believe that she is worthy of Terry's love. The most difficult challenge of all.